MOTHER
ALWAYS
KNOWS

A MOTHER ALWAYS KNOWS

A Novel

SARAH STROHMEYER

HARPER ● PERENNIAL

NEW YORK ● LONDON ● TORONTO ● SYDNEY ● NEW DELHI ● AUCKLAND

HARPER ● PERENNIAL

HarperCollins books may be purchased for educational, business, or sales promotional use. For information, please email the Special Markets Department at SPsales@harpercollins.com.

FIRST EDITION

Designed by Jamie Lynn Kerner

Library of Congress Cataloging-in-Publication Data has been applied for.

ISBN 978-0-06-335150-9 (pbk.)

25 26 27 28 29 LBC 5 4 3 2 1

For the one and only true Stiletto.

PROLOGUE

What haunts her still is the howl—a wild, animallike cry of pain more piercing than a catamount's bone-chilling scream. Instinctively, she knew it came from her mother, and she was scared. She did not like the woods when it was dark, and as a young child she was petrified of being alone. To this day, she's still afraid to be by herself, the horror of what unfolded that night having scarred her forever.

"Did Ellen give you a special tea?" her mother asked before heading into the deeper part of the forest. "Did the tea make you sleepy?"

Astraea feared Mean Ellen might kidnap her again and put her in the scary room if she tattled. So she didn't reply.

Mama mumbled a naughty word and stroked her daughter's wispy hair. "It's all right, sweetie. You can stay here while I go find the turtle."

A bad thing had happened at the turtle earlier. Astraea rubbed her bare ankles to erase the creepy sensation of tentacles gripping her feet, pulling her into the earth below. She shouldn't have gone into the woods barefoot. If she'd been a good girl and obeyed the rules, Mama wouldn't have been upset and they wouldn't have had to come here right away.

This was all her fault.

Terrified to be alone, Astraea clutched her mother's legs. "Please don't leave me," she begged with a whimper.

"Don't worry. This won't take long. I'll be right back."

"No!" Astraea squeezed harder. She and her mother were a team. Mama said so. They were each other's world and no power could keep them apart. Why couldn't they just go home? Why couldn't she show Mama the spot by the turtle tomorrow?

Mama pushed back her hood and unclasped her necklace. Prying off her daughter's grip, she pressed the smooth stone into Astraea's palm and sealed it with a kiss. "Keep this safe for me until I return. But you must stay where you are. If you wander off, I won't be able to find you and you will be lost."

Astraea was delighted and amazed. This was Mama's pendulum. It was magic. She let Astraea play with it on very rare occasions. Mama would never leave her pendulum. She'd definitely be coming back.

Her mother vanished silently down the path, and in her black robe she soon became indistinguishable from the trees. Astraea tried to focus on where she went, but she was so tired, so very, very tired from Ellen's tea. She found it impossible to keep her eyes open, and soon the revelers' whoops and chants in the distance lulled her to sleep under the honeysuckle. Grown-ups were gathered around the commune bonfire to celebrate the summer solstice, the mystical night when sprites and fairies and even gods disguised themselves as humans to join in the festivities.

The howl jolted her awake. Startled and confused, Astraea stayed put as she'd been instructed. But what if her mother was hurt? Surely if Mama was in serious trouble she would want Astraea to find her. Yes, she was scared, but she was also brave. Mama told her so over and over.

Draping the pendulum around her neck, she zipped up her windbreaker and followed the path, barely visible under the quarter moon. If only her mother had dropped white pebbles like Hansel and Gretel to show her the way. Not breadcrumbs though. The birds would eat those.

"Mama!" she called into the vast darkness. "Mama, are you okay?"

Silence. Astraea stopped and cocked her ear, her own anxious breathing louder than the babble of the stream up ahead. Perhaps her mother couldn't hear. Perhaps she needed to yell louder.

"*Mama!*"

Again, nothing. Astraea began to quake slightly. Her mother had said she'd be back. *She'd promised.* She'd given her the pendulum for safekeeping. Why wasn't she answering?

Blinded by stinging tears, Astraea stumbled forward, her feet catching on rocks and roots and tangled vines until she reached the stream. There, face down, was her mother with her arms splayed. She must have been thirsty, tried to take a drink of water, and fallen.

"Mama?"

Still no response.

Astraea stepped closer. "I'm sorry I didn't stay where you told me to stay, but I heard a noise and . . ."

Something was wrong.

Her mother wasn't moving, and that was not good. If she stayed face down in the water like this, she would drown. Astraea tried to roll her over, but when she placed her small hands on her mother's shoulder, she found the silky robe was sticky and wet. Then she saw a deep part in her mother's hair, as white as Hansel and Gretel's pebbles. Her skull was split open like a coconut.

Astraea let out a shriek and then got a hold of herself. She had to be brave, and brave girls were strong and thoughtful, not crybabies. Maybe Mama couldn't talk because she'd taken a hard fall and the wind had been knocked out of her. That had happened to

Astraea once while tree climbing, and she turned out to be A-OK. Mama would be fine after her head wound was bandaged.

She didn't hear the crunch of footsteps until it was too late. A figure, robed like her mother, but taller and with a pair of long, twisted antlers, loomed above. Astraea's heart leaped into her throat.

Cernunnos, divine protector of the forest and the god of death. Dagda had read her a story about this god who died every summer solstice only to be reborn every winter, on the longest night of the year. Was it really him in the flesh?

"Don't be afraid." Leaning down, the magnificent creature gathered the little girl in his strong arms and, humming the soothing tune he sings to the dying, carried her up the mountain.

"Say nothing about what you saw tonight," he said after sitting her against the hard, cold wall of a cave. "This is our secret. And we all know what happens to little girls who tattle, right?"

Astraea nodded fiercely and, too petrified to speak, watched him descend through the forested hill until he disappeared, leaving her in the state she feared more than witches or Mean Ellen or even Cernunnos:

Alone.

STELLA

JUNE 16, 2023

I always knew a day of reckoning would come, except maybe not so soon and definitely not because the kid of a rabid book banner was weirded out by my footwear. I blame myself.

After the popularity of the episode about my mother's murder that aired on *Dark Cults*, I should have expected that someone would make the connection. Even though I've been super diligent about keeping a low profile, of course my privacy didn't stand a chance against the internet's lust for personal details.

Let's face it. The internet knows all about us. It knows all about me—where I live, my credit score, what trains I take to work, how many steps I average in a day, my heart rate, my Netflix history, even whether I stopped off at the weed store on the way home last Friday or opted for a bottle of Chardonnay. (That would be wine. Just ask Google.)

What the internet *doesn't* know is who killed my mother in the early morning hours of June 21, 2003, in the deep Vermont woods surrounding the cult she called home. Only Mama's murderer knows the truth—just like he knows I'm the only witness.

I saw what he did to her. I saw *him*. And even though he was in a solstice costume and I was only ten, there's no guarantee I couldn't pick him out in a lineup tomorrow. He doesn't know what I do or don't know and that could be driving him crazy. I have no doubt he'd rather I were dead for his own peace of mind.

Hence, my reason for staying under the radar, and quite successfully, I might add. I've made it to age thirty without incident, even landed my dream job archiving for the Cambridge Public Library. Lately, I've been thinking of getting a cat.

Then along came Ashleigh Retter.

Ashleigh is the teenage daughter of Rhonda Retter. Rhonda runs an organization called Young Souls Matter. YSM has been going around the country badgering librarians about books their group finds offensive, including the entire Harry Potter series, *A Wrinkle in Time*, and bound issues of *Mad* magazine. They're super fun.

Why our boss, Dr. Gomez, agreed to meet with this dynamic duo earlier today beats the hell out of me. Like many intellectuals disconnected from the teeming mass of humanity, he theorized that a civilized conversation about the importance of diverse literature would bridge the gap between those who are rational and those who are crazy. Perhaps he was unaware that number one on Rhonda's list of banned books, due to its overt themes of domestic violence, in her opinion, was Dr. Seuss's *Hop on Pop*.

Having grown up among fanatics, I tried to explain that there's no use in getting them to see reason. They'll only drag you down to their level. Gomez chided me for being too cynical and invited me to attend the meeting with my colleague Figurina DiTolla, who's in charge of acquisitions for the children's department.

"Fig," as we call her, is black, gay, has been through some shit, and does not suffer fools gladly. She's often taken for a softie given her sweetness toward children and penchant for flowing boho dresses. But I've seen her go toe-to-toe with bossy adults, and I was looking forward to her slicing and dicing the book banners into itty-bitty book-banning bits.

The meeting began with Rhonda marching into the conference room clutching a red Target tote bag and wearing an oversize wooden cross over a pink gingham jumper and thick handknit socks stuffed into Birkenstocks. Granted, this is Cambridge, not Milan, but even the aging hippies in this town wouldn't be caught dead in that outfit.

As if I'm one to talk. I line the insoles of my Swedish sandals with Reynolds Wrap, which, of course, Ashleigh noticed right off. Her heavily lined gaze zeroed straight in on the shiny silver layer, whereupon she wrinkled her nose in disgust. Looking back, I bet that's what prompted her to google my name and stumble upon my true identity.

Dammit. If only I'd worn my Keds, I wouldn't be in fear for my life.

"Let's get right down to business." Rhonda slapped a file onto the conference table. "Here's a list of books our organization has categorized as corrupting the souls of our youth. They promote premarital sex, parental disrespect, paganism, immoral lifestyles, and the supernatural. In allowing them to stay on your shelves, you people are unwittingly—or wittingly—promoting Satan's agenda."

Dr. Gomez sighed. "I assure you, Mrs. Retter, we have no such agenda. The books curated for our children's collection are age appropriate. They're quality literature intended to spark young imaginations and a lifelong love of reading."

Rhonda clicked a red pen and circled *Twilight* so hard the tip broke through the paper. "Do you honestly expect me to believe this filth normalizing vampires and other unearthly creatures, not to mention adolescent hormonal urges, is *quality literature*? I'll tell you what it is, it's the gateway to the occult!"

Her ignorance was beginning to grate on me. I wanted to tell her that as a person raised by spiritual dowsers who started each day swinging pendulums and shuffling Tarot cards, I was all too familiar with the occult, and no one in our commune, adult or child, ever picked up a freaking copy of *Twilight*.

"Stella?" a voice whispered. Ashleigh was poised with her thumbs over her phone, smiling at me mischievously. "Are you actually *the* Stella O'Neill?"

That hint of gotcha instantly set me on edge. But I chose to ignore her, hoping against hope that she didn't actually know anything, and turned back to the conversation, which much to my delight, was getting heated.

Fig was resting her chin on her hand, ready to take on the book banners. "About your claim of immoral lifestyles . . ."

From her bull's-eye Target tote, Rhonda pulled out the classic *And Tango Makes Three*, about gay penguins who raise a family. Pinching it by the corners as if it were radioactive waste, she hissed, "Exhibit A."

Fig peered through her huge oversize, purple-framed glasses, her simmering anger radiating heat like summer sun off steel. "I'm confused. Do you have a problem with children reading about families like mine, or is it that you disapprove of the nontraditional penguin lifestyle?"

Boom!

Rhonda closed her eyes and appeared to mumble a prayer. Ashleigh bent toward her mother and, keeping her sights on me, whispered loudly, "Check this out. Looks like we have a Satanist among us."

Oh, shit. This was definitely gonna test the effectiveness of my antiperspirant. I slid back my chair, ready to make a quick escape.

Rhonda flicked an acrylic nail over the screen of Ashleigh's phone, her attitude brightening with each little click. "Oh, my," she said between taps. "Oh, my Lord."

Fig said, "What, more penguins?"

"Not quite." Rhonda held up her daughter's phone so Dr. Gomez could read the screen. "Turns out your archivist is a perfect example of what I've been talking about. This totally supports deep intel I've received that your staff members are devil worshippers promoting perversions among our vulnerable youth."

Crap. Crap. Crap. It was happening. The nightmare I'd spent a lifetime trying to avoid was unfolding in real time.

Here. At work. In front of my boss.

Dr. Gomez squinted at the screen. "Stella, what is this?"

Somehow, I managed to walk around to his side of the table instead of heading for the door. Rhonda folded her arms, triumphant. Fig put a comforting hand on my shoulder as I read the words until they made sense.

Mayhem Avenger @xoxoxoxo666
@DARKCULTS slandered DIVINER leader who is INNOCENT & will SUE! Real killer Dan O'Neill (55 Dolan Rd Sudbury MA) walks free while eyewitness daughter Stella O'Neill (@cambridgepl) stays silent re: dad's sick crimes. Find them! Bring them to justice for Rose Santos! Make them pay!

At the bottom of her post, I saw that Ashleigh had already shared it with her followers. Of course she had. And, wow, so did 1.8K other people who are a smidgeon of the 299K views . . . and growing.

That's when I lost it.

The quivering dread I'd had about being exposed turned into white-hot rage at the invasion of my privacy and the completely unfounded accusation. To put me, to put my innocent father, in danger like this was unacceptable. It took only a single unhinged conspiracy theorist to put us in harm's way, and if there was any place you could find an unhinged conspiracy theorist, it was in the true-crime corner of the internet. And given the original post's chief purpose seemed to be to protect one particular person, I had a feeling I knew who'd posted it: a Facilitator.

This post was bad. Really bad. I envisioned dozens of triggered vigilantes—many of them likely Diviners, members of my mother's old cult—showing up at Dad's house demanding "justice" and making life hell for him at the office, swatting him with 911 calls claiming domestic abuse and animal cruelty.

And what about me? They'd probably be flocking to the library doing the same. I'd have to quit my dream job, go underground, live on those survival-food buckets they sell at Costco.

This post threatened to destroy my carefully built life. I was super pissed at this kid Ashleigh for being such a Karen in training. It was all I could do not to take her stupid phone and smash it with the heel of my foil-lined sandal.

"It's going *viiiiral*," she singsonged gleefully. "Already it has, like, forty-two thousand shares just since I reposted it."

"YSM is closing in on three hundred thousand followers, thanks to Ashleigh," Rhonda cooed with pride. "She's well on her way to being a macro influencer."

"I already am, Mom." Ashleigh rolled her eyes, her thumbs flying over her phone screen. "After this post, I'll probably hit mega."

My stomach seized.

"Stella?" Dr. Gomez asked again. "Is this you?"

I should have just shrugged. I should have been cool. Instead, as my anger built and exploded into a fresh wave of hysteria, a fever came over me, and to my horror—and probably Ashleigh's elation—I began to reel.

"Let's get out of here," Fig murmured, hooking her arm in mine, escorting me out of the conference room before I melted into a mess.

As we made our exit, I overheard Dr. Gomez tell Rhonda the meeting was over and that he had no intention of removing any books from any shelves, and oh, by the way, Stella O'Neill was a fantastic archivist, and the library was damn lucky to have her. It broke my heart to hear, knowing I might not ever be able to return.

"It's gonna be okay," Fig said as we entered the stairwell. "I don't know what's going on, but it's gonna be okay."

We got to my office, which happens to be the size of a British water closet, and shut the door. A yellow Post-it note was affixed to my computer. It was from Heidi at the front desk asking me to give her a call ASAP.

I sank into my desk chair and put my head between my knees, breathing slowly to keep from hyperventilating. Fig left and returned with a paper cup of water. "I'd have poured something stronger if it weren't for those darn workplace rules."

"Thanks. This helps," I said, downing the water in three gulps.

"I don't think you should be alone." Fig perched herself on a banker's box of files. "You can stay with Mel and me tonight if you want. We're trying out a new pizza recipe, asparagus and feta. We'll eat on the deck. It'll be nice. We can help you decompress after all this."

I was touched. Fig's basically just a work friend, not a friend-friend. Why was she being so kind?

Her pocket binged, and she took out her phone. "It's Heidi. She's looking for you." Fig returned the text. "Uhm, there's some guy at the front desk asking if you'll come down to the lobby. He's very insistent. What do you want to do?"

Hibernating comes to mind. Slipping under the desk and sleeping until Armageddon. Teleporting to the Planet Xenon.

"Did she say who he is?" Could have been my father or a cop, I thought, trying to be positive. More likely, he was a Facilitator from the commune on a mission.

I nervously fingered the polished rose quartz pendulum Mama gave me the night she died. Its solidity has always been comforting, especially since it's the only memento I have of her.

"Heidi says she's never seen him before." Fig kept texting. "He's our age. Beard. Warby Parkers. Chuck Converse. Hawaiian shirt." She smiled crookedly at that. "Hipster stalker?"

"More like hipster podcaster." Which was a relief. Podcasters aren't usually trained to kill, unlike Facilitators.

"Yuck. Hipster podcasters are the worst. Ten to one he has an affected stutter to make it seem like he's *soooo* smart, as if his brain works faster than his mouth."

This got a laugh out of me.

"It's okay. I'll be fine," I told her, the water having restored my mental faculties. "You should find out from Gomez what the upshot was with Rhonda. I'm gonna finish some work and then maybe clock out."

Fig pursed her lips, doubtful. "Oooookay. You know how to reach me, right? Wait. Let me text you my number just in case."

I dictated my number and thanked her for the dinner invitation even if, *entre nous*, the idea of an asparagus and feta pizza was not my cup of tea. She gave me a thumbs-up and a wink and left. She was gone five minutes when there was a ding from my own phone. It was Fig's confirmation message: This is me!

It topped the list of four others, two from Heidi at the front desk, one from Webs offering a great deal on yarn closeouts, and one from my dad's wife, Heather, in a run-on sentence that's typical of her understated midwestern patois.

> At the hospital no need to worry your dad's okay just
> on the way to dinner before the game someone tried
> to run him over is all on Fenway.

I got a chill. That hit-and-run was no coincidence; that was Facilitator handiwork.

Those bastards weren't even giving us a sporting chance.

2

STELLA

JUNE 16, 2023

"How're you feeling?" I ask Dad when I finally reach him by phone while he's waiting in the emergency room. I've been so upset about him being a victim of a hit-and-run at Fenway, I haven't been able to do a lick of work.

"Fine. Absolutely fine! Heather overreacted, insisting I be checked out for a head injury. I was barely nicked. Anyway, it was my fault for jaywalking. I'm lucky I didn't get killed by those crazy Boston drivers."

Dad's doing a yeoman's job of remaining upbeat, though I definitely sense some tension. "Sorry you have to miss the Yankees."

"I won't if they'd just hurry up with the CAT scan. I'm dying to see Whitlock cream Cole." He pauses, probably listening for his name being called. "Heather says there's something on the internet about . . . *you know*. That true?"

I wish my beleaguered father didn't have to deal with this latest crisis, along with a possible TBI. "Nothing major. Same ole, same ole." I, too, can downplay.

"Uh-huh. Heather showed me the post. This is pretty major, toots. You want to stay with us tonight?"

Out of nervous habit, I unclasp Mama's pendulum from around my neck, swinging the stone from side to side. I don't buy the Diviners' theory that pendulums, like dowsing rods, can connect us to the Divine Eternal Energy that unites all living creatures. But I do like how the rhythmic back-and-forth calms my anxiety.

"Dad, you'd better prepare yourself for a shitstorm. I'm guessing you've been doxed."

He waits a beat. "Is that good or bad, doxed?"

I have to smile. How lovely to be so oblivious to the nastiness of the internet you haven't a clue about random strangers showing up on your doorstep—or in the lobby of your workplace. Meanwhile, I don't dare leave my office until I get the all-clear from Heidi in reception that my hipster stalker is gone "It's not good. There'll probably be people—Diviners and others—waiting for you when you get home, demanding you turn yourself in to the police."

He chuckles softly. "Oh, come on. You think I'm afraid of a bunch of silly cosplayers?"

I'm impressed he's aware of the term.

"I'll tell them to leave and, if they don't, I'll turn the garden hose on them."

"Sure, Dad. You do that."

Daniel? The authoritative voice of an emergency room nurse pierces the background noise.

"Hey, looks like my table's ready. Just might make the first pitch after all. Gotta go, Stell. I'll give you a call when I get the all-clear. Take an Uber home tonight, okay? *Okay?*"

But I'm barely listening because an email has been forwarded from the library general mailbox to my inbox and it appears to be from those who wish me dead.

3

STELLA

JUNE 16, 2023

FROM: info@cambridgema.gov
TO: Stella.Oneill23@cambridgema.gov
RE: Time's Up!

From: <b.machiavelli@123456789abcef.onion>
Sent: Friday, June 16, 2023 3:47 PM
To: Cambridge Public Library info@cambridgema.gov
Subject: Time's Up!

Dear Stella: Please consider this email as formal notification that considering the heightened public scrutiny concerning the circumstances of Rose Santos's death, we strongly advise you to keep your lips sealed and tell no one what you saw that tragic night twenty years ago.

The chances of you being approached by true-crime "journalists" and/or podcasters eager for an exclusive interview with the girl who witnessed her mother's murder are now all but guaranteed. It is not in your best interests to allow these vultures access. Doing so will only hasten the inevitable.

You, more than anyone, can relate to the true meaning of the phrase "living on borrowed time." Much as a death rattle signals the imminent passing of the soul from the human form to the Eternal Divine, the pendulum has revealed this online posting is a harbinger of your end is near.

We are so sorry, but there can be no escaping Destiny.

Take heart, Stella, your fate was never in your control; it has always been governed by the stars. Be comforted by the assurance that Sister Rose is waiting to greet you with open arms on the other side of the veil, and soon you two will be reunited in Eternal Love & Divine Energy.

Peace and light unto you and forever more.

Us.

4

STELLA

JUNE 16, 2023

Us.

I have no idea how long I stared at that terrifying email from my mother's killer—or *killers*. Minutes? Hours? The nuances are only beginning to sink in. This isn't merely a letter from my mother's old cult.

It's a death threat.

I should show it to the police, but that would be futile. There's nothing here that outwardly puts my life in danger. You have to read between the lines, decode the cult buzz phrases like *the pendulum has revealed* and the creepy and exploitive *Sister Rose is waiting to greet you with open arms on the other side of the veil and soon you two will be reunited in Eternal Love & Divine Energy*. That's my dead mother they're talking about!

That's *my* life they're threatening!

And the signoff about peace and light? It's the closing line of a Diviner burial, right before they ignite the corpse on its funeral pyre.

Shivers run up my arms, as intended. These cultists want me to crumble, beg for mercy, maybe even return to the Center to seek forgiveness and protection, those bastards.

They were savvy enough to send the email from the dark web so it's virtually untraceable. MacBeath's Facilitators are not about to slip up by using a proxy Gmail account.

After Radcliffe MacBeath hit the big time with his self-help books about harnessing the Divine Energy for personal and financial success, he not only got rich, he got paranoid. At least that was the explanation in *Dark Cults* for why the Center's security detail—known as the Facilitators—has become weaponized in recent years.

I have vague memories of these guys milling around the commune in hiking shorts, green polo shirts, and Timberland boots looking more like enthusiastic Boy Scouts than the Krav-Maga-trained spies portrayed in the documentary.

Mama used to warn me to stay clear of them, never to make eye contact, and to answer their questions with succinct yeses and nos. Her warnings didn't faze me since I was a kid, but as an adult I've concluded that it was a Facilitator in costume who murdered my mother—on MacBeath's orders.

MacBeath would never have dirtied his delicate hands with such a messy task, and even if he had been inclined, he wouldn't have been so stupid as to forfeit an airtight alibi by being at the bonfire until dawn before hundreds of witnesses, while Mama was taking her last breath in the forest less than a mile away.

In the twenty years since her murder, the Facilitators have apparently become the bullies of the internet, which they scour constantly for any slander against their dear leader. Woe to those who dare criticize MacBeath, because the Facilitators will launch full-on assaults, anonymously and relentlessly harassing innocents like my father.

I have no doubt they wrote the viral post that's probably as encrypted as this email.

So the police won't be helpful, but maybe Trooper John Oswald will be. Trooper Oswald worked my mother's case until he retired ten years ago. We met when I was eighteen, after I reached out to him for answers, convinced a conversation with the lead detective could solve the crime. It didn't, not even close, but he shared some insights into Mama's murder and gave me his personal contact info to use in an emergency, which this definitely is. I forward him the email and send him a text to check his inbox. I can't wait around; I need his professional advice on what to do next.

Then I go back to the email for another read.

I can't believe the day I've dreaded for so long has finally arrived. Twenty years after waking up in a hospital bed surrounded by bright lights and strange faces, the trauma of the man with horns slaying my mother so fresh in my psyche I could barely speak, I'm back to being ten again, alone and panicked and riddled with fear.

Which is exactly where MacBeath wants me to be.

He might try to pass himself off as a modern-day prophet with his long, white hair and happy Hawaiian shirts spouting harmless phrases such as "Love is energy," "Energy is love," "If the power's not within you, you're without power," and "Unplug to recharge." (That last one became a popular bumper sticker on Teslas.) But he's a ruthless charlatan determined to control his slavish followers at any cost—just as long as his hands stay clean.

Rumor has it he began his career selling time-shares in the Poconos under his given name of Doug Dudko from Scranton, Pennsylvania. Then he moved to multilevel marketing, where he clawed his way to the top of the pyramid scheme by peddling longevity vitamins to gym rats. He was king of the hill until jealous colleagues declared mutiny and ran him out of the company.

He wasn't adrift for long. Doug Dudko soon discovered divination and its potential for enticing suckers to turn over all their money. He dropped the Dudko and legally changed his name to Radcliffe MacBeath, purchased 440 acres at the edge of the Green

Mountain National Forest in Vermont, where he built the Center for Spiritual Dowsing, formed a limited-liability company called SDS, LLC, and launched his brand: Spiritual Dowsing for Success.

Within years he became the darling of daytime TV, wooing depressed housewives and the unemployed with promises of supernatural powers guaranteed to unleash unlimited wealth and happiness. People flocked to his seminars and gobbled up his self-help books. He smiled often, made self-deprecating jokes, and, on screen at least, couldn't seem more benign.

So MacBeath won't be the monster I find standing by my bed in the wee hours of the morning holding a pillow over my face. He's too crafty to make a rookie mistake like that, and he doesn't have to when his brainwashed Facilitators are willing to do his dirty deeds.

True fact: only 51 percent of murders are ever solved, my mother's case being a prime example. If Radcliffe MacBeath has his way, I'm destined to become just another statistic.

I've got to get out of here and get home as fast as possible. The sooner I'm under the covers with my door triple-locked, the sooner I'll be safe. Just as long as I can make it from Cambridge to my apartment in Somerville.

I send a text to Heidi, informing her I've clocked out for the weekend. Then I grab my backpack, Heather's handknit white cardigan, and my water bottle. I'm in the stairwell and nearly out the library's secret emergency door when my phone pings.

A text from Trooper Oswald:

> Sorry to read this Stella. MacBeath went after Rose and now he's after you, just like we anticipated. I still say if we find out WHY he killed your mother we'll be halfway to closing the case. The question and the answer are the same.

Why?

He's not wrong. But his little armchair observations aren't doing me much good this afternoon, and I can't say they did much for my mother's case.

After being assured by Heidi that my hipster stalker has left, I venture out for the fifteen-minute walk to the Harvard Square station, all senses primed for potential attack. It must be my paranoia because there seem to be bearded men everywhere. Is there an unshaven male convention in town? Or is it just that I never noticed the preponderance of men with chin hair?

More likely I'm losing my grip.

After my habitual survey of the T station, I swipe my MBTA card and hustle down the crimson-tiled steps to the outbound platform with the rest of the herd. Porter Square is one easy stop away, but it's also Friday, so everyone's out and about.

The train coming from Boston is packed. The doors open, releasing a rush of smells—body odor, sewer, bad cologne, and weed—but not enough passengers for the train to be comfortable. As soon as I squeeze in, my phone vibrates and a text fills the window.

Heidi said u left. Lemme know when you get home!

A message from Fig, my new self-appointed guardian angel.

Needed to get out. Thanks for everything. V sweet of you, I text back.

Fig returns with a clipped response: Sweet, I ain't!

The train screeches to a halt. I and the other lemmings step off onto the platform and head up the stairs.

"Astraea?"

My heart stops. I haven't heard my cult name called out loud since Mama died.

Keep moving, a voice in my head urges. *It's a trap. Don't fall for it.*

Lowering my shoulders, I push into the crowd, barreling through the commuters as if I'm Tom Brady headed for the end zone. Thank God I never wear heels, I think as I deftly skirt strolling couples studying the menus in restaurant windows and zigzag around a gaggle of teenagers staring at their phones.

I don't dare check to see if he's behind me. All I want is to get to my apartment fast, close the door, and hunker down.

My home on Hancock Street is only a half a mile from the Porter Square T, normally a ten-minute walk, though not this evening. Taking no chances, I cut through the backyard of St. James Episcopal Church, wait a decent interval, and then check both ways on Beech before heading to the strip mall, where I duck into the Star Market. Since I'm here, I opt to pick up supplies for a quick dinner. Frozen yakisoba noodles, salmon sushi, and a bottle of a cheap Pinot Grigio with a screw top.

The problem with my living arrangement—well, actually, there's more than one—is that I'm a third wheel. Logan and Mari are the actual renters. I sublet the tiny bedroom off the dining room. And though I supposedly have full use of the kitchen, they're always in there whipping up some elaborate recipe they read in the *New York Times* or throwing one of their famous dinner parties.

That relegates me to a mini fridge, a microwave, and a bowl.

The arrangement's a funky deal I found by answering a Craigslist ad last summer, when Logan and Mari were still in school working on their MBAs. Since graduating and getting jobs in the city last month, however, their fortunes have drastically improved in inverse proportion to their willingness to share a single bathroom. Their lease is up in July, and it would not come as a shock to learn they're moving closer to their work. Too bad, because the location is ideal, though there's absolutely no way I could afford the $4,400 a month in rent.

No weird stalker's waiting for me when I exit the grocery store. When I get to Hancock Street I'm fairly confident I've ditched him. Opening the ground-floor door, I'm relieved to be free and clear as I slip inside the small foyer and climb the stairs to our second-floor apartment.

Which is locked.

Odd, since Mari and Logan never lock up when they're in, unless they've gone to sleep, which, considering it's not quite six, is way too early, even for them. Plus, their car's in the designated parking space, and I can hear voices inside. So what gives?

I fumble for the key that opens the inner door. But it doesn't turn and I realize why. The brass is shiny new and there are scratch marks on the wood. Unbelievable. Those two have changed the locks.

"Hey!" I shout, angrier than a frazzled North Shore mother. "Open up! It's me." All murmuring from the other side ceases.

There is the pound, pound, pound of stockinged steps across the oak flooring and then a click. The door opens and I'm face-to-face with Logan.

"Why'd you change the locks?" I ask, trying to wedge past him.

He extends a foot. "Sorry, but you can't come in."

For a second, I assume he's joking. Then I remember this is Logan and Mari we're talking about. They only laugh at the misfortune of others. "You've got to let me in. I live here, remember?" I hold up my shopping bag as some sort of proof.

"You don't technically live here. Not legally." Logan's pudgy cheeks and pompous attitude are reminiscent of a bossy chipmunk. "You are an at-will tenant. We can evict you whenever we want."

From the living room comes Mari's irritating nasal whine. "Just let her in for now. I don't want the neighbors downstairs over-hearing all our business."

The neighbors downstairs are a nice family of three—a pro-fessor, her struggling author husband, and a kid named Henrietta. The Jamesons. I cat sat for them when they went to Costa Rica on winter break. Mari and Logan wouldn't know the Jamesons be-cause they exist in a bubble that prevents them from interacting with any humans besides their work colleagues and/or their fellow Harvard MBA alums.

Logan removes his foot and I pass by him, plunking my bag on the dining-room table as he locks the door again. Mari's ema-ciated frame is stretched out on the couch before the bay window, a steaming cup of tea on the coffee table next to her open Mac-Book Air and, unless I'm mistaken, a damp folded washcloth on her forehead. Her skin has the waxy sheen of someone deathly ill.

Shit. Maybe she's really, really sick. I've been so wrapped up in my own problems, I haven't stopped to consider there might be a perfectly legitimate reason for Logan's refusal to let me come in. Mari's ill. That's why they came home early from work. Could be COVID.

"Oh, geesh, Mari," I say, keeping a cautious distance. "Are you okay?"

Mari shoots a glance at Logan.

"No, she's not okay," he answers for her. "She's in crisis."

"Crisis?" I'm not entirely clear what he means by that. Has she been fired? Has someone died? Is she suffering disturbing symp-toms pointing to a fatal disease? I decide on the latter, the opened laptop being a giveaway. A tickle in the back of her throat can send Mari to her computer searching for dire diagnoses on WebMD.

Her husband stands by the foot of the couch, a sentinel pro-tecting his wife, and crosses his arms. "Look. We understand none of this is your doing, but you could have been up front with us from the get-go."

I pull out a chair from the table and take a seat, confused. How am I the cause of Mari's Google illness? "What are you talking about? I've been totally up front with you."

"Hah!" Mari sits up a bit and lifts the mug of tea to her lips, taking a brief sip before replacing it on the table. "We saw the post going viral today and read up on the cult it referred to. And I don't know, maybe it's just me. But if I had a whole cult of crazies who probably wanted me dead, especially if that cult *had a militant arm*, I think maybe, just maybe, that's a detail I'd have shared with people who are generous enough to let me rent from them."

So they've seen the post. And instead of being cool or asking me how I'm doing after being accused of covering up my own mother's murder, they are evicting me without warning. Boy, is that obnoxious. However, seeing as how I'm already primed to be pissed, I have to keep my escalating anger in check so I have a place to sleep. I'm going to play it cool.

"No one wants me dead," I lie in a calming monotone. "And you have no right to kick me out. I'm paid through July."

"Damn straight we can kick you out!" Logan interjects. "We've consulted legal counsel"—meaning his friend Connor, a 3L at BU Law—"and he confirmed we are not bound by a contractual obligation. You knew when we allowed you to stay here that the landlord was unaware of a sublet, that our own lease did not permit it. We've put our own necks on the line for you."

"And eight hundred dollars per month," I add.

"Look, Stella, we harbor no personal animus. That said, our health and safety are priorities, and my wife will not sleep a wink with you under our roof knowing you're mixed up with a weird cult."

"I am *not* mixed up with a weird cult. I left the cult when I was ten. I barely remember it. I spent most of my childhood at my father's home in Sudbury."

"You mean your father the murderer?" Mari shoots a guilty glance at her frowning husband. Clearly, he didn't want to broach that subject. "I don't care. It needed to be said, Logan."

"Did it?" I shoot back, now properly incensed by the unfair smear. "Don't tell me you believe everything you read online. You've met my father. He's a quality-control engineer. He wouldn't hurt a fly. His job is to keep flies from getting hurt, in fact."

Mari says "Humph" and averts her gaze, unwilling to admit she was wrong, which only ticks me off more. She should apologize. Dad schlepped their new dining-room table up a flight of stairs and nearly sprained his back in the process. She knows she's way off base here.

"Whatever," she continues, not nearly as abashed as she needs to be. "My point is people are digging into your dad's past. Your mom's too. Do you have any idea what she and those Diviners were up to? Sacrifices of young women, that's what. Sacrifices on the summer solstice to guarantee a productive harvest!"

Heat shoots up my neck. I've heard this conspiracy before, and Mari has clearly done a Reddit deep dive on the cult.

"That's categorically untrue," I fire back. "Mama's murder had no connection to the summer solstice or this ridiculous shit about sacrifices. It just so happened that she was trying to escape with me that night because there were hundreds of visitors at the Center for midsummer festivities, and she figured there'd be less chance people would notice us leaving!"

"What about the other two?" Mari will not drop this bone. "They disappeared during the solstice too. I read online that they were burned in a bonfire to appease the gods, and their ashes were stirred into potions of mead to give the cult supernatural powers!" Mari's referring to the two missing women highlighted in the *Dark*

Cults episode. Rory Davis and Willow Johnston, age twenty-three and twenty-five respectively, were homeless addicts who met in rehab and decided to hike Vermont's 276-mile Long Trail to support their sobriety. They stopped off at the Center's hostel, took part in the summer solstice celebration, and reportedly were observed dancing around the bonfire.

The following morning, they were gone, their clothes still in their backpacks, their cots undisturbed. Even their toothbrushes were dry. Police inquiries met a dead end. As with the investigation into my mother's murder, numerous Diviners willingly penned affidavits swearing MacBeath was present during the celebration and never left the compound.

The Center's statement after the *Dark Cults* episode aired was almost identical to the one they issued after my mother was killed: Rory and Willow made the mistake of defying Center rules and entering the forest at night, for which the Center could not be held responsible.

In addition to Rory and Willow, my mother's best friend, Cerise, also went missing shortly before my mother was murdered. Hence the viral post's reference to the Triangle Three. The Bennington Triangle was the subtitle of the *Dark Cults* episode and the name, coined by author Joe Citro, of a mythological area in southwestern Vermont. According to him, strange, unexplained events have occurred in the Bennington Triangle. The Triangle marks what some folklorists have described as a "thin place" prone to supernatural activity, including disappearances, rumored alien visits, and even Bigfoot sightings.

Still, as someone close to what's been happening in The Center, never, ever have I heard of cultists burning people at the stake to appease the gods, as Mari seems to believe.

"The Diviners aren't homicidal, primitive pagans, Mari, they're just a bunch of New Agers who like to meditate and swing pendulums over charts to tune in to their inner Divine Energy. Totally peaceful and harmless." Well, except for the Facilitators. But this doesn't seem like the moment to point that out.

Logan redirects the conversation. "What I don't like is your lack of transparency, Stella. You never told us anything about your mother's murder or that she was once in that cult—"

"Where the other women went missing, don't forget," adds Mari. "Probably disappeared by the cult's hitmen. What are they called again, Logy?"

"Enablers," her husband answers. He snaps his fingers. "Wait. Facilitators."

Well, color me shocked. Turns out "read up on it" actually means Mr. and Mrs. Cannes slummed it by streaming murder porn. "Wow. Did you guys really watch that awful show? I didn't think you stooped to true crime."

"Not my normal cinematic fare, true, but as a former psych major I found it mildly interesting." Mari sniffs. "If you haven't seen it, I suggest you do. Without naming names, it quite clearly implies that your mother's cult is run by a deranged lunatic. What's his name again, baby?"

"Radcliffe MacBeath. Founder of the SDS Movement. Spiritual Dowsing for Success. What a scam."

Logy baby won't get an argument from me. "Look, guys," I say, trying to inject a bit of common sense. "That *Dark Cults* episode was sensationalized to attract eyeballs. Naturally, they're gonna make stuff scarier than it is by hinting the cult follows a madman who happens to be protected by a secret security force of trained assassins." Though, to be fair, this is exactly what I believe too. But again, I want to have a place to sleep tonight, so needs must. "You are way overreacting."

"Overreacting? Then explain him!" Mari thumbs toward the window.

Logan peers out. "Shit. He's back."

Even before I see the glasses and beard and Hawaiian shirt, I know exactly the man they're talking about. There he is on the sidewalk, having a one-way conversation with the ether. My stalker has found me. My stomach does a triple somersault.

"That's one of them," Logan says. "He was there when we got home, asked if this is where you lived."

"That's when we decided to call an emergency locksmith," Mari adds.

Still, no excuse for locking me out without warning. And no excuse for not warning me of a stalker waiting at my home either. "What did he say, exactly?"

Logan does an eye roll. "He said, 'I'm looking for Stella O'Neill. Is this the correct address?'"

So much for hoping the Diviners knew only where I worked.

"We didn't answer," Mari adds. "Sweetie, I think now we should call the cops."

Logan drops to a knee by her side. "Mari-kins, I've told you we can't. If the police come, there'll be a report and the landlord will find out we violated the lease thanks to"—he curls his upper lip at me—"*her.*"

As if *I'd* posted the Craigslist ad.

"Which is why she has to leave immediately." The prospect flushes Mari's cheeks with much-needed color. "Logan, if you won't do it, I will. Stella, you've got to go, pronto." She flings a finger toward the door. "You can arrange to pick up your things tomorrow during the day. Text me a time and we'll give you an hour to clean out. Anything left by Sunday is getting tossed to the curb."

Logan runs to the door, unlocking it and flinging it wide. My Star bag is in his other hand. "Sorry," he says without a scintilla of remorse, "we have to do it for our—"

"Health and safety, yeah, yeah, yeah." I bypass him on my way to the bathroom, where I grab my contact solution, toothbrush, toothpaste, and deodorant. My phone vibrates again.

Another text from Fig. I'm beginning to think she's as psychic as my mother was.

> Taking a detour home to your apartment to make sure you're okay. U okay?

Incredible. How does she know?

> Not exactly.

My thumbs hover over the screen as I debate whether I can ask her for a ride to my parents' house twenty miles away. With rush-hour traffic, it'd be an hour's drive, way too big a burden.

What's up? Fig asks.

> Being evicted

There's a series of dots, and then:

> You can stay with us! On my way!

Wait, how does she know where I live? Maybe she asked HR for my address after everything that happened today, just in case. She's being so nice. Too nice.

Don't overthink it, I tell myself. *Be grateful for the help.*

Returning from the bathroom, I snatch the groceries out of Logan's hand and flip him the bird for old times' sake. "You guys suck."

"Class," he says, watching me from the top landing as I head down the stairs. "And don't even think about getting back your security deposit. There are definitely dings in the walls we're gonna have to patch."

Great. That means I'm out $1,600. This is the worst day ever. It's so awful, I've almost forgotten about the hipster Diviner waiting to pounce as soon as I step outside.

"Hey, Astraea!" he says, with a cheerful wave, like we've arranged to meet for coffee. "So nice to see you again."

It's the same voice from the subway.

I freeze. There's something about this guy that's familiar. He's a little older than I am and fairly normal looking in a jeans jacket and a funky pair of Nobull high-tops. Normally, I'd find that package attractive, but not when I suspect he wants to carry me off to the Center to meet my death.

"You need to leave me alone, got it?" I say firmly, holding the Star bag high, ready to swing it like a mace. That wine bottle's got to sting. "I don't appreciate being stalked."

"Stalked?" He brings a hand to his chest, as if personally offended. "I'm not stalking you."

"You show up at my work. You show up at my home. What would you call it?"

"Uhm, being concerned?"

"Well, knock it off." Pointing to the window where Logan and Mari are watching, riveted, I say, "That's my roommate. She's calling the cops and they're on their way to arrest you for stalking, so you'd better get the fuck out of here."

A crease between his brow forms. "Come on, Astraea. Don't be like that. It's me . . . Rowan. We grew up together."

Rowan? Then I remember: Rowan Ocht. Rowan was another wild kid in the cult. I can see him now, plunging off the cliff on a rope swing into Glacial Lake over and over. The guy had no fear.

"All coming back to you?"

"Sort of . . ."

He grins widely, revealing straight white teeth. Not sure where those came from. We cult kids never saw a dentist. Never got vaccinated. Never wore shoes—unless you were me, of course.

"I know who you are," I say, "but that doesn't change anything." Even if we were childhood playmates, Rowan's a Diviner and I can't trust him. He could still be under Radcliffe's influence. For all I know, he could have been promoted to Facilitator. "But how'd you find out where I live?"

As if we're about to make a drug deal, he checks over both shoulders, reaches into his pocket, and pulls out a pendulum in black agate hanging from a chain of sterling silver. "How do you think?"

There are two possible answers. Either Rowan is a genius at map dowsing or Radcliffe has been keeping tabs on me for years and gave him my address. Logic dictates the latter. "Really, the cops should be here any minute," I say, taking a step back. "The library has you on camera. You'll be in big trouble."

"You're the one in big trouble. You're not safe on your own in the city with all these rumors flying around. You need to come back to the Center. We've got the Facilitators with their top-notch twenty-four-hour security, and the Diviners will take care of you like a prodigal sister. You'll be loved and protected."

Is he high? I got the email. I know what they're after, and it's not love and protection. Of course the cult wants me to come back. That way they can have total control over my every move, make sure I'm inaccessible to journalists or podcasters or cops. And if I'm very, very good and fall in step with their philosophy—including pledging obeyance to their leader, MacBeath—they might even let me live.

Hardly an attractive offer.

"You are honestly asking me to return with you to the place where my mother was murdered on the orders of your psycho leader, *for my safety?*"

He smiles that annoyingly blissful Diviner smile. "Why would you think Dagda had anything to do with your mother's death?"

"Don't be insulting. You know they'd have arrested Radcliffe by now if his followers hadn't submitted sworn—and let's be honest, Rowan—totally fake alibis. They claimed he was at the solstice bonfire all night and, therefore, couldn't have gone into the woods to kill my mother. That doesn't matter. You and I both know the deed was done by a Facilitator, on your Dagda's orders."

"You're right about one thing," Rowan says, clearly annoyed by my accusations. "The police do know who killed your mother, and, yeah, they haven't arrested him and never will. But his name is Benjamin Winslow, not Radcliffe MacBeath."

That name catches me up short. Winslow. *Winslow.* My mother had a client named Mrs. Winslow.

I have a vague memory of an English garden fragrant with pink roses and a wooden swing set with a dented metal slide that burned the backs of my legs on a hot summer day. My first glass of sweet-and-sour lemonade. Blue Popsicles that were supposed to taste like raspberries, and my mother sitting at a circular wrought-iron table on a slate patio swinging a pendulum next to a woman with white hair pulled back in a big black bow. Their heads were often bowed in silence.

I'm still caught in my memories when a big black SUV with tinted windows snakes up the street, slowing as it nears us. Funny. That does not seem like the type of car Figurina DiTolla would drive.

Rowan puts an arm around me and pulls me to him tightly before the SUV picks up speed and turns the corner. I find I've been holding my breath and, judging from the way he exhales, so has he.

"Sorry. Knee-jerk reaction," he says sheepishly, releasing me from his clutch. "I'm kind of on edge."

You and me both, buddy.

Beep. Beep.

With a screech of brakes, Fig pulls up to the curb in her tiny green Mini Cooper convertible. Boy, am I glad to see her and her absurd straw sunbonnet. She looks like Little Bo Peep driving a golf cart.

"Don't park," I yell, sidestepping Rowan and throwing open the passenger door. I jump in, checking over my shoulder. "Just go. I'll explain later."

She shifts into drive. "Where to?"

"Anywhere," I bark, as the black SUV appears in the rearview. It must have been circling the block. "Preferably by the most confusing route possible. We've gotta ditch that car behind us."

"It's summer construction season in Boston. We have no choice but to get lost." Cranking the steering wheel to the left, she cuts off the SUV, steps on the gas, and nearly runs over a kid on a skateboard before turning right into the wrong way of a one-way side street. I'd be shocked except I'm from Boston. Fig's driving doesn't even faze me as I google BEN WINSLOW VERMONT.

The hits are intriguing. Benjamin Winslow grew up in Dutton, Vermont, near the Center, so his mother definitely could have been Mama's client. He'd be about forty now, which would have put him at twenty when my mother was murdered. A few years ago he married his second wife, a former runway model named Priti with whom he lives in Monterey. According to his Wikipedia page, he made his money founding a start-up called HeadFake. HeadFake specializes in "cutting-edge, health-monitoring tracking apps."

That's all very interesting, but none of what I've read so far accounts for why Benjamin Winslow would have wanted my mother dead, so maybe it's just the Center's latest fake-out to throw off the scent. I can't figure out how they would have met, considering at the time of her murder he was a rising senior at Stanford, at least according to my quick calculations.

But then I notice a chilling detail:

Ben Winslow played center for the Stanford University Cardinals when they made it to the second round of the Division 1 NCAA tournament in 2002. I'm no connoisseur of basketball, but I've watched enough Celtics games to know the center tends to be the tallest player on the team.

Googling his college stats, I nearly plotz. The guy's height is six feet six inches. Super tall.

Just like antler man.

5

ROSE

JUNE 17, 2003

DRAFT Welcome Speech

SUMMER SOLSTICE ANNUAL CONFERENCE
THE CENTER FOR SPIRITUAL DOWSING

Glastenbury, Vermont

(INTRO, INTRO. WELCOMING. NOTICES ABOUT
DINNER/EVENTS . . .)

*You know the question I'm most often asked by outsiders
is why did I leave all my earthly comforts to follow
Radcliffe MacBeath, better known to us Diviners as
Dagda. Judging from all the heads nodding in the
audience, I get the impression I'm not alone!*

*But you know, fellow Diviners and beloved guests,
I truly love when I'm asked this question. I cherish the
opportunity to testify about the miraculous moment when
Dagda saved not only my life, but the life of my precious*

daughter, Astraea, who has had the joy of growing up in this loving community that's so close to nature and so far from the sterile wasteland of the outsiders' society.

I was probably like you were before you attended one of Dagda's transformative seminars or read one of his bestselling books, or more likely saw his famous appearance on Sally Jessy Raphael! (Pause for laughter.)

I, too, was going through the motions of living, ticking off all the boxes on the checklist for success. I was married to a decent man with ambitions of his own, and I'd just given birth to the light of my life, our daughter, whom we named Stella. You see, fellow Diviners, even then I was aligned with the stars.

So let's turn the clock back to 1994, when I first met Dagda. Dan, my husband, was finishing up his PhD in chemical engineering at Northeastern and was always busy. We barely saw each other except at night, and by then we were almost too exhausted to talk, much less anything else.

We were living in a tiny one-bedroom apartment on the fourth floor of a brick walk-up in a sketchy section of Boston. I was a stay-at-home mom, occasionally freelancing for the local newspaper where I'd been a full-time reporter before giving birth to our daughter. I took any assignment they threw at me including, once, a ridiculous request that I attend a free seminar being offered by so-called self-help guru Radcliffe MacBeath.

Radcliffe . . . MacBeath? He sounded like a Shakespearean cartoon character. (Pause for laughter.) But I accepted the assignment and brought my infant daughter, since my husband was working.

Brothers and sisters, I don't need to tell you what

happened next. When Radcliffe began to explain about the universal energy that unites us all, when he described us as one soul separated by our human bodies, something resonated deep down inside me.

It felt like the voice of my grandmother was speaking. She'd always taught me there was magic in the world, and if you paid attention and prayed, you could tap into it. She'd been known for her ability to cure members of her community from various diseases, to ward off evil spirits, and to match soul mates.

In other words, my grandmother was simply practicing divination! If I'd been able to introduce her to Dagda's message that we are all one energy connected to the Divine Energy, she would be right here with us tonight.

Unfortunately, my fabulous grandmother died unexpectedly when I was pregnant with Stella. I felt her loss keenly. I was so lonely, so bereft, that had it not been for my baby girl, I might have chosen to walk down a dark path. Nothing felt like home, nothing gave me hope . . .

Until I met Dagda.

After his presentation, I went backstage, and before I could open my mouth, he said, "Hello, Rose, queen among flowers." Turning to my daughter in her stroller, he said, "And this little star must be Stella, though, really, she's an Astraea, the goddess of justice."

Here's the thing. There is absolutely no way Radcliffe MacBeath could have known our names.

He then took my hands in his, looked deep into my eyes, and said quite matter-of-factly, "Rose, you have been blessed with a rare power inherited from a gifted woman."

(Pause to let that sink in.)

"She is watching over you and sees you are grieving.

She wants you to know you are loved and that you two
will be together once more. In the meantime, however,
you have a divine purpose on this Earth, and that is to
use your power to help others. Reject society and all its
superficial trappings. Come with me, Rose, so I may
teach you how to reach your full potential while living in
harmony with nature and those who are fellow seekers.
Come to the Center, Rose. Come home."

Home. Such a simple yet potent word. It was then
that I realized I hadn't lived in a true home since I'd left
my grandmother. At that moment, I knew there was no
question. I had to follow Radcliffe MacBeath. It was my
destiny.

So—deep breath—I eventually left my husband
whom I loved and took our daughter to live at the Center.
I have never regretted a single minute.

On that note, please stand in gratitude for our leader,
our guru, the shepherd who's led us out of the wilderness
by leading us into the wilderness, the one and only . . .

"Mr. Dickhead himself."

"Stop it, Cerise," Rose scolded, trying not to laugh as she drew a line through *the one and only*. Too clichéd. "What if he hears?"

Cerise shuffled her Tarot cards and glanced around the dusky cabin and under her rocking chair, pretending to search for eavesdroppers. The only other person here was Astraea, fast asleep in her trundle bed and snoring slightly. "Do the walls have ears?"

"They might," Rose whispered. She didn't have to tell Cerise that one of Ellen's newly created security-force members, a so-called Facilitator, would stop at nothing to curry favor with Cliff by ratting out a follower for disloyalty.

Cerise herself had gone to bed with a growling stomach often enough to know she'd be punished with a stay in the Chi Chamber and a forced fast if Dagda decided she needed a lesson in obedience. She should be more careful.

"Do you think he'll sign off on this?" Rose asked.

"I had my doubts until you got to the glowing bullshit. He's gonna *love* that. Comes off like a god. You know he demands nothing less."

Rose feared for her friend, whose outspoken cynicism was growing bolder by the day. Cerise used to be more circumspect about her dissatisfaction with Radcliffe's behavior, reserving her quips about his latest extravagant purchases for when she and Rose were safely alone, out of Facilitator earshot.

Occasionally when their leader got on his soapbox about the importance of simple living—despite his comfy, heated home with its indoor plumbing and running water—Cerise might roll her eyes. But like the rest of them, she dared not do or say more.

Lately, however, she'd been risking Ellen's wrath and a trip to the Chi Chamber by openly questioning his increasing demands for money. In the midst of being lectured by him last week about the importance of tithing, Cerise actually said out loud, "You do know ten percent of zero is zero, right, Cliff?" It was a not-so-subtle reference to the fact that most of the Diviners labored long hours for free.

Cerise wasn't that much older than Rose, forty at best. She'd been at the Center since Cliff founded it in the eighties. Hard living had taken its toll. Her brittle hair was already going gray, and her skin was leathery from countless hours working in the fields without sunscreen, just one of the many chemicals Cliff forbade, along with Tylenol and Neosporin. These were poisons promulgated by the corporate pharmaceutical industry to make Americans sick so they'd purchase more chemicals promulgated by the corporate pharmaceutical industry, he claimed. The wild mushrooms and

Indigenous plants used by the Abenaki were far more effective, he said. Better still, they didn't require a physician's prescription.

Rose had come to understand that Cliff wasn't as concerned about Western medicine's profit motive as he was about legitimate doctors inquiring about the Center's dietary restrictions and working conditions, especially for the children. That could expose them to surprise inspections from Children's Services or a police investigation. Such raids weren't unheard of. In 1984, a commune in the Northeast Kingdom of Island Pond was stormed by the Vermont State Troopers, which removed over one hundred children from their homes. Diviners lived in fear of being next.

Cerise clutched her jaw and winced.

"Tooth still hurting?" Rose asked, as if there were any doubt.

"Nothing's working. Raw garlic. Peppermint tea bags soaked in clove oil. There doesn't seem to be a remedy."

Aside from seeing an actual dentist, Rose thought. She considered asking her wealthy client Genevieve Winslow for a referral, preferably to someone who would treat Cerise pro bono. Knowing Genevieve, she'd sneak the dentist a couple of Franklins under the table.

"Not to worry," Cerise said. "After the solstice is over, I'll get the tooth pulled and that will be that." She spread seven cards in a standard horseshoe on the table. She read the first—"the past"—and nodded in agreement. She had no reaction to the second. When she reached the seventh and final card, she slumped in the rocking chair.

"Unfavorable outcome?"

Cerise held up the final card, the Queen of Swords. "I always get this."

"Because that's you, isn't it? Quick wit. Sharp tongue. Perseverance."

"Except it was upside down." Cerise arched an eyebrow. "You know what *that* means."

A knot inside Rose twisted. An upside-down Queen of Swords meant Cerise had an enemy. It wasn't hard to guess who: most likely Ellen, Cliff's henchwoman and most trusted adviser. The witch would go to any lengths to ingratiate herself with Dagda, and seeing as how Cerise had become a thorn in Cliff's side, might be tempted to make an example of her. She'd probably lock Cerise in solitary confinement for days if she could.

"Cards are unreliable," Rose said lightly. "What does your pendulum say?"

Cerise swung the six-sided garnet pendulum that Rose had purchased for her as a birthday gift despite the Diviners' prohibition against celebrating such milestones. The stone was a deep, dark pink, in homage to the color of Cerise's name. The garnet also had grounding properties, to keep her friend from flying off the handle.

"I asked if I'd be alive to see the solstice and the answer was no."

Rose pretended to focus on the speech, her mind racing in alarm. Like her fellow Diviners, she believed in the concept that Divine Energy was a true force connecting and directing all human interactions. However, there was something to be said for a dowser's subconscious influence, and Cerise certainly hadn't been herself lately.

Turning from her speech, Rose said, "You'll be fine. It's just your tooth generating so much caustic energy. Try again when you feel better."

Cerise shrugged and placed her cards in a small silk drawstring bag she wore attached to her belt. "I'd better be going, anyway. A few days until the solstice extravaganza, and we're still way behind on supplies. The front office needs to up its game for what they're charging this year."

"I heard the entrance fee was one fifty."

"Try two fifty. Two hundred and fifty bucks to sit on the dirt listening to a megalomaniac drone on and on about our magical portal here at the Center, and how, with a monthly contribution of a small mortgage payment, they, too, can learn the secrets of tapping into the Divine path to physical wellness, spiritual fulfillment, and—lest anyone miss the bold print—*immense financial wealth.*"

She rose slowly, painfully, from the wooden rocking chair. "The hell of it is, he was awesome back in the day. Cliff didn't give a tinker's dam about fame or TV appearances or acquiring another Porsche. He was just another poor seeker trying to find meaning in this fucked-up universe, as were we all. It breaks my heart to see how he's changed."

Rose hoped Astraea hadn't heard the swear. Or the slander. Either could land them in trouble if her child innocently told a friend.

Cerise stretched. Her emaciated frame swam in her worn overalls and faded purple T-shirt. Once upon a time, she'd been Cliff's cherished sidekick, a devoted acolyte bursting with passion for the Diviners' philosophy.

Then Ellen swooped in, fanning the flames of their guru's ego while securing her own position of authority. The place had gone downhill ever since.

"Okay, I'd better go," Cerise said. "She who will not be named has apparently got me on double-secret probation. If I'm not in bed by curfew, it'll be eight hours of weeding without water for me!"

Rose gave her a sad wave as her friend unlatched the door and let herself out.

How had everything gone so wrong? What had whetted Cliff's appetite for fame and adulation? He used to be so kind, so down-to-earth. He used to mock men who lusted for wealth and prestige as duped fools. He was such a spiritual mentor—and lover.

Once upon a time long, long ago, she and Cliff had been an exclusive pair, their languorous lovemaking an expression not of physical desire but of divine spiritual connection. The night Cliff promoted her from Mentor to Realized was the night he first took her to his bed. The exhilaration of his hands over her body as he whispered mesmerizing words of adoration transcended any sexual encounter she'd had with Dan or any man.

This, she remembered thinking, letting her body give in and flow to his energy as her mind swooned in ecstasy, *this* is divine love. There'd been nothing like that moment of intense intimacy before or since; their union had been absolutely transcendent.

Now, he was just into himself as though he, alone, were the sun in the universe of orbiting Diviners.

For so long she'd been defending him to Cerise and to herself. But as Astraea sighed and turned over in her trundle bed, Rose realized there was more at stake.

Astraea was ten and precocious. She was heading toward the dangerous precipice of adolescence. With her shiny auburn hair and twinkling eyes, high cheekbones, wide smile, and merry disposition, the girl was poised to grow into a charmer. Cliff had noticed, and Rose had noticed Cliff noticing, much to her dismay.

She didn't appreciate the way he singled out her daughter for special treats, rewarding her tiny achievements with a joyride in his convertible or showering her with praise. Rose cringed when he stroked her head and chucked her under the chin. Pulling Astraea onto his lap turned her stomach.

Eight years from now, when she reached legal age, would Astraea be on his radar? The prospect was intolerable.

Cerise was right. Cliff had changed, and he wasn't likely to repent his new ways. Rose would have no choice but to leave the commune and the fellow Diviners who'd become her family.

The question was not whether she would leave, but how. Her sizable earnings from conducting readings for Genevieve Winslow had been turned over to MacBeath. She didn't have a dime to her name. No transportation either, and the commune by design was miles away from town, at the end of a twisting and difficult mountain road. Even if she did have the means to escape, there were always the Facilitators to worry about. Ellen's security force kept a close watch on the Diviners' every movement.

There was someone who could help, however, someone who Rose suspected despised her with every essence of his being, despite his generous offer of cash. To accept his proposal, however, would effectively be an admission of guilt and a blow to her pride.

Still, that might be her only option, because she and Astraea had to get out of the commune—sooner rather than later.

ROSE

JUNE 19, 2003

Rose grew increasingly worried about Cerise.

She'd been absent from two sunrise meditations, and there was no sight of her friend in the field. Rose hoped to sneak her a canteen of peppermint tea to soothe her tooth pain and a cinnamon roll warm from the oven. Not ideal sustenance for someone afflicted with a dental abscess, but that was the best she could do.

Normally, during the approach of the solstice, Cerise would have been bopping all over the place, pitching in wherever needed—hauling in pallets, setting up food and information tents, weaving wildflower crowns, and decorating the pavilion on the hill with her fabulous peonies.

Cerise was a genius at raising peonies. Named after the healing deity Paeon, the lush pink and white flowers symbolized wealth and prosperity, Cliff's new favorite things. That's why he wanted vases of them on the pavilion altar and on his table at the banquet, to send the subconscious message that his presence equaled financial success.

And yet, Cerise's carefully cultivated peony bushes were untouched, their dark-green stems bending to the ground, burdened by the weight of the blooms. She should have cut them at the snowball stage, removing the ants and placing the buds in fortified water so they'd be perfect for the solstice. At this rate, they'd be lucky to find enough for a bouquet, since most of their petals were already turning brown.

Where was she?

Visitors were beginning to invade the compound, with a record number expected to attend thanks to predictions of warm, sunny weather. Clear blue skies, mild temperatures, and a gentle breeze made for perfect June conditions. Even the nasty blackflies seemed to be on hiatus.

Rose checked the garden to see if, by chance, her friend was back at work. She waved to a pair of Diviners in handwoven straw hats picking fresh peapods and inquired if they'd seen their coworker.

"Probably reading by the swimming hole." The Diviner who went by the name Aurora pulled off her gloves and wiped her sweaty brow, her blissful smile never faltering. "Who can blame her? Days like this are few and far."

No judgment. That was a Diviner rule. Rose liked to think most of her comrades tried their best to leave their opinions at the Center's gates, just as they'd left behind careers and car payments and technology. This was not by choice. Dagda forbade power lines because they interfered with connections to the Divine Energy.

The exception was his own house, tucked on the hillside overlooking the Center, with separate access to the mountain road. The Center had paid a pretty penny to hook up his residence to the nearest power pole, over a mile away. Cliff claimed he needed electricity to operate his computer and a satellite dish so he could communicate with the outside world in order to spread his message to the masses. Rose had her doubts after learning he owned three televisions and that the dish was so he could watch ESPN. Just more evidence their leader was becoming unhinged.

Recently, he'd purchased another new roadster—a ridiculous Porsche Boxster convertible. With its low clearance, Rose was amazed he'd been able to drive it up the rocky mountain road without scraping the undercarriage. And then there was its garish color. A vivid turquoise to "generate positive energy." At least that was Cliff's excuse.

Cerise said the car cost fifty grand, about as much as hooking up to the power line. She was outraged that the rest of them had to sleep in drafty dorms and take bracingly cold showers when Dear Leader was sleeping on Egyptian-cotton sheets in either a heated or air-conditioned bedroom, thereby violating his own dictates.

"I'm not going to stand for it," Cerise told her a few weeks ago, when they were treading water in the freezing swimming hole, where not even a spying Facilitator could hear their conversation. "I'm thinking of staging an intervention, getting him to recognize that if he keeps up this manic spending and buying all these luxuries, he'll lose credibility as well as followers. Maybe he'll see reason when he realizes he's got a brand to maintain. Otherwise, this place is in the toilet."

Cerise had asked if Rose wanted in, but she'd demurred out of her own self-interest. Her little family had a pretty good setup. They enjoyed a private cabin and outhouse, and she didn't want to cross Ellen by being a rabblerouser. She was very fortunate not to have to work in hot fields like Cerise or clean out the latrines like the Novices. As a Realized member of the cult, she was high enough on the food chain to be spared such vile duties.

Her successful side hustle as a psychic and talented baker didn't hurt either. Her gooey cinnamon rolls put Café Divine on the map, turning it from a loss leader into a significant revenue source for the Center. The spotless, pink-walled restaurant with its cheerful gingham curtains and polished pine tables was now a mandatory stop for Long Trail hikers and a few tour buses. Depending on the season, Rose could bake up to a hundred rolls a day, triple that for the solstice. It felt like she'd been baking and freezing for weeks in preparation.

"Can I have one more for a friend?" Astraea asked that morning, greedily eyeing the two rolls remaining on the tray in the café. She clasped her hands behind her back and rocked on her heels, her brown eyes wide in exaggerated innocence.

"*May* I," Rose corrected, crossing her arms in feigned disapproval. "To whom will this roll be given?" Since there was no formal schooling at the Center, she made a point of teaching correct grammar whenever possible.

"Rowan." Astraea's soft cheeks blushed a pale pink. "His mama won't let him have sugar, you know."

Good thing, since Rowan was wild enough as it was. That boy was forever scaling trees and engaging in risky behavior, like cliff diving. He was fourteen, at that dangerous age when he assumed mortality didn't apply to him. Rose feared her child might be tempted to follow suit someday and end up hurt.

"Rowan's a big boy," she responded. "If he wants a cinnamon roll, he can come here himself."

Astraea's lower lip popped in disappointment. "But I promised."

She was generous, this child, another attribute Rose credited to the Diviners' philosophy that no one owns anything. Except for Cliff, who kind of owned everything. "If his mother says it's okay, then he may have one."

Rowan's mother, the resident numerologist, would not approve unless the numbers did, a fact Astraea had already deduced.

"What's the date today?" Her daughter stood on tiptoes to read the paper calendar on the wall. "June nineteenth. Six for June plus nineteen for the day equals twenty-five and two thousand three for the year equals five when you add two and three up. Twenty-five plus five equals thirty. Three plus zero equals three, and three is a lucky number. I'll go tell his mama."

Who said the Center kids didn't know their math?

Astraea ran off, her brown ponytail bouncing as her sneakered feet skipped excitedly, sparking a flash of panic. Did they forget the foil this morning? It was a constant concern.

"She's adorable." Bryanna, a new recruit as evidenced by her green robe, stacked dirty dishes left on the tables. "And smart, no?"

"More often when a cute boy's involved." Immediately, Rose chided herself for being so sexist. "Sorry. That came out wrong."

Bryanna smiled in forgiveness. She was a wisp of a willow, no more than twenty-one or -two, and judging from the scars on her wrists, already handling some heavy baggage. Rose had seen more than a few of her ilk come and go in her near decade at the Center. Runaways, recovering addicts, sex-abuse victims. They found a warm welcome and no condemnation among the Diviners.

"Boys. Boys. Boys." Shaking out a crocheted dishrag, Bryanna began to wipe a long wooden table. "More trouble than they're worth, in my opinion."

Every newbie had a story, some more tragic than others, Rose thought, taking a broom to the floor. "If you want to talk about him, I'm here."

"Thanks, but"—Bryanna shook her head and moved to the next table—"I'd rather leave the past in the past. That's why they call it the past, right?"

Another of Cliff's "insightful" euphemisms straight from the introduction to *Dowsing for Spiritual (and Financial!) Success.*

"How about you?" Bryanna asked, flipping back one of her braids. "You end up here because of a guy?"

"Not exactly, unless you count Dagda." Rose rattled off a

synopsized version of the testimony she'd deliver at the solstice ceremony. "I had to see if what he promised was true."

"And was it?" Bryanna arched her back, wincing. She was too young for that kind of ache.

"Bending at that angle can do a number on your lumbar if you're not careful," Rose said, avoiding the newbie's questions.

Bryanna gave Rose a curious look. "Was your husband okay with that? You taking off with his daughter when she was just a toddler?"

The feelings of guilt this dreaded question prompted were profound. Rose hated remembering the devastation in Dan's voice when she called him from the commune to say she'd left in the middle of the night because she needed to be free to practice her spiritual dowsing without his negative energy getting in the way.

Dan didn't share her enthusiasm for Radcliffe MacBeath or his teachings, which had captivated her from their first meeting in Boston. In fact, Dan dismissed MacBeath as a quack and Rose as a fool for following his nonsense.

Be that as it may, Rose was free to pursue her interests, or so he claimed, but she had no right to take their daughter to some godforsaken commune in the woods of Vermont. Rose promised they'd be gone for only a few months.

That was seven years ago.

Dan kept saying over and over, "I thought we were happy. Why didn't you tell me?"

She *had* told him. He just hadn't listened.

"My husband's come to terms." Rose picked up the speed of her sweeping. "In fact, I think it's for the best. He's doing what he loves, quality control if you can believe it, and he doesn't have to worry about coming home in time for dinner. He's a bit of a workaholic."

"Ah. I see."

Rose could tell Bryanna couldn't see. For some women, a husband who earned enough money so they didn't have to work a paying job was the ultimate prize. Rose was aware her former friends on the outside blamed her for doing the unthinkable—leaving her husband and taking their baby to go live in the wilderness. They must have thought she was either incredibly selfish or just plain nuts. Maybe both.

"How about you?" Rose asked, switching the spotlight onto Bryanna. "How'd you end up here?"

Turned out, Bryanna came to the Center like so many—during a pit stop on her hike on the Long Trail. The Center catered to hikers, offering them cheap accommodations in the hostel and filling vegetarian fare in the café. If they couldn't pony up payment in actual cash, then they could work off their room and board in the gardens or latrines.

Cliff likely directed Ellen to assign Bryanna to the café so she wouldn't be scared off by shit scraping and weeding. No dirty broken nails or stinky chores for this promising Novice.

Bryanna reminded Rose of herself when she first came to the Center, full of awe and admiration for Dagda and his devoted followers. She knew what the girl was feeling, this urge to please, to become one with the Divine, whether spiritually—or via Cliff, physically. The memory made Rose's heart flutter like she was still a lovestruck teenager.

Bryanna needed to take care. Dagda was a formidable figure, forever scheming and calculating to get what he wanted. And young Bryanna with her silky dark hair and almond eyes could have been Rose's twin. Cliff definitely had a type, and this newbie was it. That might have been okay seven years ago when he was a kind man. Not now.

Like Cerise said, Cliff had changed.

"Rowan can have a cinnamon roll!" Astraea announced, returning triumphant from pestering Rowan's mother.

Rose had spun around to see her innocent daughter in the doorway holding hands with Dagda.

Cliff, however, was focused solely on Bryanna, who bowed her head, nervously wiping her hands on her apron. "I wonder if I might sample this delight," he boomed, ogling his future prize.

"There's only one roll left," Astraea piped up. "And it's for my friend Rowan!"

Silence quickly descended. Cliff did not take rejection well— even if it was only a cinnamon roll and the refusal came from a child. Rose bit her lip, her mind racing for an alternative that would placate both guru and daughter.

Bryanna stepped forward. "Absolutely, Dagda. Allow me."

She lifted the glass top, pinched the roll with tongs, and placed it on a cloth napkin. "Here you go."

"Just a bite, please. I'm trying to watch my weight." He opened his mouth wide like a bridegroom waiting to be fed wedding cake by his bride.

Bryanna hesitated, unsure of what to do. Rose cringed at the awkwardness of the moment. She'd wanted to snatch the roll out of Bryanna's fingers and smush it in his face.

"Sure." Bryanna broke off a piece and popped it in his mouth.

"Delicious!" He ran his tongue over his lips seductively. "Now, Astraea, you may give the rest to your boyfriend."

Before Rose could stop her, Astraea responded with a stamp of her little foot. "He's not my boyfriend."

Cliff laughed and ruffled her daughter's lovely dark hair, a combination of Rose's black Puerto Rican locks and her husband's Irish red. It had occurred to Rose at that moment that Astraea could have been Bryanna's younger sister, the two looked so much alike.

"Go on now. Never keep a hungry man waiting."

Another disturbing change in Cliff's personality, this sudden focus on gender. Astraea took no notice, happily skipping out the door to deliver the remainder of the cinnamon roll to Rowan.

"By the way," Cliff said, addressing Rose, "Genevieve Winslow requests a consult tomorrow afternoon. I know, I know. It's the day before the solstice. Be that as it may, she is your best client, and I'd hate to let her down in an emergency. Unless you're still trying to avoid her son. I understand he's home for a visit."

Cliff studied her reaction, searching for a telltale display of emotion. She refused to give him the satisfaction.

Rose threw up her arms. "Tomorrow? We're expecting over a hundred guests for lunch. It'll be one of our busiest days. Can't she wait until Monday?"

Appeased, he answered, "Apparently no, but here's the good news. Due to the time constraints, you don't have to go on the bus. I'll drive you in the Boxster. Bring Astraea. You know how she loves the convertible."

Rose tried not to let him see her disappointment.

Reading her thoughts, he reached into his pocket and pulled out his pendulum with the glittering black stone, itself worth a small fortune. As it began to swing, his mouth slid into a cruel grin.

His message was clear: *You can't fool me. I know all.*

7

PRITI

Ben hasn't been himself all day, not since coming across some bit of bad news while he and Priti were sitting down to lunch. He stabbed his grapefruit salad, took one glance at his phone, dropped his fork, and immediately pushed back his chair. Without a word, he took the stairs two at a time to the makeshift office they'd set up on the third floor of this massive colonial house, his childhood home in the quaint town of Dutton, Vermont.

Priti knew better than to pester her husband when he was dealing with an emergency. Whether investors were threatening to jump ship or his mother was organizing a mutiny at her assisted-living facility, Ben found solutions by shutting himself off from all distractions to focus intently on the problem at hand. In the three years since they'd been married, she'd learned to let him be.

So she took her salad outside to the patio and sat under the navy-and-white-striped awning to enjoy the lovely summer day. She sipped her lemonade and admired her mother-in-law's lavish garden. Roses were in bloom, and the soft air was fragrant with their perfume. Bees buzzed over the pink flowers, and beyond the hedge abutting the country club's golf course, a lawn mower was sending up plumes of freshly cut grass.

Having come of age in the sun-dried suburbs of Sacramento, Priti had never lived in a place that was so *green*. The shutters on the uniform white clapboard houses in Dutton were painted a dark Dartmouth Green. There was a quiet town green in Dutton's center, the multicolored tulips and spring-yellow daffodils lovingly tended by the local garden society. The grass here was a bright, virulent shade of emerald, as if determined to make up for Vermont's gray winter.

Dutton was even located at the base of the *Green* Mountains. The looming hills were a majestic contrast to the pristine orderliness of the valley village once voted the most picturesque town in New England. Priti was itching to hike a bit of the Long Trail that ran up the mountain spine, but Ben, a bit of a control freak, wouldn't hear of it. It was too dangerous for her to go alone. She might turn an ankle or run into bears. Also, there were freaks up in the mountains.

"Freaks?" Priti had to laugh. "You do realize I was born and raised in California, right?"

Ben shook his head, super serious. "You never know who you'll run into on that trail. If you get hurt, there'll be no one around for miles to hear you scream for help. Seriously, people have gone missing on Glastenbury and never been found. The place is booby-trapped with pits and empty mine shafts."

Priti was sure she'd be able to avoid pits and empty mine shafts. Still, she didn't argue. The Winslow family had owned a hunting camp on Glastenbury Mountain for generations, and Ben knew the woods like the back of his hand, having trekked through them often with his beloved father. Maybe one day he'd slow down his work enough to take her up the trails himself.

Priti thought his dad's death was the reason for Ben's overprotectiveness. The renowned Judge Winslow dropped dead of a sudden heart attack at age fifty-five, while he and Ben were playing a game of Horse after dinner. Ben had been only fifteen at the time, and the loss of his dad made a permanent impression.

"Ben was a teenager when he had to step in and be the man of the family," her mother-in-law, Genevieve, once commented. "It changed him."

The idea that there had to be a "man of the family" was terribly old-fashioned and sexist, in Priti's opinion, but it wasn't her business. The older she got, the more she understood that every individual is dealing with his or her own private trauma, and there were far more harmful ways to process the loss of a parent than becoming hypervigilant.

Besides, maybe the sudden maturation had changed Ben for the better. She'd married him not for his wealth or good looks—Those royal blue eyes! The thick jet hair! The shoulders! Nor was she mesmerized by his big brain, though, admittedly, she'd always had a soft spot for nerds. And she didn't marry him because, at five feet eleven inches, she'd often overshadowed other men she'd dated. Ben was a comfortable seven inches taller than she, and though not crucial to a relationship, his height was nice.

Priti married Ben simply because he was the kindest and most thoughtful man she'd ever met. Take, for instance, his attention to Genevieve, an irascible old biddy whom Priti would have found intolerable if her solid armor didn't deflect her mother-in-law's barbs. Like Priti, Ben took Genevieve's moods in stride and doted on the woman. He spent every June in Vermont "closing out the fiscal year," as he put it, meeting with her doctors and financial advisers, and arranging for maintenance to be done on the historic family homestead.

Of course, things would be so much easier for everyone if Genevieve would simply accept his invitation to have her come live with them in Monterey. Then he could sell the Vermont money pit and be spared these annual trips.

But Genevieve stubbornly refused to move across the country. She had no interest in leaving her friends and church and the home that'd been hers for nearly sixty years, unless it was in a pine box. At age eighty-two, she almost got her wish when last spring she fell in the bathtub and broke her hip. Now she was in Hamden House, a well-appointed assisted-living facility, and she was absolutely furious.

"I'm being held against my will" was her greeting to Ben when he and Priti arrived for their annual visit a few weeks ago.

Ben kissed her powdered cheek and said, "Lovely to see you too, Mother. You're looking well."

"Get me the hell out of here!" she roared, pounding the carved arm of her Queen Anne love seat.

"Mother can be difficult," Ben said later, when they were unpacking in the guest room. "She tends to swallow a camel and strain at a gnat."

Priti thought to herself, *Apple, meet tree.* Ben might rise to challenges, but he tended to get snagged on petty issues. Which raised a nagging question: what had he read on his phone that was so earth-shattering it caused him to spend all afternoon working? When was he ever going to tell her what happened?

Around five, he burst out of his office. "Going for a run," he declared, bounding down the stairs in shorts and a T-shirt.

An hour later, he returned, drenched in sweat but still agitated. Avoiding Priti's anxious smile, he headed straight to the library, where she heard the cork pop on the Maker's Mark and the *glug, glug, glug* of several ounces being poured into one of Genevieve's Waterford glasses. This was no longer a normal reaction to a problem. Ben was freaking out.

Something was seriously wrong.

She needed to get her husband out of the house and out of his head. Maybe a trip to the inn would boost his spirits. They often went there on Fridays for fish and chips and to catch up with the locals. Many of his high school friends had returned to Dutton after college to raise their families, including Ben's first love and first wife, Charlotte.

At their initial meeting, Priti found that Charlotte was more beautiful than she'd anticipated. Though not nearly as tall as Ben (or Priti), she was as willowy and graceful as a professional ballerina. Looked like one too, the way she pulled her dark hair into a bun, a style that emphasized her long, white, swanlike neck. Despite her own modeling cred, Priti was slightly intimidated.

Until she met Charlotte's husband, Grover. Then she relaxed.

In fact, she and Grover—a flat-footed harmless doofus with slightly bucked teeth and a self-deprecating sense of humor—had become quite chummy during her June visits. She liked that he didn't take himself seriously and seemed to embrace the embarrassing nickname that'd been bestowed on him in high school: Bogey Grovey. Because he sucked at golf apparently.

If Charlotte could be happily married to an affable man like Bogey, then she couldn't be all bad. Though her relationship with Ben did strike Priti as odd, if not disturbing. Charlotte was more outwardly affectionate toward Ben than toward her own husband, frequently touching her ex's arm or throwing back her head in laughter at his lamest jokes. Priti wondered if Charlotte married Bogey just for his fat trust fund since she never seemed to pay him a second of attention.

"Everything okay?" Ben asked, putting the phone to his chest when Priti interrupted him in the library.

"Let's go out for dinner. Just down to the inn." She knew better than to comment on him needing to buck up. Ben wasn't a fan of personal critiques.

"Sure. I'll be ready in twenty. Let me wind up this call." He kept the phone to his chest.

As Priti closed the double doors behind her, she swore she heard a woman's voice on the phone. He could have been speaking to his assistant in California, except his assistant was a man who, unlike the lilting voice on the phone, sounded nothing like Charlotte.

Ben usually felt better after hanging in the inn, with its cozy fireplaces and low, beamed ceilings. According to local legend, his great-great-great-great-grandfather signed up with the Green Mountain Boys in 1775 in the back room. He was very proud of his ancestor, though Genevieve disputed this claim as an exaggerated Winslow family myth.

Unfortunately, even a night at the inn failed to do the trick. Ben was tense all through dinner, barely touching his food and getting up from their table frequently to either text or make a phone call outside on the patio. Old friends stopped by to slap him on the back and chat, and he could barely crack a smile.

In a last-ditch effort to get her husband to lighten up, Priti suggested he head over to the billiard room for a few rounds of pool. She could have joined the klatch of fellow billiards widows, but she never clicked with the blond horsey set in this town. Plus, she wasn't invited to join their royal table, probably because Charlotte was queen of the court and her ladies-in-waiting were being loyal.

So now Priti's sitting at the bar with a cup of decaf and the latest *New York Times* crossword puzzle on her phone, scratching her head at thirteen across: *Shell stations?*

"Taco bars." Bogey Grovey slides onto the stool next to her

and bumps his knee so hard against the bar that beer sloshes out of his glass and onto his madras shorts. He takes no notice, stabbing a pudgy finger on her phone screen. "Thirteen across. You think they're referring to gas stations—Shell and Mobil—but they're not. Get it?"

She gets it. Tapping in the letters, she says, "Thanks. Not shooting pool?"

"Nope. I'm so bad, the guys gave me the cue to leave." He pokes her with his elbow. "Get it? *Cue* to leave?"

Priti can't help but giggle. "Oh, man. You've gotta up your game. That's pathetic."

"Char thought it was funny." He grins and twirls on his seat, scanning the room for his wife. "Geesh. I told her to give it a rest, but there she is with Ben again. Those two have been at it all day."

Priti snaps up her head, curious and slightly peeved. "What do you mean?"

He chucks his chin to the patio outside the restaurant's double doors. "See for yourself."

He's right. Ben and Charlotte are deep in conversation under the white awning. Priti can tell from the way she's standing with an arm outstretched that Charlotte's sneaking a cigarette. Whatever it is they're discussing must be important, otherwise Ben wouldn't tolerate it. As a confirmed hypochondriac, he avoids secondhand smoke like the devil.

"They've been on the phone nonstop." Bogey takes a sip of his shaken beer, white foam dotting his upper lip. "Ever since Charlotte got a text about that post."

Priti squints, trying to understand. "I have no idea what you're talking about."

"He didn't say?"

"I assumed it was about business." But now Priti is worried. "What is it?"

"Here. Lemme show you." Pulling out his phone, Bogey scrolls down and holds up his screen for her to read.

> **Mayhem Avenger** @xoxoxoxo666
> @DARKCULTS slandered DIVINER leader who is INNOCENT & will SUE! Real killer Dan O'Neill (55 Dolan Rd Sudbury MA) walks free while eyewitness daughter Stella O'Neill (@cambridgepl) stays silent re: dad's sick crimes. Find them! Bring them to justice for Rose Santos! Make them pay!

The words make no sense. This might as well be in Martian. "Not ringing a bell?" Bogey asks.

Priti shakes her head. "What does this have to do with them? It doesn't even mention Ben. Or Charlotte. Does it have something to do with HeadFake?"

Bogey puts down his phone and bends so close that Priti can make out the pores on his sunburnt nose. "Ben didn't tell you about his mother's psychic, who was murdered here twenty years ago?"

What the . . . ? "Noooo, he didn't tell me about a murder. And I doubt Genevieve ever had a psychic. You're bullshitting me." The woman was a starched and pressed Episcopalian. The idea that Genevieve Winslow would have dabbled in the occult was inconceivable. Then again, the same could have been said about Nancy Reagan.

"I'm not bullshitting you," Bogey says. "Genevieve used to bring in a woman once a week to have her fortune told and swing a pendulum or whatever it is psychics do. I don't know why. Maybe grief made her slightly cuckoo after the judge dropped dead." Bogey twirls a finger by his temple.

Priti's still trying to picture it—Genevieve in her string of pearls and Talbot's basketweave cardigan holding out her hand to have her palm read. It doesn't track. Surely, her snob of a mother-in-law would have pooh-poohed such malarkey.

"It was a big scandal, actually. The psychic's name was Rose Santos, and she had a kid who survived in a cave for days after her mother's body was found on Glastenbury Mountain. It was a national story, though they never did catch the guy. A lot of people think the weirdo that runs the cult up on the mountain did it."

"*What* cult?" Holy shit! Why hasn't Ben mentioned they live near *a cult* when they're here, or that he's connected to a famous murder victim? He knows how addicted she is to true crime.

Bogey reaches over and snatches a cocktail napkin. With a golf pencil that tears the flimsy paper, he scribbles "Dark Cults." "That's the show. Go online and watch an episode of *Dark Cults* called 'The Triangle Three.' It kind of explains everything, though it doesn't mention Ben by name. Probably for legal reasons."

Priti studies Bogey's nearly illegible chicken scratch, feeling a sense of dread. "Do I dare ask why Ben should have been mentioned?"

"Oh, it's all ancient history now. I was in Maine finishing up at Bowdoin and was as shocked as everyone else to learn he'd even been in town during the murder, and that the cops actually considered him a suspect. I never bought it. Ben the All-American Eagle Scout? Get out."

The dread has erupted into an upset stomach. Could be from the fish or the stress or the fact that she's over a month late. Priti pushes away her coffee and takes a big gulp from her water glass.

"Sorry, Priti, didn't mean to upset you." Bogey rubs her back in slow, comforting circles. "I just assumed you knew."

"You assumed wrong."

Well, at least this explains why Ben's been so clipped and grumpy. For a man who cherishes his privacy and impeccable reputation, he must be frantic that this viral post could bite him in the butt. That's the last headache he needs with his already skittish investors.

"Hey, Bogey." Ben is back, hands shoved in the pockets of his jeans, practically twitching. He stinks of Charlotte's cigarette. "We should go, Priti. I just found out I've got a meeting in Boston bright and early tomorrow, and I need to hit the hay."

Priti glances over at Bogey to say goodbye and finds only his empty stool and the sweating empty beer mug, the cocktail napkin discreetly folded to cover up his writing. She swipes it casually and puts it in her bag—she's going to watch that episode the first chance she gets.

Ben is already waiting for her on the marble sidewalk when she steps out of the inn. Slipping her arm into his, they walk silently toward Genevieve's house in the cool night air, scented with roses and peonies, apple blossoms and fading Canadian lilacs. Blinking fireflies are beginning to rise from the grasses to meet and mate under a starry sky. A perfect midsummer evening, if it weren't for the fact that she just found out the police once investigated her husband for murder.

"What's going on, Ben?" she finally asks. "You can tell me."

He gives her arm a reassuring squeeze. "Nothing I can't handle."

"Is it business or—"

"Business," he snaps, dropping her arm. "Look, do you mind if we don't discuss it? I've got heartburn from that burger and I just want to go to sleep. I've got to get up at the crack of dawn."

With that, he inputs the security code on the alarm and unlocks the gate to Genevieve's house, marching up the driveway in a huff. Priti is so stunned and wounded by her husband's uncharacteristic snippiness that she bends over and releases the contents of her upset stomach into the box elders.

Not the fish or the stress, she thinks, dragging the back of her arm across her mouth. Pregnancy. *She is pregnant.* She doesn't need yet another test to tell her what her body is signaling.

After years of trying, after a spate of miscarriages and giving up all expectations of conceiving without artificial intervention, she is finally carrying a fetus—hopefully, this time, to term. Instead of being thrilled, she's numb.

Her flatlined reaction is self-preservation, a way of managing her expectations since she's not sure she can deal with another devastating blow when this fetus does what its unborn, undeveloped brothers and sisters did. The repeated cycles of joy and crashing disappointment have taken their toll on her, on her marriage. She and Ben have been psychologically scarred.

With the first pregnancy, they acted way too precipitously, crowing about their happy news to family and friends mere hours after those two lines appeared on the pee stick. They were more circumspect after that loss, but they didn't take care of their own hearts, throwing caution to the wind as they indulged in fantasies about their future family.

A boy would be Benjamin James Winslow III, though they'd call him James. A girl would be named after Priti's grandmother Mala. The nursery would be painted yellow with plenty of light and a comfy rocking chair. Gender-based toys and decorations were out. As parents, they'd do their best to encourage their children's passions, wherever they might lead. They even debated how much screen time, if any, James—or Mala—would be permitted.

Ben and Priti fell in love with their babies while they were little more than doomed tadpoles. With each loss she sank into deep depressions overlaid with recriminations, replaying her "failures" on an obsessive loop. She should have sworn off wine months before. She shouldn't have eaten sushi or used hairspray. She didn't believe her doctor's assurances that miscarriage was Mother Nature's way of tossing out mistakes. That made her incensed. Her babies weren't mistakes; they were perfect.

This time would be different.

This time, she'd keep the news to herself until she passed the three-month mark. Hiding such a desired surprise from her husband wouldn't be easy. At least she wouldn't have to worry about morning sickness. Ben would be on his way to Boston, and after her stomach calmed she could watch this *Dark Cults* episode without him being the wiser.

Now she'd be keeping not one but two secrets from him.

The question was, how many secrets was he keeping from her?

8

STELLA

JUNE 17, 2023

"Don't tell Mel I asked you this." Fig shakes a can of whipped cream and sprays her coffee with a thick layer. "But was it awesome growing up in a cult?"

It's Saturday, the morning after all hell broke loose, and we're sitting on the balcony of Mel and Fig's very nice third-floor apartment in Watertown overlooking the tennis courts. I'm trying to keep warm in Fig's fleece jacket while pounding coffee and carbs from a flaky *pain au chocolat*. Mel's at the gym sweating in a Cross-Fit class. I'd feel guilty except this pastry's delicious.

And I'm exhausted.

Don't get me wrong. I'm incredibly thankful for Mel and Fig's hospitality. They made me feel right at home, plying me with a delicious Pinot and three slices of asparagus and feta pizza, which, honestly, wasn't too disgusting. Mel in particular made sure not to pry into my background, even shooting Fig a dirty look when she asked if certain foods were banned at the cult. (Animal flesh of any sort and no junk, to the best of my recollection.)

But the convertible couch was a killer. It's one of those ancient models from someone's rec room, the kind with the metal bar that pinches into vertebra T6. Whenever I managed to get somewhat comfortable, I'd be jolted awake by a fact I hadn't considered. The thought that kept me staring at the ceiling from 2:00 to 4:00 a.m. was the sobering realization that I am as vulnerable as a newborn kitten.

My mother's case has gone cold. No cop is actively hunting for her killer or my intended assassin. As for my father, he can't save me. He almost bit the dust himself yesterday at Fenway. Which means I'm totally, completely alone.

My worst fear.

Fig replaces the cap and sets the can on the glass table between us, licking a spot of cream off her finger. "I mean, growing up in a cult. Like, what did they teach you?"

I take another sip of dark coffee, hoping the caffeine will kick in soon. "Mostly, we learned about the stars and astrology, Greek, German, and Norse myths. Some stuff about the Druids and a lot about how to tune in to the so-called Divine Energy. Nothing you could use to get into college—or to get a job, unless you wanted to become a professional psychic."

"Sounds like fun." She eyes me over the heap of melting whipped cream. "Was it?"

"Yeah, except when I left the cult and came to live with Dad and I discovered I was way behind other kids my age, intellectually and mentally. My stepmother, Heather, had to homeschool me starting with the basics. Multiplication tables. Long division. Thankfully, I was already a good reader. The few books Mama could sneak to me from her clients were my entertainment, since it's not like we had a television."

Fig nods, the children's librarian in her pleased to hear that. "No mystical ceremonies though? Goat sacrifice? Human?"

I have to laugh because she sounds like Mari. "No sacrifices of which I'm aware, though there were nightly dowsing rituals where all the grown-ups dressed in robes and chanted."

Out of nowhere, the soles of my feet begin to tingle, and I have to fight the urge to get out the tinfoil. Fig watches as I reach down to itch the scratch. "Do you mind if I ask?"

I knew this was coming. "About my fondness for Reynolds Wrap?"

She cringes. "Mel would kill me. She said it's probably some foot odor."

"I don't have stinky feet!" That rumor needs to be nipped in the bud.

"Sorry. Sorry." She holds up her hands in self-defense. "Didn't mean to trigger. I'm just curious."

I can hardly blame her. "Okay, this is weird. Promise you won't judge."

"Not me. I don't judge. I leave that up to God."

"Good to know." Finishing my coffee, I set it down on the glass table, fold my arms, and tell it to her straight. "You know that movie where the kid sees dead people? Well, I kinda . . . *feel* them."

Fig spits whipped cream and coffee through her nose. "Oh, gross. Excuse me." Leaping out of her chair, she slides back the patio door and runs inside, emerging minutes later with wads of tissue in each nostril. "My apologies. You kinda caught me by surprise with that one. So, you feel the presence of ghosts, like in *Sixth Sense*?"

"Not exactly. In *Sixth Sense* he *saw* dead people. I *feel* them under my feet, and not always. Only if they're buried naturally, like if they were Orthodox Jewish or Native American or planted before 1848. That's when lined caskets were patented." I have to cross my bare ankles to keep from giving in to the urge to claw at my feet.

Fig is speechless. Her lower jaw is actually open, which, when you add the white toilet paper plugs in each nostril, makes for quite an elegant portrait.

"My mother used to call it 'silly toes,' to ease my anxiety," I continue. "Even as a little kid I knew there was nothing silly about the sensation of ice-cold bony fingers poking through the soil to grab my feet. It was as frightening as hell. I forget how we figured out the foil was an effective barrier—I think she maybe took the idea from how caskets are lined? But somehow she figured it out."

Fig removes the wads of toilet paper. "That's bizarre. There has to be a rational explanation."

"There's definitely an explanation. Whether it's rational or not depends on if you believe I was born with a weird dowsing gift, like my mother believed. Since my therapist considers psychic abilities to be a bunch of bullshit, she theorized that I was misremembering about being able to dowse before Mama was killed and that I'm actually suffering from post-traumatic stress disorder from witnessing her murder. She suggested I undergo ART—accelerated resolution therapy—to remove the trauma from my memory bank. She was certain that would cure me."

"Aaaaand . . ."

"And I thought it did the trick until I went to the Boston Aquarium and stepped on the unmarked grave of what I later determined was a Revolutionary War–era woman buried near the waterfront. That was it. From then on, I didn't leave the house without Reynolds Wrap, preferably heavy duty."

Fig takes another sip of coffee and thinks. "This is so cool. Like, where else have you had this experience?"

"There was a small graveyard at the Center that had a couple of old Diviners who were buried in burlap instead of being cremated. Sleepy Hollow Cemetery in Concord. I went there to see Thoreau's grave and Louisa May Alcott's. That was a mistake. And . . . other places."

Fig leans forward clutching her tissues, peering at me with the same unnerving intensity she used with Rhonda Retter. "What *other* places?"

She's taking this shockingly well. Suddenly uncomfortable with Fig's third degree, I scroll through my phone messages, past the usual spam, until I get to Dad's. I haven't told him about being evicted. He doesn't need more stress, though it sounds like he's doing okay.

> All well on the home front except for a group of obsessives with nothing better to do who showed up this a.m. They'll get bored and leave soon. No TBI. Nothing broken. Sox creamed the DY 15–5! Call u later to discuss Plan B.

Uh-oh. Dad's coming up with lettered plans. Never good.

"Why do I have the impression you're avoiding the question?"

Because it's too scary to contemplate, I want to say, putting down my phone. "I'm not."

"All right. Then explain this. Last night after picking you up from your apartment, you got in the car and immediately googled a guy in Vermont named Ben Winslow. All night you were researching the Winslows and how they might have been involved in your mom's murder. You said you used to go to their house and play outside when your mother was doing her thing with Genevieve Winslow. Hon, I don't know if you realize this, but in the middle of the night, Mel and I heard you sobbing and murmuring the words 'Winslow' and 'Mama.'"

Oh, god. They heard that? How mortifying. "I didn't mean to. I—"

"I know. And I probably shouldn't have mentioned it. Mel told me not to. I was just so heartbroken for you. I wanted to help and I didn't know how."

See, this is why I don't have friends. It's awkward when other people care. It's too much responsibility the way they expect you to open up and let them in to riffle through your personal mess. All I want to do is pop into my shell and burrow deep into the sand like a clam. It's safer that way.

Fig puts a hand on my knee. "Would it be totally inappropriate to suggest maybe something bad happened to you at Ben Winslow's house while you were outside playing, and that's the source of your trauma? Could it be your mom found out Ben did something to you, that she was going to report him to the authorities? Think back, Stella."

The old wooden swing hanging from an apple tree, the bark having grown over the rope it'd been there so long. The bittersweetness of Mrs. Winslow's homemade lemonade. Pink roses and purple irises radiant under the June sun. Fairy homes with moss for rugs and tiny acorn hats for cups and saucers. Thick grass. Running from invisible children who tickled my toes. The mischief makers, Mama said. They won't harm you. Leave them alone and they'll leave you alone.

My phone's text alert snaps me to attention, my heart pounding as though I've been abruptly awakened from a nightmare. I never thought I'd be so glad to get a message from Logan.

He informs me he and Mari will be out at the Union Square farmers market—*natch*—from ten to eleven. That's when I may come to the apartment to get my things. No other time will work since they're having friends over tonight and will need to get the place in order. He finishes with a cheery PLEASE HAUL YOUR OWN TRASH!!

"I'm really, really sorry to ask for another favor, Fig, but can you give me a lift to my apartment?" I hold up my phone to display

Logan's message. "My delightful hosts have given me one hour to pack up all my things and get out."

"Sure, no problem." Fig hands me a tissue. I don't know why I need it until I realize my cheeks are damp.

"Thanks," I whisper.

"I shouldn't have pushed you," she says. "But something happened to you at that Winslow house. I know it in my gut. You can't dream about the place without crying for your mother. That's not normal, Stella. Not normal at all."

STELLA

JUNE 17, 2023

My life is a train wreck.

Carefree activities like riding in the passenger seat of Fig's Mini Cooper convertible with the top down should be a literal breeze. Now they're terrifying. The notion of my head being exposed is making me paranoid and anxious. Anyone could pick me off in Boston traffic and disappear into the city's maze of tunnels and bridges and one-way streets.

Fortunately, it's begun to drizzle and we have to put the top up.

"Don't even think about it." Fig moves the Mini over the fog line as she eyes my side mirror. "Won't get past me, jerk."

We're in bumper-to-bumper traffic in a logjam on Coolidge Avenue and the Volvo behind us is attempting to pull the quintessential Masshole move of cutting in front of everyone by driving up the breakdown lane.

Except the car in my sideview mirror has green plates. This isn't a Masshole. He's a Vermonter in a pricey V60 station wagon. That old anxiety ticks up again, and I slide down in the seat just in case.

Fig gives me a quick glance. "Aren't you being special."

"Vermont plates. You know, might be one of . . . *them*."

She checks her rearview. "Dude's in a golf shirt with a fancy haircut and rapper shades driving a suburban Mom car, and next to him is some woman wearing a visor. Not really giving the vibe of off-the-grid Diviners."

"I don't know what they're like anymore. The one who came to my apartment yesterday, Rowan, used to be a filthy wild child. Now he's a hipster with a trimmed beard and pricey Nobulls."

"Beard and high-tops." Fig snickers. "Can't take him seriously. In the history of the universe, there has never been a hitman named Rowan and definitely not with a trimmed beard and high-tops."

I check the side mirror again. The Volvo has backed off slightly. "The point I'm trying to make is that the car on our tail is from Vermont."

"His name is Chip."

"You know him?"

"No. I'm just saying, that's what he seems like his name would be. And I bet her name is something formal, like Katherine. Anyway, you can relax. He cut over to the left and turned onto Mount Auburn going the opposite direction."

Relieved, I give Fig a sheepish grin and return to a sitting position. "Guess I'm a little on edge."

"Yeah, well, I have bad news. I didn't want to tell you last night when you were already so stressed, but you know your library ID photo, the one where there's a small coffee stain on the front of your shirt? Hate to tell you but it's all over the internet and you're tagged as—brace yourself—Astraea O'Neill."

So much for staying under the radar.

Logan and Mari are gone from the premises when we arrive. They've even left us their reserved parking space on the street, though that has nothing to do with thoughtfulness. They're on a shopping spree to buy stuff to impress their friends now that they have an extra room. By tomorrow, my former quarters will be a trendy home office with an ethically sourced bamboo standing desk, all traces of my existence exorcised by a German beechwood air diffuser.

I can tell these two have been in my old bedroom because their winter clothes are already hanging in my narrow closet. Nothing sends the message that you've been displaced like the smell of mothballs.

I still haven't quite recovered from Fig's interrogation about the Winslows and the memory it unearthed. Could it be I accidentally came across bodies buried in Genevieve Winslow's garden? Would Ben have killed Mama to keep her from taking my discovery to the police? That could make sense.

I figured Fig was going to drop me off and go, that I'd call Dad to pick me up. Nope. She's insisting on helping me pack. This woman is strange. Wonderful, and kind, but strange.

She's Miss Efficiency, shaking out the reusable shopping bag for my clothes and yanking open the drawer of the bureau borrowed from Mari and Logan. All I own are its contents and the queen-size blow-up mattress, the bedside table from Ikea, and the multicolor floor lamp a college kid put on the sidewalk for free. I am pathetic.

"Be easy on yourself," Dad used to remind me. "You had a rough start, Stella. But you're loved and you're alive and that's ninety percent of the battle."

That last part about being alive I used to think was a reference to my surviving in the woods for three days after Mama's murder. Lately, however, I've begun to wonder if he and Heather fear my mental health is fragile, that I'm at risk of suicide due to my PTSD.

The thing is, I don't feel like I'm suffering from post-traumatic stress disorder. It's not as though I'm a shell-shocked soldier or victim from a war-torn country. Okay, so, yeah, the nightmares can be rocky and I have issues with relationships, but so do a lot of people. You don't have to witness your mother's murder to be messed up.

Ironic, isn't it? The girl who miraculously survived three days in the Green Mountain wilderness is now barely scraping by in Somerville twenty years later. And Dad calls that success. Talk about a low bar.

I slip a blouse from a hanger, fold it and drop it in one of Fig's reusable shopping bags. I'm on autopilot, folding and dropping, trying not to think. I've done enough thinking for one day.

"What's going on here?" Fig gets up from the floor where she's been conducting a last-minute sweep behind the bureau and holds up what the average person might mistake for a pair of bent coat hangers.

My heart wrenches. They were Mama's copper dowsing rods, rescued by Dad when he retrieved her belongings from the commune. He gave them to me when I turned sixteen, a sentimental hand-me-down. Shows what a lousy daughter I am, that I lost them behind the bureau.

"Wow. I've been looking for these," I lie. "They're Mama's."

They bring back memories of when my mother was called upon to locate ley lines of buried dark energy in some of the fancy houses in Dutton and Manchester. Mama used to say her clients contacted her because their home was "unhappy," whatever that meant. They needed her to expunge the evil and let in the light.

On the rare occasions when I was allowed to accompany her on these visits, I got to see Mama in action. She'd drift through rooms holding the dowsing rods at right angles to her body, her eyes closed as she entered her trance. It was spooky how she seemed to transform into another person. Her voice deepened and her shoulders sagged, even her black hair would momentarily turn white as snow. Swear to god.

When the rods crossed, that marked the site of a buried line, and Mama was back to her old self, assessing the situation and ticking off suggested remedies. My job was to have her supplies handy in case she needed a roll of sage for smudging or a handful of salt to toss in the corners.

I was proud of my mother's unique ability during these sessions. I remember once wanting to be like her, she was so pretty and magical. However, when I became a teenager and wrestled with the complex emotions any thirteen-year-old has—much less a girl who'd been raised in a cult and saw her mother murdered—Mama's approval rating took a nosedive. My grief narrowed into a type of rage that'd hit me without warning.

How dare she be so selfish as to take me away from my father, only to abandon me when I needed her most! Why did we have to go into the woods at that ungodly hour? What was so important that it couldn't wait until morning? If she'd been more sensible, she'd probably be alive today.

My rage hardened into resentment. I blamed her for raising me like a feral animal. Whenever Heather calmly reminded me to chew with my mouth closed or hold a fork correctly, in my embarrassment I internally railed at Mama. She was the reason I wasn't in regular school with regular kids, because I was so behind in my coursework. She was the reason I was so immature. She was the reason I went to sleep at night in a room lit up by blinking alarms.

And worst of all, she wasn't there to give me comfort.

No wonder I forgot about her dowsing rods.

Though perhaps I should at least make an effort to understand what Rose Santos was all about. I mean, I'm not a scared kid or a surly teenager anymore. I'm almost the same age as she was when she was killed. The least I can do is give her a chance, out of respect. Reminiscing about the cult with Fig has brought up the good memories too. It wasn't all bad. It was fun . . . until it wasn't.

"Give them a go," I say, placing the rods in Fig's hands. "Tuck in your elbows and point the rods straight ahead, like you're a cowboy with a six shooter."

Fig likes that image and begins to laugh. "Oh, please. I have no psychic ability."

"You won't know until you try." I explain she needs to connect with her rods so she can interpret their movements. "Tell them to show you yes and no. For most people, yes is when the rods cross. No is when they fly apart. You have to kind of sync them to your subconscious."

She frowns.

"Like this." Removing the rods from her hands, I grip them in mine, making an instant connection. I don't have to say out loud "yes" or "no." By merely thinking of a positive response, they cross. A negative response, they fly apart.

"You didn't ask them to show you yes and no," she says when I hand them back.

"I didn't have to say anything out loud. I just thought the questions. Okay, now you go."

We spend several minutes like this, swinging the rods to and fro until Fig is sure they know the drill. From the way she's biting her lip to keep from smirking, clearly she thinks this is B.S.

"You've got to believe, Fig, or it won't work."

She inhales deeply and nods, trying to knuckle down. "Gotcha. So what should I ask?"

"Start with something simple. Did I wake up this morning?"

"What?"

"Just ask it that. Hold the rods straight. Let the energy flow." I stand back and fold my arms, assessing her technique or, rather, lack thereof.

"Did I wake up this morning?" she repeats.

The rods do nothing.

"Guess I didn't?"

"Wait. I forgot an important step. I'm so used to thinking the question, I missed the part where you have to include the yes or no. So say, 'Yes or no, did I wake up this morning?'"

"Yes or no. Did I wake up this morning?"

The rods stay still.

"You have to concentrate!" I want this to work so she can relate to what I'm talking about when I say I can feel the dead through my feet. I want her to have an inkling.

The lines between her brows furrow and the rods begin to vibrate slightly, a sign they're activated. And then, miraculously, they cross. *Yes!*

Fig turns to me with a big grin. "I swear I didn't do that. They moved on their own."

"I know, I know," I say, taking them back and slipping them in the bag. "With a little practice, you'll be able to have these down in no time."

"What would I use them for, to ask every morning if I woke up?"

Wise guy. "You can use them for anything, whenever you're in need of direction. Like should I switch jobs or date this person."

"I'm married, Stella."

"You know what I mean." I start stripping the bed.

"Could you ask them if so-and-so killed your mother?"

That stops me mid sheet fold. As a matter of fact, I have asked this question of the rods and the pendulum more than I can count—with disappointing results. "Uh-huh." I shake out a pillow.

"And?"

"And the answer's inconclusive." Meaning no.

Fig takes the rods out of the bag and holds them like I taught her. "Yes or no, rods, did Ben Winslow kill Stella's mom?"

This is not a question I've put to the pendulum or rods because I didn't learn about Benjamin Winslow's existence until yesterday. I'm actually holding my breath, waiting and nearly exploding when the rods cross.

Fig flinches, like she didn't expect the system to actually work either. "Well, well, well!"

I don't know what to make of that result. I hate to admit this, but a part of me secretly believes. Or maybe I just want to believe. I mean, feeling the dead could be a PTSD thing like my therapist thinks. Or . . . I really *can* feel the dead. Who knows? But the way those rods crossed so easily raises the hairs on the back of my neck.

"Did *you* do that? Be honest."

Fig drops the rods on the mattress and crosses herself. "Swear to god, no. I just concentrated like you told me to."

An awkward silence falls between us. "I should have stuck to whether or not I woke up in the morning," she says, going back to her cleanout. "Two bags. No problem to fit them in the Mini." She hoists one in each hand. "I'm gonna take these down to the car. Meet you there."

When she leaves, I check myself out in the mirror affixed to the back of the door. Removing my ponytail holder, I shake out my long, wavy hair and am met with the ghost of Rose Santos. We are suddenly one and the same. Identical high cheekbones and big bug eyes. The difference is our hair color. Mine has more red, a contribution from my Irish father.

All of a sudden, the door flies open and there's Fig, breathless, her own eyes bigger than golf balls. "You were right. Chip *was* following us."

She grabs my wrist and, putting her finger to her lips, tiptoes us to the living room bay window overlooking the street. It's the same window where Mari and Logan spied on me the day before, so I know better than to press my face against the glass. Fig and I surreptitiously peek from the side.

A dark-haired man I peg in his midforties is on the sidewalk staring up at us through the rain. His head is covered by a white Titleist cap worn backward (he's way too old to pull this off) and a navy, zip-up raincoat with white piping. It's the rapper sunglasses that are the dead giveaway though. He's definitely the guy in the V60 with Vermont plates who tried to pass us. He's also super tall and bears a vague resemblance to a LinkedIn profile photo I looked at recently.

My throat tightens. "I think that's Ben Winslow."

"Get! Out! What's he doing here?" Fig hisses as he disappears from view.

We wait, our ears cocked. Then, to my horror, the door to the street creaks open without so much as a knock followed by the soft tread of steps coming up the stairs. My heart starts thumping hard.

Fig grips my wrist tighter. "It's okay. I deadbolted it."

We freeze, waiting for what's next. Fig drops my wrist and goes to the fireplace, where the set of iron tools Logan bought Mari for Christmas stand unused because Mari was too nervous about having an actual fire. Snatching a poker, Fig wields it like a sword. I take the shovel, both of us prepared to smack the crap out of him if he tries to break in.

"Holy shiiiiit," Fig hisses as the handle on the door slowly turns.

Beeeeeeep!

Fig and I jump at the blaring of a car horn from below. Dammit. Mari and Logan have arrived. Sure enough, they're parked next to the Mini, red hazards flashing, Boston style. Clearly, they're annoyed we took their space, but, to be fair, they're early. It's only quarter to eleven. We have fifteen more minutes.

The handle stops turning. Even from the living room, I can hear my cell phone vibrating where I left it on top of the bedroom bureau: Logan texting me that they've arrived.

Mari gets out and marches to the sidewalk, hands on hips. "Hey!" she shouts, her pink cotton crewneck sweater turning dark rose in the rain. "Move your fucking car!" Other cars are backed up behind their newly leased Audi. Logan is probably wetting his pants one of them will scratch the paint.

There is a clatter of footsteps down the stairs, our would-be attacker exiting stage right. Mari turns and shouts to him, "Hey, you! Are you with them? Tell them to move their effing car!"

He must not have responded, because she throws up her arms, comes inside, and bounds up the stairs. We don't have a chance to release the deadbolt before she starts pounding. "What the hell? This is our place. You can't lock me out!"

Fingers fumbling, I manage to unlatch the deadbolt. Mari falls in, furious. Her damp hair is slicked to her head, giving her the appearance of a preppy rat. "What's going on here? Didn't you hear the horn? You have to move. You're causing a traffic jam."

"You're the one causing the traffic jam," Fig says as I dart behind them, out the door, and down the steps. No longer scared and now pissed, I am determined to find this Ben Winslow asshole and make him explain what he's up to.

I turn the corner just in time to see his Volvo pull away from the curb of a side street heading toward the expressway, like he'd parked for an efficient getaway.

"Did you catch him?" Fig is behind me, doubled over.

"He was too fast for me." He must be a runner. Or it's those long legs.

When Fig and I return to the apartment, we find the two bags of my belongings plus my dorky lamp on the sidewalk getting soaked. There's also a tow truck. Its lights are flashing, and judging from the pair of legs in grease-stained jeans sticking out from under the Mini, its operator is attaching the hook.

"Stop!" Fig waves her arms. "That's my car."

The tow dude slides out and rises slowly—reddish hair, red stubble carpeting a double chin, wearing a Red Sox cap and faded Shamrock Pub T-shirt from some drunken St. Patty's Day celebration of yore. He's about as Southie as Southie can get. Ten dollars says he goes by Sully, Tommy, Mark, or Mikey.

"That'll be one fifty," he says, wiping rain from his forehead with a blue shammy cloth.

"For what?" Fig demands.

"The call. Doesn't matter if I tow or not. Ya still gotta pay."

"But I didn't call. *They* did." She flings her arm toward the second-floor bay window where Mari is perched in her favorite spot, smugly spying on us like a pampered house cat. Logan's double parked in the Audi, waiting for the tow truck to move Fig's car. He pretends not to notice other motorists leaning on their horns and flipping him the bird as they squeeze past.

The tow driver snorts and spits. "Doesn't matter. If you don't have a *pah-mit*, you can't *pahk* here. Says right *they-ah* on the sign." He points to the very visible white PERMITTED PARKING ONLY sign with the very visible drawing of a tow truck. "You got a *pah-mit* for this space?"

Fig's silence is his answer.

"Then the *pah-mit hold-ah* has every right to have you towed. Now, if you don't mind." He grabs the hook. "Lemme do my job."

Fig lets out a whimper, but I've got it covered. Always carry enough cash for a quick escape was another rule of Dad's. I count out three fifties from my wallet and hand them to the driver, who drops the hook and stuffs the bills in his pocket. Slim chance the front office will ever see that money.

"By the way, this was on your front bump-ah." He slips her a black metal square no bigger than a quarter. "I ain't seen one like that before. Not one of them *Ayah*-tags. Wouldn't have noticed it except I hit it by mistake with my flashlight."

It's a high-tech GPS tracker.

Fig and I exchange glances and I know without being psychic that she is good and truly frightened. I am causing problems. I don't want Ben Winslow or the Diviners adding her to their hit list.

Time to call Dad and find out about this so-called Plan B.

10

ROSE

Before heading to Dutton to meet with Genevieve Winslow that morning, Rose stopped by Iona House, the quarters for unpartnered adult female Diviners, and went upstairs to Cerise's bedroom. It was a cheery space, if small, tucked in the corner with a window overlooking the trail through the Glastenbury forest.

Cerise's iron cot was made up with the quilt she'd sewed by hand, the corners tucked neatly. The colorful rag rug she'd woven herself lay squarely in the middle of the swept wooden floor. Her indoor slippers were under the bed, her summer nightgown and bath towel, dry to the touch, hung from their hooks. Her grubby overalls were gone.

It had been three days since Rose had seen Cerise, a lifetime in their friendship. Normally, they met at least twice a day for a mid-morning coffee and an after-dinner, after-meditation recap. Even if Cerise had needed a well-deserved break, as her fellow field hands said, a person could play hooky reading and skinny-dipping in the mountain swimming holes for only so long. Cerise hadn't been to breakfast or dinner, work or any of the meditations. And this was the solstice week, when everyone was expected to pitch in.

The only other possibility was that Ellen had locked her up in the Chi Chamber. Rose shuddered at the prospect.

The Chi Chamber was a rusted shipping container at the edge of the compound, by the woods. It was so well hidden that many Diviners were unaware of its existence. Lucky them. Rose once spent a night there as punishment for daring to defend a Novice being mistreated by Ellen. She exited feeling betrayed and hurt, not repentant as she pretended.

Until then, she'd taken Cliff at his word that the Diviner lifestyle was to promote love and harmony. But how could a community that sent its members to solitary confinement be anything but cruel?

The windowless container was tight, no more than eight feet by ten feet. The addition of a water closet with only a toilet and a small sink was fairly new. It was uninsulated, so it was freezing in the winter and boiling in the summer. Rumor had it a Diviner collapsed from heatstroke last August and had to be packed in ice fetched from a grocery store in Manchester so he wouldn't die. Rose wasn't sure if he survived or not; the Facilitators had quickly shut down any discussion of him.

The supposed purpose of the chamber was to allow misguided Diviners the seclusion required to reset their chi, the vital life force that needs to be in balance for perfect harmony. Every inch of the metal walls was covered with brightly colored posters imprinted with Dagda's most beloved sayings. Diviners were expected to fast and pray on his words until they reached enlightenment or admitted the error of their ways, whichever came first. But before they could be released from the chamber, Dagda would have to grant—and administer—a cleanse, which normally ran about five hundred bucks.

Cerise would never survive the Chi Chamber, not with her tooth infection, Rose feared. The night she stopped by the cabin to hang out and read Rose's speech, she was getting feverish and desperately in need of medical care. She could die without antibiotics.

"What are you doing?"

Rose spun around to find Ellen holding her clipboard, her right eyebrow arched in accusation. The petite task master with the pug nose was wearing her white ceremonial robe, of which she was very proud; white robes indicated she was Realized, the highest order next to Divine's gold. (Only Cliff got to wear that.) Though Rose, too, had reached Realized, she didn't go around wearing her coveted robe like a show-off. For starters, the white would have been impossible to keep clean.

Ellen must have been spying on her. So what? That witch could go to hell for all Rose cared. "What have you done with Cerise?"

"What makes you think I did anything with Cerise?" Ellen smiled slightly, enjoying Rose's torment. Before coming to the Center, Ellen had been a claims specialist at a major health insurance company that routinely denied coverage for patients with preexisting conditions, which explained her hard shell.

"Cerise's work overalls are gone. Her bed hasn't been touched. Her bath towel's dry and I haven't seen her in days." Rose ticked off the facts finger by finger. "You run everything around here. You know what happened to her. So where is she?"

Ellen brought the clipboard to her chest and shrugged like she couldn't have cared less. "Cerise has always marched to the beat of her own drummer. She's been complaining about that stupid tooth for weeks, as you know. She probably went to town to see a dentist, in clear violation of the rules, so she'll have some explaining to do when she returns. If she can summon the courage to return, that is."

If she can summon the courage? What was that supposed to mean? Rose opened her mouth to ask, but Ellen held up her finger.

"I don't have time for this now. Dagda wants to leave for

Dutton and asked me to find you. He already has your daughter. They're waiting in the car."

Ellen must have known how that line would strike fear in Rose's heart. Rose had given Astraea firm instructions never to be alone with any man, even in what she had previously thought of as the relative safety of the commune. Without saying a word, Rose pushed past the smug henchwoman and took the stairs two at a time.

Cliff was behind the wheel of the Boxster checking his watch when Rose got to his private drive, out of breath from running. Next to him, Astraea was standing on the passenger seat jumping up and down.

"Finally!" Obviously exasperated, he turned the key in the ignition, starting up the car before Rose was able to open the door and pull Astraea onto her lap, though Astraea was too big for that now.

"She needs her own seat and there isn't one. Let's leave her here," Rose said, ignoring her daughter's pout of disappointment.

"Just hold her. Don't make such a fuss about each and every little thing," Cliff snapped, speeding down the drive to the twisting mountain road.

Astraea couldn't have been more delighted. She lifted her face to the sun, the breeze flowing through her two braids as they zigzagged down the mountain. All Rose could think was that a deep pothole or oncoming car requiring a sharp turn of the wheel could send the child flying.

Rose held Astraea tighter and said sweetly, so as not to bruise his ego, "We're so early. No need to rush. Let's enjoy the ride."

Cliff placed a hand on her left knee and squeezed, not a gesture of fondness, but of warning. "Don't tell me how to drive. I've been driving a lot longer than you."

This was unfair. Her life and the life of her daughter were at stake. But Cliff wouldn't react well if she pressed the issue, so all she could do was pray that Brigit, the goddess of protection, would keep them safe.

Finally, the bumpy dirt road ended at Route 7. Cliff hooked a right onto the smooth pavement and let loose, the Boxster doing what it was built to do—going from zero to sixty in under seven seconds.

Thrilled, Astraea raised her arms and screamed for joy. Rose bit her lower lip to keep from screaming in panic. "Oh, my god, Cliff. Slow down!"

"Why? She loves it!" He high-fived Astraea. His own long hair, more gray than brown lately, flew out of its ponytail they were going so fast. Rose was terrified, and that only spurred on Cliff to give it more gas.

"Please?" she shouted, squeezing his thigh as he'd squeezed hers, though he might have misinterpreted the gesture as an invitation. "It's near the end of the month and you know how cops like to make their quota. They'd love nothing more than to snare the famous Radcliffe MacBeath in a speed trap."

That did it. Her wise words mitigated by the flattery on which he thrived prompted him to ease off the gas. The Boxster slowed to the proscribed 45 miles per hour. "Better put her between your legs," he said, turning serious. "At least until we get off the highway."

"But she could get hurt . . ."

"Do it!" he growled. "Goddammit, must you constantly backchat? It's exhausting."

Unsnapping the belt, Rose slid her daughter under the dashboard just as they passed a dark green Vermont State Police cruiser hiding like a spider behind a granite outcropping in the median. Rose's gut tightened as she eyed the speedometer—a safe, yet cocky, two miles over the speed limit.

Cliff gave the trooper a two-finger salute.

"You know him?"

"Trooper Oswald." He tightened his grip on the steering wheel, checking the rearview, his previous cockiness replaced by simmering anger. "I've had reports that he's been asking a lot of nosy questions about us. Apparently he thinks we're up to no good. Goddammit. He's tailing me."

Rose turned to see for herself.

"Jesus Christ! Don't let him see you check! Look straight ahead and whatever you do, *keep her down.*" He nodded to Astraea, who instinctively knew to keep quiet when Dagda wasn't happy. Her eyes went wide with worry.

Rose winked and tugged her daughter's braid, though her mind was racing. Was the Center under investigation? Would it be raided and all the children taken from their parents? Would she lose her baby?

All Trooper Oswald had to do was stop Cliff for a trumped-up vehicle violation. He'd see that Astraea wasn't buckled into a seat, that there wasn't even room for her. Rose could easily be charged with child endangerment, which would be enough to notify social services, which might insist on paying a visit to the Center, putting all parents and their children at risk of separation. She took Astraea's warm little hand in hers and prayed. *Please, Brigit, mother goddess, woman of wisdom, please get us through this.*

She was steamed at Cliff for putting them in such a precarious situation. There was no reason to take the two-seater. She and Astraea would have been fine in the Center's stunted yellow school bus with their trusty driver, Joe, at the helm.

Yes, the bus sported THE CENTER FOR SPIRITUAL DOWSING on the side, and yes, that might have attracted the attention of the police if they were truly monitoring the commune's comings and goings. But they would have been legal, and it was highly doubtful a cop would have tracked the bus for five miles as Oswald was now doing to them.

"Isn't there some rule he can't follow us after a certain distance?" Rose asked tentatively as they took Exit 4 to Route 30 into Manchester.

"That's a myth. They can follow us for as long as we're on a public road and this SOB is gonna follow us all the way to Dutton."

A wave of anxiety roiled through Rose's body. Though they were fewer than eight miles from Genevieve Winslow's house, Route 30 was a two-lane country highway with tons of speed traps. Sweat began to bead on her temples and the palms of her hands as she gripped Astraea tightly. She could feel her armpits dampen when Cliff nodded in response to her question about whether the cop was still there.

Finally, Dutton's famous marble sidewalks appeared, signaling they'd almost reached their destination. They drove by white picket fences surrounding horse farms with their sweeping manicured lawns and historic homes with four chimneys, dark green shutters, and immaculate landscaping.

Cliff took a careful left at the Dutton Inn and drove one mile under the 25 miles per hour speed limit through the Dutton town square, past the gazebo with its pots of red and pink geraniums, until they reached the stone wall marking the Winslow estate.

Even supposedly cool Cliff exhaled a sigh of relief as they drove through the stone pillars and up the driveway. Rose's fears shifted from worrying about Trooper Oswald to worrying what would happen if Ben was home. That, she suspected, was the real reason Cliff insisted on acting as chauffeur.

The stately colonial home loomed above them at the peak of a slight rise. Eight windows framed by shiny black wooden shutters, four dormers, and an arched front entrance that was rarely used made for an intimidating mansion. A master gardener in her own right, Genevieve Winslow had directed the landscapers to soften the exterior with bushes of blue hydrangeas, pink dianthus, and purple irises. Fragrant white peonies framed by dark green leaves bowed heavily against their supports, while the red columbine stood like grenadiers.

"His car's gone, so you can breathe a sigh of relief." Cliff killed the engine. "You needn't worry about me running into your boyfriend."

He was wrong. Ben wasn't her boyfriend, and she wasn't worried about Cliff running into him. She was far more worried about Ben running into Cliff. She was fairly certain her aging and indulgent Dagda wouldn't survive Ben's fury.

11

ROSE

JUNE 20, 2003

"You don't have to stick around and wait. Why don't you go down to the Northshire Bookstore? There's a café there, and you can browse while I'm with Genevieve. You'll be bored silly hanging around here for an hour." Rose needed Cliff to be gone.

What she really needed was to make a phone call without him monitoring it. She didn't dare use the Center's office phone, not with so many snoops eager to tattle to Ellen.

Astraea had already taken off, running pell-mell to the swing hanging from an apple tree. Pulling back the rope as far as it would go, she swung forward, pumping her legs and kicking up her heels in an exuberant display of freedom. Next would be the slide on the swing set that, once upon a time, must have been Ben's.

Cliff was deaf to Rose's suggestion about finding something to do. Gripping her elbow with just enough firmness to let her know he was wise to her ways, he led her up the walk to the front door Genevieve rarely used. "Won't get rid of me that easy, my dear."

Dammit!

"Genevieve likes me to come around back." Rose wiggled out of his grasp and went to the side entrance. She couldn't wait to be rid of this increasingly authoritarian father figure who always knew best, and she was tired of the Diviner spies waiting to knock her down a peg. She wanted to be free. And safe. For Astraea's sake, if not her own. "The front is just for company."

"Ah, yes. She has you coming in the servants' entrance. So it seems you two aren't as close as you think."

Rose tried to brush off this dig, which did hit a nerve. She'd been bothered by Genevieve's insistence on the side door too, though Genevieve claimed only UPS and stuffy acquaintances used the front. Cliff was just trying to drive a wedge between her and her wealthy, esteemed client, a relationship he hotly envied.

The upper-crust society in the area refused to treat Radcliffe MacBeath as anything other than a slimy charlatan. The local country club denied his application, the ultimate insult to him, a bestselling author, celebrity, and entrepreneur. The year before, he hadn't been invited to a single social gala despite dashing off several huge checks to Dutton society's pet charities. He took that as a personal affront too, and worse, as a confirmation of his inadequacy—a fear left over from his impoverished childhood.

Cliff had been raised by a single mother who cleaned the houses of wealthy families in Clarks Summit, Pennsylvania, and would feed her son leftovers about to be composted by her privileged clients. In his memoir, *The Divine Right of Me*, he'd written about feeling like the kid with his face pressed to the window of a candy shop, forever eyeing the goodies he'd never be allowed to have. When Rose read that, she shook her head in pity for her guru, knowing he'd never be accepted by the society he craved. To them, wanting to be included was considered a sign of weakness. He'd have been better off giving them the finger.

Genevieve greeted them on the patio, her posture ramrod straight, her spindly arms covered by a white cardigan and folded in judgment. It was chilly for June, even for Vermont, the temperature lowered by the previous night's rain. The week before, she and Rose had been in sundresses and sipping iced tea to keep cool in the sweltering heat. Astraea had been running around barefoot, sucking on a Popsicle.

"Hello," she said in a clipped tone, directing her gaze to Cliff, who responded with an awkward bow. It was hard to tell if she was more confused by his uninvited presence or his tropical outfit.

Cliff was working on his brand, which Cerise once described as "Jerry Garcia and Jimmy Buffett meet *Miami Vice*." Expensive, tight-fitting white jeans topped by a wildly colored Hawaiian shirt, his long graying hair tied neatly in a ponytail, his eyes shaded by Ray-Ban Aviators. The shirt, Rose happened to know, was created by a famous Diviner designer in Baja specifically for him. The watch on his wrist was a Rolex that cost about as much as that Boxster, and his scent was Versace's Pour Homme.

Whipping off his glasses, he extended a hand. "Radcliffe Mac-Beath. Delighted to finally meet you, Mrs. Winslow."

Genevieve glanced at his buffed and polished nails and nodded without accepting his offer of a shake. "Won't you come in," she offered flatly.

They entered a vaulted space abutting a chef's kitchen. Despite the massive size of this historic house with its formal parlors and dining room, the judge's old study and library, it was in this relatively new, airy addition where the Winslow family did most of their living—though family was an odd term for what was left of the Winslows. Genevieve resided mostly by herself, aside from Ben's visits on Thanksgiving, Christmas, her February birthday, and the month of June. He was her only child.

At the thought of Ben, Rose's pulse spiked briefly. As much as she'd been trying to avoid him lately, he could be crucial to the plans she was forming. She would have to find a way to get him alone on one of these visits so they could talk privately.

"What a lovely home!" Cliff zoomed like a bee to a framed print of a red barn on a yellow hayfield. Pulling out a pair of readers from the breast pocket of his shirt, he squinted at the signature. "My god. It's an original Sabra Field!"

Genevieve said only, "Please make yourself comfortable, Mr. MacBeath. Rose, shall we get started?"

"Love her colors." He tapped his glasses against the frame. "Do you know, I've had dinner at her house in Barnard. Funny story. My car was stuck in the mud outside her house on a ghastly night. Rain, snow, the whole nine yards. She graciously invited me in and warmed me up with a spicy vegetarian stew while we waited for the road crew to dig me out. Did a jigsaw puzzle. A jungle, if memory serves."

If memory serves. Hah! Rose had heard Cliff's spin on this story a thousand times, and with each telling, his brush with the famous Vermont artist became more and more intimate. In the initial version, he'd merely gotten stuck in the mud outside her house and Sabra had let him use her phone to call for a tow. Over the years, it had evolved into dinner, and now, a jigsaw puzzle.

"Oh, Sabra's a dear, dear friend." Genevieve smiled, calling his bluff. "We met years ago when she attended a spring production of *On Golden Pond*, and ever since she's been a loyal supporter of the Dutton Playhouse, where I'm on the board. I'll have to ask her which puzzle."

Busted! If he'd simply stuck to the truth, that would have been a mildly amusing, if trivial, tale. But he couldn't resist embellishing the story to make himself appear like a VIP worthy of Genevieve's approval. Rose had worked with Genevieve long enough to know she would call Sabra Field, and when Sabra failed to remember ever even meeting Cliff, Genevieve would find a way to bring that to Cliff's attention in a public venue, where he'd be roundly panned as a fraud. Genevieve believed in Rose's gifts, but she certainly didn't believe in Radcliffe's teachings.

Cliff, however, would not be outdone. "You're on the board of the Dutton Players? How fortuitous!" he exclaimed. "You know, my accountant's been after me to find more write-offs, and I do love local theater, especially when it's a 501(c)3." With that, he produced a checkbook from seemingly nowhere, clicked a pen, and scribbled out a check, ripping it off and handing it to Genevieve with another dorky bow. "There you go! I realize you don't handle the books, but perhaps this is a start."

The move was so crass, so what Genevieve and her ilk detested, that Rose melted with secondhand embarrassment.

Genevieve pinched the check between two fingers and frowned. "How very kind of you, Mr. MacBeath. Too, too kind, actually."

All Rose could see was a series of zeroes. At least four. This was infuriating. Just the week before, she and the other cooks in the café had been instructed by Ellen that, due to poor cash flow, they were to reduce the food allotments to their fellow Diviners. Rose was alarmed, because those who worked long hours in the field or chopping wood were already famished and needed more sustenance. Cliff claimed inadequate caloric intake was beneficial for body and soul, but he wasn't cutting back on his portions, Rose noticed. And now here he was dashing off five-figure checks to impress some old biddy.

Cliff flicked his hand. "Oh, please. I'm happy to help. The arts enhance so much in life, don't you think?"

It was a stupid question, and Rose figured Genevieve would zing him with a barbed quip. Instead, she said, "I so agree. You know, it just occurred to me that we've been in need of an able fundraiser. I'm sure the board would love to get to know you, Cliff, and, if you're amenable, bring you on as a member of the team."

And there it was, the entrée Cliff desperately sought. He was even Cliff, not Mr. MacBeath. So typical of him. Just when Rose thought for sure he'd be put in his place, he wowed them all by getting exactly what he wanted.

"Happy to assist." Checking his pricey timepiece, he added, "I've kept you far too long from the business at hand. My apologies."

"Nonsense. You've been a delight!" Genevieve actually batted her lashes.

He was a master, Rose thought, following Genevieve out to the garden to do their reading. She was growing concerned now that executing her plan would be far more difficult than she considered.

Perhaps even impossible.

"So that's the infamous Radcliffe MacBeath," Genevieve said when they were safely out of earshot, sitting at the wrought-iron table with a pitcher of lemonade. "I've always wondered what the attraction was."

This comment wasn't really about Cliff as much as it was about her, Rose decided. Genevieve didn't give two figs about the man—aside from his potential financial contribution to the Dutton Players. What Genevieve really wanted to know was . . . *why*?

Why did Rose stay at the Center when it was clear she was unhappy there? *Why* did she tolerate Cliff's exhausting ego and demands? *Why* did Rose leave her husband to join the cult in the first place? And *why* didn't she flee after Genevieve let it be known that she was ready with money, shelter, and transportation should Rose ever say the word?

Rose had to be careful with her reaction. Dutton was a small community, and whispers of potential exploitation at the local cult could be enough to rouse police interest. For all she knew, Genevieve was in contact with this Trooper Oswald who Cliff claimed was investigating the commune.

Of course, were the Center to be raided, Rose had no doubt that, unlike the rest of them, Cliff would emerge unscathed. He'd portray himself as a victim persecuted by Big Energy for promoting a lifestyle that eschewed the powerful trifecta of oil, natural gas, and electricity. Never mind that Cliff was powering his Boxster and his house with Big Energy. The Diviners were conveniently blind to his hypocrisy and primed to be outraged on his behalf. Rose herself had let his hypocrisy get too far before allowing herself to see the truth.

Rose feared the more loyal of his followers might even take to violence. Cliff's rhetoric at evening meditations lately had been peppered with explosive phrases like "witch hunt" and vague threats of revenge against those who would come after not just him, but the Diviners and the Center collectively.

Cliff was already laying the foundation for persecuting one of his own. The other night he'd wondered aloud if the Center was putting itself at risk by welcoming all and sundry without more rigorous vetting.

"We could be harboring a troll, beloveds, a nonbeliever who is undercover on behalf of corporate America." He put up his hands to quell the murmurs among his followers. "I know. I know. I'm loath to even entertain the possibility, but we must. So I ask each and every one of you to dowse for the source of the negative energy I sense is infiltrating our community. Find the evil force and bring him or her to me so I may reverse their polarization."

This was met with hearty and, for Rose and Cerise, disconcerting applause.

"How much do you want to bet he's talking about me?" Cerise whispered in Rose's ear.

Rose had nudged her hard and scolded her to quit messing around. But Cerise wasn't amused. She was dead serious.

And now Cerise was gone. Vanished into the ether without a trace. *Poof!*

Rose smiled at Genevieve and held up her pendulum. "We're running behind. Shall we?" Best to ignore Genevieve's question. Besides, Rose assumed Cliff was spying on them from the French doors. She didn't have to *see* him to see him. As someone tapped into the Divine Energy, she simply knew.

With a resigned sigh, Genevieve folded her ringed fingers on the table and waited. They'd been meeting for so many years, they'd adopted a silent routine. While Genevieve meditated on her troubling issue, Rose swung the pendulum as she tapped into her client's vibrations.

Genevieve didn't have to be told what meant yes or no anymore. She knew that Rose's pendulum swinging side to side was negative and was positive if it switched to a circle, the pendulum rotating in a clockwise direction. If it stood still, it meant Rose wasn't doing her job.

The garden was blissfully quiet aside from the bees buzzing on the roses and a bright red cardinal tweeting from the apple trees, which were in full bud. Having grown tired of the swing, Astraea was busy playing some sort of make-believe game among Genevieve's fragrant lavender lilacs. Crafting little homes for fairies, probably.

Rose tried to concentrate on Genevieve's concerns, but her own worries intruded. She couldn't stop thinking of her escape plan, which had taken on new urgency now that Cerise was gone. Cerise wouldn't have left the Center without saying goodbye, Rose was sure of that. Even during her rare trips into town, her friend always asked Rose what she could pick up for Astraea. Rose would reply nothing, since Cerise was flat broke. That didn't matter. Cerise would return with a few modest gifts—a cherry Tootsie Pop for Astraea and a few paperbacks nicked from the free library outside the post office for Rose.

Reading mysteries and romantic suspense was Cerise's secret addiction, spiritual dowsing having banished her more sinister demons. Like many fellow Diviners, she'd stumbled upon the Center during what Cliff called "the seeking years"—that period of early adulthood when the paths so clearly marked in childhood became lost in a bramble of failures and uncertainties.

Cerise had dreamed of being a doctor until crazy expensive med school tuition dashed that plan. So she became a pharmacy assistant and was doing okay until she made the fatal mistake of dipping into her own supplies to numb a chronic shoulder injury. Fired from her job, depressed and very much alone, she ended up at the Center by accident when she stopped by for lunch at the café during a tour bus trip through Vermont.

Like the hostel system for hikers, the café was also a tool for recruitment. After lunch, a kind Diviner invited Cerise to tour the lovely commune and enjoy its peaceful simplicity. Cerise spent the rest of the afternoon basking in the sun and listening to the birds. When she was about to leave, she was invited to a free dinner followed by meditation and, since it was late, a free bed in the hostel. Feeling bad about accepting so much hospitality at zero cost, Cerise had fallen prey to the Center's most effective ploy: manipulating visitors into repaying favors they never requested.

In the beginning, Cerise was Cliff's star pupil, immersing herself in every word he'd written on the subject of divination. She believed with all her heart that all living creatures, from the king of England to the lowliest moss on the mountain's rocks, was connected by a Divine Energy that could be harnessed for personal empowerment with the aid of certain tools—pendulums, rods, forked sticks, and bobbers.

Eager to earn his approval, Cerise followed Cliff's instructions to a T, working her way from Novice to Seeker to Mentor. She fasted for days, subsisting only on spring water until she achieved a state of hallucination. On the chilly May day she was to be elevated to the coveted status of Realized, she purified herself in a mountain stream in preparation for "Spiritual Unification."

Spiritual Unification capped off the ordination as a Realized, the penultimate level one could achieve as a Diviner. Rose had been in the same state as most female Diviners in her situation, ready to submit to MacBeath in soul—and body. She, too, had been willing to "unite energies" with this extraordinary man, this demigod who seemed to understand her like no one else, ever.

Rose considered herself special until Cerise pointed out that no men, only women in their prime, made it to Realized. The revelation had been crushing. She and Cerise had been simply notches on Radcliffe MacBeath's woven gold belt.

One night, Cerise went to Cliff's house, as had been routine for her since becoming a Realized, to take a hot shower and fall into his bed. Except another woman was already between the sheets, naked. And not just any woman, a girl barely over the age of consent, and she wasn't a Realized. Cerise wasn't sure if the girl was even a Novice. But she was pretty sure Cliff was old enough to be her grandfather.

That's when the scales fell from her eyes and Cerise began to see the Center for what it was—a vehicle for Cliff to drain money from gullible devotees while simultaneously using the wealth and status he acquired through deception to boost his ego. He'd grown very rich and greedy since Cerise signed up for the program. Acquisitive too. A nice house, cars, designer duds, jewelry. The Diviners liked to say he earned these perks from his bestselling books, which might have been true. But that was beside the point.

The Diviners were supposed to be living a simple life near to

Mother Earth, without the interference of modern society's trappings, and here was their Dagda violating every rule he himself had dictated.

Cerise had told Rose that she'd have left then and there except she was underfed, overworked, dirt poor, and too crushed to fight. Her birth family had disowned her, and the Center had long ago emptied her bank account. Even if she managed to escape, she'd have had no place to go and no way to survive.

So it didn't make sense that after all these years, Cerise suddenly had found the wherewithal to leave. These were not promising signs. Rose suspected Cliff's Facilitators had put her closest and dearest friend out of *his* misery.

She suppressed a flurry of panic at the thought. Here on Genevieve's peaceful patio was not the time or place to spiral. Rose needed to zero in on the task at hand lest she disappoint Genevieve and incur Cliff's explosive wrath. Cerise's fate was a cautionary tale of the punishment a Diviner faced for displeasing their guru.

"What's wrong?" Genevieve waved to the pendulum, which dangled limply with no movement. "Is this a bad sign?"

Embarrassed to be caught lost in her own thoughts, Rose said, "It's not you. It's me. I have a lot on my mind."

She expected Genevieve to clear her throat in irritation. After all, Rose wasn't being paid two hundred dollars per hour to sit there like an idiot. She was supposed to channel the Divine Energy so Genevieve could connect with her beloved late husband.

Usually, Genevieve would mentally ask the judge a question. Rose would provide the answer after feeling the positive or negative responses descending from above and surging like electricity down through her head, neck, shoulder, arm, wrist, and finally, fingers pinching the pendulum's chain. She never knew what Genevieve asked, and since her client seemed satisfied with the results, Rose never pried. However, today's session was an emergency, and

Rose should have been more focused on Genevieve's questions than her own.

To her relief, Genevieve reached over and took Rose's hand, giving it a motherly squeeze. "I'm sorry. You do look awfully tired today. Is there anything I can do?"

"That's so kind of you. I just . . ."

Genevieve leaned close. "Is something going on at the Center? Or is this about Ben?"

Funny. Despite being so eager to see him—and so afraid Cliff would—Rose hadn't thought about Ben much since arriving. "It is and it isn't. I might need Ben's advice. Do you know when he's coming back?"

"Not really. He's off with his high-school sweetheart, Charlotte." Genevieve's lips twisted in sympathy, misreading Rose's interests. "She's home on summer break and they've reconnected while he's in town. They were quite the item back in the day, you know."

If this was Genevieve's way of gently making Rose aware of her son's romantic intentions, she needn't have bothered. Ben and Rose didn't have that kind of relationship. Quite the opposite.

"That's good. I'm glad to hear he's taking a break from working."

"Constantly. That's all he does when he's here, fixates on that goddamn computer." Genevieve let go of Rose's hand and reached for the pitcher of lemonade, pouring them both glasses. "He tells me he's going to make millions with this latest invention of his, software that can monitor a person's heart, blood pressure, even glucose, from miles and miles away." Genevieve took a delicate sip. "Good thing he's got his trust fund to fall back on when his grand plans go south."

"Mama!"

All of a sudden, Astraea was there, her tiny hands gripping

the edges of the glass table, her little lips stained pink from Gene-vieve's Popsicles. "Like bees to honey," Genevieve quipped, pouring a small lemonade for her too. "Here you go, sweetie."

Astraea wasn't there for a sugar fix. Her skin was deathly pale, her knuckles white, and worst of all, her feet were bare. Without inspecting her daughter's ankles, Rose already guessed they were likely covered with bright red scratches that were quite possibly bleeding. She'd been so afraid this might happen if she brought the child here while she was distracted. She never should have allowed Cliff to talk her into it.

"Oh, baby. What is it?" Rose held out her arms and Astraea ran to her, burying her face on her mother's chest, her tears damp-ening her cotton dress.

"They got me," Astraea blurted. "I tried to run away, but they kept pulling me down. They're cold and lonely. It was scary."

Rose stroked the soft braids of her sweet child, so innocent and unaware of her powerful divination abilities. Someday, Astraea would come to regard her gift as a blessing rather than a curse, and she would use her talents to further justice. For now, however, she needed to calm her down and make sure Dagda didn't catch wind of what was going on in the garden.

"They're merely mischief makers, honey," Rose whispered. "They want to play with your silly toes."

Over the child's head, Rose caught a glimpse of Genevieve staring where Astraea had been playing. The edge of the garden where the lilies of the valley grew between four carefully tended peony bushes had a special significance for her client. Rose knew from her readings that it was a very private, very personal, grave-yard.

"You mean"—Genevieve's jaw dropped—"she can . . . ?"

Rose lowered her lids in assent. Genevieve closed her mouth, biting her lip hard to keep from crying. After a moment, she slowly rose from her seat and walked stiffly to the sacred place. Rose and Astraea watched as she knelt and clasped her hands.

"What's she doing?" Astraea whispered.

"I'm not sure." Rose kissed her daughter's cheek. "Maybe we should give her some space."

Understanding more than Rose would have expected for a relatively sheltered ten-year-old, Astraea slid off her mother's lap and said solemnly, "I'll go tell Dagda we're ready to leave."

Not quite, Rose thought. She needed to make the call, even if she didn't have permission to use Genevieve's phone and it was long distance. In fairness, her client would never see the charge. She had accountants who dealt with such trivialities. But Ben would. He scrutinized every penny spent from his future inheritance, and he'd be upset that his mother had telephoned Sudbury, Massachusetts, at four thirty in the afternoon on June 20 for no discernible reason. He'd likely realize it was Rose who had made the call, and he'd add it to the list of reasons he didn't like her.

It would make no difference; Rose hoped she would be long gone by then.

Taking Astraea by the hand, they entered the house to find Cliff, bored and antsy, watching a golf match on the TV in the den. His feet were on the coffee table, jiggling, his jaw working back and forth as if he were grinding his teeth.

"Took you long enough." He turned off the TV and tossed the remote on the couch. "Jesus, Rose. It's the effing twentieth. I don't have time to sit around playing pattycake while you gals have a tea party. I'm scheduled to address over two hundred people at seven, unless you've forgotten!"

Astraea clenched her mother's hand. Cliff could be intimidating when he was irritated. Rose couldn't imagine how frightening this tall figure of supreme authority must be to a small child.

Rose was tempted to spit back, *Then you shouldn't have come.*

She wanted to point out their session actually hadn't been that long, having been cut short by Astraea's discovery. But as arguing wouldn't accomplish anything besides further infuriating the man who controlled every aspect of her life, she simply murmured, "My apologies. Please let me use the bathroom and then we can go."

Cliff sighed. "Very well. But make it fast."

Pig, Rose thought, dashing up the stairs.

During a brief tour of the house, Rose had noted the princess phone on the wall of her client's bathroom for use in case Genevieve slipped in the shower and hurt herself. Shutting and locking the door, she lifted the phone off the hook, listened for the dial tone, and dialed the number she'd committed to memory.

She held her breath, her heart thumping. Either Dan would be relieved to hear her voice or so disgusted he'd hang up right away. The only reason he might listen was for the sake of their daughter. Astraea was her trump card, which she'd play immediately when he answered, having rehearsed the script over and over in her head.

The phone rang four times and then the answering machine clicked on. Shoot. Of course he was still at work. It was Friday! She should have thought of that. Still, she wasn't going to blow this opportunity. Who knew when, or if, she could get to a phone again before tomorrow night. She'd have to leave a message.

"Hi, Dan, it's, it's, it's Rose." She was startled to find she was stuttering. Obviously, she was much more nervous than she realized. "Look, I can't explain now, but I need you to drive up to the Center tomorrow night and get me and Astraea, er Stella. I'll be free shortly after midnight. We'll be waiting for you in the parking lot. I'll be in a white robe. There'll be tons of visitors for the solstice so you won't stand out. Please, Dan, please be there."

"ROSE!" Cliff's voice boomed from below, his footsteps heavy on the stairs. "What the hell's taking you so long?"

"I want to come home." Then, before she could stop herself,

she added, "I made a mistake, Dan. I never should have left. Stella shouldn't have to pay for my sins. Please come, before it's too late."

Shaking, she hung up the phone, flushed the toilet, went to the sink, turned on the water, and washed her hands, regarding her haggard reflection in the mirror. Had she gone too far? It was a chance she had to take. Dan needed to realize this message wasn't made on a whim, that she was baring her heart. Her experiment in alternative living was over.

She was done. The prospect of spending a minute more than she had to at the Center was now out of the question.

Tucking a few strands of flyaway hair behind her ears, she threw open the bathroom door and froze at the sight of Radcliffe MacBeath radiating rage.

"You're not going anywhere, my dear, not without my say-so. If you thought you could outwit me, your Dagda who knows all, sees all, perceives all, you were dead, dead wrong."

Whereupon he grabbed her wrist and dragged her down the stairs, apparently not all-knowing enough to see Genevieve Winslow gripping the banister in shock as she witnessed him shove her favorite psychic and friend out the door.

So much for his debut in society.

12

STELLA

JUNE 17, 2023

The Alewife Brook Reservation is a big, beautiful marshy park along the Alewife Brook in Cambridge, best known to tourists as the start of the Minuteman hike-and-bike path. I do not go barefoot here.

According to my spotty research, in the 1600s this area was home to Native Americans who netted alewife and bluefin herring as they migrated from Cape Cod Bay up the freshwater Missi-tuk River, now known as the Mystic. Since these folk were buried before the invention of grave liners, I can only imagine what a tiptoe through the marsh would yield. I envision skeletal fingers reaching through the rich, loamy, fetid muck to grab my ankles, most likely. Whispered pleas for salvation—or vengeance. No thanks.

Maybe that's why I don't often have this experience in contemporary cemeteries. I could skip the light fandango across Forest Hills in Jamaica Plain and not feel so much as a tickle of souls on my soles.

Anyway, the reason I bring up Alewife is because Heather and I are meeting this afternoon at the Alewife T Station to execute Dad's Plan B. Dad can't come because he's being held captive in his own home.

As I predicted, the Facilitators have incited a bunch of wannabe vigilantes into a frenzy by spreading bogus claims online that my father killed my mother. Never mind that I was three when Mama took me to the Center or that the police years ago blasted this conspiracy theory as bullshit. Logic is not the strong suit of these fools, though these fools are doing an excellent job of fulfilling the Facilitators' goal of diverting attention from their Dagda.

In fact, Dad was the first suspect cleared by the police in their investigation. He was at his cousin Frank's wedding two hours away from the Center in the Berkshires in western Massachusetts. It would have been impossible to slip out and make the trek up the back roads in time to murder Mama around two in the morning, when he was closing down the dance floor at one. The police even went beyond the usual protocol to issue a formal statement proclaiming his innocence.

"It's insane," Dad said on the phone after Fig and I got back to her apartment from cleaning out mine. "Last night, these idiots shined lights into our bedroom window, making it impossible to sleep. We had to call the police. They shooed them off, but this morning they were back again. I went out to talk to them, to explain, but they actually rushed me!"

"Maybe you should post photos of you boogeying down to 'Hot in Herre' at Frank's reception." Dad's shirt was off in a few, and he was executing a poor attempt at breakdancing, head on the floor, a foot in the air. Humiliating, totally, but hardly a portrait of a man scheming to kill his estranged wife.

"My being in the Berkshires only puts me closer to the crime, in their minds. They claim there are witnesses who are too intimidated to come forward who saw me at the Center. How would they have seen me? It was the solstice and everyone was in costume."

I have no idea if *everyone* was in costume, though certainly the man in the Cernunnos getup was. He was tall like MacBeath and Dad and, as I've recently discovered, Ben Winslow. Then again, I was ten, and most grown men seemed big and scary to me at that age.

The upshot is Dad's afraid if he leaves to meet me, the mob will follow him. He refuses to take that chance. He's hunkering down at home with the shades drawn and sending Heather in his place.

She's waiting in her Kia hatchback exactly where Dad said she'd be, on the rooftop of the parking garage. Perhaps not the most ideal location, since it's still raining.

"Hey, sweetie," she chirps from the open driver's side window. She gets out and gives me a warm hug scented with Downy fabric softener. As always, she's sensibly attired. Today, she's in a pea-green LLBean rain jacket and matching rain boots, her copper-colored hair is in a smooth ponytail, her freckled face is free of makeup, and her only adornments are tiny gold hoops dangling from each ear.

Heather's not old enough to be my mother. She's more like old enough to be my babysitter. Now that I'm an adult and the years of her tucking me into bed are long gone, she's become more of a friend than a parent. Much to Dad's abhorrence, we've spent plenty of evenings knitting to true-crime junk on TV. At least, we used to before we, ourselves, became true-crime junk.

We get in the car to get out of the rain, and Heather asks if I have my stuff. By that, she means the "essentials" Dad told me to pack: a pair of jeans, a pair of shorts, a few T-shirts, one sweatshirt, a bunch of underwear (I could always buy more, right?), socks, deodorant, makeup, toothbrush/toothpaste, a brush, hair ties, and a bandanna. Why the bandanna, I have no idea. Dad seems to think it'll come in handy.

"Yup. Where we headed?"

When Dad said he'd found a safe place for me to lay low for a while, my fingers were crossed for a rocky island off the coast of Maine or a tranquil hideaway over the border in Canada. I could use a little rest and relaxation.

"Upstate New York, a tiny town near Saratoga Springs." Heather unzips her coat. "And not us, you."

I don't like the sound of that. Well, actually, I don't like the sound of Upstate New York. It can mean only one thing: Heather's sister, Debra, the dog trainer. And not just any dogs—killer poodles.

Heather confirms my supposition with a cheerful "You remember Aunt Debby!"

It's all I can do not to shudder. I met Debby only once and I can't say she was more fun than a barrel of monkeys. Years ago she appeared at Thanksgiving with a fancy trained security dog, a hypoallergenic killer poodle named Doodles who, according to her, could rip your throat out at the mention of a secret command. Aunt Debby spent the entire dinner communicating to Doodles via little clicks of her tongue while the rest of us dug into our turkey and avoided eye contact lest we trigger the canine assassin.

Debby's luxury killer, allergy-free poodles sell for anywhere from $40,000 to $50,000 a pup. Probably that's how Dad and Heather decided her place would be a safe retreat. Makes sense. Free twenty-four-hour security. But I do not want to stay with Debby. I don't want to live at the kennels with my glum stepaunt who's made it perfectly clear that humans are second to canines.

"I can tell you're not thrilled." Heather slips out of her rain jacket. "I get it. My sister's, uhm, quirky. But Deb's in Colorado introducing a dog to new clients. That's a weeklong process, you know. She has to teach them what to do, what not to do, it's a whole thing. You'll have her house to yourself, and you'll have the round-the-clock protection of her dogs to boot!"

Yippee, I'm tempted to say, though I don't want to come off as ungrateful. "So, what about the dogs? Am I supposed to take care of them too?" Feeding and walking those killers gives me the heebie-jeebies.

"Oh, no. There are only three in the kennels these days, and Deb has her helper. She'll come in the morning for feeding and exercise and training review. Otherwise, the dogs will be safely in their locked cages, though you can unlock them with a remote . . . if you feel threatened."

Not one bit of this scheme is sitting well with me. Stuck alone in a kennel in Nowheresville, Upstate New York, with killer poodles, twiddling my thumbs while waiting for the internet hoopla to die down or a Facilitator to bump me off or kidnap me back to the commune, whichever comes first, is no vacation. Also, I don't see how Deb's house is a solution. If anything, staying there will only postpone the inevitable. And by that I mean my death.

"That's really, really nice of her, but . . ."

Heather thrusts out the jacket. "Put on the coat and pull up the hood. In case anyone sees you, they'll think you're me. Here." She drops the key in my hand. "Don't worry about the car. Your father has been promising to buy me a new one for forever. I've had my eye on a hybrid Rav and passing the Kia to you is the push I've needed to upgrade."

I stare at the key fob, speechless. I've never owned a car before. I've never needed to. Dad insisted I get a driver's license when I was seventeen, but I've never driven farther than New Hampshire for tax-free shopping. "You mean . . ."

"When this nightmare is behind us, I'll sign over the title. For now, let's keep it under my name and insurance. We don't have the luxury of dillydallying with paperwork. You should va-moose."

From her own bag, Heather removes another packable LLBean rain jacket in periwinkle blue. Being chronically practical does have its benefits, I suppose. "There's a cooler in the back with sandwiches and fruit along with a six-pack of Diet Coke." Heather's favorite beverage.

"The code to Deb's gate is 1492, like Columbus sailing the ocean blue," she says, slipping on her other jacket and zipping it to the chin. "The tank is full. I've calculated that you can drive to Deb's without stopping based on forty-one miles per gallon and a two-hundred-and-eighty-mile distance. Should be able to make it on less than nine gallons, and this baby holds almost twelve." She gives the dash a pat. "I'll miss her. She's been a buddy."

It's settled then. I am to go to Bumfuck, New York, in Heather's car without question. I have barely uttered a full sentence during her speech, in which she made sure to include important details like Diet Coke and the Kia's fuel tank capacity.

Heather does this when she's upset, texts or speaks without stopping. She's also blinking rapidly in an effort to keep from crying. Above all else, my stepmother is determined to maintain the impression that she's the ultimate problem-solver. The perpetual Superwoman riding to the rescue armed with wet wipes and a mini bottle of hand sanitizer.

Heather wasn't always so in charge. When Dad brought me back to Massachusetts after Mama's murder, he worked from home for about six months to make sure I felt safe. He went overboard on security, installing alarms on all the windows and doors, taking me with him whenever he left the house.

The arrangement couldn't last forever, seeing as how it's almost impossible to oversee quality control in a lab when you're not physically in that lab. But Dad didn't want to chance it by sending me to public school, where Mama's murderer might have access to my tender neck. Besides, I was still trying to catch up to my contemporaries education-wise and required personal tutoring. So he advertised for a full-time nanny. None of the women who answered the ad filled the bill, and Dad was about to give up until his on-again, off-again girlfriend said she'd step in.

Back then, Heather was a sweet and shy Midwestern transplant who was getting by with a minimum-wage job in a daycare center and dog sitting on the side. She and Dad had met on match.com before online dating was the new normal, and from all appearances their relationship back then could best be described as casual. I doubt she expected to be thrown into the role of mothering a traumatized wild child.

And I was a tough case. I was babyish for my age, unaccustomed to living outside of the woods. I had no idea how to use a telephone or run a microwave. I found them terrifying. The constant drone of electricity, the whirring of the window air conditioner, the blaring TV commercials, or even the hum of the refrigerator made me want to crawl out of my skin. What was white noise to most kids was, for me, as annoying as a buzzing mosquito.

Add to that my physical state, which was neglected. Having never been seen by a pediatrician, I had to undergo a series of painful vaccinations. I went to the dentist for the first time and discovered the piquant joy of Novocain and the piercing whine of a diamond drill.

Then there were the night terrors when I was haunted by the ultimate boogeyman—Cernunnos. This was the monster who killed my mother, only he was coming after *me* as I lay trembling under the bushes staring up at his wild, twisted antlers. I was obsessed by how close I'd come to death. If I'd shouted for help instead of staying silent when he picked me up and carried me to the cave, if I hadn't stayed put as he'd instructed, surely he would have done to me what he did to my mother, splitting my skull in two without a second thought.

This is what I dreamt about for years after coming home to Dad's house. Almost every night I'd wake screaming.

Nothing worked. Not hot milk. Not bedtime stories. Not even Benadryl to get me to sleep. Therapy might have helped except Dad fired my therapist on the advice of his mother, my staunchly Irish grandmother, Patricia O'Neill, who distrusted all psychologists and was convinced they'd only dredge up disturbing memories that would mess me up even more. To remember is a curse, to forget is a blessing, was her stance, which Dad bought hook, line, and sinker.

Thank God for Heather. Relying on her daycare training, she knew what I needed, crawling into my bed and holding me close until I fell asleep. It must have been a year of that, her sleeping by my side every night, stroking my hair and singing silly songs until I dozed off. Eventually, I had fewer and fewer dreams of Antler Man. I learned to sleep without screaming.

Recalling the way she used to hold me close and brush away my tears fills me with sentimental nostalgia. Heather may not have been my birth mother, but in many, many ways she's been more of a mother than Mama ever was.

Impulsively, I throw my arms around her and hug her tightly. "Thank you so, so much," I murmur into her hair. "You've always been a real mother to me, you know."

Heather replies with her own snort-sob, squeezing me back. "You have no idea what that means." Then, pushing me away gently, she reaches into the generous pockets of her LLBean mom jeans for a tissue. Because that's Heather—never without a Kleenex Slim Pack.

"Go, before I lose it," she says, blowing her nose. "And don't worry about me. I'm gonna hop on the T and head into the city. Your father booked us a room at the Marriott on the wharf and we'll meet there this evening, if he can sneak out. We need a getaway from those dreadful people. I'm exhausted."

Good. They need a break.

Heather gets out and leans in the window, raindrops dripping from her hood. "Call us as soon as you get to Deb's. She's got security cameras all over the place, but even so, we'll feel better when we hear from your own mouth that you're safe and sound."

I promise to do as she instructs, making the three-hour drive to Saratoga Springs without stopping, and phoning as soon as I punch in the code and get past the killer poodles. We run through some rudimentary instructions about the car, including this model's tendency to get stolen due to a wonky ignition situation, and then she grasps my hand and urges me to "*be careful*," as if that were a revelation.

I watch as she heads to the door leading to the T, her monogrammed tote slung over her shoulder.

It hits me that with these wheels I'm completely free to go wherever I want, when I want. I'm not locked in my house or cowering in a one-room sublet or holed up in my broom closet of an office. I have no ties that bind, no rent to pay. I have enough personal and vacation time to buy me a week away from work.

But I'm not really free. I'm a fugitive.

I'm running from a man who killed my mother. More than that, in light of the creepy email from the Facilitators, I'm also running from a whole community that believes my fate is an early death, a destiny preordained by the stars, which they must help fulfill. I can already tell the stress is taking a toll on my psyche. I've hardly slept the past two nights, partially because Fig's foldout couch sucks, but mostly because everything right now is so scary.

I'm afraid to let my eyes close and drift off in slumber. I'm afraid to cross a street, get on the T, climb public stairs. It's just a matter of time before I'm pushed in front of a speeding car or onto the third rail or down the steps of the subway. I can't live like that in a city, constantly looking over my shoulder during my commute to work. I'll end up in the psych ward, where I'll probably be smothered by a pillow wielded by a Facilitator.

What did Trooper Oswald say in his text? I check my phone and scroll back to his message.

> Sorry to read this Stella. MacBeath went after Rose and now he's after you, just like we anticipated. I still say if we find out WHY he killed your mother we'll be halfway to closing the case. The question and the answer are the same.
>
> Why?

Odd that Oswald in all these years never mentioned Ben Winslow. I wonder if he ever really was a suspect, as claimed by Rowan. I ask Oswald outright in a text:

> Did you ever investigate a local guy named Ben Winslow in Mama's murder? He came to my apartment yesterday in Somerville. Tried to get in.

I wait, listening to the rain tapping on the car roof. Oswald is typing, according to my WhatsApp. Ever since a skiing accident cut short his career in law enforcement and confined him to a wheelchair, the guy's been tethered to his computer or phone. I like how he gets right back to me, though. Very satisfying.

Interesting. You file a police report?
No crime. Middle of the day, tried door handle and
fled. Was he a legit suspect?

Oswald is typing . . .

Your mother & MacBeath visited the Winslows 24
hrs before she was killed. That put Ben on my radar.
Solid alibi checked out tho . . .

I remember that day because MacBeath let me ride in his
new blue convertible. I loved driving with the top down, my hair
whipping in the breeze, sunshine overhead as I lifted my arms
to the sky. Sometimes he'd take me for joyrides behind Mama's
back. We'd snake down the mountain road to the highway and
let 'er rip. I'd shriek in delight, and then he'd buy my silence by
treating me to a root beer float at Stewart's. Mama was never the
wiser.

I'd played at the Winslows' on numerous occasions while
Mama worked, and I'd always been careful to wear my foil-lined
shoes. That day, however, I removed my sandals to feel the cool
grass under my toes. The Winslows had a fantastic lawn, thick and
green and likely chemically fertilized. It was irresistible.

What followed next was frightening, and I don't like to think
about it too much because it freaks me out. That's why I ignored
Fig's question when she was prying into what happened at the
Winslows'. Call it a survival tactic.

Except now I must force myself to remember what happened:
I was stepping into the garden to sniff some flowers when I felt
something from below slithering over my bare feet. I assumed it
was a harmless garter snake and paid no attention. We cult kids

weren't afraid of snakes or bats, like others our age. We'd been raised to believe we had a divine connection to all living beings. Snakes and bats were our brothers and sisters with souls just like ours, except in different forms.

There was no snake. There was nothing. The cold, lifeless fingers that wrapped themselves around my feet and up my ankles, pulling me down, were invisible. I remember just freezing in terror and thinking, *This is what you get for not wearing your shoes.*

My mother was on the other side of the garden with Mrs. Winslow, and I had to weigh the lesser of two evils: being dragged into the earth by these dead things or running to Mama and being punished for disobedience. I tried pulling them off, the ghost fingers, scratching at them, clawing, but they wouldn't let go.

Finally, I couldn't take it. I ran to my mother and buried my head in her lap.

You'd think I'd have learned my lesson, right? Nope. Later that day I again went barefoot. This time, I was in the woods outside the Center. A girl I'd never met before, likely the daughter of a visitor there for the solstice, talked me into taking her into the forest to see this turtle I kept talking about. That was against the rules. Only kids who permanently lived in the commune were allowed to go into the forest, and then only after we told an adult that's where we were headed.

I remember figuring it'd be okay as long as we returned while it was still light; after all, lots of the Center's rules weren't enforced during the solstice. However, shortly before I got to where the turtle was, I felt the creepy dead fingers again when I crossed a mound of freshly overturned dirt.

Having been traumatized in the Winslows' garden hours before, I was particularly sensitive and freaked, ditching my new friend and dashing back to the Center ASAP to hide under the covers. The girl was furious because I'd left her stranded in unfamiliar woods. I can hardly blame her. When Mean Ellen found out, she ripped me up one side and down the other.

As much as I dread going back there, I need to know what, exactly, is buried in the Winslows' garden. I have the feeling the buried dead under Genevieve's lovely pink peonies may hold the key to finding out who killed Mama and, like Trooper Oswald keeps asking, *why*.

13

STELLA

JUNE 17, 2023

It's already evening when I turn off Route 7 onto Route 30, a two-lane country highway leading from the crowded tourist mecca of Manchester to a Tasha Tudor wonderland of twee—and not-so-twee—clapboard houses. With each mile on the odometer, the countryside turns more charming.

To keep from chickening out, I don't allow myself to think about what I'm actually doing—returning to the font of my nightmares, the hell pit I vowed to avoid forever. My mission is too important, the stakes too high. My future and my father's safety are on the line. There'll be no peace for either of us until my mother's murderer is identified and brought to justice.

So, I swallow my mounting trepidation, ignore the flutter of anxiety in my chest, and focus on the present, hands on the wheel at two and ten, eyes on the road. Every once in a while, I glance at my surroundings, which couldn't be more bucolic.

The midsummer loaming bathes the classic New England homes in a golden light. Robins hop to the sound of worms and whistle goodnight. The air is sweet and clean. Gracious oaks and lush maples create a magical canopy for bluebirds and tiny goldfinches.

Crossing the Dutton town line I notice the sidewalks aren't made of concrete, but of marble slabs. And there are flowers everywhere. Red geraniums in clay pots. Pink roses trellised around doorways. Blue hydrangeas. Lush peonies. Purple irises and salmon-tinted columbines.

Shirley Jackson lived around here, which goes far to explain how she came to write *The Lottery*. Definitely, the only way a perfect place like this can continue to exist is if someone volunteers to be the sacrifice in an annual community stoning.

None of the scenery seems familiar, however, until I reach the heart of Dutton and its quaint village consisting of little more than a general store, a town green, and the Dutton Inn. American flags wave from every pole and streetlight in preparation for the Fourth of July. Yes, I remember this. *I do!*

I remember Mama letting me walk to the general store with a dollar tight in my fist to buy penny candy while she met with Mrs. Winslow. I didn't accompany her on every meeting, just if there was no one to keep an eye on me.

The Center owned a rusted old yellow school bus that, to my knowledge, was the only vehicle on the premises, besides Mac-Beath's secret fleet of sports cars. A Diviner would drop us off in Manchester in this commune bus, and we'd ride another little commuter bus that must have run all the way to Bennington. We'd get off in the village and then Mama would take my hand and lead me past the Dutton Inn down the marble sidewalks to a mansion with stone walls and gardens and an apple orchard with a hefty rope swing.

That walk from the bus stop to the house seemed like forever, but, according to Google Maps, it's only a mile from the general store to where Genevieve Winslow lives. I park Heather's Kia across the street, get out, and assess the situation.

The house is set back several hundred feet on a majestic rise of land. Four chimneys, plenty of mullioned windows, and that apple orchard. My heart leaps at the sight of the wooden swing still dangling from a tree bough. I spent many hours on that swing, as I recall, kicking my heels in the air, hopped up on the red licorice I'd bought at the general store, since white sugar was forbidden in the Center.

The big iron gates at the entrance are new. Or maybe I simply didn't notice them when I was a kid. There definitely wasn't an electronic keypad and intercom on a post at the curb. That seems a bit extreme for Dutton and its exploding crime rate of zero.

I bet this souped-up security is Ben's idea, seeing as how he's made a career out of producing tracking software. I'm also betting there are a bunch of remote cameras all over the property, linked to his phone so he can protect his mother.

So much for my plan to simply walk to the front door, ring the doorbell, and introduce myself to Genevieve. It crossed my mind she might have died, that her house might have sold and the garden excavated for a pool or an addition to make the big house even bigger. However, Genevieve popped up in my Google search in the "around town" section of the *Dutton Reporter* not too long ago looking pretty damned hearty. She was at a holiday fundraiser dressed in a Chanel suit, her gray hair in a classy updo, and an heirloom brooch studded with jewels on her jacket. Had to admire her bright red lipstick—the sign of a grand dame if ever there was one.

Just when I'm about to give up, get back in the Kia, and drive to Aunt Debby's, the gates open. I slip behind the stone wall expecting a car, only to spy a tall, slim woman in spiked heels and a killer saffron-colored cocktail dress clicking down the driveway. Her dark hair is pulled back in a tight bun, and as she approaches, I can make out her jeweled cascade earrings flashing in the evening sun. She appears to be on a mission, a yellow beaded clutch in her hand as she marches out the gate and takes a left toward the inn.

I'm so fascinated by this exquisite woman that I almost miss my chance. Throwing the hood of Heather's raincoat over my head, I duck inside the gate doors just as they're about to shut. This is an unbelievable bit of good fortune. It's the kind of lucky break my mother would have said came from the Divine. In her philosophy, coincidences were called coincidences because nonbelievers couldn't stand the reality that everything is a miracle.

I'm halfway up the driveway when it occurs to me, way too late, that Ben might be visiting his mother. If so, I'm literally walking into the lion's den here. I'm also trapped. I don't know for sure, but the entire estate could be surrounded by stone walls that'll be impossible to scale. He'll either call the police or shoot me as a home intruder or both.

"Okay, okay, calm down, Stella," I tell myself as, taking a deep breath, I plow ahead to the front door. "Play it as it lays." Yeah, right. As if I've ever thought quickly on my feet. My style leans more toward make-it-up-as-you-go-along because improvisation is a procrastinator's last refuge.

No one answers when I ring the doorbell. That's good. I go around to the side entrance and along the way notice the door to one of the garage bays is open and empty. Genevieve's probably out to dinner. What about Ben? Maybe the beautiful woman is a clue.

Taking out my phone, I google "Ben Winslow wife" and up comes a *New York Times* feature on Ben's wedding to Priti Suryanarayana at a beachside service in Monterey a few years before. The article gushes about Ben's accomplishments as founder of HeadFake, about his congressional testimony, numerous awards, and advanced degrees from Stanford. As for Priti, there is simply this description: "former runway model represented by the Jones & Jones Agency."

The article includes a photo of the happy couple attired in traditional Indian wedding garb. The bride is heavily hennaed, her eyes downcast, but there's no mistake. The bombshell who just passed within inches of my nose definitely is the same woman. Judging from her purposeful stride and cocktail attire, she was on her way to meet someone. I hope it's her husband. Anyway, it appears the house is currently unoccupied, so it's now or never.

Genevieve's garden is largely how I remember it, though not as vast and overgrown as it was. Either she's cut it back or I'm no longer four and a half feet tall. It's lovely, though, framing the entire patio off the back. My thumb is far from green, but even I can appreciate the thoughtful planning, how the pink June roses serve as a backdrop to the purple lupine spikes, orange flowers whose name I don't know, and big red poppies.

The showstoppers are the peonies, luxurious flowers the size of small cabbages. Even from across the lawn, their perfume is intoxicating, though a few petals are beginning to brown at the edges. There are four bushes, just like when I was ten, and they are lovingly tended, mulched and supported by almost invisible wire baskets.

Shame I might have to dig them up.

It's nearly seven thirty on nearly the longest day of the year. Too bad, because tiptoeing through the tulips, so to speak, would be far easier under the cover of darkness. Oh, well. Plus, it's not raining here like it was back in Boston. Heather's raincoat is hot, and I feel like I'm suffocating under the hood as I step out of my new Allbirds and place my bare feet on Genevieve's mulch with a sigh of delicious relief.

Most people don't think twice about taking off their shoes. For me, going barefoot outside is pure liberation. My feet are unconfined. I can wiggle my toes and sink them into the soil. It's almost . . . orgasmic.

I'm wearing shorts, so I have to be careful of the rose prickers as I delicately slide one foot between the peonies and roses. The soles of my feet are particularly tender, having been protected for most of their existence, and the rough, moist mulch is disconcerting. Wedging myself further, I take another step so I'm solidly between the two mature peonies. I inhale the sharp, pungent smell of the shredded cedar, but I sense nothing below.

I feel like a doofus standing there swatting at the occasional blackfly as I wait for the old creepy sensations to manifest themselves. Inching toward the other bush with still no reaction, I'm beginning to come around to my therapist's theory that all along my "sense" of the buried dead has been in my head. I'm not a specially gifted dowser, as my mother was convinced. I was simply traumatized, transferring a deep-rooted (not to pun) separation anxiety into a strange phenomenon in which I hallucinated corpses reaching for my ankles the way schizophrenics hear dogs speaking in human voices.

Alternatively, maybe after I accidentally discovered Genevieve's gruesome cemetery and, therefore, got my mother killed, Ben dug up the evidence and dumped it elsewhere. There's that.

Before abandoning what's turning out to be a fool's errand, I decide to try a trick Mama taught me: body dowsing. With my feet together, I close my eyes and meditate to clear my brain of random, swirling thoughts until all that remains is a vision of a clear undisturbed sea. This is my base level.

I concentrate on what's below the peonies. Mulch. Dirt. Roots. Stones. Worms. Grubs. Rotted organic matter. Fungi. Bacteria. And, most important, any foreign item. While meditating on these fascinating layers, I inhale for five counts, hold my breath for five counts, and then exhale for five counts while simultaneously breathing out the word "find."

Soon, I feel a tug, and my body lists forward to a fragrant

patch of deadly white lilies of the valley. Lilies. The flowers of the dead. With a sincere apology to Genevieve and a heaping amount of dread, I lift my right foot and step on the lushest bunch.

My foot goes ice cold. So cold, the lilies around me instantly wilt as if hit by an early frost. Their leaves curl. Their little stems wither and drop their tiny white buds. Then there's a stirring under my arch, almost like a tickling. Someone is tickling the bottom of my foot! It's as if the tips of tiny fingers are tapping on my insoles.

They're merely mischief makers. That's what Mama said when I ran to her that day so upset. *They just want to play with your silly toes.*

Because they're children.

Shit.

Genevieve Winslow, master gardener, president of the Dutton Floral Society, member of the Episcopal Church Altar Guild, wife of a renowned federal judge, has killed at least one innocent child and buried him or her beneath my feet. The possibility that I'm standing on a child's corpse makes me physically ill.

If my dowsing is correct, then she's a cold-blooded, sick psychopath no better than John Wayne Gacy, a baby-faced charmer who killed and buried thirty-three teenage boys and men on his suburban Chicago property. There's Ben's motivation for murder, I realize with a shiver rising up my freezing ankles. He needed to kill my mother to safeguard his. That bastard.

Checking my phone, I see it's close to 8:00 p.m. The Winslow crew should be returning from dinner at any moment. Leaping from the garden, I brush off my feet, slip on my shoes, and make a dash for the potting shed by the stone wall to fetch a shovel.

Finally, I'm going to prove once and for all that my mother wasn't lying when she said I was gifted in divination. I don't have PTSD and I'm not hallucinating. I am not fucked up in the head.

I am a dowser of the dead. And I'm going to use my skill to bring Genevieve and Ben Winslow to justice by texting Trooper Oswald photo evidence of my discovery.

Just as soon as I can figure out a way to unlock this damned shed door.

14

PRITI

JUNE 17, 2023

> Priti, for the love of god, call me!

Priti glances at the text on her screen and swipes it away. Let her husband twist in the wind. It's what he deserves for leaving her in the lurch so he could spend an entire weekend in Boston screwing his ex-wife!

Ben was supposed to return this afternoon. He promised. *Just need to tie up a few loose ends and then I'll be home.* That was this morning, and Priti was fine with his schedule. This would give her plenty of time to watch the stupid *Dark Cults* episode Grovey was going on and on about and prepare a special dinner to celebrate their big news.

Because who was she kidding? For the life of her, she couldn't keep a secret this big from her husband. Yes, she might lose the baby (again), and yes, that would be crushing (again). She'd do anything to spare Ben that pain. On the other hand, this one might take!

Priti ran out and purchased grass-fed rib eye for the grill. At the Saturday morning farmers market she bought asparagus, new baby potatoes, and for dessert, fresh local strawberries. She'd even splurged on a bottle of Dom for the reveal. When Ben asked why she wasn't having any, she'd give him a Mona Lisa smile and he'd immediately know.

She could see it now: the artfully set patio table with tiny votive candles and wildflowers, lightning bugs twinkling over the garden, the warm June evening. Ben would rise from his chair slowly, in awe, and take her in his arms. He'd tell her how much he loved her. He'd vow to wait on her hand and foot, and then they'd spend the rest of the night holding hands and daring to dream, yet again.

It would be perfect.

After she went shopping, she came home, put away the groceries, and settled down to watch the *Dark Cults* episode. Honestly, she hadn't been expecting much. But she was so fascinated, she took notes and drew a timeline of Rose Santos's murder in the early morning hours of June 21, 2003. Bogey was right that the show didn't mention Ben by name, though it did obliquely reference a "wealthy love interest" of Rose's who was questioned extensively and cleared when police verified his alibi.

Priti's watched enough true crime to know the aforementioned suspect must have been pretty privileged for such white-glove treatment. These shows routinely drag some poor schlub's name through the mud as a red herring. Ben, however, wasn't a poor schlub. He was the son of a federal judge and a Stanford All-American athlete who'd already launched a start-up when Rose Santos was murdered. Ben had connections to powerful lawyers who likely warned *Dark Cults* to step correct.

She tried to be consoled that he was never charged and that the cops must have done their due diligence since they were under the spotlight too. The case had made national headlines because of the search for Rose's young daughter, who was found nearly hypothermic in a cave miles from where her mother's body was discovered. Some kooks said she'd been carried to safety by Bigfoot, who purportedly roamed the woods. Others claimed aliens or ghosts of the Abenaki. Priti figured the frightened kid simply climbed the hill until she found shelter.

She was relieved to learn the two missing hikers, Rory Davis and Willow Johnston, were last seen at the Center celebrating the solstice at midnight two years ago. Not that their disappearances made her happy, just that while Rory and Willow were dancing around a bonfire, she was fairly certain Ben was on his way to Albany to catch a flight back to LA. Actually, he'd planned to leave a few days later, but Priti found out she was pregnant (again), and he was so excited he took a red-eye home.

How things have changed.

She was scrubbing the new potatoes when a text popped up on her phone. She assumed it was Ben messaging her from the road with his ETA. Instead, it was this:

Sorry, Prit. Gotta take these folks out and show 'em a good time. It'll be worth it if they commit to being on board. See you Sunday bright and early!

Dammit!

Her romantic plans *ruined* thanks to some anxious investors despite being so loaded they didn't know what to do with their cash. Priti was furious and disappointed and, finally, resigned. Managing partners went part and parcel with Ben's role as Head-Fake founder and CEO. She knew that going into this marriage, and who was she to complain? They lived a very comfortable lifestyle thanks to her husband's innovation and hard work. The least she could do was be a good sport.

So she wrapped up the food and stuffed it back in the fridge, resolving to make the most of her night alone. She'd treat herself to a long, luxurious bath, a pedicure, maybe a paraffin wax while catching up on the crap TV Ben refused to watch. She might even crack open the Haagen- Dazs and cut up some strawberries. After all, there had to be some benefits to being pregnant.

Just as Priti dumped a capful of bubble bath under the water, however, Genevieve phoned in a lather. She couldn't attend the Dutton Playhouse annual fundraiser at the inn because her doctors forbade it. She'd specifically asked Ben to go in her place and he'd agreed. Now she finds out he's in Boston!

"This is a disaster!" her mother-in-law screeched. "A disaster! The Winslows are legacy members. If I don't make an appearance and my son doesn't either, there'll be talk. I don't want people asking if I'm okay, imprisoned as I am in this horrid institution he stuck me in against my will. You know this'll fire up the old gossip about Ben. What am I going to do?"

Priti wanted to ask about the "old gossip about Ben," but exercised prudent restraint. When it came to Genevieve, she had to tread very carefully. The woman was pricklier than a cactus on a pincushion.

"I can go," she offered reluctantly. "I'll make the rounds and spread the word that you and Ben had prior engagements and extend your deep regrets."

Silence.

Finally, Genevieve said, "Well, you're not a proper Winslow, but you'll do in a pinch."

Thanks, Priti thought sarcastically, turning off the water with reluctance. Two hours, tops, and then she could be in that bath. All she had to do was dress up, smile, make small talk, and execute a quiet exit.

"May I ask you another favor?"

Priti winced. "Absolutely."

"Could you pick me up for church tomorrow morning? Ben said he'd be back in time to take me. Obviously that's out of the question. I know my son. It'll be drinks and dinner at Pier Four and then some private club after that. I'll be at the church coffee hour when he finally wakes up with a splitting headache."

Pier 4? Ben had conveniently omitted *that* tidbit. She had a flash of her husband tucking into his butter-bathed lobster and smiling at a pretty potential partner, a faceless go-getter with a killer body and a cutthroat business acumen—Ben's fantasy woman. They sure as hell had better not go out for nightcaps at some club.

"It'd be my pleasure. When should I pick you up?"

"Nine fifteen and not a minute later. I don't want to lose my seat in the front row." With that, Genevieve ended the call. Not a scintilla of gratitude.

Priti donned a cocktail dress she'd packed at the last minute, a wash-and-wear designer halter-neck sleeveless number that hugged every inch of her curves. Hopefully, she wouldn't be able to fit into it much longer. Twisting her silky black hair into a chignon, she added dangle topaz earrings Ben had brought back from a trip to Sao Paulo and headed out like she was ready for combat.

The walk and fresh air put her in a better mood—until she ran into Bogey Grovey.

He was standing on the front porch of the inn, hands in the pockets of his khakis and rocking back on his heels. The green blazer did him no favors. Perhaps he thought it resembled a Masters jacket; to Priti it made him look like a salesman for State Farm Insurance.

"There's my gal!" he exclaimed, bounding down the steps to greet her. "I'd been hoping Ben would send you in his place." He kissed her on both cheeks, European style.

Priti was confused. "How'd you know he wouldn't be here?"

Bogey touched her elbow, leading her into the hotel. "Aww, Char told me." And then, before Priti could ask how his wife would know, he added, "Those two certainly are going whole hog for her birthday. The Woods at Pier Four. My love's favorite spot."

Priti wrested herself from his grip, the blood draining from her upper body as she grabbed a lobby wingback chair to steady herself. "Ben is out with Charlotte? He told me he was out with investors."

"That's right. Charlotte's an investor." Bogey Grovey grinned ear to ear, weirdly delighted his wife was celebrating her birthday with her ex-husband. "Surely you knew."

Surely she didn't, and surely Ben had no intention of telling her. Not once this weekend did he even hint Charlotte was with him in Boston. Not once in their three years of marriage did he mention his ex-wife was an investor in his company, about which he talked endlessly.

Which is why she's ignoring his calls and texts suddenly flooding the screen of her phone. There are so many, she finally has to take a peek.

> It's important! There's someone at the house!

> I saw you leave. I saw her come in. I'm watching her on the security cam right now. She's in the backyard. Where the hell are you?

Oh, for the love of god. What the hell is going on? Excusing herself from a tête-à-tête with Bogey and Joss Willey, lead mare of Dutton's horsey set, Priti steps outside to the patio where Ben and Charlotte had been in intense conversation the night before. She presses his smiling icon.

"Finally!" he exclaims. "Where've you been? Why haven't you answered my calls and texts?"

Priti grits her teeth. She's seeing red, she's so pissed. "I am do-ing your mother a favor and you, too, by representing the Winslows at the annual Dutton Playhouse fundraiser, thank you very much."

"Shit. I totally forgot about that."

"You're welcome. Not that you—or your mother—thanked *me*. I guess this is my expected duty as the lesser Mrs. Winslow, filling in for you when you're out wining and dining your ex-wife on her birthday at the priciest tourist trap Boston has to offer."

His stunned silence is oddly gratifying. "Come on, Priti, don't be like that."

"Like what?"

"You know. Jealous. It's not becoming."

If she could reach through the air and strangle him, she would. "Going now. Bye, bye!" Her finger is on the red end call button when she hears him shout, "No, no! Don't hang up. Please. I need you."

Is this some ploy? "I am not jealous, Ben. Your ex-wife is an in-vestor in HeadFake and she's out to dinner with you on her birth-day, being treated to a five-hundred-dollar meal, facts you failed to mention . . . *ever.*"

"I know, I know. That was a mistake. I should have been up front from the beginning about Charlotte's partnership. I didn't want you to get the wrong idea."

"If I got the wrong idea, it was because you were hiding the truth from me, your *current* wife."

"Look. I can explain everything. But right now we have a crisis. The security cameras picked up a woman entering the property after you left. She's there now. She's trying to break into our garden shed."

What's he talking about? "I didn't see anyone when I left."

"She must have snuck in before the gates closed. I need you to go home and find out what she's up to."

"Me?" Priti checks over her shoulder. Bogey, Joss, and her

other horsey friend, Liz, are gaping at her through the window. "You want *me* to go back and confront an intruder alone? Why don't you just call 911?"

"Out of the question."

"Why?"

"All sorts of reasons. It'll take them an hour to get there. I don't want this on the police blotter or in the local paper. Besides, I think I have an idea what this is about. She's harmless."

"How do you know?"

"I just do. I think she's the daughter of an old friend of mine, a woman who died twenty years ago."

Ah, hah! Well, this is the closest her husband has come to admitting any connection whatsoever to Rose Santos. At least that's progress. "You mean, you think the woman trying to break into the garden shed is Stella O'Neill." *Zing!*

"Wow," Ben replies with a touch of humility. "So you've heard the rumors, I suppose."

"Not rumors. *Dark Cults*. The 'Triangle Three' episode. Bogey recommended I watch it." She pivots on her heels and finger waves at Bogey, her fellow jilted spouse, her comrade in marital discord. "I followed up with extensive googling, so now the post that went viral yesterday makes sense."

"Seems we've got a lot to talk about."

"Seems *you* have a lot to explain."

"I will. I'll tell you everything. Anything you want. But for now, could you go home and find out what she's up to? Get some contact info from her if you can. I've been searching high and low for this kid."

Kid. Interesting term since Stella would not be much younger than she is, Priti thinks. "Keep your eye on the security camera and call the cops if she gets aggressive. Sorry if saving my life ruins the birthday vibe."

Without waiting for his response, she ends the call and heads home, not even bothering to lie to Bogey and his gal pals about not feeling well or whatever. This night sucks. Tomorrow will be better, she tells herself, as long as she stays pregnant.

As long as Stella O'Neill doesn't put up a fight.

15

STELLA

JUNE 17, 2023

"What are you doing?"

Startled by the sound of a voice suddenly behind me, the rock I'm about to bring down on the padlock misses its intended target and smashes into my hand.

"Oww! Shit!" I howl, checking my wrist. The injury is red and spreading. There's gonna be an ugly bruise.

The goddess in the saffron cocktail dress doesn't seem to know what to make of me. Priti Winslow's just standing there, gawking. No sign of Ben, but he can't be far behind. I have a choice—run or act like this is no big deal. I'm going with the latter.

"You're back awfully early," I say, dropping the stone, the radiating pain subsiding to a dull throb. "That party must have been a dud. I figured I'd have at least a half hour. Wouldn't need it if I could get this shed open. Know where I can find a key?"

She shakes her head. "Oooh. You've got some nerve trespassing on private property. This is my mother-in-law's house, you know."

"I know. I just need to dig up a teeny tiny spot in her garden and then I'll be on my way. Maybe she stores her shovels in the garage?"

"My husband saw you on the security cameras. He's been trying to find you."

Now who's being bold? "Yeah. So I gather. Tell him I will not be getting in touch. If he saw me here, then he knows damn well the proverbial shit has just hit the proverbial fan."

She curls her lip, disgusted by my unnecessary vulgarity, I suppose. "You need to go." She takes out her phone like it's a threat. "I'm calling the police."

"No, you're not."

"Yes, I am."

"You won't because your husband told you not to, right?" I can tell by her sheepish expression that I've nailed it. "He probably came up with a bunch of excuses. Dutton doesn't have a police force or the state police are all the way in Rutland, blah, blah, blah."

She says nothing, the classic deer in the headlights. Except with legs up to here and bone structure for which I would gladly myself commit murder. Definitely a former model. Real women don't come in this fine a package.

"The reason why your husband doesn't want you calling the cops has nothing to do with their response record," I continue. I should keep my stupid mouth shut except the shock factor's too delicious to resist. "He doesn't want the cops involved because your mother-in-law has incriminating evidence buried in her garden that could put her away until she's dust."

Judging from the way she shoots a horrified glance at the garden, I'm confident this is breaking news for Priti.

"What?" is all she can manage. "What are you talking about? Explain what you mean."

At that moment, it occurs to me that Priti might be engaging in conversation to give her husband time to get here. That's not a risk I can afford to take.

"You'll see," I say, taking the long way around the garden and bolting toward the driveway.

I don't bother to glance back to check if she's chasing after me. I just keep running until I get to the gates. I lean on them with all my might and, to my surprise, they open wide. I'm outside the Winslow estate, and as far as I can tell, Ben is nowhere around and neither are the authorities.

I practically leap with joy at the sight of Heather's little white Kia parked just where I left it under a lush green maple tree down the street. Escape is but a few steps away, I think, as the car remote unlock responds with a satisfying *beep-beep*.

All I have to do is get in, lock the doors, pull out, and head west on Route 30 to the sanctuary of Aunt Debby's dog kennels near Saratoga Springs. When I arrive, I'll let Trooper Oswald know of my discovery. I have no idea if "feeling the buried dead" is enough to secure a search warrant, but it can't hurt to try.

And then I notice something's not quite right with Heather's car. It appears to be listing slightly, as if off kilter.

Bing! My phone vibrates with a new text. Still trying to figure out what's going on with the car, it takes me a minute to comprehend the message.

Well, hello!

It's not from a familiar number. Just more annoying spam that I'm about to delete when another line pops up.

How nice of you to pay me a visit. Please don't leave in such a rush. I was looking forward to a chat.

I gape at the words, trying to make sense of their meaning. This isn't spam. This is from Ben. Or Priti. Or Genevieve.

But Ben doesn't know my cell phone number. How could he? Email to the library information desk, that's a no-brainer. Even my work email is public. But not my phone. No one knows my phone number except Heather and Dad and Fig and . . . someone who could hack it.

Someone like software genius Ben Winslow.

Now I'm in full panic mode. I have to get out of this place, fast. I am in so way, way, way over my head. Coming to Dutton, tromping all over Genevieve Winslow's garden, and sassing her daughter-in-law were stupid gambles. Ben obviously has been following my every movement since I drove out of the Alewife train station.

Dammit. I should have checked the Kia for a tracker like the kind the tow-truck driver found on Fig's car. How could I have been so careless?

There are no other options. I'll have to go full Unibomber and ditch the technology. That's the only way to lose this asshole.

Tossing the phone to the pavement, I smash it with the heel of my sneaker and kick it into the nearest grate, where it lands with a satisfying splash in sewer water. If Ben wants to track my phone, he'll have to go through Dutton's Public Works Department.

When that's done, I inspect the car only to find the front and rear tires on the passenger side are totally flat. One tire would be an unfortunate accident from a nail in the road. Two means it's deliberate. Two means Ben's waiting to see what I'll do and where I'll go. That's when he'll snatch me.

Not if I can help it.

Fumbling with the door handle because I'm so flustered, I take a cursory inspection of the back seat to make sure it's empty and get in the car, immediately depressing the locks. Heather's cooler packed with Fluffernutter sandwiches and Diet Cokes and washed organic green grapes in a tidy Ziploc bag is still next to me on the passenger seat, touching and hopeful. I think of my poor, worried stepmother trying to keep me fed and fueled as I race to her sister's, wringing her hands as she and Dad anxiously wait for my call announcing I've arrived safely at the dog kennel.

And now, with my phone in the gutter, I am unreachable.

"I'm sorry," I whisper, my fingers shaking so hard I can barely turn the key. I don't care if I ruin the tire rims and mess up the alignment. I'll make it as far as I can to the next gas station and deal with that mess when I get there. The point is I need to go!

Click. Click.

The lights on the dash flicker, but the engine doesn't turn over.

Click. Click.

I try again, focusing on the fuel gauge, which is empty. Sweat is now pouring down my temples. My whole face is damp from it.

How? I couldn't have used more than a quarter tank of gas to get here. In the short span of twenty minutes or so, while I trampled over Genevieve's garden and fought with that shed lock, someone managed to puncture my tires *and* drain my tank.

Now my nose detects the chemical scent I should have smelled before I got in the car. Spilled gasoline. It's all around me, filling up my nostrils with its acrid, dizzying fumes. Whoever siphoned costly gas out of Heather's car just let it flow to the ground in a toxic pond.

Which, if ignited, could blow me to smithereens.

Madly punching the unlock, I throw open the door and jump out onto the street, pumping my legs as fast as possible to get away from the potential explosion. My ears are cocked for the rumble and thunder to follow.

Out of breath, I collapse at the corner three blocks away and lean against one of the navy USPS pickup boxes. The car hasn't blown up, but it's only a matter of time. Just as I'm conducting an internal debate over whether I should call 911, I remember I don't have a phone. Then I hear the crunch of gravel and turn to see a shiny black SUV pulling to the curb. It's identical to the one in Somerville yesterday, only it has an UBER sign in the windshield.

The passenger window slides down, and a guy who looks like he's headed to his high school prom in an ill-fitting suit and tie leans over. "You okay, ma'am?"

The kid couldn't come off as more harmless. Military buzz cut, ruddy cheeks, big grin—and he addressed me as ma'am. I bet his goats won a blue ribbon in 4-H and his maple syrup is the sweetest. My savior straight off a Vermont dairy farm.

"That's my car." I point to the listing Kia up ahead. "Someone slashed my tires and drained my gas tank. I lost my phone and . . . I don't know if there's a service station around or . . . I need help."

He makes a face. "Geesh. I've never heard about something like that happening around here. That's crappy. You probably should fill out a police report for your insurance."

"Not the most pressing issue at the moment, though you're probably right. Except, how do I call the police without a phone?"

"I can do you one better, ma'am. I just dropped off a group for a fundraiser at the inn and I've got to be back in Manchester to drive some VIPs to the Reluctant Panther. I'll be going right past the Manchester Police Department on Main Street and can drop you off if you want. It's only about ten minutes away. They can give you an assist."

Bless him. Bless this sweet, noble country boy. "That's awesome. Thanks so much."

Getting out, he does a quick jog around the front and opens the rear door. "Sorry. Company policy. Have to put you in the back seat."

Fine by me. Bonus, the windows are tinted, so Ben Winslow won't be able to catch a glimpse of my getaway. Win-win. I weigh the risk of going back to the Kia to grab my stuff and decide not to chance it. I don't want to be blown to smithereens because I needed my toothbrush and a clean pair of undies.

Climbing onto the luxurious butternut leather seat, I sink, literally, into the lap of luxury. Bottles of pricey French sparkling water are chilling in a center console for the VIPs, a rare peek into how the 1 percent lives.

The driver gets in, slams the door, and gives me a thumbs-up through the privacy glass. "Everything okay back there?"

"Perfect," I say, though I'm antsy. The sooner I'm out of this leafy neighborhood, the better. I hope the cops can recommend an affordable hotel where I can stay overnight since I won't be making it to Aunt Debby's anytime soon. I very much doubt I'll be able to get the tires replaced on a Sunday in these boonies. I'll have to wait until Monday.

With a quick glance at his side mirror, my hero executes a perfect U-turn in the middle of the street. I check over my shoulder to see the injured Kia. I feel bad leaving it behind.

I find I'm shaking and cold, most likely from the burst of adrenaline. Sitting up and straightening my spine, I let out a long, slow breath. The nightmare is almost over. I'll have the Manchester police contact Trooper Oswald, who'll send detectives to the garden. Even if Ben Winslow is digging up his mother's flowers, it's too late. DNA is a bitch. That stuff sticks to everything.

I'll also call Dad when I get to the police department and explain about the car. Knowing my parents, they'll pull out the Visa and book me a night at a legit hotel so my safety will be assured. Room service chicken club with an iced tea. A nice hot shower. Fifty channels. I can already feel the cool air-conditioning.

Speaking of which, it's a little stuffy back here with the windows closed. I try pressing the button, but it doesn't move. Child locks.

"Excuse me," I say, knocking on the divider. "Can you unlock the windows? I need some fresh air, if you don't mind."

The young driver says nothing. Perhaps he can't hear? There must be an intercom around here somewhere. I inspect the console between the two facing seats and the one next to me, which is marked by a tiny phone icon. Flipping open the top, I lift up an old-fashioned handset and put it to my ear. It rings and rings.

He doesn't respond. He's not reaching for his handset or anything. Just staring straight ahead as we proceed at the legal speed limit down Route 30.

Screw it, I decide, hanging up. I can tolerate some stuffiness for the next five minutes or so until we get to the Manchester PD, which must be coming up pretty soon since we're already turning left onto Main Street.

A blue sign up ahead notes the police and town hall are on the right. Gathering my purse and Heather's raincoat, I'm ready to jump out when, to my confusion, we fly right past the red-shingled municipal complex. Crap. Don't tell me he spaced. I really don't need that kind of headache.

I'm trying not to get annoyed since he's doing me a favor, but it's not much of a favor if his good deed results in yet another hassle. I'm done with being polite. I pound on the divider.

Bang. Bang. Bang. "YOU MISSED THE TURN. WE NEED TO GO BACK!"

Again, he's unfazed. Instead, he leans forward and taps his cell phone, which is attached to the dashboard. He's answering an incoming call. I can't hear what they're saying, but I can read the caller ID on his screen. Two very basic words that, combined, make up my worst nightmare.

THE CENTER.

Fuck. I fell right into their trap.

16

ROSE

JUNE 20, 2003

It was after four when they finally left Genevieve's. Cliff was in a sour mood, eyes fixed on the road, his gloved hands tightly gripping the steering wheel. The muscle in his jaw twitched, and he was as brittle as a dried twig.

"Mama?" Astraea said from her hiding place between Rose's knees. "I need to go to the bathroom."

"Keep. Down!" Cliff interjected. "Don't make me tell you again."

Rose put a finger to her lips and gave her daughter an encouraging smile, though, internally, she was seething. How dare he speak to Astraea that way. She was a little girl, and he hadn't exactly been an exemplary role model back at Genevieve's, the way he was shouting and dragging and pushing Rose into the car.

There wasn't a single generous bone in his body. All that mattered to Cliff was Cliff. He didn't care that he'd shocked and scared a child. He was more concerned about Genevieve's disapproval, which was clear from the way she stood in the doorway frowning, her arms folded in fury, as she watched them pull out of the driveway.

He was mad at himself for losing whatever ground he'd gained with that ridiculous check to the local playhouse. Once again, he'd let his temper get the better of him. So much for supposedly being Divine.

"Why were you calling your husband? I heard you say Dan," he snapped as they zoomed down the highway.

Rose kept her tone light. "Just to say hello. He asked me to check in with news about Astraea and it'd slipped my mind, so . . ."

"I'm not buying that."

Rose shrugged. "That's all it was. Swear to God."

God doesn't exist. We are God, would have been his standard retort, if he hadn't been so upset.

Rose knew he'd find a way to shift the blame to her for ruining his chances with Genevieve. Personal failure was impossible for him to accept. Anything bad was always someone else's fault.

There would be repercussions and the repercussions would be severe. Rose prayed to the Divine that Cliff wouldn't make Astraea a pawn in his war of revenge. He could separate them by locking Rose away in the Chi Chamber. But with Cerise missing, who would take care of Astraea?

Ellen. And that would mean Cliff would have full, unbridled access to her daughter to groom her as he pleased. The prospect made Rose's skin clammy cold. It wasn't the police she needed to worry about taking Astraea away from her; it was her guru.

Because who would stop him? Not Ellen. Not the Facilitators, whose primary purpose was to spy for Ellen, who then used their intel like currency to buy more perks for herself. Not even Rose's fellow Diviners, who'd been so brainwashed by Cliff's sermons and intimidated by the Facilitators that, for the sake of their own survival, they convinced themselves he always knew best.

Her only solace was timing. Cliff would be "on" from the moment he returned to the commune to the departure of the last solstice visitors on Sunday evening. He wouldn't have the opportunity to inflict his retribution, nor would he take the chance of doing so with so many outsiders there to bear witness.

If all went according to plan, Rose and Astraea would be back in Massachusetts by the end of the weekend. That is, if Dan got her message.

How to know? There was no way for her husband to contact her. She would have to try contacting him again.

"Mama!" Astraea hissed more urgently. "I. Have. To. Go."

There was only one service station before they turned onto the mountain road, and it was right up ahead. Perhaps they had a phone she could use.

"Cliff, I'm so sorry, but Astraea is desperate," she pleaded.

"Too bad. She shouldn't have drunk all that lemonade." He readjusted his grip on the wheel. "That'll teach her."

Rose bit her lip, thinking what would motivate him to pull over. Leaning toward him, she murmured, "If you don't stop, she's gonna piss all over the floor of your new car."

Cliff immediately hooked a left into the Cumberland Farms.

While Astraea relieved herself in the bathroom, Rose searched in vain for a pay phone.

"We haven't had a pay phone since, like, forever," the teenage clerk said, ringing up her order for a single pack of Dentyne, a ruse in case Cliff caught her talking to an outsider. "Don't you have a cell?"

Rose had seen only a few cell phones, having forsaken all electronics when she joined the commune. Ben had one, something called a Nokia. He'd said he'd buy her the same model, but she'd turned down that offer, along with his others. Cliff would have hit the roof if she'd snuck in a phone. Besides, like Ben noted, the chances of picking up a signal at the Center with the mountain in the backyard were nil.

When they returned to the Center after a silent drive from

Cumberland Farms, Cliff sat behind the wheel and delicately removed his leather driving gloves finger by finger. "You're not going back to the Winslows' again. You've lost your privileges."

So it begins, Rose thought. *He wants to keep an eye on me 24/7.* She motioned for Astraea to run off and play and waited until her child was out of earshot to turn on him. "Don't be a fool. Do you have any idea how much money I've brought to the Center by working for Genevieve?"

The staggering sum was fresh in Rose's mind thanks to Ben, who'd angrily confronted her with a spreadsheet earlier that month, having been alerted to the questionable withdrawals by his mother's accountants.

"Eighty-three thousand dollars!" he'd thundered. "I mean, I don't even know how that's possible."

"Nearly seven years. Twice-weekly sessions at two hundred dollars a pop. It adds up," she'd responded calmly, declining to mention the several grand Genevieve had slipped her in cash during their friendship to buy books and toys for Astraea.

Genevieve referred to her under-the-table gifts as mad money that Rose was to hide from the Center's grasping hands at all costs.

Cliff closed the door of his four-bay garage and put his hands on his hips, his cheeks flushed red with anger. "I don't care what that old biddy has shelled out. You and I both know the only reason you're so eager to see her is to get into her son's pants. I'm the most skilled Diviner on this planet, Rose. Do you actually think I don't know when you're having an affair with an outsider?"

Rose had to work very, very hard not to show her amusement. She wanted to laugh in his face and call him a fraud. As satisfying as that would have been, it wouldn't achieve her goal of getting her and Astraea out of this hellhole tomorrow night.

"I'm so sorry," she murmured, feigning shame. "I shouldn't have tried to keep anything from you. I should have known better."

"Uh-huh. Unfortunately, this sudden humility of yours is too little, too late. We'll have to address your violations of the Diviner Code of Ethics after the solstice. You should prepare yourself for a rather thorough purification process."

"Yes, Dagda. Understood."

"Meanwhile, as always, my primary concern is my flock. And though you may be the black sheep at the moment, I love you as I love all under my care. To that end, I reiterate that you are not to have any contact with Genevieve or Benjamin Winslow so that you are not further corrupted by their blasphemous ways. Is that clear?"

"Please reconsider," she replied, keeping her eyes averted. "I'll give up Ben, but Genevieve needs me. If she calls tomorrow morning, I must go." Maybe if he thinks she's sacrificing a lover, he'll be more amenable to letting her continue to visit the Winslows.

"Under no circumstance will you go. I've consulted the pendulum and the answer is firm. Ben Winslow poses a threat to you and your daughter. After you pay your penance, I may revisit my decision. But not before then. Again, I ask you, is that clear?"

"Yes," she whispered. "It's clear." She waited for him to hold out his palm and demand she turn over her earnings from the afternoon, per usual. He didn't. Instead, he went into his house and slammed the door.

Rose smiled to herself and headed to the play area to fetch Astraea to prepare for the night's ceremonies, wishing for all the world that Cerise was there to share in a good laugh at their Dagda's expense.

The summer solstice was the highest of holy days at the Center, drawing close to five hundred visitors from June 20 through June 22 and requiring months of planning and preparation. For weeks, the Diviners set up wooden pallets for tents to handle the overflow from the hostel, which had fifty beds. Portable toilets were brought in along with a trailer that served as a makeshift medical unit to deal with heatstroke, dehydration, insect bites, allergic reactions, and the occasional twisted ankle.

Water. Medicine. Food. These were the basics. As the café's head baker, food was Rose's department. She usually baked one thousand cinnamon rolls, which were stored in rented freezers powered by gas generators. Oatmeal with the Center's own maple syrup, scrambled eggs, the cinnamon rolls, oranges, and coffee and tea were served, buffet style, for breakfast. Lunch was simple fare: local cheddar cheese sandwiches with lettuce from the Center's gardens on homemade bread, with strawberries on the side. Dinner was actually the easiest of the meals since the vegetarian bean chili simply needed to be defrosted, and cornbread was a snap. The biggest pain was the salad, again from the Center's gardens.

Cerise usually made the brownies—some of which were magic. This year, with Cerise AWOL, there were none.

The expense of feeding and housing and cleaning up after so many partygoers was astronomical. The two-hundred-and-fifty-dollar entrance fee for three days and two nights barely covered the costs. To glean a profit, the Center offered private readings and guided hikes to the abandoned and mystical village of Glastenbury at the mountain's peak.

Over the centuries, several locals had gone missing in Glastenbury, a ghost town that was once a mining community and, later, a failed recreation destination. It was pitted with dangerous unmarked mining shafts that, in Rose's analysis, accounted for a majority of the disappearances. However, the Diviners considered the abandoned village to be a "thin place" with extraordinary energy that attracted mystical entities, from outer space aliens to Bigfoot, which stole hikers and kidnapped children. That's why Cliff chose this location for his center, because of the area's supernatural reputation.

This year, the celebrations began at dusk on Friday the twentieth and extended until the morning of Sunday the twenty-second. The solstice didn't always fall conveniently on a weekend, but when it did, Cliff liked to maximize his profits.

While he returned to his comfortable house to shower and meditate in preparation, Rose took Astraea home, cleaned her up, and fed her dinner. Then she did the same, washing in the stream that ran behind their cabin with a bar of soap she'd made herself with olive and almond oils, lye, and her own lavender. Her damp hair in a French braid, she stepped into a linen shift tied at the waist and then the white hooded robe of a Realized.

The Diviners wore hooded robes according to their ranks— green for Novices who were just beginning to explore spiritual divination, orange for Seekers who had committed themselves to the practice, and purple for those whose divination skills had earned them the respected title of Mentor. White robes were reserved for the few Realized, those who'd broken through the boundaries of human perception to interact with the Divine Energy directly. Rose and Ellen wore white. But only one wore gold, the color of a king, and that, of course, was Cliff.

At 6:30 p.m., she walked with Astraea to the café to join the other children. Children weren't permitted at the nighttime summer solstice ceremonies because the rituals incorporated psilocybin mushrooms and "spiritual unions." Naked participants often engaged in a simulated sexual frenzy to rhythmic drumbeats, while others, intoxicated by mead and marijuana and twinkling fireflies, often paired up for not-simulated trysts in the field.

Disney World it was not.

Astraea and the other children stayed at the café, where they held their own party, playing games, waving lit sparklers, and indulging in ice-cream cones, a rare treat. Eventually, they'd end up asleep in one happy pig pile on the floor, supervised by designated babysitters who were under strict orders not to let them go to the pavilion under any condition.

With a kiss and a hug, Rose and Astraea parted until the following morning, when the children would be treated to pancakes while the adults slept in. Then Rose went to oversee the buffet tables groaning with fresh garden salads, vegetarian chili, cornbread, and strawberries. Her crew had done an excellent job preparing the Friday night feast while she was off dealing with Genevieve, and that was bittersweet. Because this was the last solstice dinner she would ever organize.

Two hours later, the food was put away and the tables were removed. Diviners brought in rough-hewn benches they arranged in concentric circles around a lit bonfire, sage-scented woodsmoke rising through a hole in the pavilion's ceiling as the sun inched toward the horizon.

Most of the visitors were in costumes drawn from a variety of inspirations. Druids and witches, characters from *Lord of the Rings* or the Society for Creative Anachronism, and fairies were de rigueur, as were solstice-themed mythical entities. Younger women unashamed to wear diaphanous gowns and flower crowns tended toward Áine, the Irish goddess of the solstice, or Auxo, the Roman goddess of the solstice.

Men often dressed as Lugh, the Celtic god of sun and light, complete with a cape, beard, staff, and shield. Or they went as Cernunnos, the Celtic god of nature and fertility, who died every summer solstice and was reborn on December 21. Cernunnos was symbolized by his long, twisted antlers and braided brass torc, an image that the early Christian church, which was fearful of the god's strong pagan influence, coopted and corrupted into a more familiar representation of Satan.

Even the Facilitators, Ellen's security force, were getting into the solstice spirit, though Rose wasn't quite sure if they were truly celebrating or simply eager to patrol the commune in disguise.

Rose took her place in the front row as befitting a Realized. Cerise, whom Cliff demoted from Realized to Mentor as punishment for her impertinence, used to sit right behind her. That space was empty, a metaphor for the hole in Rose's heart created by her friend's absence. The only other Realized was Ellen, and she was nowhere to be found.

Cliff appeared at dusk, Ellen carrying his long train. Face hidden by his golden hood, he carried a staff carved from smoothed mahogany and spoke not a word as he entered the pavilion. All stood while he made his way to the center altar near the bonfire, which emitted bursts of colors—green, purple, orange, and blue— from the crystals he tossed into the flames.

Commanding all to sit, he produced a large, shiny onyx pendulum and swung it over the fire. Mumbling words that were supposed to be Latin, he closed his eyes and swayed as he transitioned into the state of highest energy. That's when he began to call out the names of chosen outsiders. "Paul! Kim! Marta! Chris!"

It was not by accident that those chosen for the first solstice reading happened to be the Center's most generous donors. Cerise had done a little digging and discovered the select often forked out as much as ten thousand dollars for this special treatment.

Ellen took her place on a gaudy new chair painted in white with gold trim, a complement to Cliff's throne. Throwing off her hood, she smiled at Rose, her lips parting like a snake about to strike. Something was up, and that made Rose uncomfortable. Maybe Ellen expected her to be envious that she was seated at the right hand of their guru and Rose wasn't. More likely, the bitch had done Cliff's dirty work and she was being rewarded with a plum position. The question was what Ellen had done. Rose dreaded to think.

Cliff proceeded to place his hands on the heads of each of the chosen, closing his eyes and lifting his face skyward to absorb their energies. He removed the block of negative energy that had been preventing an attendee from receiving a promotion at work. A woman who'd been trying to conceive was "cleared" by Cliff's power and declared fertile. He advised another to seek medical treatment for a possibly cancerous mass in her liver.

In prior celebrations, Rose had been in awe of Cliff's abilities to divine. She accepted his readings as proof she'd made the right move when she decided to leave her husband and take their young daughter to live in the woods of Vermont. Tonight, however, she felt none of the old magic. She felt hollow and deceived.

Radcliffe MacBeath was a fraud and a huckster. She couldn't get past that fact as she watched him swing his pendulum and wave his hands, speak in tongues and pull every trick of every hackneyed carnival magician ever. Smoke! Incense! Colored flames! She studied carefully how he was able to glean telltale details from those so eager to believe in the supernatural that they gasped in amazement when Cliff was able to repackage those same details as divine insight into their secret souls.

How had she not seen the authentic him before? Cerise had been right; they'd all been hoodwinked.

Ellen licked her thin lips in delight. Being a skilled Diviner, she'd detected Rose's discomfort and was enjoying watching her suffer. She wanted to keep Rose guessing, that was her game. What had they done to Cerise? What would they do to her . . . *to Astraea?*

Finally, Rose couldn't take another minute of agony. When the attendees applauded Cliff for another divine reading (he'd accurately deduced a woman dressed like a sprite had recently lost her grandfather), Rose slipped out of the pavilion and ran to the café as fast as her feet could carry her.

Most of the children were asleep on blankets spread out on the floor. All except for Astraea, who was sitting up wide-eyed with another curly-headed girl Rose had never seen before, likely the offspring of a visitor. The curly-headed girl was holding Astraea's hand and seemed to be comforting her, stroking her shoulder and murmuring kind words.

Rose shot a glance at her daughter's feet. Her sneakers were off, the skin on her ankles red and raw.

Alarmed, Rose rushed to her daughter and gathered her in her arms. She was all too familiar with the look Astraea got when she felt the dead—the shaking, the sickly pallor, the scratches. She'd made a mistake not taking time this evening to sit down with her and process what had happened at Genevieve's. She'd been so goddamn busy dishing up food for the ungrateful guests that she'd neglected her own child.

"Oh, baby," she cooed, lifting Astraea in her arms and taking her out of the café into the cool night. "It's okay. Don't mind the mischief makers in Mrs. Winslow's garden. They're far away. They can't get you."

Astraea wrapped her soft arms around her mother's neck and squeezed tight as Rose carried her to their cabin. "What are they though?"

"Fairies, like I've told you." This answer had satisfied Astraea in the past when she'd walked barefoot over the commune's graveyard.

Tonight, Astraea wasn't reassured. "Mama, I don't like what I felt today. It scared me. What are they?"

Rose hugged her tighter. Breathing heavily as she climbed the steps to their front door, she waited until they were safely inside their cozy home to catch her breath and let Astraea ask her more questions.

Astraea pulled out her trundle bed and sat, staring at her

mother with an expression disturbingly wise for her age. "Promise not to get mad?"

"Mad?" Rose was puzzled. "Why would I be mad?"

"That girl I met tonight. She made me go into the forest. I didn't want to. I told her I wasn't allowed, but she said she wanted to see the turtle everyone was talking about."

Rose swallowed a burst of outrage. Where was Bryanna, who was supposed to be watching over them? They could have ended up in real trouble. The other little girl was probably from the city and had no idea what kind of pitfalls were waiting in those thick woods—cliffs and swampy soil that could suck you in like quicksand, roots that could cause you to trip and fall, bears and coyotes. Even, some claimed, mountain lions.

Astraea put out her hands. "You promised you wouldn't be mad."

She had promised no such thing. Still, getting angry at a child wouldn't get to the bottom of the problem. Her daughter was upset and, as her mother, she needed to find out why. Besides, Astraea was obviously okay, if a bit rattled. "I'm not angry. Just worried. Did you wear your sneakers with the foil?"

Her daughter shook her head. "I wanted to be barefoot like the other kids."

Rose sighed. She could see where this was going. "So what happened when you went into the woods?"

Astraea's gaze drifted to the empty chair where Cerise had been sitting only a few nights ago. "She found me, Mama."

Something cold and sickening filled Rose's chest, and she had to grip the edge of her own mattress to keep steady. "Who found you?"

"Cerise."

Rose froze, stunned to hear her daughter speak that name. "Are you sure?"

Astraea nodded.

"Where?"

Astraea hesitated a bit and then, scrunching up her face like she was in pain, pointed at her feet. "Down there. I crossed a mound of dirt and, and she grabbed me!"

Rose counted to ten to keep herself composed. Tears were already burning the back of her eyes. There it was. *Cerise was dead.* Her beloved confidante and closest friend was gone forever. Rose had felt this loss deep in her bones. Now it was confirmed.

Had she died from her abscessed tooth? Had the infection that would have easily been treated in the outside spread through her body, into her heart and brain? Did she die alone and frightened?

Or did the Facilitators make quick work of what would have been a slow death?

Ever since it had crossed her mind during Genevieve's reading that Cerise had been murdered by the commune's security force, Rose hadn't been able to shake the possibility. Now that she'd had a few hours to mull this over, she'd developed a theory.

Cliff and Ellen must have decided that allowing Cerise to wander around the commune delirious and in obvious pain during the solstice would have tarnished the brand they were trying to build. Or perhaps they were worried that she was angry enough to start mouthing off to visitors about the corruption that had infected the Center. Visitors flocking here for peace and harmony would have been disturbed to see a Diviner obviously maltreated. They would have inquired as to why she hadn't seen a doctor, and knowing Cerise's outspokenness, she wouldn't have pulled her punches.

She would have loudly and proudly revealed that Cliff forbade any Diviner from seeking outside medical treatment to avoid scrutiny of the nefarious activities here. Reports of adults indulging in hallucinogenic mushrooms and marijuana while fornicating in the open as their children ran around unschooled and neglected would have sent the Division of Youth and Family Services rushing in. His reputation as a benevolent and wise self-guru whose passion was teaching humans how to reach their full potential by connecting with the Divine Energy would have been trashed. He might even have been arrested for fraud and abuse.

The Chi Chamber alone was evidence enough of that.

Cliff had gone too far. Cerise was dead, her corpse discarded in a makeshift grave discovered by Astraea's gifts. She was dead because Cliff refused to let her seek medical treatment, because he'd ordered her execution.

Radcliffe MacBeath was nothing but pure, unadulterated evil, and he needed to be put behind bars where he belonged. But that wouldn't happen unless Rose took action.

She was all Cerise had had in the world, and she couldn't let her friend be buried in an unmarked grave, never given justice.

She needed Astraea to tell her exactly where Cerise was buried. She couldn't leave her like this.

Rose had intended to escape discreetly during the peak celebrations the following night. The plan had been to gather Astraea from the café, but instead of going home, they'd go to the parking lot to meet Dan.

But she couldn't simply walk away knowing her best friend was rotting in the ground, discarded like compost. She'd have to find Cerise first and then call the authorities before Cliff and Ellen found a way to spin the story.

It was a huge task, and Rose realized the odds of attempting this feat alone without being detected and stopped by the Facilitators would be nearly impossible. She'd need assistance, and not from a Diviner who'd rat her out to Ellen.

There was only one outsider who lived nearby and could help: Ben.

It was to her advantage that Ben already despised MacBeath and the Center. A nice chunk of his inheritance had been siphoned from his mother's accounts into Rose's pockets and then to Mac-Beath, Ben claimed. He was livid that his mother had been swindled by people he considered charlatans, and he was itching to make all of them pay, even her. Rose had managed to talk him out of filing a lawsuit by pointing out that it would be way too stressful on his mother, who might also be embarrassed by a public revelation that she regularly saw a psychic.

He'd then tried bribing Rose to get her to leave Genevieve alone, and she'd refused. Now she was ready to return his offer with an alternative she hoped would be more enticing. She'd be sad never to see Genevieve again, but she had no choice but to forgo their friendship—and swallow her pride—for the sake of her daughter.

Rose was certain Ben would leap at an opportunity to bring MacBeath down. But she couldn't wait to find out. She needed to ask him immediately.

"Mama's going out for just a minute," she told Astraea, who was already in her trundle bed, immersed in the recently released *Harry Potter and the Order of the Phoenix*, a precious gift Genevieve had snuck into Rose's tote bag during a visit when Cliff wasn't there to supervise.

Rose hated to leave her ten-year-old daughter by herself after a day of trauma, but she didn't have a choice. She'd need to slip in and out of the Center's office undetected to use the phone, and that meant going now while Ellen and Cliff were otherwise occupied. If Cerise were around, she'd gladly babysit.

Except Cerise would never babysit again.

A lump formed in Rose's throat. She could barely speak. "I'll be right back, but I'm going to lock the door, okay? Whatever you do, don't answer it. Even if it's Dagda or Ellen."

Astraea looked up from her book, her eyes red-rimmed from crying yet sparkling with excitement from the tale J. K. Rowling was unraveling on the pages. Her daughter was growing into an avid reader, which normally filled Rose with joy—aside from now. She needed Astraea to pay attention, to take her instructions seriously.

"Understand?" Rose prodded.

Astraea nodded. "I won't answer the door. Promise." Then she went back to her book.

Rose pulled the door shut and turned the key.

Within the hour, Astraea would be gone.

17

STELLA

JUNE 17, 2023

No one knows where I am.

We climb the twisting dirt road higher and higher up the mountain. The few houses near the highway are miles away, so it's not as though I can count on whoever lives there to come to my rescue, even if I manage to escape. I can tell from the way the SUV is bumping along that the road is getting rougher and narrower, that we're headed into the heart of the Green Mountain National Forest.

No doubt now. I'm definitely being taken to the Center.

The driver isn't talking, just bobbing his head to whatever's coming through his AirPods, which, I'm pretty sure, are illegal to wear while operating a motor vehicle. So much for being a fresh farm kid with 4-H goats and Mom's apple pie waiting for him after a hard night of chauffeuring a $100,000 vehicle. Either MacBeath made him an offer he couldn't refuse or he needs to support a serious coke addiction.

"Hey!" Again, I bang on the divider, caustic panic rising up my esophagus, constricting my throat. "Hey. Stop!"

Still, we continue spinning stones from under the tires. The sun is low in the sky, with darkness on the eastern horizon though we've almost arrived at the longest day of the year, the summer solstice, the twentieth anniversary of my mother's murder. I try the handles once more and am met with the same dull resistance. I'm being kidnapped and taken to a remote commune *and nobody knows where I am*.

Okay. All right. I can handle this. Likely, the Kia has a built-in tracking device. Either that or, if it hasn't exploded, the abandoned car will alarm the local cops, who'll check the registration and call Heather. That's good.

Knowing Dad, he'll immediately rush to the Center since it's so close to Dutton and the source of all evil. He's a smart guy. He'll make an educated guess that I'm here.

Why, though? What do the Diviners and MacBeath hope to accomplish by dragging me up here against my will? Do they plan on brainwashing me, convincing me to join the cause? Or is their goal simpler and more sinister: kill me and dump my body in one of Glastenbury's abandoned mine shafts to ensure my remains will never be found. That's a guaranteed method of eliminating me as a potential witness.

"You're making a big mistake," I tell the driver as we pass through an enormous gate marking the Center for Spiritual Dowsing and enter a dirt parking lot, my pulse fluttering with fear. "You've committed the crime of kidnapping, you know. That's a hardcore felony."

My chauffeur keeps the engine running and the doors locked. I know he can hear me, and maybe my statement has him re-visiting this poor life choice. What I don't know is what we're waiting for.

Until *they* appear.

Muscled men in dark-green shirts and gray hiking shorts suddenly flank the SUV. Their eyes are hidden by aviator glasses, though I recognize their tattoos of suns and lightning bolts—signature branding of the Facilitators.

My stomach lurches. All my life I've lived in fear of these monsters who've loomed large in my nightmares, and now I'm actually in their clutches. With no way out.

I do the only thing I can think to do—leave evidence. Yanking several strands of hair, I tuck them into the crack behind the seat cushions, the small, cramped space that more often serves as the repository for cracker crumbs and bottle caps. Should I not survive this ordeal, at least there'll be DNA to make the cops' job easier if someone reports I was last seen being led into a black SUV.

Finally, the doors unlock. Before I can make a break for it, a hood is thrown over my own head. My fingers claw at the rough cloth, trying to yank it off, but a Facilitator's grabbed my wrists and is twisting my body in a black-belt move that lands me face down on the seat. When heavy material is draped across my shoulders, I get it. I'm to be hidden in a hooded robe.

"Be careful! This is leased," the driver whines. "If the leather's ruined, it'll come out of my paycheck."

Whereupon I sink my teeth as hard as I can into the seat hoping to leave a telltale bite mark, another little gift for the police.

"Be still," a woman's voice whispers in my ear. "It'll be far better for you if you cooperate."

Cooperate? As if! I kick as hard as I can under the robe when they pull me out of the SUV, a Facilitator on either side holding my arms in a death grip.

"Don't say a word," the woman hisses. "To witnesses, you're an initiate. They have no idea who you are, and you want to keep it that way. Trust me. For your own preservation, do as I say."

I try imagining how this must look, me hooded and being pulled toward God knows where by a bunch of gym rats on steroids and MacBeath's bullshit. How could a passerby not have concerns? Is everyone here so brainwashed they never ask questions? Well, of course they are. They're in a cult!

Through the hood, I detect faint whiffs of pine trees, dirt, and woodsmoke combined with spicy burning sage and lavender. These are the smells of my childhood. I remember the other cult kids and me rushing around to gather kindling for the bonfire, giggling with glee.

Summer solstice was our equivalent of the Fourth of July. We were so excited to watch fireworks and ignite sparklers, to play hide-and-seek in the thick fields amid the twinkling lightning bugs before being allowed to camp out at the café. It was the most magical night of the year.

Until my mother was murdered.

"Step up." The male Facilitator to my right lifts my elbow slightly as my toes meet something hard. A railroad tie, I bet. The paths to the cottages were constructed from old wooden ties pilfered from the defunct railroad that ran through the ghost town of Glastenbury. Tripped on them many a time.

The temperature's dropped due to the elevation and the setting sun. That's another thing about the Center, how dark it got once night fell. With no electric or ambient lights for miles around and only the flames from various lamps, some powered by oil, others by batteries, it could be as black as pitch. The stars were amazing. I recall the Milky Way being so dense that it was like a band of white sparkles across the sky.

We stop. There's the squeaking of a door hinge and I'm pushed forward, my feet landing on a bare plywood floor. The door slams shut and there's the unmistakable clink of a deadbolt. I wait, breathing hard. I have no idea what could be next.

My wrists free at last, I pull off the heavy robe, the rough hood, and blink. A super bright LED lantern illuminates the writing on the wall, literally. Barely an inch of space in what appears to be a windowless room is spared a motivational poster. The pat phrases of MacBeath wisdom in electric blue, green, orange, and red blare in all caps, no exclamation point spared.

ABANDON "SELF" TO BECOME SELF-REALIZED.

TURN OFF, UNPLUG, AND . . . *FEEL*!!

YOU HAVE ONE LIFE, MAKE IT DIVINE!!

TRANSITIVE PROPERTY: ENERGY IS NEITHER CREATED NOR DESTROYED. YOU ARE ENERGY. THEREFORE, YOU WERE NOT CREATED, NOR CAN YOU BE DESTROYED!

TO GAIN YOU MUST GIVE.

BE OPEN TO MIRACLES FOR WE ARE, ALL OF US, ONE WITH THE DIVINE.

PRAYER OPENS THE CHANNEL TO THE DIVINE; DOWSING PLACES THE DIRECT CALL.

LIGHTEN YOUR LOAD; DUMP YOUR NEGATIVITY.

IMAGINE IT. BELIEVE IT. MANIFEST IT.

And another that gives me pause: SOMETIMES TO LIVE YOU MUST DIE.

A ridiculously large poster shows the seven chakras, from root to crown, in an outline of a genderless human in the lotus position. Overhead, the ceiling is painted a mystic purple. Someone's taken it upon themselves to paste glow-in-the-dark stars and moons. Four screened vents way high up and no bigger than a business envelope seem to be the only openings for fresh air, which explains the suffocating stench of mildew.

A narrow cot in the corner is covered by a vibrant, handsewn crazy quilt. The bedside table is draped in a cloth featuring a detailed dowser's wheel. It's as though I've entered the bedroom of a hyperactive New Age preteen.

Out of the corner of my eye, I catch sight of a looming figure dressed head to toe in gold and jump, only to realize it's not

Radcliffe MacBeath in the flesh, but Radcliffe MacBeath in a life-size cardboard cutout, pointing an extended finger like the old-fashioned Uncle Sam poster. *I WANT YOU TO FOLLOW ME!* is inscribed across his middle, right above the gold belt.

Next to him is a crude shelf of boards and bricks. There are about five books, and though I haven't perused the titles, I'm willing to bet they're penned by him too. What better bedtime reading than long, boring treatises on how swinging a pendulum can help you navigate the stock market?

"These are your quarters." The voice from the other side of the door belongs to an older woman who may have been the one to warn me not to make a scene.

"What's the point of all this?" I ask, spreading out my arms, my fingertips touching each metal wall, the room is so small. "You think locking me in a cell stuffed with material from the Diviner gift shop is gonna bring me to Jesus?"

"Not Jesus. Something—and someone—much bigger."

Classic Diviner blather.

"We've found a few initiates need the simplicity of the Chi Chamber to transition," she continues. "It helps them block out distractions from the outside world and meditate on the words of wisdom from our Dagda."

Dagda. Right. For a half second, I forgot they came up with a goofy name for the deranged guru. "I'm not an initiate! Initiates want to join your cult," I shout back. "I have no interest in being held against my will. That's a felony, you know!" I keep pointing this out, but no one seems to care.

"We don't abide by the laws of men at the Center," the voice on the other side replies in an aggressively peaceful drone. "The universal laws of energy are timeless and eternal. Those are the only laws we follow because they are true and pure and not made by humans for their shortsighted purposes."

My fingers ball into fists at the outrage being perpetrated upon me by a bunch of unthinking hypocrites.

"How many times am I gonna be victimized by you people?" I scream, my own anger getting the better of me. "First your so-called Dagda has my mother killed and then escapes the rap by getting you lackeys to lie on affidavits. Then your Facilitators dox me and my father, who had to leave his own house, for heaven's sakes, to find some peace because you've bought into a stupid conspiracy!

"So spare me your pompous speech about obeying only the laws of the universe. Guess what? The laws of the universe can't lock you up in prison, but the laws of Vermont can. Think about that, why dontcha, when you're reading your crystal balls tonight!"

My impassioned speech is met with silence.

To my disgust, I feel a slight dampness on my cheeks and realize I've started crying. Shoot. I don't want to be unstable. I want to—*need to*—be strong. Clear thinking is my only hope of salvation.

"There's food for you in the icebox," says the voice. "Along with a jar of well water. We suggest rationing your intake to ease your body into fasting."

"Fasting? Are you fucking serious?"

"It's mandatory for initiates. All of us have been through the process, and many of us continue to practice calorie restriction. We've found it to be the most effective and immediate path to enlightenment. When the body isn't consumed with sorting and digesting nutrients, the mind is unburdened from earthly tasks and able to explore the higher realms."

I hate this place.

"We don't hate you," the voice responds, much to my shock, since certainly she couldn't have heard my thoughts. "We love you,

Astraea. Once you've been purified, you'll be a member of our eternal family, and you'll lose all desire for the outside temptations. Welcome home."

Home my ass, I think, as my stomach emits a noisy grumble. I don't know when I last ate. Around three? On the drive over I downed a Heathernutter sandwich (Fluffernutter with peanut butter and banana). Drank a Diet Coke and ate a couple of grapes.

I'm thirsty, famished, desperately in need of the bathroom, and suddenly painfully homesick. I even miss Mari and Logan, hard as that is to believe.

"You're making a huge mistake. You need to let me out now!" I shout, banging on the deadlocked door.

"Good night," the woman says. "If you have any questions, consult your mother's pendulum. I was pleased to see you wearing it."

My mother's pendulum won't get me out of this firetrap, I think, again trying the handle, which doesn't budge. If this place goes up in smoke, I am cooked. Literally. No windows, aside from those vents, which are useless.

And then it hits me: I'm actually locked in solitary confinement. This is the kind of punishment that can cause even the most balanced person to scale the walls in desperation.

Well, nothing I can do about that tonight, I tell myself, trying to keep calm. I'll have to wait until my minders return tomorrow for a chance to escape.

At least there's a tiny bathroom with a composting toilet. It appears to be fairly clean, though the battery-powered light allows barely two minutes for me to wash up and brush my teeth with the complimentary toothbrush and toothpaste.

The battery-powered LED lamp on the bedside table is the single illumination in my ten-by-ten cell. The icebox is literally a box of ice—a red cooler with a tub of homemade hummus and crudités on top. A flimsy plastic carafe of water covered with a piece of cloth tied with string is stuck in the middle, next to a green Granny Smith apple.

Ease into fasting, the woman said. She wasn't kidding. I ate more when I was starving myself as a teenager trying to squeeze into size 3 jeans. Fed up, drained, and thoroughly spent, I throw myself onto the hard cot and rest my head on the flimsy pillow, staring up at the phrase in all caps painted in Day-Glo orange on the ceiling:

ALL THINGS ARE POSSIBLE WITH POSITIVE ENERGY.

So what's my positive takeaway here? If the Diviners truly want to keep me safe, then being stuck in what was probably once a steel shipping container in the middle of the woods is a handy way to make sure I'm unharmed. On the other hand, if MacBeath ordered my kidnapping and arrest because he wants to kill me at his leisure, then I am fucked.

Whoops! I forgot I'm supposed to be positive.

I close my eyes and focus on Dad and Heather, who won't let me disappear without a fight. I pray they don't dither, that they leap into action. Though maybe they're not too worried. Maybe they've finished a romantic dinner and are walking hand in hand along Boston's waterfront before going to bed in their luxury suite, and I'm not even on their radar.

Thump. Thump. Thump.

The steady sound of drumbeats drifts through the screened vents. A call to gather, if memory serves. I try to block out the noise by covering my head with the pillow, but I can't. The beats are growing louder as if they're intentionally trying to torment me.

Tossing the pillow onto the dirty plywood floor, I practice mindful breathing, anything to stop my heart from exploding out of my chest. Anything to keep the flood of panic at bay. *In. Hold. Out. Hold. Rinse and repeat.* It helps somewhat—until I stop. Then the questions slither out like venomous snakes.

Why am I here? What will the Facilitators—what will MacBeath—do to me? How can I possibly get out? Why is this prison cell called the Chi Chamber?

And more disturbingly, *Why is this room familiar?*

There is a palpable sadness here beyond the dank mildew and lack of air circulation. The sense of dread is amorphous. I can't pinpoint exactly why this room is so awful, despite the obvious fact that it's a locked and rusted shipping container. Maybe I've been here in my dreams.

Unclipping my mother's chain, I assume the position and dangle the pendulum over the edge of the cot. I ask it to show me yes, and it immediately circles clockwise. I ask it to show me no, and it switches, moving side to side.

A sense of serenity permeates my body, flowing from my head, down my arms, through my torso, and into my toes as I fixate on the swinging dark-pink stone. I can see how a pendulum can be used in hypnosis.

I ask it a question—am I getting out of here? Whereupon it does something it's never done before. The stone wobbles. I assume this is because I'm so nervous. Except when I ask it to show me yes, it goes right back to the clockwise circular motion. When I ask if I'll get out of here alive, again it wobbles.

This is not a good sign.

Standing, I hold the pendulum out in front of me and begin to pace slowly across the floor, repeating the same questions. The pendulum continues to wobble or goes dead still until I return to the cot. The wobbling picks up steam, bobbing up and down. It reminds me of the game we used to play when I was a kid, Hot and Cold.

Except the energy rising from the pendulum and into my arm is more akin to the experience I had hours earlier in Genevieve Winslow's garden when the dead children reached for my feet. It's definitely a force and definitely otherworldly.

For lack of a better phrase, the sensation is *divine*.

Is this what attracted my mother to spiritual dowsing? If so, I might be beginning to understand. Maybe. It's as if a curtain has been parted, allowing me a peek into her thoughts. To connect with a supernatural power this amazing is simultaneously awe-inspiring and comforting.

Perhaps Mama was right when she preached that within each body—whether human, animal, insect, or plant—lies Divine Energy that longs to meld with every other Divine Energy. That's what love is. Energy yearning for energy. And that's the gift of death, which releases the energy so it can finally be free to merge into the one, big Divine.

The pendulum's stopped bouncing and is now vibrating so intensely the chain is getting hot. I have to let go before it sears my fingertips.

Something's under the bed.

With little effort, I drag the cot away from the steel wall, revealing dust bunnies and a couple of desiccated spiders over a worn carpet. Lifting up the rug, I can barely make out incisions carved into the floor, the marks darkened by dirt and time. There's definitely a cutout in the plywood. No sign of hinges and certainly no ring to lift up the piece. I try prying it out with my fingers and fail. It won't budge due to warping over the years, but I'm pumped, because once it was an actual escape hatch.

More than that, it seems to be a message board from the past. A list of letters, likely of former prisoners, has been carved into the slats.

C. D.

M. K.

B. B.

And finally, barely visible in worn purple crayon, a star. A star for Astraea.

I know that's what it means because I drew it.

ROSE

JUNE 20, 2003

Rose pulled up the hood of her robe and headed down the winding stone path from her cabin to the Center's campus below. Tiki torches brought in for the solstice weekend were lit, their yellow flames flickering in the slight breeze.

The path ended at the boxy wooden hostel, its narrow casement windows opened wide to capture air. To the left of the hostel were the latrines, one for men, one for women, connected by shared shower booths. Damp towels left over from swims in the mountain's streams hung limply on wash lines strung between a corner of the hostel and a corner of the latrine.

Colorful tents erected for the solstice were pitched on pallets dotted across the commune. Rose counted at least thirty. And yet, with everyone gathered under the pavilion for the welcoming ceremony, the area was as deserted as a ghost town.

Too bad. It would've been better if she'd been here earlier while visitors were milling around the quad after dinner, sitting and talking, displaying their pendulums and rods, or simply throwing Frisbees. On the other hand, the sun would've been out in full force, and surely someone would have noticed her slipping into the office.

Keeping to the edge of the fence, she made her way to the far end of the complex. The office was attached to the gift shop/bookstore, which was attached to the café, her intended point of entry. The kids were sleeping in the café. The question was whether from there she could get into the office without being stopped by a babysitter. If the inner doors were unlocked, the coast would be clear. If not, she'd have to rely on a tip from Cerise.

Cerise knew how to pick locks with bobby pins, a library card, even her dowsing rods. She credited a ne'er-do-well former high school boyfriend for teaching her the tricks of his trades, useful for all sorts of sticky situations.

That's how Rose learned. She'd lost the key to the padlock on the café's icebox and went to Cerise for help. Cerise grabbed a couple of paper clips, bending one into a loop and the other into a 45-degree angle. It took her a while, but she managed to release the lock along with a steady stream of swears.

"Guess that's one advantage to living off the grid," she'd said, raising the lid on the icebox. "No electronic locks. No electronic surveillance."

Though Rose wouldn't have put it past Cliff to have surreptitiously installed hidden cameras. She knew he had them at his house.

Cerise used to find that hysterical.

"The dude has a satellite dish with a hundred channels," she once scoffed. "He's got a hot tub and sauna on his back porch. Last I checked, you don't need a hot tub and a plasma TV to preach about the beauty of living off the grid!"

"Blessed evening, Mentor."

Rose had been so lost in thought she didn't notice the Diviner in orange crossing her path until she nearly bumped into him. She was about to correct him for calling her a Mentor. Then she remembered she was wearing her old purple robe so as not to stand out in her rare white one reserved for the Realized. The Center was lousy with Mentors, but there were only a few of her elite status.

"Blessed evening," she repeated, keeping her head low so her hood would hide her face. She kept walking slowly toward the café.

He stopped and turned. "Shouldn't you be at the ceremony? Attendance is mandatory, you know."

"Yes, I'll be right there." Rose's heart was pumping so hard she could hear it.

Orange robes were worn by Seekers, the most grasping of all the Diviners. Most would do anything to be promoted to Mentor, including ratting out a disobedient Diviner to Dagda, or worse, Ellen or Ellen's Facilitators.

"Where are you going?" he had the audacity to ask.

Rose kept her back to him. "Who are you, a lowly Seeker, to question a Mentor? I shall have to report you to Ellen if you persist in being so disrespectful. You are not privy to all that goes on here yet, and my official business has nothing to do with you." Her harsh tone surprised even herself. Would he obey? Or would he be even more suspicious?

He said nothing. There was the scrape of gravel as he turned and his footsteps stomped off. Rose feared she'd just earned herself an enemy.

Whatever. A friend was dead, perhaps murdered. She couldn't be wringing her hands over whether she'd rebuffed a mansplainer who'd taken offense to her attitude.

The café was dark, the children fast asleep, along with the two sitters. At least, she hoped they were asleep. If not, this time she had a plausible excuse: she'd forgotten to defrost rolls for tomorrow's breakfast. Never mind that she was headed toward the adjoining gift shop in the opposite direction from the kitchen. It's doubtful they would have questioned her.

She tiptoed toward the gift shop door. *Please may it be unlocked. Please may it be unlocked,* she prayed as she slowly, carefully turned the handle.

Voila! It opened easily. Just one more door and she'd be in the office calling Ben.

She passed the manual cash register with its paper receipt book in triplicate and guest ledger. She passed the display case of quartz pendulums and copper dowsing rods. She passed the other case of crystals and geodes, and the shelves and shelves of Cliff's books, until she reached the wall of apparel—T-shirts and water bottles printed with Diviner sayings and baseball caps embroidered with *The Center.*

In the corner by the robes in Diviner colors and various sizes was the door to the Center's office. It was rarely used. Most authorized Diviners entered by the front door near the parking lot. Occasionally someone might pop from the office into the gift shop with an inquiry, but not often.

She gave the handle a twist. It didn't budge. *Dammit.*

She had to get in there. It was the only place with a phone—if you didn't count Cliff's house. The alternative was to hitchhike down to the highway and hope to catch a ride into town, where she could use the pay phone at the gas station. She'd done that before to call Dan and give him an update about their daughter, but she didn't have time.

Those alternatives were unacceptable. Already, she'd left Astraea by herself for too long. How soon before the child got scared and went to find her at the ceremony?

Removing Cerise's mangled paper clips from her robe pocket, she'd just stuck one into the door lock when she felt a feminine presence behind her radiating hostile vibes.

"What in the world are you doing?" a haughty voice demanded.

Ellen. She must have been tipped off by the spurned Seeker.

"None of your . . ." Rose started and stopped when she saw her accuser wasn't Cliff's right-hand henchwoman, but Bryanna, the babysitter who'd let Astraea explore the woods without adult supervision.

Bryanna's hands were on her hips. "What are you doing *here?*"

She'd been caught red-handed with a paper clip in the office door lock. Defrosting rolls was not going to fly. "I forgot something in the office," she whispered, though there was no valid reason why she, a Realized, should have to explain herself to Bryanna, a Novice. "I'll be in and out."

"The office will be open tomorrow. You can get whatever you need then. You need to go. There are children sleeping in the next room and only their parents are allowed here."

She was quite bossy for a Novice, this Bryanna. Rose had half a mind to teach her a lesson.

Slipping the twisted paper clips into her robe pocket, she folded her arms and lifted her chin. "Speaking of which, you must have been sleeping on the job this evening."

Bryanna squinted. "What?"

"That's the only explanation for why you allowed Astraea to leave the café with another child. They went all the way into the woods. Not only was that a violation of the Center's rules, but they could have ended up hurt."

"Spare me. You always let your kid run wild. I've seen you toss her a muffin in the morning and off she goes. Now all of a sudden I'm the bad mommy for doing the same?"

Absolutely, because you allowed her to go without her foil-covered shoes, Rose thought, though she couldn't say that. No one must learn about Astraea's special gifts, especially now, when her daughter had accidentally stumbled upon the buried body of a Diviner.

"You can't question me. I'm her mother."

"Barely. Everyone talks about you behind your back, you know, about how selfish you were to take Astraea from her dad and come here just because you had a crush on our Dagda."

Rose grew hot at the impertinence and the biting truth of the newbie's words. Even Cerise, who loved her unconditionally, once inquired if the real reason Rose had left Dan was because she'd fallen hard for Cliff's charms. Rose had instantly denied the implication, claiming she'd been drawn to the Diviner way of life, its simplicity and authenticity, its goal of uniting with the Divine Energy.

But had she?

"Hit a nerve, didn't I?" Bryanna smirked.

"You're free to disrespect me any way you want, Bri." Rose sucked back her wounded feelings. "It's not the Diviner way to do so, but, hey, you're wet behind the ears and in other ways. You'll learn sooner rather than later what a mistake you made letting my daughter go into that forest."

Bryanna's expression darkened. "I don't know what you're talking about. The children returned safe and sound."

Good. I got to her, Rose thought, refocusing on Cerise and the reason why she was trying to break into the office. She couldn't let herself be dragged into a petty, juvenile snit by a jealous Novice when there were far more important matters to address. "I don't know about safe and sound. My daughter was traumatized. Consider yourself forewarned. There will be consequences."

"I did nothing wrong."

Rose took great pleasure in responding with a shrug. "That'll be for the police to decide, I suppose." She was needlessly taunting the girl now, but she deserved it after making that crack about her being a selfish mother who neglected her child.

"I'm going straight to Dagda to tell him exactly what you said."

"Go ahead. There are over a hundred outsiders here, including several wealthy donors he wants to impress. Your complaints mean nothing to him. Now, run along." She flitted her fingers, waving her off. "Tomorrow's a big day and you'll need your rest."

Bryanna hesitated slightly, wavering between standing her ground and tattling to her guru. Finally she said, "This isn't over. You'd better bet I'm going to report you to Ellen for breaking into the office after hours."

"I'm sure you will." With that, she brushed past Bryanna toward the gift shop's exit.

She didn't look back when she stepped outside. Merely pulled up her hood and marched toward her cabin, frustrated and annoyed and still sad over what the Novice implied about her being a bad mother.

Was it true? *Had* she been too permissive? If only Cerise were there for reassurance. Cerise always said exactly the right thing to banish Rose's anxiety. She would have told this cocky little bitch exactly where she could stick her attitude.

"I miss you, friend," she whispered into the humid night air as she climbed the steps to her rustic cabin, her thoughts elsewhere until she arrived at the porch and saw the front door was wide open.

Her heart dropped. *Astraea.* She'd told her to stay put. She'd told her to stay!

Rushing inside, she had a full-blown panic attack when she saw the trundle bed was empty, the covers thrown back. It was a one-room cabin, every corner visible from the doorway. And yet, Rose screamed and screamed for her daughter.

"Astraea! Astraea!"

Perhaps she'd stepped into the outhouse. Yes, that was it. Rose chided herself for overreacting. She made it to the outhouse in ten strides. Empty.

Unable to breathe and overcome with nausea, she bent over and grabbed her knees, trying to clear her head so she could think. It would be okay. Astraea had simply gotten worried and went to look for her mother at the pavilion. Taking a deep breath, she righted herself and headed in that direction, practically blind with hysteria.

A figure in a white robe intercepted her on the path.

"Hey, hey, hey." Ellen reached out and grabbed Rose by the shoulders. "Where are you off to at this hour?"

Rose tried to break free, but Ellen's grip was strong. "Let go of me. I came home to find Astraea gone. She must have headed to the pavilion."

"There's no one at the pavilion." Ellen's tone was eerily trance-like. "The ceremony's over. Everyone's returned to the hostel or their tents."

The tents on the quad. Astraea could be in any of them with god knew who. It's not as though the Center conducted back-ground checks on visitors. And Astraea was so trusting. She had no fear of strangers—or of Cliff.

"I've got to go. I've got to go!" She twisted so fiercely she finally broke free. Immediately she took off for the quad, screaming her daughter's name.

"Astraea is perfectly fine," Ellen called after her. "She's with us."

Us?

Rose came to a halt, breathless. She didn't like the sound of that coming from Cliff's henchwoman. "What do you mean, *us?*"

Ellen tucked her hands in the arms of her robe, lending her the appearance of a monk. "It's come to our attention that little Astraea experienced a disturbing episode, shall we say, that dis-rupted her tender young energy. We thought it best to have her chi corrected."

No! No, they didn't. They did not throw her innocent child into that hot box. Rose licked her dry lips and balled her fists to keep from strangling the horrid woman. "Do you mean to tell me you put my child, who's only ten, in solitary confinement?"

"It's not solitary confinement. It's the Chi Chamber. It's where she needs to be right now, under the loving watch of dear Dagda."

"She's ten!" Rose shouted, already hoarse from screaming her daughter's name. "She's a baby!"

"Actually, though outwardly immature, she's quite advanced for her age in some regards. Don't worry, Rose. She's safe. When Dagda is satisfied her energy balance has been restored, he'll bring her right back to you."

How could they do this? Astraea was hers, not theirs. In a million lifetimes, Rose wouldn't have put anyone, much less a frightened child, into solitary. These people were animals.

One night of being locked in that airless room, being forced to live on nothing but water and whatever scraps of food Ellen deigned to toss to her, had been the most terrifying twenty-four hours of her life. Cerise had spent an even longer incarceration, a whole week for showing disrespect to the Center by having the nerve to collapse from heat exhaustion.

"It was either weed the field, reset my chi, or die. Anyway, it got me out of the sun." Cerise had tried to make a joke out of her imprisonment. Rose hadn't laughed. She'd grieved for her friend's suffering, her hate deepening for their supposed omniscient, loving leader.

This was the man now in control of her baby.

Rose emitted a long, slow moan. She would kill him. She would. When the time was right, when they were alone, when she could lead him into the woods and push him off a mountain ledge or down one of the infamous coal shafts, she would murder that evil sumabitch. Gladly too.

One thing was for certain, she would not be twiddling her thumbs waiting for Cliff to return with her daughter. Cerise had mentioned a secret hatch used by imprisoned Diviners over the years, a hidden way of getting in and out—it had helped her survive her week there. Hopefully, Cliff and Ellen hadn't sealed it yet, since this was her only chance of saving Astraea.

"At least I know now where she is, and that gives me peace," Rose lied, mimicking Ellen's monotone. "If she's with Dagda, then she's in good hands."

A slow smile crept across Ellen's lips. "I thought you'd see it that way. As we say, let go and let Dagda."

Rose nearly barfed. She loathed that stupid, egotistic mantra. "Yes."

"Besides," Ellen said, "Astraea is growing out of childhood. Soon the time will come for our loving leader to fully induct her into the Diviner communion so she will belong to all of us, not just you."

19

STELLA

JUNE 18, 2023

I have been here before.

This is my final thought before I finally drift off to sleep and the first when I wake to a thin, watery beam of sunlight shining through a vent. The room where I'm being held against my will is as stuffy and dark as when I arrived.

I'm starved and desperately need to pee. The toilet closet is a mere four steps away, so that's convenient. I make a mental note to mention that in my Yelp review. Only giving them one star though. There's absolutely no view, the bed is rock hard, the food sucks, and the customer service is terrible.

Parched and likely dehydrated, I down three quarters of the lukewarm water left in the bottle. I don't even care if it's poisoned, I'm so thirsty. I'm staying away from the food because I'm not sure my digestive system can handle it.

Pushing back the cot, I make another stab at prying open the hatch. It doesn't budge no matter how hard I stomp on it or hit it with a hardback copy of *More Dowsing for Spiritual (and Financial!) Success*, the sequel to MacBeath's original bestseller.

Could be my hosts found out about the hatch and have super-glued it shut. If they haven't, then I don't want to be the fool who ruins this for future guests of *Le Chez Chi*.

It hits me hard when I see the prisoners' initials ending in my crayoned star. I feel so bad for the little girl who drew the symbol, because I can't fathom that we're the same person, that twenty years ago or so I was in this very room being held against my will, petrified and alone and missing my mama.

The memories of that night are slowly emerging from the shadows, triggered by this visit. I vaguely remember being awakened by old Mean Ellen, who smelled of boiled potatoes and reminded me of a human shoebox. Everything about her was like a block, from her helmet hairstyle to her square shoulders.

That night, I was sitting up in bed reading Harry Potter when the door opened. I didn't even look up because I thought it would be Mama and was surprised to find Mean Ellen standing in the middle of our cabin, a finger to her lips. She said something about Mama being needed at the pavilion, which meant I'd have to return to the café with the other kids. That sounded fun, so I went.

I don't recall anything after that, including staying at the Chi Chamber. I must excel at suppressing trauma, because I definitely would have remembered drawing on the floor.

I'm about to make another go at the hatch when I hear footsteps crunching outside the door and quickly shove the cot into the corner. I'm lying in bed, pretending to be fast asleep, when the door opens.

"Hey," a voice whispers softly.

I open my eyes to find a man kneeling on the floor. Rowan.

He looks slightly different than when he accosted me in Somerville. He's shaved off his beard, for starters. With his five o'clock shadow, mop-top haircut, and wire-rimmed glasses, I think he'd still look more at home flipping through vintage record albums in Williamsburg than swinging a pendulum in Vermont.

"Figures you were behind this," I say, sitting up, irritated. I can't help but feel betrayed by a former friend. "I thought you said I'd be *safe* if I came to the Center. You left out the part about me being tossed into a locked storage container."

"Sorry about that. Not my idea." Unzipping his jacket, he produces coffee in a paper cup and a cinnamon roll wrapped in a napkin. "For you. From the café."

I'm such an emotional mess, I nearly lose my shit over the cinnamon roll, bursting into tears as Rowan places it on my lap. The sweet, warm cinnamon smell leaves me aching for my mother.

Taking a tiny bite, I'm swept back to the sunny mornings of my childhood, sitting with Mama on the café porch after the breakfast rush, her sipping tea from an earthenware mug while I happily grooved on the intense butter and cinnamon flavors, crumbs all down my front. I can see her wide smile, the way her brown eyes crinkled at the edges, her soft lips kissing me on the cheek. I can actually feel her love.

MacBeath stole her, robbed me of years of happy memories like that one. If it weren't for him, I wouldn't have been raised as a shut-in. I wouldn't be here in this metal box sobbing over something so silly as a cinnamon roll. I despise him with a vengeance.

Rowan sits next to me on the cot and leans in. He smells freshly showered. In a commune where water is solar heated and soap is made from wood ashes, that's an achievement. "I wish I could get you out of here" is all he says.

I laugh so hard at the absurdity of that statement, I nearly spit out my coffee. "Have you thought of opening the door?"

"No. Can. Do. You're being watched."

"Why?"

He takes a sip of his own coffee. "My understanding is it's for your protection. We are all about making sure visitors feel safe. It's our policy."

"Did your insurance company mandate that policy before or after three women went missing?"

He cocks his head, like I should be ashamed for making a crack.

"Too soon?" I ask with my mouth full, having nearly inhaled the roll. I'm so starved, I could down four more.

Rising from the cot, Rowan leans against the cardboard Mac-Beath and folds his arms. He's wearing the tortured expression of someone who's about to deliver bad news. "As you know, there's a certain faction here that's convinced you're out to destroy Radcliffe."

"They're not wrong." I sip the coffee, impressed that Rowan knew I preferred two shots of half-and-half, no sugar. When it comes to dowsing, it's the details that sets the pros apart from the amateurs.

"These folks are willing to go to jail for Dagda. Maybe even willing to die."

"Can't help stupid." I'm wondering where he's headed with this speech. It seems like a big lead-up.

"Personally," he says, putting his hand to his chest, "I've got issues with Radcliffe. I'd like to do away with the hierarchy here and rebuild from scratch. No one gets to be the supreme commander. We rotate leading the meditations. You know, kind of like the Lutheran Church."

"What, more casseroles and Jell-O? Not sure that's a winning pitch to people who like to dance around naked and high on mushrooms."

He dismisses that slam with a wave and in so doing nearly knocks over cardboard MacBeath. "Shit. Just assumed he was nailed to the wall," he says, readjusting the figure. "Anyway, the point is the Center's going through a period of transformation, and I have managed to make some inroads. People respect me, even the extremists, and they've agreed to a compromise."

At last we have arrived at the reason for this carb-laden visit. I scoot back on the cot and hug my knees. "Can't wait to hear this."

"They promise to leave you alone if you sign a statement swearing, once and for all, that you didn't see Radcliffe MacBeath anywhere near your mother when she was, you know . . ."

"Bashed in the back of the head with a rock before being axed."

Rowan is visibly appalled by my bluntness. "I'm so sorry. That must have been devastating."

"To be clear, I didn't witness the actual attack, only the bloody aftermath, and that was pretty gruesome."

He closes his eyes.

"Rowan, I get where you're coming from. You want to have your cake and eat it too," I tell him, feeling rather magnanimous for taking the high road when, really, I want to kick him in the balls. "Save your guru while dialing down the chances your wacko compatriots will go crazy and kill me in my sleep. Admirable diplomacy, really. But I'm not letting MacBeath off the hook, if that's what you're asking. I saw what I saw that night, and that was a masked man in antlers the same height as your deranged guru in the woods surrounding your deranged guru's commune. Those are facts."

"But that's why he couldn't have been Radcliffe! He was by the bonfire all night. There were hundreds of witnesses."

"So maybe a Facilitator was doing his bidding, or Ellen's. What's the difference? The point is MacBeath wanted my mother dead and he killed her, either directly or indirectly. The end result is the same. I trust no one, not even you."

"If you're so certain Radcliffe killed your mother, then why were you at Ben Winslow's yesterday snooping around in his mother's garden?" He grins, clearly proud that he ferreted out this juicy detail. "Don't be shocked that I know. There are Diviners everywhere. Not like you ended up in that Uber by happenstance."

I have a vision of Heather's Kia listing to the side with two slashed tires. "Who's gonna pay for what you did to my stepmother's car?"

"We'll figure it out. Let's get back to my question. You snuck past the Winslows' gate. You tromped all through their garden."

He's making me super uncomfortable, which is significant considering I haven't exactly been relaxed. "Do you guys have drones or what?"

"We're dowsers, Astraea. Seeing with our third eye is what we do. You could too, if you applied your considerable talents."

Throwing my legs over the cot, I get up and inch past him, ostensibly to visit the icebox for a swig of water. Along my arduous three-step journey, I do a quick ocular pat down of the door, trying to determine if it's unlocked. If it is, I could make a run for it, scoot through the woods to the parking lot, and persuade an outsider arriving early for the solstice to drive me into town. I'd prefer to escape under the cover of darkness, but prisoners can't be choosers.

Rowan puts one hand against the door, shutting it for good. "Oh, and we also read minds."

"Cute, not."

"My theory is you went to the Winslows' to see if you felt what you felt the day before your mother was murdered." He chucks his chin at my bare feet. "I know you can dowse the dead, Astraea. You might as well own up to it."

It takes every muscle in my face to remain impassive. I'm not owning up to anything.

Rowan soldiers on. "Cliff told me you and your mom were running from Ben Winslow that night because you'd detected buried corpses while you were playing in Genevieve Winslow's garden. That's why Ben came to the solstice ceremony. He was in a blind rage, determined to keep Rose quiet about your discovery. Ellen was a witness to the entire exchange."

"And I'm sure Ellen would never, ever lie to cover for Mac-Beath," I fire back sarcastically.

"Don't be so hard on her. She's mellowed since we were kids and she's really worried."

"Worried I've got the goods on her guru."

"Worried that Ben's coming after you too." Rowan takes a step closer. So close that I'd be claustrophobic if I didn't feel strangely at ease with him. I guess that's the way it is when you became friends as children. Or so I've read.

"You know those two missing hikers? Ben was in town when they disappeared," he says. "The day after they were last seen, he abruptly changed plans and took a red-eye back to California via Albany."

I will say the Facilitators' research skills are outstanding. "That's probably just a coincidence."

"There are no coincidences in divination." He peers into my eyes through his wire frames. "Are you aware that Ben Winslow has been to every solstice here since your mother's murder? *Every. One.*"

That *is* chilling. "Are you sure?"

"I'm sure. He's in costume, which is why he mistakenly assumes we don't know who he is. Since we have tons of visitors, he probably thinks we won't notice him. He usually goes straight to the woods. My theory is he's searching for something he dropped that night twenty years ago, a key bit of evidence that could put him away for good. Maybe you have a better idea since you were there. *Think!*"

I close my eyes, meditating on what might be in the woods.

Beams of sunlight filtering down through thick trees as I climbed over mossy rocks. The evening trill of a hermit thrush, the babble of a brook. Cool air on my bare arms as I followed on the heels of another little girl running to the "turtle." It's just up ahead, I shout. And then

*something catches my foot. A hand. The sound of terrified screams,
mine.*

"Enough!" I hear myself say as my brain switches into defensive mode, shutting down the entire system.

"You okay?" Rowan's by my side, smoothing back my hair and lifting the water bottle to my lips. Somehow, I have ended up sitting on the plywood floor, my head against the cooler.

I take a slight sip and fall back again, dizzy. "The day before my mother was murdered, not only did I sense a buried child in Genevieve Winslow's garden, but that evening I came across a body in the woods here."

He nods, like this isn't a revelation. "You know who?"

"I have an idea." My ankles have started itching at the mere memory. "Not that I'm willing to speculate at the moment." Again, I trust no one, especially not a devoted Diviner like Rowan. Not only does he drink the Kool-Aid, he mixes it up by the pitcher.

He's silent, contemplative. "We're gonna get to the bottom of this, Astraea. Either you uncovered a hidden crime at the Winslows', in which case there's Ben Winslow's motive, or you uncovered something here, in which case . . ."

I finish the sentence for him. "In which case MacBeath ordered a Facilitator to kill my mother."

Rowan clears his throat. "Doubtful. But we have to find out once and for all. This shit needs to come to an end for your sake as well as Radcliffe's and, for that matter, all of us Diviners. It's divisive. We're not nearly as united as we should be."

Way to flip your priorities, I think, sliding up the wall until I'm back to standing. "Sorry about the lack of camper spirit, but I happen to believe my mother's murder takes top billing."

"Fair enough." His cheeks redden slightly in rightful chastisement. Then, he brightens. "Look, I want answers too. How about I come back this afternoon when I can find a break and I'll sneak you out of here. The two of us can go into the forest and you can show me the spot where you thought you found the body."

"If it's still there. MacBeath could have had it dug up and buried elsewhere."

"Can you detect, uh, residue?"

"Residue? That sounds gross."

He rolls his hand. "Whatever. Traces."

"No clue. It's not like I make a habit of walking around purposely stepping on bits and pieces of dead people."

"Maybe you should," he says. "Could open up a whole new career."

20

PRITI

JUNE 18, 2023

"Do you mind taking my mother to church?" Ben asks through the speakerphone in Genevieve's Volvo. "Stuck in traffic on Storrow Drive on a Sunday morning. Can you believe it?"

Priti's astonished that he's only now leaving Boston. He should be walking through the door of his mother's house, considering he promised to leave bright and early. Rolling over in bed, she reaches for the packet of saltines she left on the side table. She doesn't dare move without something to combat the morning sickness.

"Yes. I told your mom yesterday I'd take her." Priti bites off a corner of a saltine and chews quietly. She'd kill for a cup of ginger tea.

"Thanks so much. You're a trooper." He lets out a sigh of relief. "Hey, if you don't mind, please don't mention Stella O'Neill's visit, okay? It'll be upsetting."

"I'm not an idiot."

Priti's still unsettled by the woman's crazy accusation that some sort of apparently criminal evidence is buried in the garden, right below their bedroom window. Ben dismissed that as absurd when she phoned last night to report on the encounter, though in Priti's view he didn't seem exactly stunned. She would have expected him to laugh. Instead, he blurted out quite defensively, "That's not true!"

Then he asked if she'd remembered to get Stella's contact info, as if that's a normal follow-up question. "No," she'd replied dryly. "Stella took off."

"Disappointing," Ben had said.

It was all very, very bizarre.

Now he's acting as if nothing's amiss besides being stuck in traffic. "Charlotte and I are gonna stop and have coffee with a client, and then we'll be home."

The idea of him and Charlotte driving together after what some might consider a rather romantic evening in the city isn't calming her morning sickness. She doesn't even bother to say goodbye. Simply ends the call and makes a dash for the bathroom, the saltines being no match for the roller coaster she has found herself unwillingly riding.

Genevieve is already waiting in the lobby of Hamden House, the brick mansion built by a nineteenth-century robber baron who summered in Dutton with a coterie of New York society folks. She is perched at the edge an upholstered wingback chair, her posture ramrod straight, her thin ankles crossed, wearing what Priti has come to recognize as her summer church outfit: white blouse, navy skirt, and a pale blue cardigan tied around her shoulders. Pearls in the ears and around the neck. Lipstick pale pink. Her favorite sand-colored Ralph Lauren satchel on her lap.

Priti tries to imagine this epitome of decorum being a common criminal and can't.

Upon seeing her ride, Genevieve rises too swiftly for an eighty-four-year-old woman with osteoporosis and recovering from hip surgery. "Ow!" she gasps, clutching the arm of the chair, wincing in pain.

Priti runs to hold her before she falls, but Genevieve beats her away. "I can do it. I can do it!" Grabbing the brass-topped cane—a gift from Ben—she forces a brave smile. "Getting old is not for chickens. I see Ben didn't make it, just as I predicted."

"You know your son," Priti says.

Genevieve bends toward her, her eyes narrowing, and sniffs. "Are you feeling all right? You seem a bit peaked."

Instinctively, Priti covers her mouth. True. She'd had to pull over by the side of the road to vomit on the trip over here, a relatively quick five miles. But she'd rinsed with a tiny bottle of Scope and popped in two Dentyne. "I've been taking those prenatal vitamins and they're murder on my gut."

Genevieve links her arm in Priti's as they walk out the door and pulls her in tightly. "Does that mean what I think it means?"

"Only in preparation. Doctors' orders." She'll be damned if her mother-in-law learns about the pregnancy before Ben does, though that might be easier said than done. Genevieve's strangely intuitive about stuff like this.

During their visit last June, Genevieve poured Priti a glass of sparkling water at dinner instead of the delicious Barolo Ben selected. Ben didn't seem to notice, but Priti did and was immediately insulted. She was about to reach for the bottle when Genevieve flashed her a sly wink. Priti took a pregnancy test that very evening, and it was positive.

They chat about mindless trivia on the drive to Christ Church, a stone Gothic structure at the far end of Dutton's green, across the street from Genevieve's home.

Ben and Charlotte were married here when they were too young to realize they had no idea what they were getting into. Apparently there were over two hundred guests in attendance, including a few Vermont Supreme Court justices who were old friends of Ben's late father and several other esteemed members of the state's judiciary.

Priti can't help thinking about Ben's legal connections and the privileged social status of the Winslow family as she sits quietly next to Genevieve on the velvet church cushions. She should be in prayerful meditation focusing on the sermon, on her sins, on how she should go in peace to love and serve the Lord, but she keeps fixating on the dedication to Ben's father carved on a brass plaque under a stained-glass window a few pews up.

In loving memory of the Honorable
Benjamin Prescott Winslow II
ROMANS 12:19

While Genevieve's at coffee hour catching up with her old-lady friends after the service, Priti wanders back to the nave for a closer read of the plaque. She's typing the Bible citation into the Google search bar on her phone when a human Humpty-Dumpty in a bright-green sweater toddles down the aisle in her direction.

"Well, hello there!" Bogey Grovey calls out cheerfully. "Glad to see you're feeling above the weather this morning."

Had she been feeling under the weather? Then she remembers leaving the inn last night without saying goodbye. "What are you doing here?" she replies, ignoring the inquiry. "A die-hard golfer like you, I figure you'd be on the links on this bright June morning instead of inside a dark church."

"Oh, I'm headed there soon." He pinches his golf sweater. "The way I see it, if I'm gonna ask the big guy to keep me under par, I'd better hold up my end of the bargain and show up here first!"

She can't help but smile. "You're a delight, Bogey."

"That's what I keep telling my wife. Does she buy it though?" He throws up his hands good-naturedly. "Nope!"

Priti lets out a soft laugh. There's an adorable puppy-dog quality to this man that's very endearing.

He runs a stubby finger under the script on the plaque. "Romans 12:19. 'Avenge not yourselves, but rather give place unto wrath: for it is written, vengeance is mine.' Appropriate for a judge who served two decades on the bench, if you ask me."

"I'm impressed! Do you often go around quoting Bible verses?"

"Only those Reverend Whittingham made us commit to memory in confirmation class. Harder for a camel to pass through the eye of a needle. In my Father's house are many mansions; I go to prepare one for you. Judge not lest ye be judged. Thou hypocrite, first cast out the beam out of thine own eye; and then shalt thou see clearly to cast out the mote out of thy brother's eye. That's the best."

"Really. Why do you say that?"

He bites into a cookie pilfered from the coffee hour. "Because it sums up how people are in this town, always acting like they do no wrong, when behind closed doors they're up to no good." Brushing crumbs off his sweater, he adds conspiratorially, "You'd be surprised what's gone on within a stone's throw of this hallowed ground on which we stand."

That must be a not-so-oblique reference to Ben, who grew up "a stone's throw" across the street.

Priti's tender stomach does a flip-flop, thinking of Genevieve's mysterious crime. She places a hand on Bogey's arm as a way of signaling that she senses his pain, that she understands what it's like to be an "other," even as a former fashion model. That while he may be portly and chinless, flat footed and daft, he is still deserving of love and respect.

"I'll say it again. You're a delight."

Blushing slightly, he says, "I'm really not, but you seem to me to be a good person, Priti. I don't know how Ben keeps getting so lucky with women."

"Seems like you ended up okay. You're married to Charlotte, after all."

"Depending on how you define marriage."

Not the answer she expected—or wanted. "If you ever need to talk, Bogey, I can be trusted to listen without judgment. My sister, Neha, says I missed my calling as a therapist."

He gives her a pitying smile. "Oh, lovely Priti, I'm not the one who needs support. I'm fine. You're the one I fear for, being married to Ben. There is *soooo* much you don't know."

Prickles shoot up her spine, though thanks to skills she learned as a professional model, she's able to maintain a serene façade. "Yeah? Like what?"

Glancing at his wristwatch, he says, "It's a long story, and I've got to be going, so this conversation will have to wait for another day, I'm afraid." He takes a few steps backward, obviously eager to extricate himself after overstepping his bounds.

Now she's almost desperate. What doesn't she know? What would Bogey tell her if they had more time? "How about just the short and sweet."

"Short and sweet. Hmm. Not sure that's possible."

"A hint?"

Bogey shuffles his feet, clearly uncomfortable with the situation. He's a bon vivant who engages in superficial patter and pratfalls. Revelatory discussions in church aisles are not his forte. "Okay, here's a hint that might lift your spirits. Ben never loved Charlotte."

That's an unexpected revelation. "And how do you know that?"

"Oh, once Charlotte had a few too many martinis and told me their whole story. Here's irony: they wouldn't have gotten married if Rosa Santos hadn't been murdered. Isn't that wild?"

Priti grips the edge of a pew, unable to speak.

"It's true," Bogey continues lightly, as if they're discussing the weather instead of the brutal slaying of an innocent woman. "Char and Ben were dating off and on that summer. Nothing serious. Basically as a way to pass the time until they each returned to college. But on the night of the murder, Ben just showed up at the back door of her parents' house. She was shocked."

"By his rudeness?"

"'Cause he was a sight! Sweaty, dirty, completely disheveled, and rambling about going to the Center to confront his mother's psychic about all the money she'd swindled from Genevieve. Only he'd found Rose dead, and then he freaked. But that didn't explain the blood on his clothes, did it?"

Blood on his clothes? Priti teeters slightly, blinking to keep focus. "What? How did he explain the blood on his clothes?"

Bogey seems not to have heard her. "Ben was certain the cops were gonna point the finger at him 'cause there were witnesses up at the cult who'd seen them arguing earlier. He was babbling like a baby, according to Char, not making any sense. She had no choice but to step in and take control. Threw his clothes in the wash, got him cleaned up and his car too!

"The next day when the cops came a-knocking, she was ready. Convinced the police Ben drove straight to her house after confronting Rose Santos. Even went into extreme detail about the sex they'd had, seeing as how her parents were out of town and they'd had the whole house to themselves. The cops were so uncomfortable they closed their notebooks and left."

Blood on his clothes. Priti can't get past that, though somehow she manages to ask Bogey how all this led to a marriage proposal.

"Well, Ben felt obligated, didn't he? Here's his old girlfriend who'd been dying to marry him since grade school saving his life, and how can he repay her? With a ring, natch. Plus, everyone knows a spouse can't be forced to testify against a spouse in court and . . . win-win! Ben got what he wanted, or so he assumed. And Charlotte got what she wanted, or so she assumed. Turns out, they were a couple of dumb kids who didn't know squat."

Blood on his clothes. Everything else is meaningless. *Blood. On. His. Clothes.*

"There you are!" Genevieve announces from the entryway to the parish hall, leaning heavily on her cane. "I've been searching everywhere for you, Priti."

"Look, I'll call you later," Bogey says, clearly grateful for the interruption.

He abruptly turns and slides through the pew to Genevieve. Taking her by the elbow and leading her toward the door, he says, "Stay here. Priti will bring the car around and I'll take you out."

Bogey is doing what Priti should be doing, and she feels bad about that. She should be taking care of her mother-in-law and keeping watch on her fatigue. But she can't. She's frozen in place. She's nauseated. She's suddenly very afraid this spike in anxiety will cause her to expel this fetus.

"Priti!" Genevieve taps her cane on the tile floor. "Are you going to get the car or am I going to have to wait around here all day? I'll miss lunch if we don't hurry."

Priti surfaces from her crisis, pushes aside all ponderings about Ben, and refocuses on her mother-in-law, who's standing by the door alone. Bogey has made like a banana and split.

"In a minute," she says weakly. "I just need to pull the car around."

She practically stumbles out the double front doors into the clear morning light and down the sidewalk toward the parking lot. That's when she catches sight of an odd pair hovering by a clearly damaged car.

A white Kia hatchback with deflated tires lists crookedly

against the curb. Two women about her age—one short and dark and attired entirely in black, the other Black, tall, and full-figured in a flowing printed dress—are leaning against its side as if waiting for a tow truck. They're obviously in trouble, and they're obviously in for a wait. The nearest service station operating on a Sunday is miles away, in Rutland.

"You guys okay?" she inquires, taking out her phone to call Ben, who might know of a local mechanic.

But the short one is already on her own phone. She sticks a finger in her ear and continues talking.

"This is our friend's car," Boho Dress says, pushing a stray curl off her face. "We found it, but we can't find her."

Priti has a hunch this car might belong to Stella, especially since it has a Massachusetts plate. That it's in bad condition, that it seems Stella might be missing, that her friends are circling, acting alarmed, puts her on high alert. "Who's your friend?"

"Her name is Stella O'Neill." Boho Dress steps closer. "And I bet you're Priti Suryanarayana, aren't you? Ben Winslow's wife."

Every nerve in Priti's body fires hot. Back in her modeling days, it wasn't uncommon for her to be recognized simply as Priti, her professional name. Strangers asking her if she's Ben Winslow's wife is an unsettling twist, especially if they're friends of the daughter of the woman her own husband might have murdered.

"Did she come to see him?" The woman juts out her chin. "I bet she did. I bet that's why her stepmom's car's here. Stella probably drove over here to confront Ben about why he was trying to get into her apartment yesterday when we were there. What happened?"

Priti is stunned by the accusation and instinctively rises to Ben's defense. "My husband is a very successful entrepreneur with a multimillion-dollar company. He doesn't go around breaking into people's apartments. However, I did find your friend trying to break into my garden shed while I was out to dinner last night. So you might want to check yourself."

Without another glance, she heads to the parking lot, unlocks Ben's Tesla, and gets in. Then she rests her forehead on the steering wheel and tries very, very hard not to have a nervous breakdown.

21

PRITI

The pair is at the same spot when Priti pulls out of the church exit with Genevieve. Only a tow truck has arrived and a mechanic is chaining the Kia with Mass plates to a flatbed trailer. The short, dark woman seems to be ripping him a new one, hands flying all over the place in gestures, while Boho Dress is shielding her eyes, her shoulders heaving in sobs.

"What the hey-ho's going on there I wonder?" Genevieve inquires, squinting out the passenger window.

"I haven't the foggiest," Priti replies, crossing the street and turning up Genevieve's driveway instead of down Main toward Hamden House.

Genevieve grips the dashboard. "You're going the wrong way. I'll be late to lunch if we stop off at the house."

"I thought I'd make you lunch instead. Chicken salad, the kind you like, with white grapes and almonds. Perhaps a glass of prosecco to go with? They don't serve that for lunch at Hamden House, do they?"

A naughty smile plays on Genevieve's lips. "No, my dear, they do not. How delightful!" The woman beams as they pull up to the door, she's so tickled.

Priti's very well aware she's disobeying her husband's directives. Ben believes it'll only confuse his mother in her declining mental state if she visits her home. She needs to adjust to the fact that from now on the senior-living facility is her permanent residence, not a temporary rehab, as she's been told. Or rather, misled, in Priti's opinion. Anyway, Ben will never be the wiser since he's in Boston and the spying maid has the day off.

Granted, Priti *may* have an ulterior motive. She *may* want to lead Genevieve down the literal and figurative primrose path to twenty years before, when Ben, according to Bogey, was in need of an alibi. She *may* want to inquire about his relationship with Charlotte, and also whether it was true, as Ben apparently alleged, that Rose Santos had defrauded Genevieve. She also might link her arm in Genevieve's and lead her to the garden just to see her reaction.

But also, it is a lovely June morning and a lunch alfresco on the patio will be delightful.

She leaves the car on the driveway instead of parking it in the garage so it's easier for Genevieve to walk around back. Priti's by her side, complimenting her mother-in-law on her spectacular flowers, the blooming roses and peonies, the irises and hydrangea.

"The white peonies smell divine." Genevieve puts her nose to one. "The pink, not so much."

"Do you use any fertilizer? The garden seems so lush." Priti can't help it. She had to ask.

Genevieve frowns. "How the hell do I know? Ask the landscapers."

Did they find buried evidence?

Priti's keeping watch over activity across the street. The tow truck is pulling out, and now the two strange women are in some sort of heated argument. Disturbingly, the hippie chick keeps pointing upward at the house despite being yanked back by her shorter friend.

What the hey-ho indeed?

Priti sits Genevieve at the wrought-iron table and brings her a glass of water and another of prosecco, popping the cork dramatically before pouring.

"Aren't you partaking, my dear?" her mother-in-law inquires, almost knowingly.

Priti rubs her belly, the faint smell of the alcohol already making her ill. "I'm afraid my stomach still hasn't settled from the vitamins. I'll be right back with our lunch."

From the refrigerator, she brings out a container of chicken salad courtesy of Le Petite Poule Rousse, Dutton's extremely overpriced and fabulous gourmet market. Cracking open a box of croissants, she slices two in half and pops them in the toaster oven for a quick warm-up. Meanwhile, she pours herself a half glass of orange juice, to which she adds two ice cubes and a splash of soda water. Then she takes a long, slow, refreshing drink.

This magic beverage is the only hydration that keeps her sustained and vertical. If this fetus survives, she wouldn't be shocked if the baby came out orange from all the juice and carrots she's already ingested.

The toaster oven dings and Priti places crisp lettuce leaves on each half and a scoop of the chicken salad in the middle. A few local strawberries for garnish along with a couple of orange slices and that's a lunch that would cost more than fifty bucks at the inn, not including the ten-dollar glass of prosecco. This is Priti's favorite hobby, guesstimating how much a meal at home would cost if they'd ordered out.

Placing the plates and glass of juice on a bamboo tray, Priti heads to the French doors leading to the patio and stops short at the sight of the boho chick in deep conversation with her mother-in-law.

"Shit," she mutters, annoyed by the stranger's intrusion. How bold and inappropriate to barge in on someone's Sunday lunch like that. Some people have zero manners.

"Oh, let me help you." Boho chick nearly knocks over her chair as she jumps up to open the door.

Priti gives her what she hopes will be accurately read as a dirty look. "Thanks."

"No problemo!" Boho chick chirps, either oblivious or intentionally not getting the message.

"Priti, I don't know if you've had the pleasure of meeting Figurina DiTolla." Genevieve gestures for the intruder to return to her seat, as Priti sets down the tray.

"Please," the intruder says, extending a hand for Priti to shake, "call me Fig. Only my grandmother calls me Figurina."

"Figurina is the best friend of the daughter of one of my own closest friends long dead, can you believe it?" Genevieve shakes her head. "What a coincidence."

Coincidence my ass, Priti thinks, forcing a smile, disappointed she won't have a chance to grill Genevieve solo. "There's more chicken salad if you'd like to join us, Fig."

Fig wrinkles her nose in disgust. "Chicken? Oh my god, no. I haven't eaten meat since I became a vegetarian in kindergarten."

"Good for you!" Genevieve pats her hand. "I always wanted to be a vegetarian, but I lived in a house of male carnivores. You're lucky, being married to a woman, that you don't have to put up with that."

How did her mother-in-law find out so much about this intruder so quickly? Perhaps it's the prosecco. Genevieve's champagne flute has been refilled to the brim, and she's dumped out her water glass and filled it with prosecco for this Fig person. Quite generously too.

"Perhaps you'd like a PB&J?" Genevieve offers.

"No, no, that's fine. Thanks. I really just stopped by to ask after my friend Stella. That's her car that's being towed, and didn't you say, Priti, she stopped by here last night?"

"Really?" Genevieve puts down her sandwich half and wipes her lips. "Well, isn't that interesting."

Priti slides into the chair next to her mother-in-law with resurrected hope for info about Ben and Rose. Better a stranger ask the tough questions than she.

Fig sips her prosecco and sets down the glass with enough force to shatter on the iron table. "Why is that interesting?"

"Because Stella—or Astraea, as she was called back then—knew my son, though I doubt she remembers. She was just a child when she used to accompany her mother on her visits. Sometimes, not always. Often Rose preferred to leave her at the commune so she wouldn't be bored."

"Visits for what?" Fig folds her arms expectantly, displaying no qualms about probing into a personal and, in Priti's view, very odd relationship.

"Oh, she helped me deal with the profound grief after my husband died suddenly of a massive heart attack. Dropped dead at fifty-five. Boom!" Genevieve slaps the table, rattling the plates and glasses. "It was quite a shock, as you can imagine. My husband and I had dated since high school, married the week after he graduated from Williams and I from Smith. We practically grew up together."

Priti knows none of this, and for a second, she forgets about her own husband, so focused is she on the father-in-law she never knew.

"I worked the perfume counter at Filene's in Boston while he attended law school. After he graduated, we moved here, to Dutton, where he had family connections going all the way back to the Revolutionary War. He opened a small practice in Manchester, and eventually he was appointed to the bench. When he passed, he was a highly respected judge based in the federal courthouse in Rutland. Such a smart man. Wise beyond his years. Not a day goes by when I don't miss him."

"But what does that have to do with Stella's mother?" Priti asks, intrigued that her in-laws hadn't been born into wealth, as she'd assumed, that Genevieve with her Smith degree had put her husband through law school by peddling Chanel No. 5.

"Stella's mother was a woman named Rose Santos. She was a fabulously gifted psychic who could connect me to my Ben. It sounds silly, I know, but I don't care. I firmly believe in life after death, that only a thin veil separates us from our loved ones who've passed." Genevieve does not seem ashamed of blithely admitting to this quackery. "We would sit at this very table, and she would facilitate a discussion, speaking for my husband since he couldn't."

So Rose was nothing but a two-bit con artist who preyed on a widow's grief for years and, undoubtedly, for thousands and thousands of dollars, Priti decides, revolted. This explains why Ben decided to confront her. He had every right to be angry that Rose was sucking up his inheritance and duping his mother.

"Were you aware that there's a TV show on Rose's murder?" Fig says.

Priti zeroes in on Genevieve's response, which is hard to read.

"Hmmph." She picks at a bit of chicken salad with her fork. "That doesn't surprise me. The Keystone Kops in this area botched that investigation from the get-go. There were tons of search parties trampling all over the crime scene looking for your friend's mother, destroying evidence left, right, and center. You knew about that, didn't you?"

"That Stella was gone when they found her mother's body, and that they didn't find her for three days? Yeah. So sad," Fig says.

"Pitiful."

Fig continues, undaunted. "Did you know your son came to Stella's apartment in Somerville Friday demanding to see her? I was there. He banged on the door, insisted we let him in."

Priti gasps. Was what Fig kept saying true? Could Ben have rushed off to Boston for a confrontation with Rose Santos's daughter instead of doing what he said, meeting with investors—and Charlotte—about HeadFake? Because if so, that was a pretty damn big lie.

A chill has descended on their festive atmosphere. Genevieve is sitting straight as an arrow, her lips pursed tightly, her gaze fixed on the garden, tears pooling in the corners of her eyes. The simple joyful summer luncheon has, in an instant, become an awkward fiasco and Priti won't have it.

"Perhaps you should leave," she hisses at Fig, who shows no sign of budging.

"Yes, perhaps you should."

Ben's stern voice booms from behind them. Priti turns to see her husband in the same clothes he wore when he left Friday, the day, she realizes, he went directly to Stella's apartment. Unshaven. Pale. A grease stain in the middle of his polo shirt. Eyes bloodshot. He looks like a man who's come off a weekend bender instead of wheeling and dealing with billionaires.

"Hi, honey." Priti jumps up to give him a hug. He returns her affection with a weak embrace.

"What's going on?" he asks, his stare fixed on Fig. "What's Mom doing here?"

"It's my home!" Genevieve says. "How dare you ask me what I'm doing in my *own home!*"

Ben turns to his wife with a disapproving frown. "I thought we agreed Mom would stay at Hamden House. I thought I explained my reasoning very clearly about how to best deal with *my* mother."

What he said is true. Deep down, Priti knows she had no business overriding her husband's orders simply because she wanted to get Genevieve alone for a gossip fest, even if she justified doing so by convincing herself they deserved a nice lunch on the patio. Priti feels guilty and also not guilty.

After all, she might have erred by bringing Ben's mother here, but he's hardly in a position to judge.

Fig pops up from her chair and flounces over to Ben, drawing so close, they're practically nose to nose. "Did you kill my friend's mother on June twenty-first, 2003, somewhere between the hours of midnight and nine thirty a.m. the following day, when Rose Santos's body was found? Did you bludgeon her skull with a rock in the woods outside the Center for Spiritual Dowsing ten miles from here, up the mountain?"

Genevieve's fork clatters to her plate in shock. Priti places a reassuring hand on her forearm, bracing for her husband's outburst over such an outrageous accusation, and made on his own turf, no less.

Ben, to her surprise, is unperturbed. "Don't be crazy. Who the hell are you anyway?"

"My name is Figurina DiTolla, and I am the manager of Children's and Young Adult Literature at the Cambridge Public Library, where I work side by side with our archivist, Stella O'Neill, though you might know her as Astraea, the daughter of Rose Santos, your mother's psychic."

"You need to leave before I call the police." Coolly, Ben steps past Fig and kneels by Genevieve. "I'm sorry about this, Mom. I hope you're not upset."

Genevieve tosses back the rest of her prosecco and reaches for the bottle. "It's about time someone put the question to you, my son. Lord knows the chicken-shit police around here didn't have the cojones!"

"Genevieve!" Priti blurts. This could not be the same prim and proper socialite who once had to take to her bed when she learned the thank-you notes Priti sent after the wedding had been typed instead of hand-printed.

Removing the bottle from his mother's liver-spotted hand, Ben sits in Fig's place. His demeanor is placid, his voice calm. "We've been over this. I told you I went to the Center that night because Rose called looking for me, saying she was in trouble, that she and Astraea needed to get out of that place immediately."

"Nonsense," Genevieve retorts hotly. "You and your greed got the better of you after those pencil-pushing accountants made such a fuss about how much I was paying Rose for her sessions. That was none of their business. It was my money to spend as I pleased. You should have butted out and left Rose alone."

Ben nods patiently, as if they've been down this road before. "That's true. Initially I took notice of her because of the eighty thousand or so siphoned from your account to pay for her readings. It was definitely a red flag."

Vindicated, Genevieve goes, "Hmmph."

"But that was before you described how MacBeath dragged her down the stairs that day, how you witnessed him being abusive to her in your own home. Rose and I had already discussed how that chiseler had pocketed all the money you'd paid her over the years. That's when my attitude toward her changed, and I offered to get her and her daughter out of a bad situation. That's why she called me the day she was murdered and asked for help, because I was the only one who could give her any assistance."

"If your intentions were so noble, then why did you need Charlotte to provide you with an alibi?" Priti blurts, surprising herself. She didn't expect to ask him this with his mother and a stranger present, but she couldn't resist the impulse.

Ben half grins. "Who told you that?"

"Bogey Grovey. This morning, after church." She realizes Fig has her phone out, that she's recording this interchange. "Put that away!"

Ben reaches over and snatches the phone out of her hand. Priti's afraid he'll smash it. Instead, his thumbs dance over the screen. "Erased." He doesn't hand the phone back to her though. He keeps it on the table. "You're on thin ice here," he says to Fig.

"Uhm, seems like you're the one on thin ice." Fig chucks her chin at Priti. "What's this about fabricating an alibi?"

"I didn't fabricate anything. I spent that night at Charlotte's because I couldn't go home in the state I was in."

"Which was?" Genevieve asks.

"Upset. I went to the Center as Rose asked and rescued her daughter from this prison where she was being kept, the poor kid. I thought for sure the three of us would go back to Dutton, where Mom had plenty of room for them to stay until we worked out a plan. But Rose refused to go, and we made quite a scene arguing back and forth. People saw us get heated, and I was told to leave."

The women are listening, rapt. Priti finds she's been holding her breath, mentally comparing Ben's story to Bogey's. So far, Ben hasn't mentioned that he was dirty and disheveled, that his car needed to be cleaned of all evidence. He hasn't admitted that Charlotte lied when she told the police he was with her during the hours of Rose's murder.

He hasn't said anything about blood on his clothes.

"I sat in my car a long time debating what to do. I was so torn. On the one hand, I thought, fuck it. Who is Rose Santos to me? I should let it go. On the other, I couldn't abandon this desperate woman and her child, who'd been taken away from her mother and locked up in a metal box. These people, these so-called Diviners, were animals. Who does that to a kid?"

Priti thinks of her husband, then all of twenty, wrestling with this moral conundrum, and her heart swells with pride. Ben is a good guy. A really good guy. She reaches for his hand and he clasps hers tightly. Whatever the outcome of this saga, they're a team. They're in this together.

"So what did you do?" Fig presses.

Ben shakes his head. "Not enough, let's put it that way. Not enough. If I hadn't been such a coward, weighing the pros and cons of doing the right thing instead of simply doing the right thing, Rose would be alive today. I'll never get over that."

Priti wants more details, but Ben is done. "Someday I'll explain everything. For now, I need to find Stella so we can talk. Until then, for her sake and, frankly, mine, that's as far as I'm willing to go. She and I are both in danger now that her identity's been leaked—her especially."

Fig says, "That's why you came to her apartment yesterday, just to talk?"

"Yup. I wanted to tell her my side of the story before Mac-Beath put his spin on it, and also to warn her. I know what it's like to be in the crosshairs of those nuts at the Center. They're crazy and delusional. I hope she's far, far away in a safe hiding spot."

Priti, Fig, and Genevieve exchange glances.

"Actually, that's why I'm here," Fig says. "Stella was in Dutton last night. She left her car parked outside this house."

Ben says, "That's bizarre. I don't get why she made the three-hour drive to confront me when she just could have answered the door when I knocked."

"Not sure you, per se, were the reason for the visit," Fig says. "More like this place. Stella can't talk about it without tearing up. Like maybe she experienced some sort of trauma here? I have a hunch she might have been trying to re-create a moment."

"She was caught on our security camera walking all over the garden," Priti adds. "It was weird."

"She was walking in my garden?" Throwing down her linen napkin, Genevieve slides back her chair, grabs her cane, and slowly goes over to inspect her flowers.

"Stella's dad contacted me early this morning asking if I'd heard from her," Fig continues. "I guess she was supposed to be staying with an aunt in Saratoga Springs and hadn't arrived. Anyway, when I told him she wasn't responding to my texts either, he got understandably upset. He'd been trying to reach her, and On-Star reported that the car hadn't budged all night.

"We told Dan we'd take a Sunday drive to Vermont, my wife and I, and see what was up," Fig continues. "Dan would have come himself but, like you said, the cultists are crazy. They've been camping outside his house, making it impossible for him to go anywhere without them following and harassing him. I played down the situation to her dad, said Stella just let her phone battery run out and couldn't find a mechanic on the weekend. Then Mel and I broke the land speed record getting here."

"Did you find her?" Ben asks.

"Unfortunately, no. Found her stepmom's car though. Two tires slashed. Gas all over the place. All our calls going straight to her voicemail. Speaking of which." Fig snatches back her phone, gets up, and walks off to make a call.

"Shit," Ben curses. "This is not good. Not good at all."

"They're trampled!" Genevieve shakes her cane. "She pounded my lilies to mush."

Not a flicker of guilt or remorse or fear, Priti thinks. *Interesting.*

"Was she wearing shoes?" Genevieve barks.

Ben turns to Priti. "You were there. You spoke to her. Was she barefoot?"

"What?" Priti looks from Ben to Genevieve. "Does that matter? I don't know."

"Well, what did she say?" Now Genevieve seems concerned, if not outright panicked.

All eyes are upon Priti, whose blood has drained into her shoes. Ben blinks rapidly, a surefire signal not to mention Stella's comment about the buried evidence. "Nothing," she lies. "Just ran."

"Welp, the car's in the garage." Fig returns and fetches her bag by the chair, finished with her call. "Still no word from Stella though. Mel's gonna swing by and pick me up, and then we're gonna go to the state police."

"And tell them what?" Ben leaps up from his chair. "That your friend had her tires slashed, that she hasn't been seen since last night? They won't do anything. It's a Sunday. The state police are understaffed as it is, and they need at least twenty-four hours for an adult to be missing to issue a report."

Fig puts a hand on her hip. "You have a better idea?"

Side-eyeing his mother, he says, "Mom. Maybe you should get ready to go so I can take you back to Hamden House."

"Bugger." Genevieve leans on her cane. "Just when things were getting good. Best I skip to the loo before the long drive."

"I'll fill you in later," Priti whispers as she accompanies her mother-in-law to the French doors. Closing them after Genevieve's inside, she says to Ben and Fig, "I certainly hope you're not thinking of doing what I think you're doing."

"I have to, Priti. If Stella was here and her car was vandalized then that means they got her," Ben says.

"Who, the cultists?" Fig says this so loud they could have heard her ten miles away in the Center.

Ben puts a finger to his lips. "Keep it down. I don't want to upset my mother more than she already is. Yes, the cultists. Who else? Not like Dutton is a crime center. I can't remember the last time—*any* time—someone's car was vandalized in this town. That was not random."

"Crap!" Fig rubs her temples. "This is unreal. This is exactly what we were trying to avoid. This is her worst nightmare."

"It's the only explanation," Ben says. "It's not as though the cult hasn't made people disappear before. You do read the news, right? You do know that a few years ago two women who visited the Center went missing. It's always around the summer solstice too."

"That was what the *Dark Cults* episode was about," Priti says. "Those women and Rose's murder. I suppose that's how it got the title 'The Triangle Three,' because the disappearances and death happened within the Bennington Triangle."

"What about Rose's friend Cerise?" Genevieve's back at the open French doors.

Priti suspects she was eavesdropping all along, the call of nature no match for the siren song of a real-life murder mystery.

"She was very upset about Cerise," Genevieve told them, "who vanished from the Center out of the blue the week before that horribleness happened to Rose. I told the police there must have been a connection, but they bought Cliff MacBeath's story that Cerise had left the Center of her own volition to seek dental treatment a week before and never returned. His followers backed him up."

"Per usual," Ben says. "That's how this guy gets away with everything. He's totally insulated from prosecution thanks to the people he keeps close. There are lawyers in his cult willing to defend him. Stockbrokers willing to bankroll him. This guy made his millions peddling a debunked theory that dowsing could lead to financial and professional success, so that's the type who buys his hype."

"Law of attraction," Fig interjects. "Stella told me that was one of their key principles. Successful people attract successful people. Wealth attracts wealth. Envision being rich and soon you'll be rich too."

"It's brilliant until someone like Rose pulls back the curtain and reveals the all-powerful Wizard of Oz is a time-share salesman from the Poconos," Priti says. "I'm betting that's why Mac-Beath had her killed, to keep her from destroying his city on the hill."

Fig smiles. "As a die-hard *Wizard of Oz* fan, I'd appreciate the metaphor if my best friend weren't in the clutches of the Wicked Witch of the West, as your husband thinks."

"Not thinks. Knows," Ben says. "Okay, guys. We're out of options. The only choice is to go to the Center and find her. I owe that to her mother . . . and mine." He smiles sweetly at Genevieve, who is shaking slightly, from anger, fear, distress, or the aftereffects of the wine, Priti's not sure. "Don't worry, Mom. I'll be fine."

"Because I'm going with you," Fig says. "She's a friend, and I promised her father I'd track her down. Just do me a favor, folks, and don't tell my wife. The woman's a control freak who happens to love me to death. It's an awful combination."

"A wonderful combination," Genevieve says. "Take it from a widow who lost her best friend and soul mate way too soon."

Ben walks over to his mother and slides an arm around her bony shoulders. Genevieve leans into him, resting her head against his. It's a beautiful mother-and-son moment Priti never imagined she'd see and is so glad she did. The two need each other. They're family. The only family Ben has besides her, and therefore, should be treasured like gold. She's been trying to tell him to pay less attention to work and more attention to his aging mother, but apparently it took a car with flat tires and a missing woman to get that to sink in.

Brrrring!

Fig jumps. "Jesus. Is that, like, a real phone?"

"A landline in the kitchen," Priti says with a laugh. Slipping past Ben and his mother, she goes inside and answers the old beige princess phone on the wall.

"Hi, Priti. It's Bogey."

Calling so soon? "How come you're not teeing off?"

"I should be. You're right. Look, I think I should follow up on our conversation. I didn't give you the whole story because . . . well, you never know who's listening in a public space, right?"

"Actually, now's not . . ."

"It's about Ben and Charlotte. I, I didn't have a chance to finish our conversation. There's more you need to know about what they've been up to."

Like going to Somerville to corner Stella O'Neill? Curious, but also frustrated by the conflicting stories, Priti doesn't know what to say. She pastes on a smile as Fig passes by on her way to the powder room. "Bogey, I'm not . . ."

"If you can get away this afternoon, meet me across the street behind the church at four. Just tell Ben you're going for a long walk. Which isn't far from the truth. I need you to dress for a hike, but don't make it too obvious, okay? We don't want him to think you're going up the mountain."

Mountain? This was sounding crazy. Covering the phone's mouthpiece, Priti says, low, "I thought this was about what Ben and Charlotte were up to in Boston."

Pause. "It's all related. The thing is, Charlotte isn't who you think she is and neither is your husband. But you have to see for yourself."

"See what?"

"What I came across in Ben's hunting cabin. It's not for the faint of heart, Priti, which is why you can't breathe a word of our walk to Ben. . . . Not unless you want to end up like Rose Santos."

22

ROSE

Rose didn't sleep that night. How could she, knowing her precious little daughter was locked up in a repurposed storage container—a suffocating firetrap—within her arms' reach. Her heart ached so painfully she feared it would burst.

She felt like she was clawing out of her skin with anger and frustration as she paced the worn pine floor of her cabin, biting her fingernails, praying, dowsing, and scheming. It was too late to call Ben. That would have to wait until morning. But there was action she could take now. She could plan.

At initiation, every Diviner was bequeathed a spiral-bound notebook to keep track of their dowsing practice sessions by tool, focus, and time spent. Ellen occasionally collected them for grading like a pop quiz to ensure the Diviners were doing their homework. The highest marks were given to those who wrote extensive passages praising Dagda for his wisdom and insight. Ellen would photocopy those passages and collect them in a stack for Cliff to read whenever he was in a sour mood.

Rose had learned long ago to keep two books since Ellen, being naturally suspicious and paranoid, would actually count the pages to ensure none had been ripped out and used for private correspondence. The second book was Cerise's idea, after she emerged from her first confinement in the Chi Chamber a different person, a little broken, a little sad, and very determined to make Cliff pay.

Rose needed to find Cerise's secret notebook. If Cerise had run so afoul of Cliff that he'd had her "negative energy" permanently exterminated, then surely she would have documented his cruelty. The question was whether he and Ellen had found Cerise's notebook and destroyed it.

If Rose could get her hands on Cerise's notes and free Astraea so she could lead her to Cerise's grave in the forest, then she'd have enough ammunition for the cops, even if Cliff got wind of her efforts and had Cerise's remains removed. Cliff was armed to the teeth with lawyers who, being devout Diviners, would mount a vigorous defense on his behalf, trashing Cerise as a mentally unstable former addict who left the Center of her own free will. Rose would need every shred of evidence to put him behind bars.

Donning her everyday black robe, Rose headed into the night to search Cerise's room. The mission couldn't have been more risky. She would have to sneak into the resident dorm and then upstairs silently. This might not have been a problem if Seekers didn't sleep in adjacent rooms.

Cerise had served as the Seekers' dorm mother, answering their questions and assisting them with their dowsing practices. She used to hold meetings on Monday evenings to discuss concerns ranging from the mundane (someone's toothbrush had gone missing or another's snoring was out of control) to more serious issues (complaints that they hadn't been promoted from Seeker status and whining about the latrine-cleaning schedule).

Which was why Rose's plan was so dangerous. Any Seeker who caught Rose riffling through Cerise's personal belongings would report her to Ellen, who would immediately report her to Cliff, who'd reward them with an upgrade of status to Mentor. Mentors didn't weed until their fingers bled or scrub rotted wooden toilet holes in outhouses. However, Mentors or Realizeds who were found to have violated Article 1 of the Diviner Code of Conduct—one shall not question Dagda—would be punished severely.

Rose might be thrown in the Chi Chamber too, in which case there'd be no chance of escape for either her or Astraea.

Fortunately, the door to the dorm was kept unlocked so residents could enter and exit to use the latrines. Rose turned the handle and began quietly climbing the narrow wooden staircase. The third step from the top, she knew, had a squeak. She avoided it successfully, made it to the second floor, and took a left toward Cerise's room.

It, too, was unlocked, thankfully. She stepped inside, a faint light from the waxing moon outside the window providing the only illumination. The room had changed from when she'd been there the day before, though Rose couldn't put her finger on exactly how.

Perhaps she was simply feeling the absence of her friend's presence. Gone was the small vase of wildflowers Cerise used to keep by her cot. The pegs that once held her robes and farming overalls were empty, and any lingering scent of the rose oil she used to dot on her wrists to make her feel "human" had evaporated. The room was stuffy, and Rose sensed the presence of evil lurking in the corners.

There was only one place where Cerise could have hidden her notebook. The floorboards were useless, seeing as how this room was on the second floor and the building was so ramshackle there was no insulation. The floor was the ceiling of the room below. The nightstand had no drawers. Which left the space between the thin mattress and the cot. Rose lifted the handmade quilt common to all the Diviners' beds and ran her hand under the mattress.

That's when she heard footsteps lightly coming up the stairs. Rose's mind raced, sweat running down her neck as she tried to gauge if she could fit under the cot. Slowly, carefully she slid beneath the iron bedstead and lowered the quilt. Dust bunnies tickled her nose, and it took all her years of meditation to keep from sneezing.

The hinges on the door creaked and soft footsteps entered. Rose held her breath, waiting for the visitor to leave. It was 2:00 a.m., hours before the sunrise devotion all Diviners were required to attend. There was no conceivable reason for someone to be here—unless she'd been followed.

At last, the door closed again. Rose didn't dare move an inch until she heard the footsteps disappear down the stairs. Still, it wouldn't be safe to leave now. She'd have to stay put until the hermit thrush welcomed the dawn's first light with its magical trill, the Center's collective wake-up call in June. Others would rise, including the visitors sleeping in the tents on the quad. Once people got going and moving, Rose could melt into the crowd without being noticed.

She ran her fingertips under the cot's wire frame until she found something—a folded piece of paper, which she pulled down through the slot. Clutching the note in her hand, she let herself drift off until she was awakened by a screaming robin and the clanging of the dorm residents getting up, getting dressed, and hurrying outside for morning devotions.

Only then was she able to slide from under the cot, her cramped muscles aching and sore as she unfolded the note and read in the faint light words written in Cerise's distinctive slanting penmanship:

To whomever finds this: Get. Out. Now.

Rose studied the words, fighting back tears as she folded the paper into eighths and stuck it in her bra. Even in her darkest moments, Cerise hadn't been thinking of herself, but of her fellow Diviners, warning them to save themselves while they could.

Rose pulled off her black robe and stuffed it under the cot. After making sure the coast was clear, she exited Cerise's room wearing only the dress she'd had on the night before. Anyone would understand why she hadn't changed and why her normally tidy bun was a tangled mess when she explained her child had been kidnapped and carted away to the storage container. She had no intention of spiffing up her appearance. She wanted the world to know what Cliff had done to her and to Astraea. The more outsiders who were made aware of his twisted soul, the better.

Her mind was made up. She would have to contact Ben. Fueled by outrage and determination, this time she marched straight to the office. No tiptoeing in like she'd done the night before when she was caught by Bryanna. This was do or die.

Lucky break. The gift shop was packed with so many solstice visitors lined up at the old manual cash register, the Diviners on duty didn't notice her opening the door to the office and slipping inside, then closing the door softly behind her. She'd have to act fast. No telling when Ellen might pop in to check a registration or make copies of the night's program on the hand-crank mimeograph machine.

Picking up the landline, she put it to her ear and dialed the number on the rotary phone. Genevieve Winslow's line rang three times. Rose closed her eyes and prayed her client wouldn't answer and nearly jumped for joy when Ben's gruff male voice said, "Winslow residence."

Rose took a deep breath. "It's me," she whispered. "I've decided to take you up on your offer. First, I need your help."

Even though she was nervous about defying Dagda and facing the consequences if her plan failed, calling Ben had been empowering. She'd taken the first step in breaking free from the Center. After years of griping to Cerise about how the place was going downhill and they should leave, she was finally taking action instead of just talking. She told herself everything would work out. Ben was smart and so was she.

By tomorrow night, she and Astraea would be far away in Massachusetts, back in civilization, where there'd be electric lights and air-conditioning and all the comforts she missed. No creepy Ellen and her frightening Facilitators. No dogmatic Dagda to dictate her every move.

But when she entered her cabin riding high from her talk with Ben, all hope vanished. She found Ellen sitting in the rocker, hands folded in her lap, her expression placid, per usual. Something had happened to her daughter. *Something bad.*

"Is Astraea okay?" Rose blurted, her knees weakening as she prepared herself for the worst.

Ellen slowly rose from the chair. "You weren't here when I knocked this morning, so I had to let myself in. It's been quite inconvenient. Really put a crimp in my schedule, which, as you know, is jam-packed on this the most important day at the Center."

These people were heartless demons. Just answer the freaking question, she wanted to scream. "Where. Is. My. Daughter?"

"She's fine. She's had a healthy breakfast of juice and oatmeal. When I left her, she was happily coloring."

Rose was so lightheaded, so shaky, she had to rest against the wall for support. "Thank God," she whispered.

"Don't thank God. God has nothing to do with it. Thank Dagda."

Rose knew that for political purposes she should repeat the mantra. She just couldn't, though Ellen was crossing her arms, expecting the golden words. "I need to see her."

"Your daughter will be released once she draws her pictures. Dagda feels it would be therapeutic for her to purge the dark energy of her discovery yesterday by expressing her trauma through art."

In other words, they want to know if Astraea can draw a map to Cerise's grave, those bastards. "I see. Can I at least visit her?"

"Dagda feels any interruptions would disturb the flow of Astraea's creative energy. I'll stop at noon to give her lunch and check on her artwork. She knows she can't go outside and play until she's finished."

Stay strong, Astraea, Rose telepathically messaged her daughter. *And, Cerise, if you're hovering around this plane, please look after my baby.*

"Is that what you came to tell me, that my imprisoned daughter is coloring?"

Ellen pursed her lips so tightly they went white, the only indication of disapproval in her otherwise serene bearing. "I came to tell you there's been a change of plans. Instead of delivering your personal testimony about how you came to be a Diviner and follower of Dagda shortly before the solstice at ten past three, Dagda would like you to hold your presentation at the stroke of midnight. Dagda feels yours is compelling enough to keep the crowd awake at that hour and motivated to see the ceremony to the end when the new sun rises. It's quite an honor."

It was quite a trap, you mean. Rose clenched her jaw.

Cliff was skilled enough to have tapped into her thoughts and picked up on her plans to escape with Astraea once darkness fell.

Actually, Rose wouldn't have put it past him to have installed a bug on the office phone so he could monitor all the outgoing calls, including hers to Ben just now. Ugh. She'd been so careless! Then again, it wasn't as though she had any other options.

But learning of her plans would explain why all of a sudden he wanted her front and center at midnight, and why he insisted Ellen tell her about the change in the night's schedule. Cliff wanted her to know he was onto her, especially since he couldn't leave the ceremony and track her whereabouts.

If that was true, then it also followed that the chances of Astraea being freed from her prison tonight were nil. In a way, her daughter was being held for ransom, Rose thought, much to her abhorrence. The man needed to be locked up as a child abuser—as well as a murderer.

Rose knew that until her daughter was back in her arms she would have to play the game perfectly. And that meant pretending to be a devoted acolyte of their deranged leader.

"Such an honor to speak at that hour," Rose said with a gracious smile. "Blessed be."

"Yes, blessed be." Ellen nodded and headed toward the door. Pausing, she squinted at the robes hanging on hooks. "Where's your black one?"

A question Ellen never would have asked in a million years if she didn't already know the answer. "I have no idea," Rose lied. "I haven't worn it since Marcus's funeral."

Marcus had been a ninety-year-old Diviner, one of Cliff's first followers, who threw himself into a deep ravine instead of dealing with the terminal cancer consuming him from within. To have sought standardized medical treatment would have been to reject Diviner principles that the body could heal if negative energy was purged and the channels to healthy energy were opened. Instead, he committed suicide.

"You should find it," Ellen said. "For the passing into eternal life is an inevitability we all must face, some of us sooner than later."

The parting shot was essentially a death warrant and chilled Rose to her bones.

23

PRITI

JUNE 18, 2023

Priti can no longer discern if her persistent nausea is due to pregnancy hormones or stress exacerbated by Bogey's stunning phone call.

Driving Genevieve back to Hamden House was pure torture. She had to pretend as if nothing were wrong. Twice, she'd had to pull over, open the door, and bend over to keep her head from spinning, along with the car.

Genevieve appeared oblivious to her daughter-in-law's inner turmoil. Clutching the handbag on her lap, she kept up a constant prattle about the neighbors' lawns and whether strawberries were past season and when she'd be able to drive herself again so she wouldn't be dependent on Ben and Priti for rides.

Not until the end of the trip did Genevieve turn her attention to this "Figurina person" and what she and Ben thought they'd accomplish by going to the Center to find Stella O'Neill.

"I mean, they don't even know for certain that's where she is. She could be anywhere. She could have taken a bus."

Though there's no bus from Dutton, Priti thought to herself as they blessedly pulled into the long drive up to the assisted-living center.

"And what's Ben going to do about the no trespassing order up there? How does he expect to get around that?"

Priti slammed on the brakes so hard, Genevieve's seat belt snapped. "What did you say?"

Genevieve's hand was at her chest, as if she were trying to keep her heart in place after such an abrupt stop. "The no trespassing order. The Center filed one after Rose's death, to keep him off the property."

"Why would there be a no trespassing order?"

"I assume Cliff MacBeath didn't want him on the premises. Isn't that the purpose of no trespassing orders?"

"Yes, but"—Priti tried to block the term "psychopath" from dominating her thoughts—"he didn't do anything wrong."

"He went up there that night and caused such a scene they had him escorted from the commune. Maybe it won't be a problem now. After all, it's been twenty years, and he's matured out of that angry-young-man phase, thank God. For a while there, I worried he was going to end up with his father's explosive temper. That man used to get so mad, I threatened to leave him if he didn't get control of himself."

Priti decided to file that bombshell away for later. She needed to get Genevieve settled into her apartment and back home in time to meet Bogey, provided Ben and Fig had already left for the Center.

They're gone when she arrives home. Ben's Tesla isn't in the garage and Fig's pink cardigan with blueberry buttons is no longer hanging off the back of her chair in the garden. Priti sends a text to her husband, wishing him good luck, and debates whether to end with her standard "I love you!"

For all she knows, after meeting with Bogey she might be on the next flight to LA before those two return. Her family will welcome her home, no question, though the prospect of raising this baby with them and not Ben is too depressing right now to contemplate. First, hear what Bogey has to say, she tells herself, and take this situation day by day, hour by hour, minute by minute.

Changing into a pair of comfortable leaf-green jeans, a natural linen top, and a jeans jacket, Priti pulls her silky dark hair into a ponytail, which she threads through the back of a white baseball cap, and slips on her favorite Jackie Ohh II sunglasses. Only when she assesses her outfit in the mirror does she realize she's subconsciously dressed in upscale, casual camouflage instead of backwoods hiking.

In case a passerby catches sight of her, it'll help to be disguised, she rationalizes. Dutton is a small town and people do talk. Sometimes too much, sometimes not enough.

Then she takes a deep breath and sends Bogey the text he requested.

Meet you in thirty is his quick response.

To be extra careful, she cuts through the backyard of Genevieve's house to where her property line meets the Dutton Country Club and crosses the playing field, keeping to the hedgerows. She feels silly making this extra effort, but you never know who's watching from the mullioned windows. Better to enter the church parking lot from the rear, undetected.

Bogey is waiting for her in his white BMW SUV with the engine running. "Hop in," he says, opening the passenger-side door.

She hesitates slightly. But Bogey isn't dangerous. A doofus, sure, but the polar opposite of an axe murderer.

"Hurry," he chides, checking his rearview. "We don't want to be seen. And you'd better get down."

She takes a seat, lowers the visor on her cap as he backs out of the church parking lot, hooking a left and then another. She feels ridiculous.

"Where are we going?" she asks, adding to herself, *Why are we going?*

"You didn't tell Ben or anyone we were going for a hike, right?" Though the air-conditioning's running full blast, a trickle of sweat is dripping down his right temple from under his own baseball cap. "I don't want him to tip off Charlotte so she runs to her lawyer. We've gotta look after our own interests, Priti, you and I, which means we have to strategize. *Capisce?*"

Capisce? No one she knows uses words like "capisce." "I don't even know what's going on," she says, sitting up slightly. She has to look out the front window or she'll barf.

"I'll tell you when we get there."

"Where?" They've left the Dutton limits and are on a dirt road she's never been on before.

"Where I found the evidence of their crimes." He turns to her and she sees her own reflection in his mirrored glasses. "Brace yourself. It's not gonna be pretty."

Okay, now she's gone beyond curious to outright panicked. "This sounds so bad, Bogey. From the cryptic way you were talking on the phone, I assumed you meant they were using the cabin just to hook up." *Just*, she thinks. What a stupid thing to say. There's nothing *just* about this situation. This is her marriage at stake, the future happiness of her unborn child. A tryst is grounds for divorce.

"Here's the truth." Bogey shifts in his seat, his right wrist propped on the wheel. "Your husband wasn't lying when he told you my wife was investing in HeadFake. No dispute there. She is. Additionally, this weekend they met with potential investors solicited by Charlotte, who managed to talk them into dinner with her and Ben at Pier 4 the other night."

So far, so good. Priti sits up a little straighter. Glad to know it wasn't a romantic dinner with just the two of them. "Okay . . . ?"

"That's not the whole story though." Flipping on his blinker, though no car's behind them, he takes another left onto an even rougher dirt road. A small brown sign is marked GLASTENBURY WILDERNESS TRAIL 1.5 MI. "We're almost there. Stay with me."

Where else could she go?

"You saw the *Dark Cults* episode, right?"

"I did, yesterday." Priti closes her eyes as they bump over the rocky road, every jolt sending her gut reeling.

"So you know about the two other hikers who went missing from the Center around this time of year."

"Yup." Priti can't understand what those cases have to do with anything. Gripping the door handle, she tries focusing on road markers—a tree, a rock, a post—anything to keep her stomach settled.

"The solstice that year was around midnight on the twentieth. After the ceremony, the two women were seen leaving the Center with a tall man dressed as some sort of Druid god with antlers. Matched the description of the suspect in Rose Santos's murder."

A cold chill runs up Priti's arms. Surely Bogey can't be suggesting what she thinks he's suggesting. No, that's too much of a leap. "Where are you going with this?"

"That's why we're here. Just be patient." Bogey turns into a small dusty lot by the trailhead and kills the engine. Another mile of those bumps and she would have lost it.

He gets out, opens the door to the back seat, and fetches a backpack. Lowering the rear hatch, he shrugs on the pack and assesses her outfit. "New boots? Not a speck of mud."

Priti glances at the pair she'd purchased a few weeks ago. "Yeah. Is that a problem?"

"If you don't mind blisters it's not. And you'd better douse yourself in serious insecticide. The blackflies where we're going are murder." He uncaps a can of Cutter and begins coating her legs with the smelly stuff.

Shit. She's beginning to regret accepting his offer. She doesn't like how the trail disappears into thick underbrush and that it's made up of rocks, not flat ground. This won't be a stroll in a sunlit, dappled forest. If they're headed to the Winslow hunting cabin, then they are going deep into the woods. Ben refused to take her there because the trek was too grueling, or so he claimed.

Maybe that was an excuse . . .

Bogey opens the car door, reaches for the center console, and pops it open, removing a small gray pistol, checking the safety before tucking it into his cargo shorts. "Just in case we run into a bear."

She's horrified. Priti's never seen a real gun before, at least not something that wasn't an antique firearm like the one hanging over the mantelpiece in her late father-in-law's study. "Where'd you get that?"

Bogey flicks his gaze at the gun like it's nothing more than a grease stain on his tie. "This? It's Charlotte's. Ben bought it for her when they were first married and he was traveling a lot for work. Now she keeps it in her car for safety. Totally legal in Vermont, by the way, for good reason. Never know what you're gonna run into on the trail, especially out here where you're far more likely to encounter a wild animal protecting her babies than a fellow hiker."

Suddenly Priti feels very much out of her element. And very much wary. She can't shake the question of what has she gotten herself into.

Bogey pops the top off a Nalgene bottle and shoots a stream of water into his mouth. Gone is the flat-footed doofus and butt of his buddies' jokes. Bogey Grovey no longer resembles a human platypus. He's a strong man in his early forties. Capable. Experienced. And now, armed.

"The trail's a steep three-mile climb with challenging terrain, to the abandoned village of Glastenbury, where the Winslow hunting camp is," he explains, tossing her a set of hiking poles before turning to the trailhead. "I hope you're up to the task."

Though every nerve cell is on alert, warning her to resist, to run, she doesn't see many options. Where would she go? They didn't arrive here by familiar routes or paved highways with numbers she's seen before. She honestly has no idea where they are, especially since, according to her last check, her phone has zero cell service. It's not as though she could just take off. That would be totally embarrassing, her jogging down the access road like an idiot, not to mention insulting to poor Bogey, who's gone through all the trouble of bringing her here.

He motions for her to hustle. "We have to hoof it if we want to be back by dark. It might be almost the longest day of the year, but you never know what trouble lies ahead. I sure as hell don't like to stick around after nightfall."

24

STELLA

JUNE 18, 2023

This is some bullshit.

Rowan was supposed to come by after lunch with a robe for me so we could slip out undetected among the early festival folks and into the woods. But he's not here yet. He's late. Super late.

I don't know the exact hour because the light filtering through the vents isn't enough to set up a sundial. But I can count the minutes since Ellen slid a tray of two celery sticks and another bottle of water through the door slot. It must be at least four.

I'm getting restless. The walls feel like they're closing in. Even the ceiling seems lower. I can't take this dank air, it's so unhealthy. The stench from the compostable toilet has begun to permeate the storage container I now call home, and it's getting hot in here.

It should be hot. It's the summer freaking solstice, not the happiest of anniversaries to begin with and certainly not improved by my incarceration in a human toaster oven. I need to get out. OUT! Whatever it takes, even being spotted by the Facilitators, who would love to serve my head on a platter to MacBeath, I don't care.

I. Want. Out.

The sheets. I've been thinking about them, wondering how

they could be used to my advantage. They're white, which is helpful, and all I really need is cover to get me to the showers. Once there, I can maybe snag someone else's robe. That'd solve a bunch of problems.

If I could only pry open that damned hatch.

Pushing back the cot, I take another gander at my little purple crayon star and at the other initials carved into the floor. C. D. is the first. I'm betting the C. D. stand for Cerise Danyew.

It'd be sweet if the other initials matched the two more recently missing women, but they don't. According to the *Dark Cults* show, Willow Davis went missing after a solstice celebration in 2021. Ditto for Rory Johnston. Both were seen at the Center's solstice festival; both were never seen after that. So there has to be a connection.

But if there is, they weren't held in this tuna can or they didn't think to scratch their initials in the wooden floor. That would tie everything together easily. Maybe too easily. MacBeath might be a killer, but he's wily.

What I need is a pry bar of some sort to get under the slats and jimmy open the hatch. My captors haven't been very accommodating in this regard. The plates on which my measly meals are served are constructed from paper. MacBeath's bestsellers are inadequate and . . .

MacBeath. That's it!

Turning over the life-size cutout of their dear leader, I examine the bottom for what I hope is a metal stand and hit pay dirt. Sure enough, two metal strips six inches long have been bent at the ends to support the cutout. It takes nothing to rip them out, though that means MacBeath's no longer towering over the Chi Chamber as he lies helplessly on the floor, his thumb still extended in a positive-energy, can-do attitude.

I slide a metal support into the cut around the hatch and begin to saw. The space has definitely been glued, and the aged glue is now cracking with ease. See now, if my captors archived articles for a public library like I do, they'd know from indexing *Fine Woodworking* magazine that superglue does not provide long-lasting bonding. Your coffee cup handle, sure, but a plywood hatch this close to the ground that's susceptible to moisture and temperature fluctuations? No way. It's bound to corrode.

Within minutes, the hatch is off and I'm peering into a dark, dank hole with a faint shimmer of light at one end. There were solid reasons, I'm sure, for setting the storage container upside down. Ease of construction. Instant roof. Et cetera. But if they really wanted to build a prison, they should have bolted it to a concrete pad, not to a flimsy plywood foundation. Then again, these are dowsers we're talking about, not Bob Vila.

To my pleasant surprise, I'm able to wiggle through the hole. An equally rickety crosshatched fencing to keep out varmints is a breeze to break. Snatching my sheet bundle, I shimmy out on my belly into the relief of fresh air. I am glad to see this part of the prison is backed against the fence along the woods.

I can't dawdle, especially if Rowan finally arrives like he's supposed to. I wrap myself in the sheet and get oriented.

The Chi Chamber is at the top of the hill near the cabins, one of which used to be my home. Part of me would love to visit the old place, but now is not the time for a stroll down memory lane. I need to find the showers, which I vaguely recall are between the boxy dorm and the boxy hostel.

Unfortunately, my surroundings hardly resemble my hazy memory. It's not only that I was so young and the details are fuzzy or that I last lived here twenty years ago. What's really throwing me for a loop are the crowds.

I've never been to Coachella, but that's the closest comparison that comes to mind. This place is like a hippie rock concert from days of yore, complete with the pungent odor of burning cannabis and gray-bearded types chanting and swaying in rhythm to music only they can hear.

On top of that, nearly everyone is in costume. Lots of flower crowns with trailing colorful ribbons. Stag headpieces too, and loincloths. Too many loincloths, frankly. Sorry, these are not CrossFit bodies.

I can pick out the resident Diviners because they're wearing different-colored robes appropriate for their status in the Center. For the outsiders, it's a free-for-all—from elaborate medieval gowns to sparkling fairy costumes with gossamer wings to heavy, hot capes straight from wardrobe for *Game of Thrones*. Though, to give them credit, they do seem pretty happy.

The relatively small quad of the Center's campus is packed with back-to-back tents of various shapes and sizes. To the left, a class that might be mistaken for yoga is under way, only instead of downward dog it appears to be downward rod. The students are struggling with their forked branches while a Diviner patiently teaches them how to tune in to underwater sources.

To the right, folks are gathered around two circular wooden tables. At one, a Diviner is demonstrating how to use a pendulum with a map. At the other, a Diviner is laying out tarot cards, the gateway drug to more intense divination.

The gathering is festive and joyful and, on the surface, extremely harmless. I can see why the Diviners take objection to their Dagda being accused of murder. How could someone who envisioned a commune built on peace, conservation, and the simple meditative act of tapping into the Divine Energy possibly take a life so violently? To his devoted followers, who've embraced this off-the-grid lifestyle, that's impossible. More than that—to entertain such notions would be blasphemy.

If it's true that Cliff MacBeath ordered my mother's death,

then that would unravel the Diviners' entire existence and make a mockery of the sacrifices they've made—quitting their jobs, pulling up stakes, shunning the comforts of modern society, and leaving loved ones to move here. I can relate because that's what my mother did, never expecting she'd meet her end on a stream bank, the back of her skull sliced in two.

That thought fills me with outrage. My loving mother trusted this community. She believed in its gentle principles. She wanted nothing more out of this life than to exist in harmony with the natural order of things and to raise me among like-minded people and their children. Rose Santos wasn't out to get rich or stick it to the other guy. She was a good person.

She was my mother, and whoever stole her from me needs to be brought to justice—once and for all.

I need to find out why we were in those woods. All I have to do is be brave. Sometimes forcing yourself to dig deep and confront the trauma takes more courage than seems humanly possible. I'm reminded of one of my mother's favorite sayings—the Universe never lays more on your shoulders than you can handle.

Throwing the sheet over my head, I head to the showers.

The morning rush has passed seeing as how it's midafternoon and, let's face it, the water, as I recall, is directly from the well and bracingly frigid. Warm and relaxing it isn't, and I doubt bathers are eager to linger under its icy spray.

To my delight, two stalls are occupied and, even better, a green robe hangs on a hook by one of them. I feel bad about leaving the newbie Diviner buck naked, but what's an escapee from a Chi Chamber supposed to do?

Dropping the sheet, I'm reaching for the robe when a strangely familiar voice behind me shouts, "What the hell do you think you're doing, Ms. O'Neill?"

I turn and there of all people is Figurina DiTolla in a green

Novice robe embroidered with I FOUND MY BLISS AT THE SOLSTICE! grinning like an idiot. This doesn't compute. Why would Fig be at a solstice festival, unless, shit, she's been a secret Diviner all along?

"Surprised?" She reaches into a paper bag and pulls out a matching robe. "They sell these at the gift shop for an outrageous hundred and twenty-five bucks. You can Venmo me later."

"Get back!" I hiss, searching the shower for a weapon. "Get the fuck away from me."

"What's wrong with you?"

"What's wrong with *you*?"

"Uh, nothing. Your dad called to say you hadn't made it to your aunt's in Upstate New York and said their OnStar detected the Kia on a side street in Dutton, and you weren't returning his texts or voicemails. So Mel and I drove down here to look for you—you're welcome—and found Heather's car with slashed tires and no sign of you. What happened?"

"I got kidnapped. That doesn't explain why you're here." I know I'm sounding ungrateful, but I don't trust her because, at this stage of the game, I trust no one.

"Kidnapped!" Fig drops her jaw in shock. "I knew it. I just knew some bad shit went down. Mel and I . . ."

The other shower turns off and Fig thrusts the robe at me. "Put this on, fast!"

I have no idea what's going on, whether Fig is friend or foe. But I do as she says, pulling the hood up, leaving the sheet on the floor, and following her out of the showers.

Fig checks both ways and then hooks her arm in mine, leading me toward the hostel. I keep my head low as we pass two Facilitators deep in discussion. They look so innocent with their shiny name tags and squeaky-clean smiles. They'd drag me back to the Chi Chamber in a nanosecond if they knew it was me under this robe. Probably break my kneecaps for good measure.

Instead of going into the hostel, Fig does a detour around the rear abutting the woods. We have total privacy, for now. "I'm so sorry you were kidnapped. What a nightmare. How are you?" she asks.

I don't know how to reply. I still can't believe she's here, that we're having this discussion in, of all places, the Center. I want to be happy to see her. I want to be thrilled. But it's like something inside me has broken and I'm afraid to put my faith in anyone anymore, even a children's librarian.

"They didn't hurt you, right?" Fig presses. "Your dad called the cops, but they were useless, natch. Chalked it up to vandalism and recommended a garage where he could have the Kia towed. He was gonna come down here and search for you, but Mel and I talked him out of it. It's too crazy where he is."

"At the hotel?"

Fig squints. "No, at their house in Sudbury. They didn't say anything about a hotel."

Dad and Heather must have changed their plans about a blissful night on the waterfront, which just adds to my guilt. If it weren't for me, they wouldn't be on self-imposed house arrest. I hate being the cause of everyone's misery.

Yet this doesn't explain how Fig, a work colleague, ended up at the Center. "How'd you know to come here though?"

"Logical deduction. Mel called around to all the hotels, even as far as Rutland, and you hadn't checked in anywhere. Then we met Ben Winslow's wife, who told us she'd come across you trying to break into their toolshed . . ."

I stop her. "Wait. You spoke to Priti?"

"At length. Ben, too, and his mother! She was having lunch at the house. Really nice people. Ben figured you'd be at the Center and that they might have locked you up in some big storage container. He dropped me off and gave me directions to where I might be able to find you, since apparently he's not allowed on the premises. I saw you crawl out and head to the showers and . . . here we are!"

My blood goes cold. Fig has no idea who or what she's dealing with. Ben will do anything to keep me from exposing the little bodies his mother buried under her flowers. And by anything, I mean what he did to Mama.

Shit!

I have to get out of here. I need to get into the woods, find whatever my mother was seeking at two in the morning twenty years ago, and go to the cops. This madness needs to end now.

"Gotta go," I say, pulling up my hood.

Fig is right on my heels. "Not without me. Where are we going?"

"The woods." I'm picking up my pace as we walk along the perimeter of the compound. "I don't know how to get there. The whole commune is fenced in."

It wasn't like that when I was a kid, I swear. We used to be able to run into the woods whenever we wanted. Probably Cliff's insurance underwriter insisted on a fence due to the literal pitfalls. That and, you know, my mother being killed.

And then a thought. "Is Mel here?"

"No, she drove up to Rutland. That's where your stepmother's car is."

"Then how did you get here?"

"I told you. Ben drove me!"

My brain is spinning. Forty-eight hours ago, Fig and I were dead-bolting my apartment door to keep that psychopath from killing us, possibly from adding our remains to the collection in his mother's garden. And now these two are carpooling?

"Are you insane? There's a very good chance Ben killed my mother. Rowan told me Ben came up to the commune that night, tried to convince Mama to leave with him. When she refused, he flew into a rage. Also, get this. He might *say* he's not allowed on the premises, but according to Rowan, Ben's been visiting the Center's solstice ceremonies in disguise every year. He doesn't participate, just goes into the woods. It's like he's looking for evidence that might incriminate him."

Fig is unfazed. "You're going to take the word of the Diviner who wanted you to come here with him because he was concerned for your own 'safety'?" She puts air quotes around the word "safety." "Lemme ask you something. If he's so great, why did he lock you up in a metal box?"

She has a point. "In all fairness, he was supposed to get me out this afternoon."

"He didn't, though, did he?"

Fig's right. "So is Ben still here?"

"Nuh-uh. He dropped me off and gave me his number so I can text him to pick us up. I don't think he's the killer, personally. His concern for you seemed pretty legit." Fig rattles a slightly rusted part of the chain-link fence that has clearly been cut through. "Looks like the work of teenagers. Messy. Hard to find. Ideal. You game?"

Prying open the fence, she stands there holding it wide, waiting for my response. And though this is the opening I've been searching for, literally and figuratively, I freeze.

It seems awfully convenient that Fig's here, that she's convinced of Ben Winslow's innocence, and yet so familiar with the Center that she found the fence opening before I did. I have to wonder, how much do I really know about my work colleague who's gone out of her way for me ever since Rhonda and Ashleigh Retter from Young Souls Matter upended my life?

Before that, Fig and I rarely saw each other out of the office, aside from the occasional retirement party or library staff softball game—and now she's rushing to my rescue.

No. Something is definitely not right.

My instincts are vibrating on high. I should walk away. Maybe I should run! But where would I go? Already I'm risking my own neck by being among Diviners who're convinced I'm out to destroy their guru. Just wait until Mean Ellen and the Facilitators discover I've escaped and they start rounding up the search parties.

Fig's still holding the fence open. "What's the holdup, O'Neill?"

Since politeness keeps me from replying "you," I step through the gate and into the woods.

25

ROSE

JUNE 21, 2003

Rose looked over the sea of Diviners and solstice visitors packing every inch of the pavilion, waiting for her to begin her introduction. She swallowed hard, her throat so dry she ended up coughing instead. She dreaded public speaking. Despite meditating beforehand and asking the Divine Energy for composure, inevitably her voice would crack and tremble, which would unsettle the listeners, who'd shift in their seats or study their hands in embarrassment for her.

She hated standing up in front of a crowd with all those eyes upon her. No matter how often she pleaded with Cliff to spare her the agony, he never cut her a break.

"Ease with public speaking is necessary if you're going to elevate from Realized to Divine," he'd say. "You can't reach that level without conquering this demon, Rose, which you can do if you put in the hard work and merge with the Divine Energy."

But that wasn't why he wanted her to introduce him. The sick truth was that Dagda enjoyed watching her stutter and squeak in torment. Rose's ineptitude served as the perfect foil to his brilliance.

Cliff gravitated to the spotlight, connecting to the audience in ways she couldn't conceive. Each attendee came away from Cliff's presentations with the false sense that he'd been speaking directly to him or her, that he saw into their souls, read their innermost thoughts, and knew their sins.

Tonight, however, Cliff had another reason to make sure she was front and center at midnight. He could sense her maternal desperation, as feral and intense as a mother bear missing her cub and had correctly intuited she was scheming to break her young daughter out of the Chi Chamber. He was determined to teach her a lesson that he, and only he, was in control of Astraea's fate.

As she sat next to him on the dais awaiting her turn to speak, Rose concentrated on what emotions she wanted to send to the Divine Energy. Panic. Loss. Grief. Hopelessness. Cliff smiled slightly, and when he squeezed her knee reassuringly, she suspected he'd tapped into her lies.

"Be strong. It'll be over soon," he murmured, giving her an encouraging smile as she stood to deliver her speech.

He wasn't referring to her introduction.

Rose placed her papers on the podium, readjusted the battery-powered microphone, and scanned the audience lit by hanging oil lanterns and melting candles. Most of the attendees were robed, their faces hidden in the dim light, so it was impossible to determine if by some miracle her last-chance savior was among them. He hadn't returned her phone call, which was disturbing. She told herself that with all the solstice activity, no one had had a chance to check the commune's only message machine.

"Welcome!" she began, throwing her arms wide in greeting. "This weekend we celebrate the Divine Energy of midsummer, which grows our crops and trees that will be harvested for winter food and warmth. Let us bask in the radiance that links us all. Let us join with one another. Blessed be."

"Blessed be!" the audience shouted in reprise.

Would Dan be waiting for them in the parking lot? She wouldn't want to leave right away, of course. She'd have to explain to him that Astraea needed to show her where she found Cerise's grave first. Dan wouldn't like that. He knew nothing of their child's powers, and the idea that their sweet young daughter had stumbled upon the buried corpse of her closest friend would be horrifying to him. He might sweep her up, put her in the car, and drive back to Massachusetts then and there, leaving Rose in the dust. Honestly, she couldn't fault him if he did.

Sweat was pooling in her armpits, popping out on her temples as she tried to quell a steady thrum of panic. Cliff cleared his throat, a signal she needed to get on with the business at hand. She returned to her notes.

"You know the question I'm most often asked by outsiders is why did I leave all my earthly comforts to follow Radcliffe Mac-Beath, better known to us Diviners as Dagda. Judging from all the heads nodding in the audience, I get the impression I'm not alone!"

The audience chuckled. Rose turned to Cliff, who winked in approval.

"Okay, let's see a show of hands. How many of us gathered here today have had to explain what cannot be explained to those who have not been shown the way?" Rose took advantage of the situation by pretending to count the lifted hands while searching for his face. Nothing. She continued. "See, yes! Again, we are united in more ways than one." She raised her own fist. "Huzzah!"

"Huzzah!" the crowd repeated loudly.

"Huzzah!" cried one man a beat too late. *On purpose?*

Rose gripped the edges of the podium, trying to gauge whether this was the signal. She could feel the heat of Cliff's gaze burning into her mind, probing, searching. To block him, she imagined a thick iron wall encasing her skull. She would not let him invade her thoughts.

She got an idea. It was off script and Cliff would realize that, but there was nothing he could do. Nor could he find objection when she ad-libbed, "I'll be honest, beloved. I would be lost were it not for the north star who is our Dagda, leading the way."

Her risk was rewarded with a single clap. A clap for *star*. For Astraea. Yes, he'd received her message and rescued her child.

Now refreshed in cool relief, giddy with joy, Rose managed to deliver the rest of her prepared speech without so much as a hiccup. When she handed the mic to Cliff, he practically snatched it out of her hand, annoyed by her perfect delivery and dubious about the move she'd just pulled.

"Don't go too far, Rose," he said into the mic over the thunderous applause. "The bonfire's about to be lit and we've got a long night ahead until sunrise."

Actually, fewer than three hours, she thought, bowing in deference as she backstepped away from the podium. She would have to hustle if she hoped to get Astraea in and out of the woods and the two of them out of the commune to meet Dan. That is, if Dan agreed to come after listening to her voicemail. Of course he would come. He was Astraea's father. He would die for that child.

"Where are you going?" Ellen hissed as Rose was about to step off the stage.

"Too much tea. I'll be right back."

Ellen shot out of her seat. "I'll go with you."

Cliff paused from his presentation and frowned in disapproval at the two women murmuring. Rose's panic returned as she calculated her narrowing options. This was no place to mount a protest and yet, under no condition could she allow herself to be escorted by Ellen.

"If you insist," she whispered with a shrug.

Both women left the pavilion and set off for the latrines, which were nearer to her cabin than the rented portable toilets. Ellen stayed close by her side, keeping pace with Rose's quick steps.

"I know you're up to something," her minder snapped. "And so does Dagda. He ordered me to keep close to you and so I shall. I'm sticking like glue, girl."

Rose's heart thumped as they left the golden glow from the pavilion and entered the deep darkness that'd settled over the commune. "You're right." She picked up the hem of her robe so she could walk faster. "I'm ill from tonight's dinner. Pray it's not food poisoning and we've sickened guests with poorly refrigerated chili or it'll be a catastrophe."

Ellen stopped, hand clasped to her chest. "You're lying."

"Why do you think I'm practically running? If I don't make it to my outhouse soon . . ." Rose bent over and clutched her knee-caps. "Oh, god. I might puke right here."

"Geesh!" Ellen covered her mouth with the sleeve of her robe and shrank back as Rose secretly inserted a finger as far as possible down her throat and gagged, immediately unleashing the contents of that night's dinner. She stayed in that position, gasping until she heard Ellen's footsteps clatter to the pavilion.

So much for sticking like glue.

Rose wiped her mouth with a handful of fresh grass and, checking to see she wasn't being followed, turned and ran smack into a Diviner stepping out of the shadows. He grabbed her by the shoulders so tightly she couldn't break free.

"She's in the cabin," Ben Winslow said quietly. "She's safe and sound asleep."

So it was true. She'd interpreted the clap and the huzzah correctly. Ben had saved her daughter. "How'd you do it?"

"Broke in from underneath the storage container like you suggested. Cut through the plywood and got her out. She was a total trooper. I took her to your cabin and put her to bed. She was fast asleep before I left. Rose, I'm afraid she might have been drugged."

Those bastards! Hot tears rolled down her cheeks. The gratitude she felt for him at that moment was so profound, it ached. "Thank you. Thank you so, so much."

"All you have to do is fetch her and a few things and we can get out of this shit box. Mom has plenty of room. You can rest and recoup."

Rose breathed in deeply, preparing herself for what was to come. In fact, if all went according to plan, this would be their last encounter.

"I'm parked right by the café. We should go now," he said, taking her by the shoulders and giving her a slight shake, emphasizing the urgency.

"I can't."

He held her at arm's length. In the darkness, she could barely make out his heavy eyebrows and angular Grecian nose, his features hidden by the hood. "Rose. You have to. There's no other choice. You said so yourself. You have to leave for your daughter's sake. My god, what they did to her, locking her up like that, was child abuse!"

She couldn't disagree. "I will leave, but not yet. I need to take Astraea into the woods tonight. She has to show me something."

"At this hour?" he exclaimed so loudly they probably heard him in the pavilion, where Cliff was winding down. Soon, the audience would start filing out, heading to the bonfire at the top of the hill, parading right past them. Rose was getting nervous.

"I'll explain later. I have to go now." She tried pulling away from his grip, but he kept holding on.

"Then let me go with you."

That would be a mistake. Rose knew those woods like she knew every sweet curve of her child's face. She'd been mushroom hunting under new moons more often than she could count. Ben would be a liability. He'd slow them down. Worse, he'd draw attention.

"Dan is coming to get me." Though she was uncertain if this was actually the case. "Yesterday, I left a message for him to fetch us tonight. He's going to take us home to Massachusetts."

Ben let go of her and took a step back. "Are you sure? Where is he?"

All she could do was shrug. "I hope he's in the parking lot."

"I didn't see him there."

Rose tried to stay calm. Fretting over Dan would serve no purpose. "I called him from your mother's. There was no way for him to call me back and confirm. I just have to assume he got the message and is doing what I asked. I can't imagine he wouldn't, knowing that he'd get a chance to be with Astraea."

"This is a mistake," Ben shot back angrily. "You need to call the authorities, Rose, and report what MacBeath and these assholes did to your daughter. You can't run away and pretend that nothing happened. These people need to be locked up for child abuse!"

She didn't reply. If only he would shut up or quiet down or, better yet, go home. She needed to hold Astraea and get the grim task ahead of them over with. Though she couldn't explain that to this man, an outsider who'd probably drag *her* to Child Services for believing her ten-year-old could sense the dead buried beneath her feet.

Ben slapped his forehead. "Oh, wait. Now I get it. You're not really leaving. You have no intention of leaving!" He was boldly shouting now. "You just wanted me to free your daughter so you could go on living with these fanatics. You know what? You're as bad as the rest of them." He stuck a finger in her face. "Actually, you're worse because you're her mother and you care more about your guru than . . ."

"What's going on?"

They swung around to find Ellen holding a torch, whose light blocked out the faces of the posse bringing up the flank. Facilitators in solstice costumes. Rose went weak. She had to think fast and couldn't. "It's nothing."

"It's not nothing," Ben countered. "You people are perverted child abusers who need to be put behind bars, all of you." He waved the finger that he'd been pointing in her face. "My father was a federal judge with friends in the highest levels of the FBI, and I'll see to it that they raid this fucking cult and round up all of you creeps if it's the last thing I do!"

Ellen wasn't cowed. "I order you off this property, Benjamin Winslow. Rose, go to your cabin. Dagda will deal with you tomorrow."

Ben took a step and was instantly surrounded by so many Facilitators, Rose lost sight of the top of his head as they dragged him across the crowded quad. She didn't bother to apologize to anyone, simply picked up the hem of her robe and headed toward her cabin where Astraea, hopefully, was waiting.

They'd have to leave tonight no question. Hopefully, Dan got the message and was coming for them.

Provided she hadn't burned that bridge too.

26

PRITI

"Ben was obsessed with Rose Santos. That's what kicked it all off, I think." Winded, Bogey pauses from scrambling over the next outcropping of rocks to catch his breath. He's been keeping up a fairly steady patter on the trail, Priti following silently, taking in his every word and wondering when they'll finally reach the camp, but nothing Bogey has been saying is making much sense.

The sun is lower in the sky, which has helped cool the temperature, but the air is still humid, the uneven ground beneath is pocked with mudholes, and the blackflies are merciless, just as he'd forewarned.

Priti had never encountered a blackfly until she came to Vermont. She and Ben went out one evening after they first arrived to play a few sets of tennis and returned covered in little red circles. An hour later, she was in agony from the irritation and itching. She even spiked a fever.

"They double dose you with an anticoagulant that keeps the blood flowing. Then they actually chew off your skin and suck out the blood," Ben explained, dabbing her inflamed sores with clear calamine lotion. "You don't feel it because the anticoagulant contains a numbing agent. How's that for evolution?"

Sucky, Priti thinks, fingering her sweaty hairline for possible bites. Every once in a while, she does a tick check on her legs, though Bogey assures her that isn't necessary. Deer don't hang around these woods, dropping their dangerous, Lyme-disease-infected parasites. Even they know enough to stay away.

Wiping sweat off her brow, she says, "Kicked what off?"

Bogey reaches for a boulder and pulls himself up. "You'll see."

"Oh, come on. This is whacked. Please tell me this isn't a prank." Because she does not have the patience or stamina in her pregnant state to take much more of this grueling trek.

"No prank." He leans over and holds out his hand so she can get up the boulder. Scrambling is tougher than she expected. The Pacific Coast Trail was a piece of cake in comparison, though she was a spry college student when she attempted that.

The boulder crested, Bogey stops at a slate sign that reads GLASTENBURY WILDERNESS AREA, along with a list of helpful dos and don'ts posted by the National Forest rangers. Beyond the sign is a relatively flat, well-trodden grass path through thick overgrowth in every hue of green. Tall trees as far as she can see. It's beautiful and, she notices, dead silent. No birds or buzzing flies. Even the steady breeze flows through the trees in utter quiet.

Something about this place is definitely not right. It even smells odd, of decay and rotting things.

"This is the old logging road to the Winslows' hunting camp." Bogey is like a tour guide, moving forward at an impressive stride. "Be careful. There are a lot of crumbling foundations underfoot. One wrong move and you can end up falling into a sinkhole or a mine shaft. Better use your poles."

Priti checks her phone. No service despite the higher elevation. Even her GPS is out of commission, the blue dot showing she is in Bennington, nowhere near here. Strange since they hadn't even driven through Bennington. At least, not that she is aware.

Rationally, she knows better than to fall for the Bennington Triangle myths. But how else to explain the chill in the air, the fact that her GPS isn't working?

Dammit. She should have left a note for Ben, who'll be beside himself when he returns from the Center to find her car there, but her gone and no clue as to where she went. She should have told someone. Why didn't she at least send a text?

"You can understand how people go missing here, can't you?" Bogey says over his shoulder, striding with confidence. "Aliens. Bigfoot. A time portal. Supposedly, a man-eating rock. All sorts of wacky theories to support the claim that this forest is so haunted, even the Abenaki refused to hunt here. And yet, it makes sense once you're on the trail. Or rather, once you get off the trail. The most weathered hiker could get lost and never be found in this wilderness if he didn't stick to the path."

She is desperately thirsty. "Do you mind if I take a sip of your camel?"

"Be my guest." He quits walking and waits for her to catch up to him. "Make sure you squirt it into your mouth. Don't suck on it."

Priti bristles. She doesn't need to be lectured about common hiking knowledge, but she doesn't bother arguing. She depresses the lever and squirts the warm water into her mouth, noticing as she does that there's a mosquito feasting on her right arm and Bogey is sporting two buck knives on his belt.

They keep trudging forward, Bogey every once in a while pausing to point out a crumbled foundation or the rusted bones of an old thresher. Priti is growing increasingly frustrated. They've been hiking for well over two hours and have yet to reach the cabin. Yet Bogey refuses to tell her why she needs to see the place for herself.

Finally, having had enough, she plunges the tips of her hiking poles into the earth and comes to a halt. "Bogey, stop. I don't see what this hike has to do with anything."

"I told you to be patient."

"I'm not taking another step unless you give me something concrete. This is ridiculous." She doesn't mean to come off so stubborn and ungrateful, but she is done!

Bogey lets out a long sigh. "If I tell you, you won't believe me. It's as simple as that. You need to see what's inside the cabin for yourself. You won't be convinced otherwise."

"Try me."

"Okay." He glances upward thoughtfully. "Those two women who went missing two years ago last June that we were talking about on the drive up. You remember them, right?"

She does. And she's growing weary of his obsession with them. "Willow Davis and Rory Johnston. Last seen with a figure wearing antlers. I still don't get what they have to do with Ben and Charlotte . . . or this slog up the mountain."

Bogey stabs the ground with his own pole. "Did you know they ended up on this trail headed down to Williamstown, Massachusetts? They might even have been standing where you are now when they were attacked."

"Geesh!" Gasping, she hops like she has hot feet, as if she's stepping on their corpses. "That wasn't on *Dark Cults*. Where'd you learn that?"

"This is what I'm about to show you. But we have to hurry." He nods down the trail. "It's gonna get darker before it gets lighter, you know." Without waiting for her response, he motors on.

More confused than ever, Priti quicksteps to catch up to Bogey, suddenly very well aware that she is completely defenseless. Not that she'd know what to do with a gun and knives if she had them.

"I still don't get what their disappearance has to do with Ben and Charlotte," she says.

"You mean their murders? Well, to answer that question, you have to understand Ben and Charlotte's history. I told you Ben was obsessed with Rose Santos, right?"

"Uh-huh." Though, again, Priti doesn't see the relevance.

"Ben and Rose had been having a fling. You know, older woman, younger man." Bogey chortles to himself. "Not that I was green with envy or anything."

Priti doubts this version of events. At lunch, Ben made it sound as though Rose crossed his radar only when the accountants informed him of the huge sums Genevieve had been paying her. There was no indication of a romantic relationship. Actually, if anything, the opposite.

"The weekend of her murder, Rose broke up with Ben without warning," Bogey continues. "He went to the Center that night because she called and asked for his help. Seems the cultists had taken her daughter and locked her away. Why? I'm not sure anyone knows. At any rate, Ben freed her daughter, and after that heroic act is when she dumped him, claimed she was leaving the cult, going back to her husband in Massachusetts, and giving her marriage another go. According to Charlotte, Ben didn't take it well."

Priti keeps walking. Up ahead is a clearing. Maybe they've reached the cabin.

"The cultists kicked him out of the Center. Ordered him never to return. Ben sat in his car, stewing with rage, and then, consumed with jealousy, went after her."

Priti stops, her mouth instantly going dry as sandpaper. "What do you mean, after her?"

"I mean, he followed Rose into the woods outside the Center, pleaded with her to reconsider, and when she told him to get lost, that's when he put his hands around her throat and strangled her until she passed out. Then he bashed her head in with a rock."

No. No. This can't be true. Even if he turned up at Charlotte's with blood-spattered clothes, there had to be a rational explanation. Ben never would have acted so violently—or with such strength. This was a man who cringed when his mother's mousetrap caught a rodent. Priti had to dump it in the trash because he couldn't stand the sight of its broken body. The suggestion that he would have strangled Rose and then bashed her head in with a rock was absurd. *Crazy.*

So was Bogey.

"Bullshit," Priti declares, not budging an inch. "If that's true, then why haven't you gone to the police?"

"Hearsay. Everything I just told you came straight from Charlotte, and she'd never back me up if I took that to law enforcement. Those two have been best friends and playmates since nursery school. She gave a sworn alibi to the cops that Ben was with her the entire night, and she'd be in almost as much trouble as Ben if the truth came to light."

Suddenly, the forest begins spinning. Priti feels like she's pressed against the wall of an amusement park Turkish Twist. She tries to find her center and can't. Bogey is mistaken. He misunderstood. Charlotte was fucking with him. There was no blood, never was. Those are the only logical explanations.

Bogey continues, determined to make his case. "The reason why Ben and Charlotte went to Boston was because for the first time they knew who Rose Santos's daughter was and where she lived." A vee of sweat is darkening his navy T-shirt. "As the only living witness, Stella O'Neill alone has the power to put them away, and they are not going to let that happen, not after what they've done."

Priti refuses to accept Bogey's theory. He is simply unaware of the facts. "Ben went there to warn Stella and to explain what he saw the night her mother was murdered. Only Stella wouldn't answer the door."

"Awww, Priti. The dutiful trad wife, gullibly believing in her husband the provider." Bogey clicks his tongue. "Sweetie, Ben didn't make a secret trip to visit the only living witness to the murder he committed because he wanted to have a chitchat. He was trying to save his ass by shutting up the witness . . . permanently. And for good reason. Rose Santos isn't the only woman he's killed, as my dear wife is very well aware."

Oh, forget it. This is nuts, Priti thinks. This whole hike has been a mistake. If she hadn't driven Genevieve to church, if she hadn't run into Bogey, they wouldn't be here in the middle of nowhere having this stupid argument. It's like she's in a bad dream except she can't wake up because she's already awake.

"The cabin's right through that stand of maples. See?" Bogey crouches and points to where, sure enough, a rough-hewn shack is barely visible between the leaves. "That's where you'll finally see what I saw—evidence. Didn't I say you wouldn't believe me unless you saw for yourself?"

Priti takes a step forward, but Bogey swings out a hiking pole to stop her. "Not quite yet. First, you have to check this out." He waves his hiking pole toward a circular wall constructed of fieldstones. "Prepare yourself, Priti. Like I warned, this is not for the faint of heart. Last week when Charlotte thought I was asleep, I overheard a conversation she had with your husband. The true-crime episode had just aired and she was beside herself, unable to sleep, pacing the floor downstairs, the whole nine yards."

Ben hadn't been sleeping last week, too, come to think of it. He wasn't a good sleeper anyway, often working on programs in the wee hours. But this latest spate of insomnia was different. He wasn't hyped on a project, he was anxious, biting his nails and snapping at her over the least little thing. Priti blamed the financial woes at HeadFake, that key investors were jumping ship. But maybe that wasn't the real reason he was on edge.

Because she'd heard him talking on the phone at 3:00 a.m. too. Maybe Bogey really is onto something. "Go on."

"Charlotte specifically said, 'Those two addicts were ready to rob us blind and slit our throats when they found us in the cabin that night. We did what we had to do for our survival and I'm not sorry.' Then, and this was chilling, lemme tell you, she said, 'We've got to get their bodies out of that well if the cops come after us on the Santos murder.'" Bogey's eyes begin to water. "Trust me, Priti, I didn't want to believe it either. I don't even care if Charlotte and Ben are having an . . . you know. I love her. She's the best thing that ever happened to me. Who knew a loser like Bogey Grovey would end up with Charlotte Winslow? But I had to check for myself. So while those two were in Boston, I hiked up here."

Clicking on a flashlight, Bogey directs the beam down into the well. "Look."

Priti doesn't want to. The prospect of seeing actual corpses is simply too much. The possibility that Bogey might not be lying is too daunting. Could it be true that Ben has killed three times and gotten away with it?

If so, then her entire world is shattered.

She closes her eyes, already burning with tears, and puts out a hand. "Let's just go, Bogey. Let's leave this place, hike back, and drive directly to the police. Let them take it from here."

"I wish I could," Bogey says with a regretful smile. "But I'm afraid it's too late."

"That's not true. It's almost the longest day of the year." Priti gestures to the thin sunlight filtering through the leafy canopy. "If we hurry, we can make it to the car by dark."

"You're not getting it. No one's going to find out about these bodies, not if I can help it. Why do you think I brought you here?"

At that horrifying moment, Priti realizes he's no longer holding a flashlight in his hand. He's holding his gun. Charlotte's gun.

Now pointed directly at her—and Ben's unborn child.

27

STELLA

JUNE 18, 2023

I've been in plenty of forests since I was ten. Dad was eager to make sure I didn't develop a phobia after my bad experience at the Center, so as a kid we'd often drive to Walden Pond and take nature walks. Some of my happiest memories are of padding on the pine-needle paths, hand in hand with Dad amid chattering blackbirds and the occasional warble of the Baltimore oriole. It was also some of the only times I was allowed out of the house.

We'd find a spot far from the unsafe crowds and read side by side on our respective towels, periodically flicking off black ants after my Doritos. When it got hot, I'd jump in the clear, fresh water, and sometimes we'd stop for ice cream on the way home. Thanks to him, I've never been afraid of dark forests, though considering my past, I have every reason to be.

Like now.

These are not the sunny, dappled pine woods of Walden Pond. Once past the fence, the trees and thick undergrowth seem to close in on us in a threatening manner. Here the path isn't sandy and covered by dry pine needles. It's rocky and, in places, swampy, mosquitoes and biting flies rising from puddles Fig and I have to stretch our legs to cross.

Green moss covers rotted logs and rocks protecting lush ferns and unfurling dark-green fiddleheads. And there are mushrooms. Lots and lots of mushrooms. Coral-colored hen of the woods climb old stumps. Golden chanterelles and pink lobster. Brown puffballs, smoky with spores, and the delicate white stalks of powerfully poisonous death caps. Also, spongy morels.

The morels trigger the first flashback.

I remember Mama waking me that night from a sleep so sound it couldn't have been natural. It's possible Ellen or someone slipped a sedative into the milk they gave me in the Chi Chamber to ensure I wouldn't alarm the solstice visitors by screaming through the door slot to be let out. That's also why I barely remember that hot metal prison or how I got out of there. All I recall is my mother shaking me awake in the dark cabin, urging me to hurry.

I didn't want to leave. I wanted to stay warm and cozy in my own bed. "Why now?" I probably asked.

"Because we're going mushroom hunting."

I loved hunting mushrooms with Mama in the middle of the night. Bundling up and heading into the woods with nothing but a basket, a trowel, and a lantern was our special bonding moment. Mama claimed coveted morels lit up under a full moon and hid during the day. Looking back, I doubt that was true. I think she simply didn't want the other Diviners to discover her secret sources.

"No need to foil your shoes," she said, tying on my sneakers to speed up the process. For some reason, I was still sleeping in my shorts and lucky T-shirt, as I recall. "You'll be fine."

Really? I'd gone into the woods the day before with a new girl, the daughter of a solstice guest, and gotten into trouble for not wearing my foil. The bad thing that happened in Mrs. Winslow's garden had been repeated in the woods, except a hundred times worse, as I recall, and Mama was not pleased.

This grave in the woods was different from the "mischief makers" Mama said lived under the lilies of the valley in Genevieve Winslow's garden. This one was newly dug, the overturned soil springy instead of hard, and what lay beneath exuded violent energy that was far more powerful than anything I'd encountered before. It was a woman, her corpse vibrating with outrage. She was furious and vengeful, but also pleading for help.

I was so scared that I tried to run away, except at first I couldn't. I fell as if I'd been tripped, falling face forward onto the pile of leaves and debris that had been raked over the small hill. Her pull was magnetic, and she refused to let me go. To this day, I have nightmares.

"You okay?"

Fig's question is like a lifeline, hauling me up from the deep, dark depths of my repressed memories to the surface of here and now. I'm surprised to find I'm on the ground, propped up against a birch, the gray light of evening casting patterns on the forest floor.

"I was having a flashback." I can feel the beginning of a headache pressing against my temples and no wonder. Having not had enough water in the Chi Chamber, I'm very likely dehydrated.

Fig kneels and hands me a bottle of seltzer. "Here. When did you last eat?"

Unscrewing the plastic cap, I take a swig, the bubbles making me burp. "When Rowan stopped by with lunch." I'd kill for a sandwich, I realize. I'm starved. Handing the bottle back to her, I say, "Thanks. That helps. Sorry. I don't know what happened."

"Unprocessed trauma. That's what happened. Totally understandable. I'm sure you'd rather be anywhere but here, but now's our opportunity, when everyone's at whatever's going on at that pavilion. Let's keep going." She extends a hand and pulls me to standing.

I brush myself off and assess the woods, the path barely visible in the thicket. "What was my mother thinking bringing me out to a place like this in the middle of the night?"

"Welp, that's the big question, isn't it? Cops can't answer it. *Dark Cults* couldn't answer it. That's why everyone's looking to you."

"And that's why we're here."

"Yup." Fig gives me a quick hug. "Three hours until the sun sets. We don't want to be stuck out here when it gets dark."

It's already dark. I have the feeling even on a bright sunny morning this forest would be shaded thanks to the thick canopy overhead. Still, there's nothing to be gained from sitting around having flashbacks. So I turn my attention to the task. "Something that sticks out in my memory—aside from the antlered man—is a turtle."

"A turtle?" Fig knits her brows. "Like in a pond?"

"No. I don't think so. Just a turtle. That's it. The little girl I was with earlier that day wanted me to show it to her. That's why we were here."

Fig surveys the area. "You know, the Native Americans are really into turtles. You ever read the children's book called *Old Turtle*? It's excellent. The author, Douglas Wood, was inspired by Native American legends about turtles, including the creation story about turtle island, otherwise known as America. Anyway, I'm wondering, if your turtle isn't a real turtle, then maybe it's an Indigenous peoples' holy symbol."

Stay here, Astraea. Let me find the turtle, and I'll come and fetch you. At least they put her in a sacred spot.

Mama's voice is crystal clear and so real it's as though she's right by my side. "Shit, I could swear she just spoke."

"Who?"

"My mother. No, seriously." I recount her words flowing back to me from decades long gone as if she'd whispered them in my ear just now. "A sacred turtle."

"Hah. Then I was right!" Fig does a fist pump.

"The Abenaki were all over these parts and prized turtles as sacred creatures. They sometimes carved turtles in totem poles or . . ."

"Assembled rock formations. That's it! The grave you walked on is near an Abenaki turtle. Slam dunk!" She raises her hand for a high five, but I can't slap it.

"Hardly a slam dunk. It's getting dark. How are we gonna find a bunch of rocks positioned in the shape of a turtle?"

"Um, would *that* be a turtle?"

I follow to where she's pointing to the left and up a rise, where a smooth domed boulder sticks out of the hillside, two smaller boulders on either side, and what could be construed as a beak-like head in front. Once I see it, I can't unsee it.

"That's a turtle all right," I agree, excited.

"Pretty big one too. Come on. It'll take us a while to get there."

Swinging her flashlight like a machete, Fig takes the lead, swiping away ferns and branches, busting through spiderwebs and sharp brambles as we go off the trail. Somehow the children's librarian in the patchwork skirts and treasured collection of delicate mismatched china has the bushwhacking skills of an Australian crocodile hunter.

However, I fear we're making a mistake going off trail. That's a dangerous move when you're in twenty-two thousand acres of thick wilderness, though I'm not sure we have a choice, since the path would lead us in the opposite direction.

"Can I ask you a personal question?" I say as Fig easily lifts a tree limb for me to duck under. "Why are you doing this?"

"Doing what?" She lets the limb fall and returns to the charge.

"You could have just told my father when he called that you

hadn't heard from me and that would've been that. Instead, you drove all the way down from Boston, took care of Heather's car, then tracked down Ben Winslow, and now you're here picking off slugs and getting the shit bitten out of you by mosquitoes . . . Why?"

"So, there's a funny thing called friendship. Ever hear of it?"

I'm silent and skeptical as we trudge on.

"Oh, guess you haven't. Let me fill you in." She swats at a hatchling of gnats and coughs. "Keep your mouth closed. Ugh. Anyway, I aspire to be what one calls a true friend. I'm fairly confident you don't have any true friends and never have because you grew up as a shut-in. This is what true friends do, Stella. They help each other out. See how that works?"

"I had friends when I was living here. Rowan was one, kind of."

Fig slices through a sticky spiderweb. "Rowan was a cool older boy you had a crush on. Pro tip, that's not the same. Cool older boys are usually interested in cool older girls or guys and are actually more interested in themselves and what bones they can break by taking out their immortality for a test drive and have no idea how to shake off ten-year-old girls who follow them around like puppies."

That makes me laugh. "Yeah, that was probably little me. A tagalong."

We arrive at a massive fallen tree that's too large to climb over and too low to the ground to climb under. "This is my chance to try out this friendship stuff of which you speak so highly, Figurina." Linking my hands, I bend down. "I'll give you a boost."

"Why, thank you, ma'am." Fig steps on my hands with her clodhopper boots, nearly breaking my fingers and my back as she hoists herself over the tree. Over the edge, she grabs each of my forearms, and with more strength than I'd have predicted, hauls me over. I scramble, slipping in my sneakers, and make it to the top of the tree.

"Slide down," Fig says. "Your ass will be covered in moss, but that's okay."

Except it's not.

As soon as my foot touches the ground, I'm overcome by a great swelling of grief, a gut-wrenching sadness I haven't felt since Dad told me in the hospital I'd never see my mother again. And I know why.

Directly ahead, a babbling brook snakes down from the hillside, coincidentally—or not—near the turtle rockface. I have been here before, on this very spot, the slim moonlight illuminating the white pieces of Mama's skull that had been split so neatly in two.

Fig reaches out to steady me. "Jesus, Stell. You look like you've seen a ghost!"

"I have." My breath is so shallow I can hardly speak as I fight off the images dive-bombing my mind. "This is where my mother was murdered."

Her jaw drops as she takes another look at the stream. "For real?"

The sensation I'm getting from the earth isn't like anything I've had before. The only way to describe it is I'm on a river of sadness. And blood. "For real."

"Oh my gosh." Wrapping me in her pillowy arms, Fig touches her head against mine. "I'm so sorry. This must be so hard for you."

"It's necessary." I break from her grasp and smile at her gratefully. "I'm so glad you're with me. I'm not sure I could handle what I'm feeling alone."

"You've been handling a lot alone, Stella. I have no idea how you kept all of this . . . *shit* . . . inside you. Who knew the quiet archivist on the second floor was dealing with so much pain? You're pretty amazing to be as together as you are. You know that, right?"

Now I'm crying. Crap.

Fig is sensitive enough to look the other way, toward the rock-face. "Well, I think that definitely answers why your mother dragged you out here in the middle of the night. She'd have made it to the turtle . . ."

"If she hadn't been killed."

"You told her about the grave, and she was determined to find it. Unfortunately, she never lived to be able to bring you to this spot."

"Which meant it was never found. Until now."

Kicking off my sneakers, I take the lead this time, my vision blurry with tears of grief and self-pity as I head toward the turtle, my tender feet unaccustomed to the rough surface. It makes total sense that that's where two children were headed. The turtle is a tempting climb, better than a rock wall. I bet cult kids have been all over this, scrambling like mountain goats racing to see who could get to the top first.

I can see it now, everything that happened that day twenty years ago. I can see the little girl with the curls daring me to scale the rockface. I remember being slightly frightened, but also not wanting to be a wimp. I remember putting one foot on the turtle's foot and another on the ground and . . .

Gotcha.

The shock that runs up my calves makes the hairs on my arms stand on end, literally. My bare foot is stuck in place as the icy fingers grab hold of my toes, then my ankles, pulling me downward. Though the ground now is hard and covered with debris, I am in danger of being yanked into her grave. I am breathless.

Cerise has found me—again—and this time she's not letting go.

"Stell?" Fig's voice comes from far away as I try to extricate my foot and can't. When I try to step forward with my left, I find she's gotten hold of that too.

Get. Me. Out!

Did Cerise actually speak those words or am I going insane? I can't believe I'm asking this question. Of course I'm insane. *This* is insane. I scratch my ankles, trying to tear off her claws.

"Honey. What the hell . . . ?" Fig's got me by the arm, pulling me toward her. But it's like I'm in quicksand or a leg trap. I'm stuck.

Free me. Freeeeeeee me.

"You can't feel it?" I ask, since Fig's right beside me on the same desecrated ground.

She shakes her head. "So, this is it, huh? This is what you've been talking about? This is a . . ."

"Grave. Cerise's grave. My mother's friend. I can even hear her talking to me. Her voice is so familiar. She used to read me bedtime stories!"

Fig smiles weakly. I don't know if she completely buys what's going on, but I can tell she's worried. "What's old Cerise saying?"

"She wants me to free her."

"I bet. Tell her we'll get right on it." Fig gives a hard tug and I go flying. As soon as I'm out of the corpse's clutches, I scramble onto the rocks and go back to scratching and scratching. I scratch so hard, tiny drops of red blood erupt through my skin and stream down my foot. I can't rid myself of the sensation, even after I pull on my socks and lined shoes.

Fig, meanwhile, has dropped to her knees and is clearing leaves and debris from where I was standing.

"That won't do any good. She's too far down. The Diviners didn't want some animal digging her up. They put her at least six feet under. We'll need a shovel."

"Probably," chimes in a voice from overhead.

Rowan is sitting at the top of the rockface, swinging his legs. What's he doing here?

"What are you doing up there?" Fig asks, shielding her eyes to watch him descend like a monkey, hopping from rock to rock.

"Following you." He jumps down and brushes off his hands. "I grew up in these woods, and I hate to inform you ladies that there's a way easier path to this place than the slog you took. There's a lookout up there with a maintained trail that goes right back to the Center. It's very popular."

Fuck.

"You remember Rowan, the guy outside my apartment when you came to pick me up the other day," I say, feeling stupid that we went through all that effort for nothing. This is it. It's over. Rowan's going to march us back to the Center, and Cerise will be stuck here forever.

"I remember Rowan." Fig wipes sweat off her brow. "Hipster cultist."

"Hey, I resent that. I am not a hipster."

The joke falls flat. Only Rowan's grinning.

"How'd you know this is where we'd be?" I ask.

"Uhm, 'cause that's what you said this afternoon. You said, I want to go into the forest and find whatever it was that's buried in there. Why didn't you wait for me?"

"Because you were supposed to show up and you never did," I answer hotly. "Pardon me for not wanting to stick around in a sweltering metal box."

"Okay, okay." Fig holds up her filthy hands, her nails already caked in dirt. "I don't know what's going on, and frankly, I don't care. I'm filthy and my boots are muddy and my socks are wet. I'm really uncomfortable, so can we get this over with?"

Rowan strokes his five o'clock shadow. "You sure this is the spot?"

I show him my red and raw ankles. "Check this out. I had to claw off her fingers."

"Seriously. She couldn't move," Fig says. "It's like she was in quicksand."

"Wowza." He squints at my bloodied feet and curls his lips in disgust. "So, you definitely know who it is?"

"Cerise. My mother's friend. Her grave was what Mama was trying to find the night she was murdered. I'd found it earlier in the day, I guess."

Going over to the fallen tree near where my mother was killed, he breaks off a branch that's as long as a broom handle and returns. "Tell me where to stick it."

Fig and I exchange looks. She has to bite her lower lip to keep from answering.

"Right there." I point to the area Fig cleared. "Try it."

Rowan drives the branch into the ground. I'm surprised it hasn't broken, considering the force he's using. "No telling how far we've got to go and what we'll find." A dark patch of sweat is darkening the front of his 2023 Summer Solstice orange T-shirt.

Orange.

It hadn't crossed my mind until now that Rowan could be a Seeker desperate for an upgrade. And wouldn't turning me in to Cliff MacBeath be a sweet prize? If so, then we are well and truly fucked.

"What's that?" Fig leans close and reaches into the hole Rowan's made. I have to give her credit. It'd be a cold day in hell before I reach into what might be someone's grave. Removing her hand, she unclenches her fingers and reveals a glittering object in her palm.

It's a cherry-red, six-sided quartz pendulum.

"It looks exactly like yours," she says, lifting her face to me in curiosity. "I thought you said your mother gave it to you?"

I touch mine to make sure it's still around my neck. "She did. The one you're holding is a darker pink."

Fig smiles.

"It's . . . cerise."

We all look up to find none other than a short, gray-haired

woman in a white robe sighting a rifle in my direction. Oh my God. I haven't seen that witch since my last nightmare. Mean Ellen.

My insides instantly turn to jelly.

"Excellent work," Ellen says dryly. "You did exactly what I told you to do and let her lead us to the site. Dagda will be very pleased if you do the honors and finish them off."

With that, she tosses the rifle down not to Rowan, but to my new best friend, Fig.

28

PRITI

JUNE 18, 2023

Funny how a pointed pistol stops time, Priti thinks, the dire reality of the situation slowly settling into her consciousness. Bogey Grovey, the good-natured butt of everyone's jokes, was crafty enough to lure her to the most godforsaken, desolate part of Vermont to kill her the same way he obviously murdered those two innocent hikers and planted their bodies conveniently near the Winslow family cabin. And she didn't even make it hard for him.

No, this has to be a prank. A tasteless one, that's for sure, but it can't be real. *Can it?*

"Stop kidding around, Bogey," she says, forcing a casual chuckle. "You're scaring the shit out of me, you know."

"I didn't want to have to do this." Bogey's bulbous head is bathed in perspiration that is running down his beet-red neck. He looks like a fatted cow on the verge of a heart attack. Eyes bulging. Lower lip quivering. Hand shaking. "But I don't see much of a choice."

Shit. This is for real. She can hardly believe it, her disbelief quickly turning into anger at herself. All those true-crime shows she's inhaled over the years, and she falls for a textbook ploy—the promise of photos, accepting a ride with a stranger, going to a second location. Now she's going to end up a statistic, a line in Ben's Wikipedia page.

Ben Winslow's second wife, Priti Suryanarayana, a former runway model, was found dead in an abandoned cistern in southern Vermont.

No one will care that she'd majored in history at Berkeley before catching the attention of the most prestigious modeling agency in LA. Her love of animals, her desire to be a mother, her legendary lemon tart, her entire life will be overshadowed by her untimely and violent death.

She's alone and isolated in a dangerously remote part of a wilderness so vast, people have disappeared in it and never been found. Her cell phone has no service, which Bogey was well aware would be the case when he devised his plan. She didn't tell Ben where she was going. She's made every foolish mistake in the book.

This is what she gets for being suspicious of her husband, for sneaking around and investigating him behind his back. She could simply have asked him about Charlotte. Ben would have given her an honest answer . . . eventually. As for the bodies supposedly at the bottom of the well, she's not about to take a chance and peer down. That's what Bogey wants her to do. It'll make his job so much easier.

Appeal to his humanity, Priti thinks, raising her hands. "I don't want any trouble, Bogey. If you don't want to go to the cops with whatever or whomever is in that well, that's okay. I get it."

"Do you? I don't think you do." Swiping his forearm across his brow, he takes a step closer.

She takes a step back, her feet crunching on the overgrowth, leaving her little room. It feels like the forest is closing in around her.

"You would have found out about Ben flipping out and going all mental on that psychic who was scamming him and his mother.

Ben told Char that night he didn't do it, but she figured out the truth. His clothes were covered in blood, for Christ's sake. If my wife hadn't taken action and washed them, your husband would be on death row."

There's no death row in Vermont, Priti thinks stupidly, before zeroing in on the key point. Ben told Charlotte he didn't kill Rose Santos. Ben must have gone into the woods after Rose, found her dead, freaked, and ran. He assumed he would have been busted for murder because everyone had seen them argue earlier. That's why he went to Charlotte looking for an alibi, and Charlotte lied on his behalf. It makes sense, but more importantly . . . her husband is innocent.

And if he didn't kill Rose, then surely he didn't kill Rory Davis and Willow Johnston. Because her husband is not a murderer. Never was. Never will be.

Vindicated and relieved, Priti feels a surge of empowerment. This is going to be okay. She and Ben are going to be just fine. All she needs to do now is assure Bogey she won't snitch to the cops. "Look. If Ben said he didn't murder Rose Santos, then there's no reason to go to the police."

Bogey also takes a step backward, like he's scared of her, an unarmed pregnant woman. "You didn't ask me about the clothes. Charlotte kept his bloodied socks as collateral in case Ben didn't do what she wanted."

"You mean marry her?"

He nods. "She was head over heels about the guy, and Ben, well, he was raised to do the right thing, I guess. He felt he owed Charlotte a ring and so he popped the question. It was the least he could do to repay her for saving his life, in a way."

The evening breeze has turned into a stiffer wind, sending green leaves fluttering, tree limbs bowing. If only one would fall on Bogey, that would solve all her problems.

As if reading her thoughts, Bogey cocks Charlotte's pistol and lifts his chin. "But the marriage ended because they got married too young." He shrugs. "Char grew bored. Ben didn't want to do any of the things she wanted to do, like throw big parties or hit the clubs. His idea of fine dining was Chinese takeout while working at the computer. She was tired of sitting at home while he worked on HeadFake and being ignored. Turns out, your rock-star husband is a big ole nerd."

Exactly why she loves him, Priti thinks, feeling a rush of warm feelings as she flashes back to a particularly pivotal moment in their relationship. It was after their third date, when they chatted so long about his plans for HeadFake they were startled to find the windows in his living room turning pink from a breaking dawn. She loves when Ben's in his creative zone, when he's so charged she can't help but be caught up in his enthusiasm. It's fun. It's thrilling. How Charlotte could find his innovations dull is beyond her.

"Bogey, so far nothing you've said is a reason to kill me. My husband's innocent. I'm not going to the cops. I don't get it."

This time he steps so close, the gun barrel is mere inches from her navel. "What about me?"

She shakes her head, not following. "What about you?"

"Exactly. What about me? No one cares, do they?"

Oh, dear. Now she's beginning to understand. Bogey has more than a chip on his shoulder; it's a boulder. "Everyone loves you. I don't know what you're talking about."

"Yeah? Then consider my nickname, Bogey Grovey. You know who came up with that? Your fucking husband, that's who. Stuck with me through high school, college, even now. People have forgotten that I was named Robert Asa Grover after a great-great-great uncle who was a famous senator. I've traced my ancestry back to England before the Norman Conquest. There's more blue blood in my right toe than in your husband's entire body, and yet he had the audacity to make my life hell by calling me . . . *Bogey Grovey?*"

Priti lowers her lids and silently curses Ben for his adolescent cruelty. "I'm sorry."

"Sorry doesn't cut it. That nickname cursed me. No one respects a man called 'Bogey.' I vowed to get even with the sonofabitch someday and goddamn if I didn't."

The gun is quivering. If only she had the nerve to reach out and grab it.

"I started by picking up his leftovers. Charlotte was a prize. It put me in another category. I thought she'd be enough. Then, after a few too many Christmas champagnes, she told me about the bloody socks and how she lied. I didn't stop hunting for those socks until I found them in the last place the cops would look. Let's just say there was only one other boy Char loved as much as Ben and that was her cat, Snowball, God rest his soul."

He dug up the grave of her pet cat? Priti lowers her aching arms to clutch her stomach in pretend nausea. "Oh, that is so gross."

"That was only the beginning." Bogey seems not to have noticed how close her hands are to the barrel because he doesn't move, just keeps on talking. "I needed more. Your mother-in-law's scam psychic was killed too long ago to make headlines.

"So, when your husband was in town for his annual visit to Dutton two years ago, it just so happened I came across a couple of dirty hikers fresh from the Center's solstice celebration, thumbing for a ride on Route 7. Couldn't have been much past six a.m. The highway was deserted and, well, they were easy pickings. I offered them free lodging, a sweet camp owned by a friend of mine who lived in California and never visited. They hopped in the car, no questions asked. You were almost as bad."

He is disgusting. It's all Priti can do not to reach out and kick him in the groin. She hates him. Hates every aspect of his being, from his bulbous alcoholic nose to his rotted core. She would leap at the chance to strangle him, if she could summon the courage.

"I took care of them just like I'm gonna take care of you." He nods over his shoulder to the well. "Ben bought Charlotte a pistol for protection when they were in LA. It's registered to him in California."

They simultaneously look at the gun. "It won't take much for the cops to find their DNA in your vehicle," Priti says.

"Or in the Volvo Ben drove that summer, before you came on the scene and he had to rent another car. Do you know how easy it was to plant those skanks' earrings without anyone being any the wiser? Bet they're still there.

"I heard Ben was planning to sell the car 'cause he sent his mother to Hamden House. That bothered me. Then *Dark Cults* came out with the 'Triangle Three' episode. I knew the time had come to act. I was gonna anonymously post a teaser online, but then you showed up at church this morning, and I realized you'd be the icing on the cake. Pretty model and wife of murder suspect disappears? Yes, please!"

There is no cogitation about what takes place next. Priti doesn't plot out her next move. To do so would sow doubt and doubt would not help. Her foot seemingly rises on its own, straight into Bogey's crotch as she reaches for the gun . . .

. . . and misses.

The shot that rings out is deafening, the bullet whizzing past her ear before she can comprehend that Bogey has done the inconceivable. The crack it makes striking the tree above them is only half as earth-shattering as the thunder that follows.

"What the . . . ?" Bogey's weak chin falls in bewilderment as he looks up to find the ten-foot limb of a rotted ash tree break off and crash into his body with such force his shoulder snaps back like a rubber band before he falls flat on the ground, the top of his head grazing the old well, leaving a nice red slick of blood. Bogey's eyes roll back so far, only their whites are visible.

Priti doesn't bother to check his vitals. With superhuman force, she lifts the heavy limb off his chest and tosses it aside. Then she kicks the pistol into the underbrush. Finally, praying for strength and pelvic resilience, she squats down, hooks her arms under his knees, and stands, forcing first his feet, then his legs, then his torso over the edge of the stone cistern, his body landing with a thud and a crunch.

Bracing herself for the worst, she bends over the rock wall and assesses what's below. The cistern has been filled in over the years with stones, mud, leaf litter, and a few pieces of trash, so that the bottom is only about ten feet down. On top of that mess lies Bogey, splayed like a Gumby who lost his wires, his feet twitching.

No one in that pit, either dead or with a broken shoulder, has a chance of getting out.

The question now is whether she can make it down the mountain to safety before this forest turns pitch black.

Using two rocks to mark the spot where the gun's hidden, she grabs Bogey's backpack and heads down the mountain, taking the same trail. She doesn't think about what she saw at the bottom of the cistern, the scrap of a red flannel shirt peeking out from under the debris next to Bogey. She doesn't think about Bogey or Ben or Charlotte or the rapidly dividing cells in her womb. She just walks, one foot in front of the other, and doesn't think. As darkness falls, the trail grows fainter and fainter. Only an hour remains until sunset. If she's not at the trailhead by then, she'll have to stop where she is and make camp for the night and pray that somehow, she and this precious fetus survive until dawn.

29

STELLA

JUNE 18, 2023

"Eeeeeep!" Fig shrieks in horror at the sight of the long black gun that's landed in her arms, immediately letting it fall to the ground.

"Thank you." Rowan swiftly snatches it, cocks it, and aims it directly at me.

"Bad throw," Mean Ellen says dryly.

I could kill Fig for dropping the gun, though I am glad she's not a traitor. That weapon really could have come in handy.

Sorry, she mouths, her face scrunched up like she's about to cry.

"It's not your fault. It's mine. You're not even supposed to be here, Fig."

"SHUT UP!" Rowan shouts, skittishly waving the rifle between us. He looks about as comfortable holding it as Fig was. He might be a Diviner fueled by Cliff MacBeath's Kool-Aid, but he's no killer. That's what I have to emphasize.

Slowly raising my hands, I say evenly, "You don't want to commit murder, Rowan. Think of all the negative energy that . . ."

"Don't listen to her," Ellen barks. "She's toxic. She'll ruin us all with her dark power."

Dark power. *Really?* That's a bit over the top. "This isn't a D and D game, Ellen," I shoot back. "I'm standing on the corpse of my mother's best friend. You guys killed and buried her twenty years ago and now you think doing the same to us will hide that fact? It's too late. Everyone knows I'm here."

This is not true. No one knows I'm here, aside from Ben Winslow, and I don't trust him one little bit.

Though there's one person who might get us out of this mess—Fig's wife, Mel. The question is whether she's on the ball or killing time in a café waiting for word from Fig to pick us up. I glance at Fig, who's gone all to pieces and is sobbing like a baby. I wish she'd get a grip and text 911 on her cell. Service might be shoddy, but it'd be worth making the effort.

"Don't move," Rowan says, continuing to swing the rifle back and forth like a lawn sprinkler. "Stay exactly where you are or I'll shoot."

Honestly, bunnies are more threatening.

"This is ridiculous." Ellen proceeds to half jump, half slide down the outcropping with confidence. She's a tough old bird, I'll give her that. Decades of hiking through these woods and living off the land have left her with short nails and firm calves. She might be in her fifties, but she's fit.

Rowan stands back to give her space. The color's returned to his features, a little boy relieved Mommy has come to his rescue, perhaps. Ellen lands, brushes off her hands, and reaches for the gun. "Give me that."

Once she gets hold of the gun, we're done for, and I can't let that happen. Stupidly, I jump off the rock and throw myself at Rowan just as he raises the rifle and, barely missing my skull, brings it down on Ellen's head with a thunderous whump. She lets out a squawk of surprise. Her arms fly outward, and she collapses right on top of me.

"Oh my god, I'm so sorry! I could have killed you!" Rowan shoves her off me. Ellen rolls over onto the dirt with a groan. "You okay, Astraea?" Leaning close, he says, "Don't go. I'm gonna need help keeping her down."

I'm totally confused. I can't tell if this is a line to save his own skin or if he's joined our side. Whatever, I wriggle up and, being careful to avoid Cerise's grave, push him so hard, he loses his tentative grip on the rifle.

Before I can grab it, Ellen extends an arm and snags the butt. She would have kept her hold on it if Fig hadn't brought her clod-hopper boot down hard on Ellen's wrist with a satisfying crunch of snapping bone.

Aaaaayyy! Ellen writhes in agony as she lets out a moan of pain. In an instant, her complexion goes from ruddy to deathly white as she rotates from side to side, clutching her flopping hand. A trickle of blood from the head wound is running down her left temple. The scene is so gruesome, all I can do is gape in horrified fascination.

"Shit!" Fig seems more surprised than any of us. Wiping away her tears, she says, "I'm so sorry. That was a lot harder than I expected."

"You fucker!" Ellen cries, still thrashing in pain, her white robe filthy with ground-in dirt. "You fucking, fucker. I don't have health insurance. Who's gonna pay for the hospital bill?"

"How about your boss?" I say without sympathy. "Seems like he has plenty of cash."

"No one move!"

At first, I assume Rowan said this, but then I see Fig's face is raised upward. There against the fading light at the top of the outcropping are two Vermont state troopers. I must be hallucinating, because neither Fig nor I called 911. Rowan's right. It's a popular trail.

"On the ground," a trooper commands, hopping down the rock like a nimble mountain goat. "All of you."

We do as they say. "This isn't our fault," Fig protests. "They tried to kill us!"

The cops aren't taking any chances, securing the rifle and ordering us to put our hands on our heads. To Ellen he says, "Ma'am, are you okay?"

Ellen suddenly and annoyingly looks twenty years older than her fifty or so years. "Thank you, officer," she says with a whimper. "I do believe I should go to the hospital. I've been attacked by these hooligans."

"Uh-huh." The trooper calls up to his buddy still perched above us, gun pointed in case there's funny business below. "We've got a ten-thirty-five requesting a ten-fifty-two and backup stat. Okay, I'm going to ask all of you to stay where you are until the EMTs arrive. Don't move. Which one of you is Figurina DiTolla?"

"That's me," Fig mumbles into the dirt.

"Your wife asked us to check on you. Seemed to be under the impression you were in some sort of physical danger."

Fig doesn't bother to dignify that remark with a response.

The cop kneels next to her. "Also, we've received a report of a missing woman. Her husband believes you may know of her whereabouts. Does the name Priti Winslow sound familiar?"

"Uhm, yeah. We just met." Fig turns her head so her cheek is on the ground. "Like, just this morning. What's going on?"

"Her husband advised he gave you a lift to this location at approximately fifteen hundred hours and that when he returned home to Dutton his wife was gone. As of nineteen hundred hours she still hadn't returned, and he advises she might have mentioned to you where she went."

This seems a bit extreme. I mean, Priti could have gone shopping or . . . anywhere. "That's only four hours," I point out.

The cop takes no notice of this. "It doesn't appear she drove, since her car is in the garage. He's been unable to reach her on her cell phone. Her husband is concerned she might have met with foul play."

Or gone for a walk. If they think a suburban housewife who hasn't checked in with her husband during a Sunday afternoon is a cause for concern, wait until they hear about our news.

"Priti got a call while we were at our house," Fig says, spitting out dirt. "She was on the landline and I overheard her say something about a . . . bogey?"

I try to remember what a bogey is.

The trooper chucks his chin at Fig. "And what time would this have been when the call came in?"

"I don't know exactly. Noon, maybe."

Apparently, I'm not alone in thinking the police response is extreme, because Rowan says, "You put out an APB for all grown women who leave the house for a few rounds of golf or just for privileged white women married to venture capitalists who are also sons of federal judges?"

The cop turns to him. "And you are?"

"The thug who tried to kill me," Ellen growls.

Rowan sighs. "Rowan Ocht. Ask retired Trooper Oswald who I am. We've been working together on the missing women's cases for months."

"In fact," I add with sick satisfaction, "you happen to be standing on the grave of one right now."

Darkness falling in the forest is very different from darkness falling on a city street, Priti is beginning to realize as she stumbles forward blindly down the trail. The shadows descend first, coloring in gaps of light like charcoal on paper. Then there are the birds.

A robin's goodnight call, tweeting in reply to the hermit thrush's song from the pines, feel more like warnings than lullabies. An owl's random hoot. A flushed grouse. These are signals that she's in their territory, not hers, and once they sign off for the evening, she'll really be in trouble.

Bobcats roam these woods. Moose. Bear. Do bears still have cubs this time of year? Priti decides not to contemplate encountering a protective mama. Hard enough to keep from tripping over these damned roots in addition to running for her life.

Unable to see her own feet, she turns on her phone and activates the flashlight. The battery's at 12 percent so she turns off wi-fi, keeping her GPS on, on the off chance it might start working.

God, she's hungry. Bogey packed no food, only water. The pack's empty and, judging from the price tag she found inside, newly purchased from a store in Albany. Likely with cash.

Thinking about Bogey keeps her mind off her hunger and the precarious state of the precious life she's carrying. He's probably still alive in that cistern trying to get out. She tries not to think about him successfully scaling the wall with his remaining good arm, finding the gun, and coming after her.

Though it's a possibility, isn't it?

She should have shot him, but she couldn't. Taking another life, even in self-defense, goes against every principle inculcated in her since childhood. She can't stand the thought of eating an animal much less killing one. If mercy is her downfall, then so be it.

Except for the child.

She can't die because he—or she—will die too. And Ben won't learn until they're both gone that he could have been a father at last.

Ben. Will he forgive her for doubting his fidelity so readily that she went off with a man she hardly knows simply because he tempted her with proof her husband was sleeping with his ex-wife? Would *she* in his position?

She's not sure. Oh, she can rationalize her behavior. After all, Ben wasn't completely up front about what he and Charlotte were doing in Boston, spying on Stella O'Neill, breaking into her apartment! At least that's been verified.

They should have left Stella alone. She was probably jittery enough to begin with, thanks to the *Dark Cults* notoriety, without a stranger invading her living space. Ben should have used more sense. Charlotte too.

What did they hope to accomplish?

If it's true that Ben didn't kill Rose Santos—of course he didn't—then why didn't he go to the police and tell them about finding her body right away? Why did he run to Charlotte, his clothes caked in her blood, seeking an alibi? There were so many, many questions that needed to be answered.

So many . . .

Crap!

In the darkness, the toe of her right boot hits something hard, and before she can steady herself, Priti tumbles forward, going ass over teakettle, jagged stones stabbing her spine as she rolls and rolls down the rocky trail, finally coming to rest at the base of a towering pine.

She ends up lying there, staring through the needles at the gray sky above, the wind knocked out of her, waiting for the cramping she knows all too well. The dull ache at the back of her hip. The twinges followed by the warm trickle of life flowing from her. It supersedes the other pain radiating up her right ankle, her foot twisted in the wrong direction.

Hot tears of self-pity fill her eyes and stream down her cheeks as she covers the spot tucked way inside her. This is their sacred moment, hers and her unborn child's. She will honor it with all the reverence and love she can manage as the rare trill of an Eastern whippoorwill ends their last moments together.

30

STELLA

JUNE 19, 2023

Fig, Rowan, and I are interviewed separately by the police, a process that's so lengthy I'm not able to leave the Center until almost 2:00 a.m.

Sitting alone in the back of the cruiser as I'm escorted to the hotel my anxious parents booked, the cold, hard facts worm their way into my exhausted brain despite my best efforts to block them out. When this is over, the sad truth is I have no place to go. I've been kicked out of my apartment, and seeing as how I simply walked out of the library, I doubt I have a job.

Yes, we made progress. Finding Cerise's grave was huge. The coroner hasn't confirmed the remains definitely belong to her, but considering the grave's age, and the fact that she was wearing a cerise-colored quartz pendulum and that she's never been found, chances are fairly good this was the last resting place of my mother's best friend.

I'm also satisfied that the reason my mother took me into the woods at that godforsaken hour was so I could use my death-dowsing skills to verify the newly dug mound was Cerise's grave. What my mother expected to do with this information is unknowable. She must have kept her plans close to her chest. I assume she would have gone to the police.

If that's true, then that's a comfort. At least I managed to help fulfill Mama's goal of finding justice for her friend, even if, from what the cops told me, Cliff MacBeath has already lawyered himself up to the teeth.

My bet is the prosecutors will try to flip Ellen, a key witness to her boss's shenanigans. Good luck. Ellen is a Diviner nun, a bride not of Christ but of MacBeath in every sick sense. His words are her commands, and the more she subjugates herself to his authority, the closer she believes she is to pure divination, the ultimate goal of every Diviner.

Yesterday when she appeared in the woods, I saw not a broken, aging victim of MacBeath's mind control, but a cautionary tale of what my mother might have been if she hadn't fled.

As for me, I'm, ironically, in more danger than I was when the true-crime episode aired and all the wacko Diviners came out of the woodwork. By refusing to do what Ellen wanted—issuing a public statement clearing her master of all wrongdoing—and by getting her busted for attempted murder and MacBeath investigated for ordering the murder of Cerise, I'm the sole object of the Diviners' outrage.

And worse, the Facilitators'.

The Center will never recover from a scandal of these proportions. The peace and tranquility of what was intended to be a meditative community is ruined, thanks to me. I can't check what's up online since I don't have a phone, but I expect the news of Cerise's remains and Ellen's arrest is already lighting up Google. This is a national, possibly international, story. TV news crews will be all over it like white on rice, their vans grinding up the winding dirt road to the Center, their reporters badgering all the solstice attendees fleeing for civilization before their good names are dragged through the mud.

Give it a year and I predict HBO will turn it into a four-part series.

So, yeah, the target on my back has just grown a lot bigger, and I've made the Facilitators' jobs way easier.

"I wish we had the staff to provide protection," the trooper says when he lets me off at the entry of the Manchester Hotel. "I know that'd make you feel safer, but we simply don't have the budget."

Right. I'm not a celebrity, not yet. That'll happen when I'm found with my throat slit.

The weary desk attendant hands me a key card along with a complimentary toothbrush, toothpaste, and hairbrush. "A chicken club sandwich, cut fruit, and chocolate chip cookie have been delivered to your suite courtesy of your mother," he says with a sad smile.

In my delirium, I briefly wonder if Mama put in a room service order from the beyond and then catch myself. He means Heather, and he's not mistaken. When it comes to brass tacks, Heather has fed and cared for me most of my life without any expectation of reward or compensation, and isn't that the very definition of a mom?

I thank him and take my tired carcass up the stairs to the second floor, tiptoeing past room 212, Mel and Fig's. It's nice knowing I'm right down the hall from those two. It makes me feel not so alone.

There's another positive! I now have an honest-to-God friend. That's my final thought as, teeth brushed, clothes off, body showered, sandwich uneaten, I lay my head on the pillow and pass out.

"We'd like you to come home with us and stay for a bit." Dad's fork and knife are poised over the fluffy waffle dripping with maple syrup when he makes this proposition. He nods to Heather, sipping her coffee beside me, and adds, "Your stepmother and I would love nothing more."

"Just until you recover," Heather adds, putting down her coffee and turning to me with a gaze filled with sympathy. Her eyes are particularly blue today, set off by a new LLBean cotton sweater. The woman has an addiction to that place. "We promise we won't impose any of the old restrictions. You can come and go as you please and we won't pry."

"You need to feel safe," Dad continues. "I've even gone so far as to hire round-the-clock security. Seriously. No more gadgets or cameras. We're talking the real deal. A full-time bodyguard."

Geesh. What must that cost? At least a thousand bucks a day. I put down my own coffee, determined to refuse. "That's nuts, Dad. Don't do that. It'll eat up your entire retirement savings in a year."

"Half of it," Heather says, placing her hand on my arm and quickly adding, "But that's okay. That's what money's for."

"MacBeath should pay. He's to blame," I say perhaps a little too loudly. The other guests in the quaint hotel dining room trying to enjoy their brunches quit talking and stare. I dig into my omelet as if nothing is amiss.

And then the paranoia takes hold and I begin to shake. Any of our fellow twelve diners could be a disguised Facilitator waiting for the opportunity to strike. There's no way to tell.

Unless . . .

Excusing myself from breakfast, I head for the bathroom. There in the sanctity of a stall, I sit on the toilet, pull out my mother's pendulum, and dangle it from my fingers. As it swings back and forth, I ask it to show me yes, and it promptly rotates clockwise. Good. I ask it to show me no, and it switches to side to side. Good. We're on track.

Taking several deep breaths, I let myself relax into a meditative state until the background noise of the hotel disappears. "Is my intended assassin in this restaurant?"

Slowly, the pendulum begins to move and, to my consternation, starts a slow rotation clockwise. *Shit*, I think, but also, *good*. Knowledge is power, and foreknowledge could make the difference between life and death.

I take another breath and ask, "Will this assassin follow me home?"

Again, the pendulum swings clockwise.

"Will I be safe there even with a bodyguard?"

On a dime, it swings back and forth. *No.*

That's enough for me. I drape the pendulum around my neck, wash my hands, and regard my weary visage in the mirror. With my unwashed hair pulled into a ponytail and my face unmade, I could be my mother, and my mother, at this moment, is sending me a message from the beyond that's so ardent I swear I can hear her whispering in my ear again.

Get. Out. Now.

Somehow I manage to keep it together through the rest of breakfast, though my shoulders burn from the sensation of my would-be killer's gaze upon them. We engage in light conversation, I pick at my omelet, Dad finishes his third cup of coffee, and then he pays the bill. Finally, we can leave. I'm sweating so much, I leave a wet mark on the inn's chair cushion.

Outside the inn, we go to the parking lot and pile into his Honda CRV. "We're gonna drive to the repair shop and pick up your mother's car. Then we'll caravan back to Sudbury," he says, plugging the repair shop's address into his GPS.

"Sure." Anything, just so we get out of here fast.

I sit in the back seat and keep my mouth shut until we get to the shop. Heather's poor abused Kia is dutifully waiting and sparkling in the sunshine, having been kindly washed by the mechanics.

It occurs to me I should have thanked Mel for arranging the car repair and Fig for putting her own life at risk to save mine. I'm still fairly new at this friendship business, so those kinds of gestures are still foreign for me. I hope they'll forgive my rudeness, which is what friends do—or so I've read.

Heather gets out, blows me a kiss, and clicks open the Kia with her fob while I move up front to sit next to Dad, who's in the shop, paying the bill. When he gets back, he gets in and leans over to pop open the glove compartment, where he stores such receipts. "No problem, chicken, insurance is gonna pick up the tab," he says, shoving the receipt under a gun.

That's a surprise. "Since when do you have a gun?"

He shuts the glove compartment door. "Since when do you think?" He gives Heather a thumbs-up out the window and we turn onto Route 7, headed south to Massachusetts and home, Heather in the lead.

"The guy in the station just told me the cops found Priti Winslow this morning," Dad says. "She was on a hiking trail somewhere around here with a broken ankle. So I guess her husband and the police were right to be worried."

"Is she okay?"

"Supposedly. I don't know how much of this is true, but the mechanic said she was kidnapped or something by a local who may or may not be involved with those two missing hikers from the Center. Cops are pretty tight-lipped, as they often are when it's a big case. For now, it's just a rumor. But what if that local guy knew Rose? He could be the killer, Stella, and that'd be the end of this fiasco."

"Wouldn't that be nice." Though, now, the suspense is killing me. Who is this mystery man? "So, it wasn't her husband."

"Who kidnapped her?" Dad gives me a look. "No, I just said it was some other guy. A local."

A local. "And not Radcliffe MacBeath."

Dad flips on his blinker. "Why don't you kick back and get some sleep, Stell. You're exhausted."

I do as he suggests, reclining the seat back as far as I can, and stare at the sky, the trees, and telephone poles passing by until sleep sets in. Dad's right. I'm not thinking straight, and I drift off blissfully until I'm jolted awake by the car rolling to a stop.

"What's going on?" I ask groggily, sitting up to get my bearings. It appears we've pulled into a deserted rest stop surrounded by woods with a couple picnic benches and a few garbage cans. We must be in Mass already.

"Heather needed to hit the john. All that coffee. Me, too." He opens the door, gets out, and stretches. I watch as Dad and Heather exchange a brief conversation, now and then glancing my way. Heather's tapping her hand and Dad's gesturing. Something's going on.

Since there's no one following us, I decide this might be a good opportunity to test the veracity of Mama's pendulum. Unclipping it from my neck, I ask it to show me yes. It rotates clockwise. Then no. It swings back and forth. Okay. Good to go.

"Is my mother's killer following me?"

The pendulum seems to hesitate a bit and then, much to my relief, swings side to side. No. Excellent. Mission accomplished.

Dad's back so I quickly stuff the pendulum in the pocket of my jeans out of respect. He's not a fan of anything related to my mother's former life. Opening the door, he leans in and says, "I'm trying not to get mad, but your darling stepmother left her wedding ring back at the hotel. Why for the life of me she took it off to begin with, I dunno. Anyway, she won't hear of me going back to get it."

"You want me to go back to get it? Heather can go with you and I'll take her car."

He shakes his head fervently. "Jesus, Stell. That's the last thing I want, for you to go back in the lion's den alone. But actually, it might make sense for you to go with her. She's just added a couple of hours to her trip and could use some help with the driving. That okay?"

"No problemo," I say, getting out and stretching. "That nap did wonders."

"You slept for an hour, you know. See you back at the homestead!" he calls out the window before driving onto the highway.

Heather's behind the wheel and on her phone. "Sorry about this," she says, shrugging. "What can I say. My fingers were swelling last night so I took it off and left it on the bedside table. I'd misplace my head if it weren't attached to my shoulders."

I nod to the facilities. "If you don't mind, I'm gonna pee and then I'll be right there."

"Do what you have to do and thanks!" She goes back to her phone. Candy Crush. Her other addiction in addition to Diet Coke and LLBean. I love Heather, but sometimes she can be a trope.

No sooner do I pass her car than the pendulum in my pocket heats up and vibrates. At first I think I must have imagined it. Then it does it again—a brief *zzzzz*. Like a buzzer. It did the exact same thing back in the Chi Chamber when it wanted me to push the cot from the wall to expose the hatch. It's trying to tell me something.

I look back at Heather, who's still playing with her phone, before heading up the broken concrete path to the low redbrick building. On one side is the men's room. On the other, the ladies'. In between is a water faucet with a rusted bowl that looks like it was installed by the Works Progress Administration.

Welcome to the Berkshires, I think, yanking open the heavy door to the decidedly gross bathroom. Two metal stalls. Two rusted metal sinks. An overhead yellow light encrusted with dead bugs, a floor painted a high-gloss gunmetal gray, and a dried urine stench so pervasive I doubt this place has been cleaned since the last century.

Class choice for a whiz, Heather, I think, not paying too much attention to my surroundings as I do what I have to do and wash my hands in icy cold water.

Bzzzz.

All right, already. Taking out my strangely hot pendulum, I run through the old routine. Show me yes. Clockwise. Show me no. Back and forth. And then I ask the question:

"Is my mother's killer following me?"

Again, it hesitates, and ever so slowly the rose stone begins a slow swirl clockwise. A chill runs up my arms.

Taking a deep breath, I ask:

"Is my mother's killer here?"

This time there is no hesitation, and the answer is a swift and powerful circling of the stone.

Shit. Shit. Shit.

What do I do? I need to warn Heather. And she needs to call the cops, since I don't have a phone. She won't though. Call 911 because a pendulum said I should? Heather's extremely practical. She'll tell me to stop being silly and to put away the toy. Unless I can convince her that whoever's just pulled in followed us here intentionally.

I crack open the door expecting to see another car, a Facilitator in a MacBeath-owned roadster, and stop cold.

Heather gives me a finger wave.

No one else is here.

I jump back into the bathroom, my heart pounding, sweat

breaking out all over. My mind racing, I try to think. *Heather?* No. That's impossible. She's, what, five feet five inches at most. The monster who killed Mama was over six feet, before the antlers. And how would she have known to come to the Center?

But hold on. Fig told me Ben told her that the day before she was killed, my mother made a call to Dad from Genevieve Winslow's house asking him to pick us up the following night after the summer solstice ceremony. Unfortunately, Dad was either at his cousin's wedding or on his way there. He wasn't home to get her call. Still, the message would have been recorded on his answering machine . . . unless it had been erased by the one person who didn't want my mother to come home.

The epiphany is chilling. Heather and Dad's relationship at the time could be described as casual at best. In fact, I don't think Dad was all that interested—plus, he was still legally married to Mama, not to mention in love with her. Heather must have realized that.

And hadn't she been dog sitting for him that weekend while he was at the wedding? I think so. So she plays his messages, hears the one from Mama asking Dad to pick us up, and instead of alerting him to my mother's plea, she presses erase. Then Heather decides to take matters into her own hands. After all, here's her golden opportunity to eliminate my mother once and for all, and what better way to do it than during a summer solstice celebration when strangers flooded the Center and she could sneak in undetected.

Which means, the Cernunnos, the antlered god of the summer solstice, wasn't my mother's killer.

He was my savior.

"I thought you might want some Wet Ones."

I'm so lost in thought, I don't hear the door open and Heather step in. I turn to her in a fog. She couldn't look more innocuous, with her neatly brushed copper-colored bob, the same small gold earrings she's worn forever, the smattering of freckles across her cute nose in her tidy outfit—blue cotton sweater, white jeans, Hokas. She extends an offering of wipes.

"Are you okay, sweetie? You look upset."

My eyes are already stinging with tears and my throat is swelling. "Why did you kill my mother?"

Heather scrunches up her face in feigned puzzlement. "What?"

"You heard the message my mother left on Dad's answering machine. You knew she'd be waiting for him at the Center so she could come home and they could rebuild their life." My cheeks are wet and I get the sense I'm blubbering, but I don't care. "We could have been a family. Mama, Dad, me. You robbed me of that, Heather. You killed my mother for no other reason than you wanted Dad to yourself. How could you be so selfish?"

Fluttering her lashes as though I'm the one who's crazy, she says softly, "You're very, very tired. You've been through a lot of trauma. You know what? After we get my ring, let's go up to Deb's. It's closer than Sudbury. We can talk and work it all out without upsetting your father. Just you and me."

And the killer dogs.

Suddenly, I snap to attention, Heather's morbid scheme becoming crystal clear. I'm sure she would have preferred that I'd gone to Deb's alone as planned so she'd have a nice alibi when she somehow remotely unlocked the cages and delivered the command over Deb's security system to kill me. I would have been torn to shreds in minutes. It would have been an unfortunate tragedy that would have wrecked my father.

But I'd be eliminated once and for all—and Heather no longer would have had to live with the constant anxiety of being busted for murder.

Only, in order for her plan to work, I needed to be scared. Dad, too. Both of us had to be convinced that the only way I could be safe would be if I ran in panic to the security of Heather's sister's dog kennel, where I'd be protected by trained attack dogs.

And how did Heather make me so paranoid? By sending a cryptic email implying my end was near. Then, having tracked the Kia to where it was parked outside the Winslows', she upped the ante by sending that obscure text, thereby prompting me to trash my cell phone, which would be a super handy device to have right about now.

"I'm such a sucker," I say, laughing slightly at my own gullibility. "You sent that email to the library. You wanted me to believe the Diviners were going to kill me so I'd run. You know, I bet it's still on your computer somewhere deep in your hard drive. It'll take nothing to find it."

"Awww shit." She shakes her head the same slow way she used to do when I tracked mud across her newly vacuumed carpet. "Now you've gone and spoiled a perfectly fine day."

And with that, she locks the bathroom door.

31

ROSE

JUNE 21, 2003

Rose didn't hesitate.

As soon as she returned to the cabin, she found Astraea's little pink sneakers, removed the insoles and the foil liners, crumpling them into tiny balls she stuffed through a crack in the floorboards.

She donned a pair of black leggings and a long-sleeved dark top. "Mom clothes," Cliff would have called them. Then she slipped on her own sneakers and grabbed the flashlight she and Astraea used to negotiate night trips to the outhouse.

"Darling," she whispered, shaking her daughter lightly by her shoulders. "We've got to go."

Her heart broke at the thought of rousing this traumatized child from a peaceful slumber. More than anything, Astraea needed to be warm and rested. Dragging her out into the woods in the middle of the night to show where she'd found a buried body would compound the stress she was already under from being trapped in the Chi Chamber.

All they needed to do was get past this ugliness, find the evidence of MacBeath's psychopathy, go to the police, and go home to Dan's.

"No," Astraea murmured, pulling up a cover, tucking in her legs. "I'm so tired."

"It won't take long. I want you to show me the turtle."

At this, the child awakened slightly. "The turtle can wait until tomorrow."

"We have to go now, before the morning. Like mushroom hunting, there are some things best done at night."

Astraea loved mushroom hunting and so she roused herself, allowing her mother to slip on a windbreaker, brush her hair into a ponytail, and give her a sip of water. Then, hand in hand, they slipped out the door, making sure to shut it quietly.

Rose put a finger to her lips and the two of them set out. Astraea was so exhausted she could barely walk, her feet dragging in the grass as Rose pulled her along, sticking to the edge of the forest and keeping her flashlight off. Fortunately, waning fires from the flickering torches provided enough light for her to locate the narrow path into the woods.

Drums banged rhythmically in the distance, the sparks from the huge bonfire on the hill cracking and snapping in an upward shower of golden flecks. Voices, many of them drunken, ebbed and swelled in an ancient Celtic song of lust and love, rebirth and fertility. Rose was sad that she'd never experience the magic of a solstice festival, but she was wise enough to know that the one truism of a human life is that nothing lasts forever.

"Mama, can we stop a minute?" Astraea asked in a small and pitiful voice.

They were deep in the woods, so far in that the drumbeats had faded to a distant thrum overtaken by an owl's hooting and the steady cacophony of chirping tree frogs above. Rose kept her yellow flashlight beam on the muddy trail, though she wondered if she'd have more luck turning off the light and letting her eyes adjust to the darkness. The beam was blocking out her surroundings.

That put her at a disadvantage, considering bears still had young cubs they'd fight to protect while they were out at night foraging for food.

She, too, had a cub to protect.

Switching off the light, she knelt and took Astraea onto her lap. A cold feeling passed through her, a sad premonition that this would be their last moment together, that either she or Astraea would not survive. "Can you go on, sweetie?"

Her daughter shook her head. "I can't. I'm too tired."

This level of exhaustion was unusual for Astraea, who, at age ten, occasionally woke up in the wee hours ready to play, she had so much youthful energy. Had they drugged her child in the Chi Chamber? Then Rose remembered something Ben had said.

"Did Ellen give you a special tea?" She smoothed back her daughter's delicate hair. Mermaid hair. "Did the tea make you sleepy?"

Astraea averted her eyes, and Rose knew the truth. She wrapped her daughter in her arms and held her tight. "It's all right, sweetie. You can stay here while I go find the turtle."

Astraea squeezed hard and whimpered, "Please don't leave me."

Rose wavered. They could go back to the Center, meet Dan, and simply call the cops later. But if she did that, she was certain Dan wouldn't let her return. Or maybe Cliff would move Cerise's body. Better to stick with the plan and just get the awful business over with. "Don't worry. This won't take long. I'll be right back."

"No!" Astraea protested.

Perhaps if her daughter had a distraction while she hunted for the grave. But what? Her hand rested on her pendulum, her only valuable possession. A gift, in fact, from Cerise. Unclasping it from her neck, she pressed the smooth stone into Astraea's hand and closed her tiny fingers around it. "Keep this safe for me until I return. But you must stay where you are. If you wander off, I won't be able to find you and you will be lost."

That seemed to do the trick. Astraea had been forever fascinated with the pendulum, and now it was hers to keep fast. Rose took advantage of the moment to gently slide Astraea off her lap and set her down by a bush of fragrant, wild honeysuckle.

Astraea looked like a fairy child, innocent and so pure Rose's heart burst with a mother's love . . . and guilt. She regretted every mistake she'd made, from dragging this child into the deep, dark forest and allowing Cliff and Ellen to lock her away in a metal box to taking her away from a loving father to live in a cult of delusional followers.

Rose didn't get a pass. Not long ago she would have leaped off a cliff, if that's what her Dagda wanted, so deep was she in his thrall. Now that the spell had been broken, she could see how she'd put her own interests above her baby's, an unpardonable sin. Her only chance at redemption was to ensure Cliff MacBeath was sent to prison and never allowed to destroy anyone else's life again.

Clicking the light back on, Rose swept the forest with its beam until it landed on a rock outcropping on a rise past the stream. Yes, of course. There was the head, the dome-like body and two feet. Slowly, she rose and moved forward, confident no bear would bother a quiet child, not with her so nearby.

Reaching the rock outcropping turned out to be harder than she estimated in the darkness. For one thing, it was off trail and the brambles were thick. Fallen trees she hadn't noticed required scrambling under or over and vines snaking over their rotted bark caught her feet.

At one point, she thought she heard footsteps coming from above the rock wall and paused, her ears cocked for sound. But it must have been a deer, so she plowed on until she reached the stream.

The babbling brook had cut a chasm through the rock wall. Rose understood exactly what had happened. The children must have been playing in the shallow water, placing rocks for a dam, when they caught sight of the turtle wall with its irresistible footholds for climbing. Astraea wouldn't have attempted that on her own unless she was persuaded by a more adventurous child. Her daughter hated being left behind by older kids and was forever eager to prove she was a big girl.

And then her daughter stepped on the newly dug earthen mound and suffered her experience. Understandably frightened by the vengeance of the dead, she fled down the brook, to the path and back to the café, where she arrived dirty, wet, and visibly upset. Few knew of her dowsing powers aside from Cliff, Ellen, and, well, Cerise, Astraea having been firmly instructed to keep that secret to herself. So she would have told no one of her frightening experience . . . hopefully.

Rose put one foot out to step on a rock in the water when she heard the footsteps again. Only they were behind her, not above.

Swinging around, she expected to find a woodland creature; much to her alarm, she found a hooded Diviner instead. She'd been followed. Frustrated that she'd been so close to finding the truth, Rose switched on the flashlight and shined it at the intrusive Diviner to identify Ellen's lackey.

The round young face that peered out from the green hood was unfamiliar, however. Rose relaxed. This wasn't one of Ellen's henchwomen, merely a curious solstice guest who'd bought a souvenir robe in the Center gift shop.

"What are you doing here?" Rose asked.

"Following you," the woman said in an even tone.

"Well, don't. You'll get lost."

"No, I won't." The woman didn't move. It was weird the way her voice was devoid of emotion. Like maybe she was on mushrooms or whatever hallucinogenic substances the Diviners were passing around the bonfire.

No matter, Rose needed to ditch her. "I want to be alone."

"You don't know who I am, do you?" The woman pushed back her hood and flicked on her own light, shining it up from her chin. She was a bottle-dyed redhead and pale with freckled chipmunk cheeks and a button nose that made her oddly reminiscent of Miss Piggy.

Rose didn't have the energy for games. "I'm sorry, if you . . . "

"Three days a week for over a year I took care of your baby, Stella, and yet you don't recognize me, do you, Mrs. O'Neill?"

Trepidation replaced annoyance. This was no accidental encounter, Rose thought. This stranger had come to the Center and now to the forest for some sort of showdown. Apparently, she was insulted Rose didn't remember who she was. She racked her memory trying to recall who'd taken care of Stella when she was a baby.

Three days a week she'd taken Stella to Sunshine Daycare after Dan finished his PhD, landed a high-paying job, and they were able to move out of inner-city Boston to the suburbs. That was mere months after she'd first met the mesmerizing Radcliffe Mac-Beath, and she hadn't been able to get him or spiritual dowsing out of her head.

Dan didn't approve; he preferred Rose to stay at home with the baby. But devoting herself solely to motherhood was driving her mad. Three days a week to concentrate on practicing dowsing, to study MacBeath's texts and develop her spiritual growth seemed like a reasonable compromise, considering she'd be with Stella for the remaining four days. Happy mother equals happy family, right?

Not to Dan. He dismissed spiritual dowsing as quackery and called Rose a simpleton for falling under the spell of an obvious charlatan. He didn't want that nonsense around their child; Rose told him to respect her beliefs as their fights devolved into nastiness. Finally, one night Rose couldn't take it any longer. She left with three-year-old Stella. If Dan wouldn't let her practice spiritual dowsing at home, then the solution was to simply change her home.

"I'm waiting," the stranger said, actually tapping her foot. "I'll give you one more minute to remember my name."

Much to Rose's shame, she couldn't pick out Stella's caregivers in a lineup. They all blurred into one "type." Pleasant, innocuous, cheerful girls with names like Kaylee and Crystal, who spoke in silly singsong voices and discussed diaper rashes and napping habits in dire earnest.

"Heather," the woman finally answered. "Heather Donnelly. I was your daughter's caregiver for over a year. I saw Stella take her first steps."

No, that couldn't be true. Rose exhaled, her trepidation waning back to irritation. "Look, can we discuss this later? I'm . . ."

"I knew it." This Heather shook her head in disapproval. "You don't deserve to be her mother and you certainly don't deserve Dan. You'll come back and ruin everything, the life we're going to build together. He still loves you, you know. That's why he didn't get a divorce when he could have. He should have sued you for abandonment long ago."

Prickles ran up Rose's arms as it occurred to her that maybe this woman, this daycare worker Heather, had followed her into the forest to do her harm. Was she with Dan? Had he brought her here to pick them up like she asked? If so, where was he? Rose's mind raced along with her pulse. She prayed Astraea would stay asleep until she was done handling this.

"How did you know I was coming back?"

"Heard your super long message on the answering machine. *'Oh, Dan, I'm so sorry. I made a mistake. I want to give us a chance if you're willing. I looooove you.'* So sincere." Heather let out a breath. *"Not."*

This woman was off her rocker. Rose scanned for a weapon. A stick, maybe, or even a rock. Anything to use to defend herself until she could de-escalate the situation. "Where's my husband?"

"Oh, he's your husband now, is he? That's convenient. Um, I assume he's still at the wedding. Can't take me because he's married and I guess it looks bad to show up with the woman you've been sleeping with who's not your wife. People look down on that kind of shit, turns out."

That's what she wants, Rose thought, Dan. Well, she can't have him. "My husband's on his way to pick up his daughter. He'd move heaven and earth for her. Probably, he's here now. So, you might want to . . . "

"No, he's not. He didn't get your message. I've seen to that. You don't think I scan everything to make sure some slut doesn't try to get her hooks in him? Your husband is a pretty popular guy, I'll have you know. Makes a good living. Has a nice house. Doesn't yell. Sober. Chips in with the laundry. And not bad in bed. Plus, the story of how you up and left him, taking his daughter, that right there's the clincher. No warmhearted woman can resist that. Except you, I suppose, you cold bitch."

Dan wasn't here. He wasn't coming either. Rose stifled a wave of panic. For Astraea's sake, she needed to keep her head clear, her wits about her. She needed to extricate herself from this situation, tell her anything to make her disappear.

And above all, make sure she doesn't know Astraea is fast asleep nearby.

"Look, I'm just out mushroom hunting, okay? I'm about to go back and go to bed. If Dan's that important to you, fine. I only said that stuff so he'd come to get us. Trust me, the last thing I want is to be Mrs. O'Neill living in fucking Sudbury, Massachusetts, going to PTA meetings and baking cupcakes."

There. That should do it.

Rose hoped that would be that and resumed crossing the stream. Heather would be satisfied and return to Massachusetts a happy camper. Rose would find another way out of the Center, and then she'd go to Dan and explain what had just occurred. Surely he wouldn't want to marry a woman as delusional as this chick. That's probably why he hadn't pursued a divorce, because it gave him an excuse.

The blow to her ankles that sent her teetering felt almost rude. Rose didn't realize she'd been tripped until she slammed into the creek with barely enough wherewithal to break her fall. The rock she'd been planning to step on to cross crashed into her diaphragm, leaving her breathless and gulping in the frigid water.

She had to get up. She had to get out of here to save Astraea. Every bone in her body ached as she brought up her right knee and then her left, crawling through the brook like a wounded soldier, her mind a blank slate, survival her only motivation.

Just when she was about to reach the other side, an earthquake erupted on the back of her head. Searing pain radiated across her skull and rattled her brain. A burst of white light shattered the darkness, so bright it was blinding.

"Astraea," she pleaded, suddenly struck by a vision of her daughter running through the long, swaying green grasses of the Center's field, yellow buttercups and purple violets clutched in her tiny hand, so filled with love and joy Rose even smiled as a second blow, sharper, more exact than the first, split her cranium like a cut melon.

"I've got you."

Cerise, lovely Cerise, draped in the flamingo red of her name, took Rose's hand.

"Come with me."

She helped her up so effortlessly Rose felt as light as air. Together, they elevated out of the water, up the mountain, and into the sky like two leaves blowing in a summer breeze.

"It's okay. Astraea will be fine. Everything will be fine," Cerise said. "We are, all of us, one with the Divine."

And then, just like that, they flowed into the ebullient white light of eternal bliss, Rose's fears and worries evaporating like raindrops in the sun.

STELLA

My mother made some poor decisions, there's no doubt of that. Leaving Dad, hitching her wagon to that charlatan MacBeath, and maybe even letting me run wild like a street urchin was not what you'd call wise parenting. I cut her a break because she was younger than I am now when she made that decision and simply didn't know better.

That aside, learning that she went into the woods to find the buried body of her best friend has changed my estimation of her. Mama wasn't simply fleeing the Center like I've always assumed; she was trying to prove MacBeath had Cerise killed. In the process, she lost her life too.

Dying for a friend is a noble cause, and it makes me so proud of her. Rose Santos may have had her moments of foolishness, but she was brave too, and smart and loyal and loving. All qualities I'd like to improve on when it comes to my life. And when I do, I can take heart that her blood runs through my veins.

"Love this place!" Fig exclaims, slamming the door to her Mini Cooper way too hard for this neighborhood. "You need help with the cake?"

"Got it." I gently lift the lemon cake from the back seat, delighted that it made the trip from Boston to Dutton without getting smooshed by Fig's stop-and-go driving. It seems like an inadequate thank-you gift for a man who not only saved my life as a kid, but then tried to save it again as an adult, while I continued to spread rumors faster than lawn fertilizer that he was my mother's killer.

"Hello! Hello, dear people!" Genevieve Winslow, ever the grand dame, steps out of the side entrance of her magnificent home leaning a little less heavily on her exquisite brass cane than when I last saw her. She paints a pretty picture in her red brocade jacket, flanked by potted purple mums. "How lovely to see you again, Figurina."

"I think she loves saying my name," Fig whispers, striding toward her, arms wide open. "You're looking well, Genny."

I'm sure no one has called Genevieve Winslow "Genny," ever. They exchange air-kisses and proceed inside while I survey the grounds. I don't remember having been to the Winslows' in the fall, but it is postcard perfect. Falling yellow and red leaves, a clean brisk snap of autumn in the air, fading blue hydrangeas. Fig's right, it's straight out of a Hallmark movie.

"Can I help you with that?"

I turn to see Ben Winslow, hands clasped behind him in a humble pose. This is our first meeting in person since that night twenty-plus years ago when, worried about Mama and me, he disguised himself as Cernunnos and came to find us.

What he found instead was my mother dead and me alone and quivering by her side. He reacted to the best of his young ability, I suppose, carrying me to safety and then, fearing cops would pin my mother's murder on him, fleeing to Charlotte for help. Not the best move, but perhaps understandable given his youth.

Placing the cake on the warm hood of Fig's car, I go over and stand before him feeling awkward and grateful and happy. "How's your wife?"

"Very well, thank you." He grins widely. Like many tall men, he stoops slightly, I notice. Despite his broad shoulders and those killer blue eyes and vast wealth, there's an endearing humility to him. "We're just past the three-month mark so Priti's given me permission to go public. Our baby's due to be born in February. Since it'll be a leap year, maybe on the twenty-ninth!"

Nerd. Big time. "That's great. Boy or girl?"

"Boy. But no more Benjamin Winslows. We're done with that. We've been leaning toward Vijay, after Priti's grandfather."

"Vijay Winslow. It works." I grimace in preparation of bringing up a sore subject. "And her attacker?"

"Bogey's in state custody awaiting trial. It's gotta be tough for him, seeing as how he's lost the use of his legs," Ben says dryly. "Not that I have any sympathy for a man who killed two innocent women in cold blood and tried to do the same to my wife."

"At least all the murders are solved. If Cliff MacBeath were here, he'd tell us that now the universal energy can be let in to begin the healing process."

Ben rolls his eyes. "If I never hear that name again, it'll be too soon. Look, I want to just say this about your mom. She was a very special person. Typical kid, I had no idea what my mother was going through after Dad died. Your mom got her through those dark years, and for that I am forever grateful."

"That makes two of us," I say awkwardly. "If you hadn't saved . . . "

He puts up his hands. "Please. You were a little kid. I could have done so much more."

"How's Charlotte dealing with all the fallout?" I ask, to get us off an obviously sensitive subject for him.

"In therapy. Finally. Bogey's crime . . . it was shocking. Sick motherfucker, that guy. And your stepmonster?"

"In state custody awaiting trial just like Bogey." I shrug. Another sad ending to a story that could have been far worse. "I've never been more grateful for broken door locks on public restrooms. What're the chances that a female member of the Massachusetts State Police decided to powder her nose at that very moment?"

"Is it true Heather had a gun?"

"A tiny pistol. Dad bought it for her after the doxers came out of the woodwork. Not sure she would have used it then and there. Glad I didn't have to find out."

He nods. "Quite the wild ride."

"At least MacBeath got his comeuppance. Those fraud and abuse charges will be hard to beat, and I understand he's broke."

"Flat broke. Though the homicide count on Cerise Danyew will probably be reduced to mishandling of a corpse. Every indication is your mom's friend died of natural causes, even if they were preventable. He should have allowed her to go to the emergency room for that abscessed tooth."

My gaze drifts to the garden where Genevieve, Fig, and Priti are standing before the lilies. The mischief makers.

As if reading my mind, he says, "You really thought my sweet mother was capable of killing children and planting them under her roses?"

"I dunno. My mother was slain by my stepmother who then sent me a threatening email pretending to be cult members, basically. All options were open."

He laughs slightly, picks up the cake box, and nods to the garden. "Come on."

We join the women, my new friends despite so many differences. Genevieve puts an arm around me and pulls me close. She smells like talcum powder. "Do you know you were my favorite little girl in the whole wide world? You were the granddaughter I never had."

I don't care if she's treating me as if I'm ten again. Genevieve and my mother were friends, and being with her is like being with part of my mother. I want to treasure every second. "I'm so sorry about your babies," I say.

"Back then, we didn't treat miscarriages the way we should. Doctors told us miscarriages were nature's way of culling deformities. We should be grateful, not sad. How could you ever be grateful about losing a baby you desperately wanted? Your mother understood, Stella. She helped me process my profound loss by connecting me with each child and letting them go. She was a godsend."

Priti's lower lip quivers slightly, and Genevieve extends a hand to clasp hers so that I'm squeezed between the two loving mothers brought together, strangely enough, by the loving mother I lost.

What was MacBeath's line from the poster in the Chi Chamber? Oh, right.

BE OPEN TO MIRACLES FOR WE ARE, ALL OF US, ONE WITH THE DIVINE.

ACKNOWLEDGMENTS

Vermont is home to plenty of obscure cults from which I drew inspiration for *A Mother Always Knows*. From the remote wilderness of the Northeast Kingdom to the isolated hollows of the Green Mountains, groups of like-minded souls have found havens where they can practice their beliefs undisturbed. The Diviners and their leader, Radcliffe MacBeath, are simply amalgamations of these inspirations.

Danville, Vermont, is also home to the American Society of Dowsers, who provided boundless materials and assistance. A thin volume entitled *Letter to Robin: A Mini-Course in Pendulum Dowsing* by Walt Woods published in 2002 by this organization taught me pendulum dowsing in detail. They have a fascinating bookstore you can access online for ordering dowsing equipment and books you might not find elsewhere.

The late Betty Sincerbeaux of Hanover, New Hampshire, introduced me to dowsing in Woodstock, Vermont, when she was in her nineties, God bless her. I can still see her to this day, impeccably attired as she explained that pre-Columbian settlers had placed standing stones to mark the solstices, her dowsing rods flicking decisively. Had it not been for my late brother, Mark, and his mutual association with the New England Antiquities Research Association (NEARA), I might have dismissed her as a crackpot. That would have been a mistake.

For those interested in learning more about the sacred landscape of New England, I highly recommend *Manitou* by the late

James W. Mavor Jr. and Byron E. Dix, published by Inner Traditions in 1989. It laid the foundation for my initial research.

Dowsing has been used in this state to find water for generations, though the late (geesh, I guess everyone I know is dead) well-digger Rick Purchase of Calais, Vermont, argued that if you dug deep enough around here, you were bound to hit water. Our neighbors located their own well after some crusty farmer cut off an apple branch and walked their property, pausing only when the branch bent so far to the ground and with such force the bark ripped off in his hands.

Spiritual dowsing is a New Age evolution of this practice. To research that, I relied on deep internet diving (don't judge!) and the invaluable book *The Psychic Witch* by Mat Auryn (Llewellyn Publications, 2020). I also made up a bunch of stuff. *Ley Lines and Earth Energies: A Groundbreaking Exploration of the Earth's Natural Energy and How It Affects Our Health* by David R. Cowan and Chris Arnold (Adventures Unlimited Press, 2003) was another great find at the American Society of Dowsers bookstore that helped me understand this phenomenon.

As for the creepy Glastenbury Mountain, most of the credit for that goes to famous Vermont folklorist Joe Citro, who coined the concept of a Bennington Triangle. I highly recommend Joe's *Green Mountain Ghosts, Ghouls & Unsolved Mysteries* (Houghton Mifflin Harcourt Publishing Company, 1994) for an enjoyable and enlightening read. I also had a personal—and humorous—experience related to Glastenbury Mountain, which I'm sure I'll share in future readings and on my website (sarahstrohmeyer.com).

Of course, no published book is written in a vacuum. Editors, the unsung heroes of the literary world in this age of DIY publishing, make or break a novel, and I was fortunate to have not one, but two sharp minds steering me in the right direction. Before leaving for Holt, my beloved editor Emily Griffin put me on course and summoned another dimension to *A Mother Always Knows* that was sorely missing in the original manuscript. And while I was sorry to lose her, I was fortunate enough to be entrusted to Harper's Caroline Weishuhn. Caroline got the concept right away and made this book even better. Jane Cavolina was a spectacular copyeditor. I am so grateful for your tweaks and catches. Great editors make magic and I've been luckier than most. Thank you, Emily, Caroline, and Jane.

Heather Drucker, preeminent publicist extraordinaire, has more energy than a bitcoin factory. Thank you for your faith, contacts, and belief in my work, Heather. If this book becomes a success, I have no doubt that'll be because of your valiant efforts to get it in the hands of independent booksellers. And speaking of independent booksellers, Katya d'Angelo and Jenna Danyew of Bridgeside Books in Waterbury, Vermont, are champs. Not only did they choose the right green for the cover font of *A Mother Always Knows*, but they host killer reading retreats twice a year at Sterling Ridge Resort in Jeffersonville, Vermont. Keep your eyes peeled on Instagram for the next retreat because you will not want to miss an opportunity to hang out amid beautiful scenery and cozy cabins with bestselling authors and fun readers. Also, bonfires.

A million kisses to my wonderful, warm, patient, and savvy agent, Zoe Sandler of Sanford J. Greenburger Associates. Somehow between babies and agency moves, she's been able to stay on top of all the tiny details necessary to transform a vague concept into a living, breathing novel. You are a delight and a savior. Thank you. Thank you! I so look forward to embarking on the next adventure.

I'm also grateful for the tolerance of my colleagues in the Middlesex Town Clerk's Office when I was on deadline. Cheryl and Dorinda may have rolled their eyes when I didn't show up exactly at "the crack of nine," but they were kind enough to keep their opinions private. I only hope and pray that a third flood doesn't follow in the wake of this book's publication. Think dry.

Finally, *A Mother Always Knows* could not have been written without the input of our daughter, Anna Merriman, herself an experienced editor, and the support of my wonderful husband, Charlie, who read through all the drafts and never lost faith. The life of a book widower (or widow) can be damn boring when your partner spends every weekend holed up in a room attached to a keyboard. It takes a special person to tolerate being married to an author for thirty-five-plus years.

If you've gotten this far in this lengthy author's note, then bless you too. Readers like you are the lifeblood of this wacky profession and, frankly, the best hope for civilization. I know it sounds cliché but it's true: we authors LOVE you. Please stay in touch and visit me on Instagram, Facebook, BlueSky, or my good old-fashioned website. Until then, may we be united in the Divine Force that connects us all.

ABOUT THE AUTHOR

Sarah Strohmeyer is the award-winning, national bestselling author of nineteen novels for adults and young adults, most recently *We Love to Entertain*. Her first mystery, *Bubbles Unbound*, won the Agatha Award for Best First Mystery. A former newspaper reporter, she is the elected town clerk of Middlesex, Vermont.

READ MORE BY
SARAH STROHMEYER

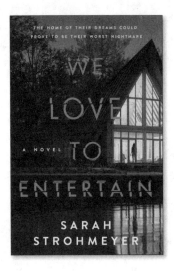

"A diabolical and deliciously twisty romp through reality TV home renovations infused with humor and warmth. Sarah Strohmeyer does murder and suspense in all the best possible ways!"

—WANDA M. MORRIS,
award-winning author of *All Her Little Secrets* and *Anywhere You Run*

"A fabulous read packed with suspense, unexpected twists, glamour and humor. Prepare to be gripped from the first to the last page!"

— LIANE MORIARTY,
#1 *New York Times* bestselling author of *Big Little Lies*

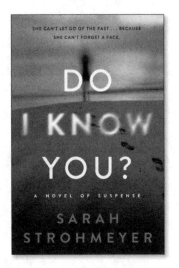